THE TREATMENT

THE TREATMENT

Mo Hayder

First published in Great Britain 2001
by
Bantam Press, a division of Transworld Publishers

Published in Large Print 2006 by ISIS Publishing Ltd.,
7 Centremead, Osney Mead, Oxford OX2 0ES
by arrangement with
Transworld Publishers
a division of The Random House Group Ltd.

British Library Cataloguing in Publication Data
Hayder, Mo
The treatment. – Large print ed.
1. Police – England – London – Fiction
2. Abduction – England – London – Fiction
3. Suspense fiction
4. Large type books
I. Title
823.9'14 [F]

ISBN 0–7531–7588–6 (hb)
ISBN 0–7531–7589–4 (pb)

Printed and bound in Great Britain by
T. J. International Ltd., Padstow, Cornwall

CHAPTER ONE

(17 July)

When it was all over, DI Jack Caffery, South London Area Major Investigation Team (AMIT), would admit that, of all the things he had witnessed in Brixton that cloudy July evening, it was the crows that jarred him the most.

They were there when he came out of the Peaches' house — twenty or more of them standing in their hooded way on the lawn of the neighbouring garden, oblivious to the police tape, the onlookers, the technicians. Some had their beaks open. Others appeared to be panting. All of them faced him directly — as if they knew what had happened in the house. As if they were having a sly laugh about the way he'd reacted to the scene. The unprofessional way he was taking it too personally.

Later he would accept that the crows' behaviour was a biological tic, that they couldn't see into his thoughts, couldn't have known what had happened to the Peach family, but even so the sight of them made the back of his neck tingle. He paused at the top of the garden path to strip off his overalls and hand them to a forensics officer, pulled on the shoes he'd left outside the police tape, and waded out into the birds. They took to the air, rattling their petrolly feathers.

Brockwell Park — a huge, thrown-together isosceles of forest and grass with its apex at Herne Hill station — rambles for over a mile along the boundary of two very different parts of South London. On its western perimeter, the badlands of Brixton — where some mornings council workers have to drop sand on the streets to soak up the blood — and, to the east, Dulwich, with its flower-drenched almshouses and John Soane skylights. Donegal Crescent lay snug up against Brockwell Park, anchored at one foot by a boarded-up pub, at the other by a Gujarati-owned corner shop. It was part of a quiet little council estate, rows of fifties terraced houses bare to the sky, no trees in the front gardens, doors painted chocolate brown. The houses looked on to a horseshoe-shaped piece of balding grass where kids skidded their bikes in the evening. Caffery could imagine the Peaches must have felt relatively safe here.

Back in his shirt-sleeves, grateful for the fresh air outside, he rolled a cigarette and crossed to the group of officers next to the Scientific Support Command Unit's van. They fell silent as he approached and he knew what they were thinking. He was only in his mid thirties — not a senior-rank warhorse — but most officers in South London knew who he was. "One of the Met's Young Turks", the *Police Review* had called him. He knew he was respected in the force and he always found it a bit freaky. *If they knew half of it*. He hoped they wouldn't notice that his hands were trembling.

"Well?" He lit the cigarette and looked at a sealed plastic evidence bag a junior forensics officer was holding. "What've you got?"

"We found it just inside the park, sir, about twenty yards from the back of the Peaches'."

Caffery took the bag and turned it over carefully. A Nike Air Server trainer, a child's shoe, slightly smaller than his hand. "Who found it?"

"The dogs, sir."

"And?"

"They lost the trail. At first they had it — they had it good, really good." A sergeant in the blue shirt of the dog handlers' unit stood on tiptoe and pointed over the roofs to where the park rose in the distance, blotting out the sky with its dark woods. "They took us round the path that scoots over the west of the park — but after about half a mile they just drew a blank." He looked dubiously at the evening sky. "And we've lost the light now."

"Right. I think we need to speak to Air Support." Caffery passed the trainer back to the forensics officer. "It should be in an air-drying bag."

"I'm sorry?"

"There's blood on it. Didn't you see?"

The SSCU's dragonlights powered up, flooding the Peaches' house, spilling light on to the trees in the park beyond. In the front garden forensics officers in blue rubberized suits swept the lawn with dustpans, and outside the police tape shock-faced neighbours stood in knots, smoking and whispering, breaking off to huddle around any plain-clothed AMIT detective who came near, full of questions. The press were there too. Losing patience.

Caffery stood next to the Command Unit van and stared up at the house. It was a two-storey terraced house — pebble-dashed, a satellite dish on the roof, aluminium-framed windows and a small patch of damp above the front door. There were matching scalloped nets in each window, and the curtains had been drawn tight.

He had only seen the Peach family, or what was left of it, in the aftermath, but he felt as if he knew them. Or, rather, he knew their archetype. The parents — Alek and Carmel — weren't going to be easy victims for the team to sympathize with: both drinkers, both unemployed, Carmel Peach had sworn at the paramedics as they moved her into the ambulance. Their only son, nine-year-old Rory, Caffery hadn't seen. By the time he'd arrived the divisional officers had already pulled the house apart trying to find the child — in the cupboards, the attic, even behind the bath panelling. There was a thin trace of blood on the skirting-board in the kitchen and the glass in the back door was broken. Caffery had taken a Territorial Support Group officer with him to search a boarded-up property two doors down, crawling through a hole in the back door on their bellies, flashlights in their teeth like an adolescent's SAS fantasy. All they found were the usual homeless nesting arrangements. There was no other sign of life. No Rory Peach. The raw facts were bad enough and for Caffery they might have been custom-built to echo his own past. *Don't let it be a problem, Jack, don't let it turn into a headfuck.*

"Jack?" DCI Danniella Souness said, suddenly at his side. "Ye all right, son?"

He looked round. "Danni. God, I'm glad you're here."

"What's with the face? You've a gob on you like a dog's arse."

"Thanks, Danni." He rubbed his face and stretched. "I've been on standby since midnight."

"And what's the SP on this?" She gestured at the house. "A wain gone missing, am I right? Rory?"

"Yes. We're going to be blowing fuses on it — he's only nine years old."

Souness blew air out of her nose and shook her head. She was solid, just five foot four, but she weighed twelve stone in her man's suit and boots. With her cropped hair and fair, Caledonian skin she looked more like a juvenile dressed for his first court appearance than a forty-year-old chief inspector. She took her job very seriously. "Right, the assessment team been?"

"We don't know we've got a death yet. No dead body, no assessment team."

"Aye, the lazy wee bastards."

"Local factory's taken the house apart and can't find him. I've had dogs and the Territorials in the park, Air Support should be on their way."

"Why do ye think he's in the park?"

"These houses all back on to it." He pointed towards the woods that rose beyond the roofs. "We've got a witness saw *something* heading off into the trees from number thirty. Back door's unlocked, there's a hole in the fence, and the lads found a shoe just inside the park."

"OK, OK, I'm convinced." Souness folded her arms and tipped back on her heels, looking around at the technicians, the photographers, the divisional CID officers. On the doorstep of number thirty a camera operator was checking his battery belt, lowering the heavy Betacam into a case. "Looks like a shagging film set."

"The unit want to work through the night."

"And what's with the ambulance? The one that almost ran me off the road."

"Ah, yes — that was Mum. She and hubby have both been trundled off to King's. She'll make it but he hasn't got a hope. Where he was hit" — Caffery held his palm against the back of his head — "fucked him up some." He checked over his shoulder then bent a little nearer to her, lowering his voice. "Danni. There're a few things we're going to have to keep from the press, a few things we don't want popping up in the tabloids."

"What things?"

"It isn't a custody kidnap. He's their child — no exes involved."

"A tiger, then?"

"Not a tiger either." Tiger kidnaps meant ransom demands and the Peaches were not in an extortionist's financial league. "And, anyway, when you look at what else went on you'll know it's not bog standard."

"Eh?"

Caffery looked around at the journalists — at the neighbours. "Let's go in the van, eh?" He put his hand on Souness's back. "I don't want an audience."

"Come on, then." She hefted herself inside the SSCU's van and Caffery followed, reaching up to grip the roof rim and swinging himself inside. Spades, cutting equipment and tread plates hung from the walls, a samples refrigerator hummed gently in the corner. He closed the door, hooked a stool over with his foot and handed it to her. She sat down and he sat opposite, feet apart, elbows on his knees, looking at her carefully.

"What?"

"We've got something screwy."

"What?"

"The guy stayed with them first."

Souness frowned, tilting her chin down as if she wasn't sure whether he was joking or not. "*Stayed* with them?"

"That's right. Just — hung around. For almost three days. They were tied up in there — handcuffed — no food and water. DS Quinn thinks another twelve hours and one or other of them'd be dead." He raised his eyebrows. "Worst thing's the smell."

Souness rolled her eyes. "Oh, lovely."

"Then there's the bullshit scrawled all over the wall."

"Christ." Souness sat back a little, rubbing her stubbly head with the palm of her hand. "Is it sounding like a Maudsley jobbie?"

He nodded. "Yeah. But he won't be far — the park is sealed now, we'll have him before long."

He stood to leave the van. "Jack?" Souness stopped him. "Something else is worrying ye."

He paused for a minute, looking at the floor, his hand on the back of his neck. It was as if she'd leaned over and peered keen-eyed through a window in his head. They liked each other, he and Souness: neither was quite sure why, but they had both fallen comfortably into this partnership. Still, there were some things he didn't choose to tell her.

"No, Danni," he murmured eventually, reknotting his tie, not wanting to hear how much she guessed of his preoccupations. "Come on, let's have a shufti at the park, shall we?"

Outside, night had come to Donegal Crescent. The moon was low and red in the sky.

From the back of Donegal Crescent, Brockwell Park appeared to ramble away for miles into the distance, filling the skyline. Its upper slopes were mostly bald, only a few shabby, hairless trees across the backbone and at the highest point a clutch of exotic evergreens, but on the west slope an area about the size of four football pitches was thick with trees: bamboo and silver birch, beech and Spanish chestnut, they huddled around four stinking ponds, sucking up the dampness in the soil. There was the density of a jungle among those trees — in the summer the ponds seemed to be steaming.

At 8.30p.m. that night, only minutes before the park was sealed off by the police, one solitary man was not far from the ponds, shuffling among the trees, an intent expression on his face. Roland Klare's was a lonely, almost hermitic existence — with odd tempers and periods of lethargy — and sometimes, when the mood was on him, he was a collector. A human relative of the carrion beetle, to Klare nothing was disposable or beyond redemption. He knew the park well and often wandered around here looking through the bins, checking under park benches. People left him alone. He had long, rather womanly hair, and a smell about him that no one liked. A familiar smell — of dirty clothes and urine.

Now he stood, with his hands in his pockets, and stared at what was between his feet. It was a camera. A Pentax camera. Old and battered. He picked it up and looked at it carefully, holding it close to his face because the light was fading fast, examining it for damage. Roland Klare had four or five other cameras back at his flat, among the items scavenged from skips and dumpsters. He even had bits and pieces of film-developing equipment. Now quickly he put the Pentax in his pocket and shuffled his feet around in the leaves for a bit, checking the ground. There'd been a summer cloudburst that morning, but the sun had been out all afternoon and even the undersides of the long grass were dry against his shoes. Two feet away lay a pair of pink rubber gloves, large ones, which he slipped into his pocket with the camera. After a while he continued on his way through the fading light. The rubber gloves, he decided when he got them under a street-light, were not worth keeping. Too worn. He dropped them in a skip on the Railton Road. But a camera. A camera was not to be discarded lightly.

It was a quiet evening for India 99, the twin-engined Squirrel helicopter out of Lippits Hill air base. The sun had gone down and the heat and low cloud cover made the Air Support crew headachy: they got the unit's twelve fixed tasks completed as quickly as possible — Heathrow, the Dome, Canary Wharf, several power stations including Battersea — and were ready to switch to self-tasking when the controller came through on the tactical commander's headset. "Yeah, India nine nine from India Lima."

The tactical commander pulled the mouthpiece nearer. "Go ahead, India Lima."

"Where are you?"

"We're in, uh, where?" He leaned forward a little and looked down at the lit-up city. "Wandsworth."

"Good. India nine eight's got an active, but they've reached endurance, grid ref: TQ3427445."

The commander checked the map. "Is that Brockwell Park?"

"Rog. It's a missing child, ground units have got it contained, but look, lads, the DI's being straight with us, says you're a tick in the box. He can't promise the child's in the park — just a hunch — so there's no obligation."

The commander pulled away his mouthpiece, checked his watch and looked into the front of the cockpit. The air observer and the pilot had heard the request and were holding their thumbs up for him to see. Good. He noted the time and the Computer Aided Dispatch number on the assignment log and pulled his mouthpiece back into place.

"Yeah, go on, then, India Lima. It's quiet tonight — we'll have a look. Who are we speaking to?"

"An, um, an Inspector Caffery. AMIT —"

"The murder squad, you mean?"

"That's the one."

CHAPTER TWO

There were marks on the camera casing where it had been dropped and, later, at home in his flat on the top floor of Arkaig Tower, a council block at the northerly tip of Brockwell Park, Roland Klare discovered that the Pentax was damaged in other, less visible ways. After wiping the casing carefully with a tea-towel he attempted to wind on the film inside and found the mechanism had jammed. He fiddled with it, tried forcing it and shaking it, but he couldn't free the winder. He put the camera on the sill in the living room and stood for a while looking out of the big window.

The evening sky above the park was orange like a bonfire and somewhere in the distance he could hear a helicopter. He scratched his arms compulsively, trying to decide what to do. The only other working camera he had was a Polaroid. He'd acquired that, too, in a not totally honest fashion, but Polaroid film was expensive, so this Pentax was worth salvaging. He sighed, picked it up and tried again, struggling to unjam the mechanism, putting the camera between his legs to hold it still while he wrestled with it, but after twenty minutes of fruitless struggle he was forced to admit defeat.

Frustrated and sweating now, he made a note of it in the book he kept in a desk next to the window, then placed the camera in a purple Cadbury's Selection tin on the window-sill where, along with a neon-pink-handled screwdriver, three bottles of prescription pills, and a plastic wallet printed with a Union Jack that he'd found last week on the upper deck of the number two, it would remain, its evidence wound neatly inside, for more than five days.

All prisons in London insist on being informed about any helicopter that passes. It keeps them calm. India 99, seeing the familiar glass-roofed gym and octagonal emergency control room ahead on their right, got on to channel eight and identified themselves to HMP Brixton before they continued towards the park. It was a warm and breathless night; the low cloud cover trapped the orange city light, spreading it back down across the roofs so that the helicopter seemed to be flying through a glowing layer of heat, as if its belly and rotor blades had been dipped in hot, electric orange. Now they were over Acre Lane — a long, spangled, untangled row of pearls. On they went, out over the hot, packed streets behind Brixton Water Lane, on and on, over a warren of houses and pubs, until suddenly, on a tremendous rush of air and aviation fuel — *flak flak flak FLAK* — they floated out into the clear darkness over Brockwell Park.

Someone in the dark cockpit whistled. "It's bigger than I thought."

The three men peered dubiously down at the vast expanse of black. This unlit stretch of wood and grass in the middle of the blazing city seemed to go on for ever — as if they'd left London behind and were flying over an empty ocean. Ahead, in the distance, the lights of Tulse Hill marked the furthest borders of the park, twinkling in a tiny string on the horizon.

"Jesus." In the little dark cockpit, his face lit by the glow from the instrument panel, the air observer shifted uncomfortably. "How we going to do this?"

"We'll do it." The commander checked the radio frequency card in the plastic leg pocket of his flying suit, adjusted the headset and spoke above the rotor noise to Brixton divisional control. "Lima Delta from India nine nine."

"Good evening, India nine nine. We've got a helicopter over us — is that you?"

"Roger. Request talk through with the search unit on this code twenty-five."

"Roger. Use MPS 6 — go ahead, India nine nine."

The next voice the commander heard was DI Caffery's. "Hi there, nine nine. We can see you. Thanks for coming."

The air observer leaned over the thermal-imaging screen. It was a bad night for it — the trapped heat was pushing the equipment to its limits, making everything on the screen the same uniform milky grey. Then he saw, in the top left-hand corner, a luminous white figure holding up its hand into the night. "OK, yes. I've got him."

"Yeah, hello there, ground units," the commander said into his mike. "You're more than welcome. We've got eyeball with you too."

The observer toggled the camera and now he could see them all, the ground units, glimmering forms strung out around the perimeter of the trees. It looked like almost forty officers down there. "Jeez, they've got it well contained."

"You've got it well contained," the commander told DI Caffery.

"I know. Nothing's getting in or out of here tonight. Not without us knowing."

"It's a large area and there's wildlife in there too, but we'll do our best."

"Thank you."

The tactical commander leaned into the front of the cockpit and held up his thumb. "OK, lads, let's do it."

The pilot put the Squirrel into a right-hand orbit above the southern quarter of the park. About half a mile to the west they could see the chalky smudge of the dried-out boating-lake, and from among the trees the basalt glitter of the four lakes. They took the park in zones, moving in concentric circles five hundred feet in the air. The air observer, hunched over his screen, steeled against the deafening roar of the rotors, could see no hotspots. He toggled the controls on his laptop. The ground crews had been easy, hot and moving and outside the trees, but tonight the thermal return was as poor as it got and anything could be hiding under that summer leaf canopy. The equipment was virtually blind. "We'll be lucky," he murmured to the commander, as they moved on through the rest of the park. "Peeing in the wind." Peeing, not pissing, careful what he said — everything up here was recorded for evidence. "Peeing in the wind is what we're doing."

On the ground, next to the TSG's Sherpa van, Caffery stood with Souness and stared up at the helicopter lights. He was relying on the Air Unit to crack this — to find Rory Peach. It was an hour now since the alarm had been raised. It had been the Gujarati shopkeeper who had dialled 999.

Most of the Peaches' dole money went on Carmel's Superkings — by the weekend the money had run out and there was usually a tab to be settled at the corner shop. This weekend nobody had paid off the bill so on Monday evening the shopkeeper went down Donegal Crescent to demand his money. It wasn't the first time, he'd told Caffery, and no, he wasn't afraid of Alek Peach, but he had taken the Alsatian with him anyway, and at 7.00p.m. had rung the Peaches' doorbell.

No reply. He knocked loudly but still there was no reply. Reluctantly he continued into the park with the dog.

They walked along the back gardens of Donegal Crescent and were some distance into the park when the Alsatian turned suddenly and began to bark in the direction of the houses. The shopkeeper turned. He thought, although he wouldn't swear to it, he *thought* he saw something running there. Shadowy and wide-beamed. Moving rapidly away from the back of the Peaches' house. His first impression was that it was an animal, because of how furiously and nervously the Alsatian was barking, straining at the lead, but the shadow disappeared quickly into the woods. Curious now, he dragged the reluctant dog back to number thirty and peered through the letterbox.

This time he knew something was wrong. There was junk mail scattered on the hallway floor and a message, or part of a message, had been spray-painted in red on the staircase wall.

"Jack?" Souness said, over the roar of the helicopter above. "What're ye thinking?"

"That he has to be in there somewhere," he yelled, jabbing his finger at the park. "He's in there."

"How do you know he didn't come back out of the park?"

"No." He cupped his hand around his mouth and leaned into her. "If he did come out I can promise you someone's going to remember. All the park exits lead into main streets. The little boy's bleeding, probably terrified —"

"WHAT?"

"HE'S NAKED AND BLEEDING. I THINK SOMEONE WOULD PICK UP THE PHONE FOR THAT, DON'T YOU? EVEN IN BRIXTON."

He looked at the helicopter. He had other good reasons to think that Rory was in the park — he knew the statistics on child abduction: most studies would predict that if Rory wasn't alive he would probably be found within five miles of the abduction site, less than fifty yards from a footpath. Other worldwide stats would tell a more chilling story: they'd predict that

Rory wouldn't be killed immediately, that his kidnapper would probably keep him alive for anything up to twenty-four hours. They'd say that the motive in an abduction of a boy within Rory's age range would probably be sex. They'd say that the sex would probably be sadistic.

If Caffery had more than a passing knowledge of the habits and lifecycle of the paedophile there was a simple reason: he could reach back twenty-seven years into his own past and find a mirror image of this in another disappearance. His own brother, Ewan — the same age as Rory — had been sucked out of the middle of a normal day. From the back of the family house. Rory could be Ewan all over again. Caffery knew he should say something about it to Souness, he should take her aside right now and tell her, "Maybe you should cut me out of this — give it to DC Logan or someone — because I don't know how I'm going to react."

"WHAT IF THEY DON'T FIND ANYTHING?" Souness yelled.

"DON'T WORRY. THEY'LL FIND SOMETHING." He lifted the radio to his mouth, lowering his voice and getting on to the helicopter commander's channel. "Nine nine, anything happening up there?"

Five hundred feet overhead, in the dark cockpit, the commander moved as far forward as the coms lead, which tethered him like an umbilicus to the roof of the helicopter, would allow. "Hey, Howie? They want to know how we're doing, Howie." He couldn't see the air observer's face, hunched over as he was, his attention on the screen, the helmet obscuring his eyes.

"I'm struggling. Looks like an effing snowfield. Unless it moves it just blends in. Has to pretty much stand up and wave at me." He tried switching so that heat showed black on his screen. He tried red, he tried blue, sometimes a different colour helped, but tonight the thermal washout was beating him. "Can you give us some more right-hand orbits?"

"Rog." The pilot nosed the helicopter over, turning in circles, both he and the commander looking out of the right-hand side of the craft at the dense wood below. The air observer narrowed his eyes on the screen. He moved the laptop joystick and under the cockpit, in the sensor pod, the gyroscopically mounted camera, deathly stable, rotated its cool eye across the park.

"What you got?"

"I dunno. There's something at about ten o'clock but . . ." Without depth perception it was difficult to tell what he was seeing on the screen, and every time they got near the helicopter made the leaf cover shift. He thought he had seen an odd, doughnut-shaped light source, about the size of a car tyre. But then the leaf cover shifted again and now he thought he'd dreamed it. "*Scheisse*." He leaned intently over the screen, moving his head from side to side, flicking the screen from wide field to narrow and back again. "Yeah, maybe get them to have a look at that." He tapped the screen. "Can you see it?"

The commander leaned forward and looked at the screen. He couldn't see what the observer was talking about but sat back and tuned the radio control into DI Caffery's loop. "Ground unit from nine nine."

"Yeah, have you got anything?"

"We think we might've got a heat source but we can't quite confirm. Do you want to have a look at it?"

"Will do."

"Right, well, there's a pool, or a paddling-pool or something . . ."

"The boating-lake?"

"The boating-lake — and the forest starts, I dunno, two hundred metres away?"

"Yup — sounds about right."

The commander leaned forward and looked to where the observer held his finger over the screen. "If you could start at that edge of the forest and move in about a hundred metres . . ."

"Rog. Got you."

The commander held his hand flat, instructing the pilot to hover, and the three crew members sat forward, not speaking, only the sound of their breathing in the headsets as they watched the glimmering forms of the TSG, the Territorial Support Group, streaming across the screen in the direction of the heat source.

"Right," the commander muttered. "Let's give them some help, shall we?" He threw a switch and powered up the Night Sun — the gargantuan spotlight dangling from the helicopter's belly. Thirty million candle power — it could burn through concrete at close range: the ground units followed it like the nativity star, yomping towards it through the trees. But on the screen the observer had lost the glowing ring-shaped heat source and now he was starting to wonder if he'd imagined it.

"Howie?" the commander said from behind. "Are we in the right place?"

The observer didn't reply. He sat hunched forward, trying to relocate the source.

"Howie?"

"Yeah — I think, but I —"

"Nine nine from ground units." Caffery came through on the radio. "We're drawing a blank down here. Can you help us out?"

"Howie?"

"I dunno — I dunno. There *was* something." He threw the screen into narrow field once more and shook his head. The noise of the engines and the rotor blades, the heat and the smells were oppressive tonight and he was having trouble concentrating. On the ground the TSG officers stood looking up at the helicopter, arms open. "Shit," he muttered under his breath. "Howie, you sodding idiot." He was going to have to back down. "I — look — I don't know —"

"OK, OK." The commander was getting impatient. "How are we for fuel?"

The pilot shook his head. "About twenty-five per cent."

He whistled. "So we need to be going somewhere in about, what? Twenty minutes. Howie? What are we thinking?"

"Look, I — nothing. I imagined it. Nothing."

The commander sighed. “OK, I’ve got you.” He switched to the CAD controller’s frequency. “India Lima, we’re low on fuel so we’re going to slip into Fairoaks for a slurp. I think we’ve got a no-trace. Haven’t we, Howie? Got a clear?”

“Yeah.” He ran a finger under his chin strap, uncomfortable. “I guess so — a no-trace. I guess.”

“Nine nine to ground units, if you’re clear down there so are we.”

“You sure?” DI Caffery sounded tense. “You sure we’re in the right place?”

“Yeah, *you*’re in the right place but we’ve lost the source. It’s a hot night — we’re fighting interference up here.”

“Rog, if you’re sure. Thanks for trying.”

“Sorry about that.”

“It’s OK. Good evening to you all.”

The commander could see Caffery on the screen waving. He adjusted his headset and switched back to the CAD controller. “That’s a no-trace in the open, so we’re complete on scene at grid ref TQ3427445, now routing to India Foxtrot.” He noted the time on his assignment log and the helicopter banked away into the night.

On the ground below, Caffery watched the helicopter disappear across the rooftops, until its light was scarcely bigger than a satellite.

“You know what it means, don’t you?”

“No,” Souness admitted. “No, I don’t.”

It was late. The TSG had zoned off the area where the air observer had imagined a heat source, got down on their hands and knees and covered every square inch of it. Still no Rory Peach. Eventually they'd given up, and Caffery and Souness had finalized arrangements for a specialized search team to come in the next day: a Police Search Advisory team would start at first light in Brockwell Park.

There was still an emergency team briefing to get through and search parameters to establish before the night was out and so, at 11p.m., they drove back to AMIT headquarters in Thornton Heath. Caffery parked the car and swung the keys into his pocket. "If he's in the park and they can't see him then he's not much of a heat source and he's not moving." In spite of what it meant professionally, part of him secretly hoped, for the boy's sake, that he was already dead. There are some things, he believed, not worth surviving. "Maybe we're too late already."

"Unless," Souness climbed wearily from the car and together they crossed the road, "unless he's not in the park."

"Oh, he's in the park. I promise you he's in the park." Caffery swiped his pass card and held the door for Souness. "It's just a question of where."

"Shrivemoor" was how most officers referred to this old red-brick building, after the unexciting residential street in which it stood. AMIT's offices were housed on the second floor. Tonight lights were on in all the windows. Most of the team had arrived, called away from dinner parties, pubs, babysitting duty. The HOLMES database operators, the five members of the intelligence cell, seven investigating officers, they were all here, wandering between the desks, drinking coffee, murmuring to each other. In the kitchen three embarrassed-looking paramedics in white-hooded forensic suits — nonce suits, the team called them — waited while the exhibits officer photocopied their boot soles and used low-tack tape to lift hairs and fibres from their clothing.

While Souness made strong coffee, Caffery put his face under the tap to wake himself up and quickly checked his in-tray. Among the circulars, the memos, the post-mortem reports, someone had left this week's copy of *Time Out*. It was folded open at a page titled: "The Artists who Turn Crime into Art." A photograph of Rebecca — eyes closed, head tilted back, a prison number painted on the centre of her forehead where a bindi spot would go.

> Rebecca Morant, tabloid totty or the genuine article? You have to be a long way out of the loop not to have heard of Morant, sex-assault victim turned art-world darling. Suspiciously beautiful, the critics found it difficult to take lynx-eyed Morant seriously, until a nomination for the ultra-cool Vincent Award and a short-listing by Becks confirmed her as a key player in the post YBA pack . . .

Caffery closed the magazine and placed it face down in the in-tray. *How much more publicity do you need, Becky?*

"Right, crew. Listen up." He used an empty Sprite can to bang on the wall. "Come on, listen, everyone. I know you're all on short notice but let's get this bit done. We'll do it in the SIO's." Holding the videotape above his head, he started towards the office he and Souness shared, beckoning the officers to follow. "Come on, it'll only take ten so you can have your piss breaks later."

The senior investigating officer's room was small — for all the team to cram in, the door had to be left open. Souness stood against the window, coffee mug cupped in both hands as Caffery plugged in the video and waited for everyone to gather.

"Right. You all know the basics. DCI Souness is doing the search and house-to-house parameters so whoever's on the knock come and see her after this. First light we've got the search-team meeting in Brockwell Park so I want everyone ready. SPECRIMs go out as usual, but bear in mind what I'm going to tell you now for hold-back on the press bureau. Exhibits, family liaison, organize yourselves. What else? We've got primacy but we'll appoint a liaison officer for, I'm sorry to say, the paedophile unit and the risk-management panel at Lambeth and, uh, someone better have a whisper with the child-protection lads at Belvedere, make sure Rory hasn't made an appearance there before. Now . . ." He gestured at the blank TV screen and took a deep breath. "When I show you this, the first place you're going to wonder about is the Maudsley." He paused. At the mention of the Maudsley — the mental-health clinic on Denmark Hill — one or two of the civilian workers had sucked in a breath. He didn't want that: he wanted the team thinking and functioning and not overreacting to the nature of the crime.

"Look," he said, "I don't want you writing him off as a psycho just yet. I'm only saying that's how it looks." He glanced around at the faces. "Maybe that's how it's *meant* to look. Maybe there's some trail-covering here — maybe he's your common or garden paedo who's trying to throw up a smokescreen, pave his way to an insanity plea if he gets caught. And keep in mind that he's been in play for three days. *Three days*. That's controlled, isn't it? Have a think about those three days and what they mean. Do they mean, for example, that he knows he's not going to get disturbed?"

Or do they mean he was enjoying himself so much with Rory that he'd decided to stay on for the long weekend?

He pointed the remote control at the video. Donegal Crescent appeared on screen. It was dusk. Beneath the time-code a crowd jostled the cordons, trying to get a better glimpse of the little terraced house: blue ambulance lights flashed silently across their faces. Caffery, standing back against the wall now with his arms folded, watched the AMIT detectives out of the corner of his eye. This was the first they had seen of the crime scene and he knew they'd find something terrible about the Peaches' house. Something terrible about its normality.

"This is on the edge of Brockwell Park," he said evenly. "Just to give you some geography, that tower you can see in the distance is Arkaig Tower on Railton Road, which the divisionals know and love as Crack Heights."

The camera tracked down the path to the doorstep of number thirty, and turned to pan across the street, the little scrap of grass opposite, the neighbours' faces shocked white ovals against the evening sky. Any point that could be observed from the Peaches' house could also be a vantage-point for a potential witness. The camera recorded everything then swung 180 degrees and faced the house head on. The number "30" in gold screw-on numerals filled the screen.

"All the doors and windows were closed." The camera ran itself around the splintered front door — opened with the Enforcer battering-ram — zooming in on an intact lock. "The Territorials had to batter their way in. The only thing not locked was the back door — we think it's our point of entry. Watch."

They were inside the house now, the camera flooding the hallway with halogen light. Slightly worn wallpaper, a grey cord carpet protected by a heavy-duty plastic runner. Two badly framed prints cast long, bobbing shadows up the hall and a child's turbo water-gun lay on its side on the bottom step. Up ahead, at the end of the hall, a doorway. The tape blurred for a moment, helical scan traces across the screen, and when the picture steadied the camera had gone through the doorway and was in a small kitchen. A glazed terracotta chicken eyed the camera beadily from next to the breadbin and a checked curtain over the door wallowed in the breeze, revealing a broken window, flashes of the darkened yard, a glimpse of the trees in the park beyond.

"Right. Important." Caffery rested his elbow on the monitor, leaning over to point at the screen. "Glass on the floor, door unlocked. This is not only the point of entry but also the exit point. Intruder breaks window and lets himself in — we think this is some time after seven p.m. on Friday evening." The camera zoomed through the broken window and out into a small yard beyond. A carousel clothes-dryer, a child's bike, some toys and four overturned milk bottles, their contents rancid and yellow. "The intruder then stays in the house with the Peach family until Monday afternoon when he's disturbed — at which point he picks up Rory Peach and leaves through the same door." The camera pulled back into the kitchen and panned the room, pausing at a set of bloody drag marks on the doorpost. Caffery tapped the remote control on his leg and looked around the silent faces, expecting a reaction. But no one spoke or asked questions. They were staring at the blood on the screen.

"The lab thinks his wounds aren't fatal at this point. The received wisdom is that the intruder carried him out of the house — through this broken fence here and into the woods. He's probably found a way to staunch the blood flow, maybe a towel or something, because the dogs lost him early. Right." The camera was moving. "Good, now I'm going to show you where the family were found."

A woman's face came briefly in and out of shot: DS Quinn, the crime-scene co-ordinator, the most experienced CSC in South London. After she and Caffery had orchestrated the video she had returned to the kitchen to ensure that the glass from the break-in was carefully photographed and removed. Then she had called the Specialist Crime Unit biologists down from Lambeth. While Caffery was with the helicopter crew the scientists had come through the house, dressed in protective suits, applying their specialized chemicals: ninhydrin, amido black, silver nitrate.

"Alek Peach — that's Dad — was found here, handcuffed by the wrists to this radiator, and by the ankles to this radiator. You can tell the position he was in from the mark he's left." Caffery pointed it out to the team — a large dark stain on the shag-pile carpet, stretching between the two radiators in the living room. "He's got a wound to the back of his head so we won't be talking to him for a while. Maybe not at all. And the second place — watch, you'll see it now we're going upstairs — is where Carmel was held."

Carmel, who was now sedated at the hospital, had given something of a statement in the ambulance. Although a cursory examination showed no head wounds it was assumed she had lost consciousness at some point: apart from making dinner at 6p.m. on Friday, she remembered nothing until she had woken gagged and cuffed to a water-pipe in the airing cupboard on the first-floor landing. There she had remained until the shopkeeper had called through the letterbox three days later. She hadn't seen or spoken to the intruder, and, no, there was no reason, business or personal, that someone would want to hurt her family. When the paramedics helped her out of the cupboard they angled the stretcher so that she faced the stairs. They didn't want her to turn and see what was spray-painted on the wall behind her.

"And when you see it," he looked around at the faces, "I think you'll agree that, in spite of the heavy traffic through the house, it's what we should keep from the press."

He turned back to the TV. The camera operator was climbing the stairs, the shadows danced across the landing ahead. When Caffery had seen the spray-painting he had instantly recognized it as a tool to weed out false confessions.

The camera wobbled, someone in the hallway said, "Fuck," and then in a louder voice on screen, "Have you seen this?" Darkness. A brief fumble then a flare of light, the camera aperture closed down momentarily, flinching like an iris. When the image came into focus the detectives in the SIO's room inched a little closer, trying to read the spray-painted message.

♀ HAZARD

Caffery paused the tape, allowing each member of the team time to bend in and examine it. "Female Hazard." He flicked off the video and turned on the light. “We want this bottomed out by tomorrow — I won’t insult your intelligence by telling you why.”

In the kitchen at the Fairoaks base the air observer took off his helmet and rubbed his ears. He still wasn’t sure what he’d seen. “I’d like to have done that on maximum endurance, y’know.”

The commander patted him on the back. “They said we were just a tick in the box, Howie. They don’t even know if he’s in the park.”

“It’s a kid, though.”

“Maybe when we lift we’ll go back, eh?”

But in the time they took to refuel, a traffic officer in Purley had been hit by a car while deploying a stinger. The offender was out of the car and running towards Croydon airfield, so India 99 rerouted to that instead. When his shift finished at 2a.m. the air observer was finding it a little easier not to think about the hazy white doughnut shape he thought he’d seen among the trees in Brockwell Park.

CHAPTER THREE

Protocol at the Jack Steinberg Intensive Care Unit in King's Hospital kept all head-injury victims on a Codman intercranial pressure bolt and a ventilator for the first twenty-four hours, whether the patient could breathe unaided or not. Even without the heavy dose of medazolam sculling through his veins, AMIT's key witness, Alek Peach, wouldn't have been able to speak with the endotrachial tube down his throat. His wife, Carmel, was still sedated but Caffery would have gone to the hospital and paced the corridors like an expectant father all night, had DCI Souness not pulled rank.

"They'll never let you near while he's on that thing, Jack." She respected this in Caffery, this hungry, stray-dog determination, but she knew her hospital consultants well. She knew not to push it. "If he needs blood they've promised us a pre-transfusion sample. We've got the consultant's statement, and that's the most we can ask."

It was 1a.m.: now that the team knew their parameters for the search, overtime had been assigned and the Brockwell Park area was secured, Souness and some of the other officers went home to catch a precious hour or two's sleep before sun-up. Caffery had now been awake for twenty-five hours but he couldn't relax. He went into the SIO's room — found a bottle of Bell's under the desk, slugged some into a mug and sat at the desk, jiggling his knees and tapping his fingers on the phone. When he couldn't stand it any longer he picked up the receiver and got through to the ICU.

But the consultant, Mr Friendship, was losing patience. "What part of 'no' don't you understand?" And he hung up.

Caffery stared at the dead receiver. He could redial — spend twenty minutes bullying the hospital staff — but he knew he was up against a brick wall. He sighed, put down the receiver, refilled the mug, put his feet up on the desk and sat with his tie undone, staring blankly out of the window at the Croydon skyscrapers lit up against the sky.

This case might be the one he'd waited his life out for — he already knew that because of what had happened to his own brother, more than quarter of a century ago —

Quarter of a century? Is it really that long, Ewan? How long before they can't get any DNA at all? How long before a body disappears into the surrounding soil? Becomes silt . . .

— he knew that he was going to have problems with it. He had felt them already, in the quiet interludes of the day, multiplying like bacilli.

Ewan had been just nine. The same age as Rory. There'd been an argument — two brothers in a tree-house arguing about something unimportant. The older boy, Ewan, had shuffled down out of the tree, walked off in a sulk down the railway cutting. He was dressed in brown Clark's sandals, brown shorts and a mustard yellow T-shirt (Caffery knew these details were true — he remembered them doubly: once directly and once from reading them later on the police appeal posters). No one ever saw him again.

Jack had watched the police search the railway cutting, determined one day that he would join them. *One day, one day, I'll find you, Ewan . . .* And to this day he lived in the same little South London terraced house, staring out across the back garden and the railway tracks to the house still owned by the ageing paedophile whom everyone, including the police, suspected of being responsible for Ewan's disappearance. Ivan Penderecki. Penderecki's house had been searched but no trace of Ewan was found, so there they lived, Penderecki and Jack Caffery, like a bitter married couple, locked in a wordless duel. Every woman Caffery had ever slept with had tried to prise him away, tried to loosen the complex fascination between him and the big Polish paedophile, but Caffery had never wasted a moment considering the choice — there was no competition. *Even with Rebecca?* Rebecca, too, wanted him to forget all about Ewan. *Is there no competition with her?*

He swallowed the Scotch, refilled the mug and took the *Time Out* from his tray. He could call her — he knew where she'd be. She rarely slept at her Greenwich flat — "Don't like to be with the ghosts." Instead she often came late to his house and simply went to bed, her arms wrapped round a pillow, a Danneman cigarillo smouldering in the ashtray next to the bed. He checked his watch. It was late, even for Rebecca. And if he called he'd have to tell her about the Peach case, about the similarities, and he knew what her reaction would be. Instead he tipped the chair forward and opened *Time Out*.

> On the now infamous sexual assault last summer, Morant says: "*Yes, the experience informed my work, I suddenly realized that it's easy to look at fictionalized rape in a film or in a book and think you've understood. But in fact these are mere representations and act as safety nets against the brutality. I decided it was patronizing to give mocked-up representations*." Adopting this mantra, in February she stoked controversy and media frenzy when it was revealed (strategically leaked?) that the moulds of battered and mutilated genitalia in her "*Random*" exhibition (inset) were casts taken from genuine victims of rape and sexual abuse.

In private Rebecca would never talk about what had been done to her a year ago. Caffery had been there, had seen her close-up, unconscious and displayed, suspended from a ceiling: a killer's bloody, valedictory exhibit. He had sat patiently through her statement for the inquest of her dead flatmate, Joni Marsh, in a little hospital room in Lewisham. It had been a rainy day and the maple tree outside the window dripped steadily through the interview.

"Look, if you find this difficult . . ."

"No — no, it's not difficult."

At that point he was already half in love with Rebecca. Seeing her bent head, those slender hands fidgeting in her lap as she tried to put it into words, tried to explain the indignity performed on her, he took pity and prompted her through the statement, broke every rule in the book to lessen the ordeal. Fed her what he knew so that all she had to do was nod. She remained shaken — at the inquest she dried during her testimony and couldn't start again, and eventually the coroner had to allow her to step down from the witness stand. Even now, if Caffery tried to coax her into talking about it, she would pull up the drawbridge. Or, more infuriatingly, laugh and swear it hadn't affected her. In public, however, she used it almost as an accessory, like part of her wardrobe:

> Cue outraged women's groups, salivating glee from the tabloids and schizophrenic cat and mouse, press-dodging games from Morant. On future ambitions? "*Being banned by Giuliani — that would be quite fun.*" And most oft-repeated hack question? "*When are you going to chuck in the art and do what you really want to do — model?*" *Random 2* opens at the Zinc Gallery, Clerkenwell, 26 August - 20 September.

As long as the world thinks she's resilient, that's all she cares about. He closed the magazine, rested his face for a moment in his hands and tried not to think about her. Out of the window London's midnight lights sparkled like luminous-spined sea creatures. He wondered if Rory Peach was looking at the same lights.

"Coffee?"

He jerked a little where he lay. Opened his eyes. "Marilyn?"

Marilyn Kryotos, the manager — the "receiver" — of the cumbersome HOLMES murder database, stood in the doorway staring at him. She wore pink lipstick and a navy-blue dress, one lapel pinned with a mother-of-pearl brooch in the shape of a bunny. "Did you *sleep* here?" She sounded half impressed, half disgusted. "In the office?"

"OK, OK." He straightened from the desk, pressing knuckles into his eyes. It was a little before dawn and the night was pink around the bottom of the Croydon skyscrapers. A fly floated feet up in the mug of Scotch. He checked his watch. "You're early."

"First light. Half the team are here already. Danni's on her way to Brixton."

"Fuck." He groped for his tie.

"Do you want a comb?"

"No, no."

"You need one."

"I know."

He went to the twenty-four-hour filling station opposite the office, bought a sandwich, a comb, a toothbrush, and hurried back, past the area maps lining the corridor, stopping to pick up the spare shirt he kept in the exhibits room. In the men's he stripped off his shirt, splashed water across his chest, under his arms, and bent to put his face under the tap, wet his hair, then went to the air dryer, lifting his arms, pushing his head under it to dry his hair. He knew he was in the silent eye of the storm. He knew that as the country woke, as televisions came on and the news spread, the incident room phone would begin to ring. Meanwhile there was red tape to wade through, community-impact assessment meetings to be arranged with the borough commander, and case reviews to think about. The stopwatch had started and he had to be ready.

"Did you get that thing about Rebecca?" Kryotos stood in the incident room, holding a coffee mug and a cake tin.

"The *Time Out*, you mean?" He took the coffee and together they went back into the SIO's room.

"She looked lovely in it, didn't she?"

"She did." He put the coffee on the desk and picked up the new murder manual — the blue and white loose-leaf file that had appeared on the window-sills of every police station since the Lawrence inquiry — and leafed through it, running a mental check list of all the tasks he should complete today.

"I called the hospital," Kryotos said. "Alek Peach made it through the night."

"Seriously?" He looked up. "Can he talk?"

"No. He's still got that tube thingy down his throat, but he's stable."

"And Carmel?"

"Came out of her sedation and she's busy getting herself discharged."

"Jesus, I wasn't expecting that."

"Relax. There's a woodentop with her. She's going to a friend's."

"OK. Speak to the uniform and tell him to call when she's settled."

"*Her*. It's a WPC."

"Her. Tell her to call when Carmel's settled and say I'll be on my way, and then, Marilyn, can you get a Quest Search off to Hendon for me?"

"Yup." She put down the tin, found a pen in his desk-tidy, sat down in Souness's chair and jotted down the key search words he gave her. "Abduction", "intruder", "handcuff", and "child", with an age range of five to ten. He didn't have to be careful what he said to Kryotos — she was probably the most level-headed member of the team — no matter what the crime, she handled the details that passed through her hands with a calmness he sometimes envied.

"Is that it?"

"No." He thought for a moment, closing the murder manual and putting it back on the window-sill. "Let's see, sex offenders. Include that, OK? And do the usual check of the nonce register."

"Right." She recapped the pen, pushed herself to her feet and picked up the tin. She paused, smiling at his hair, which was still slightly rumpled. If anyone suggested she had an unprofessional fondness for DI Jack Caffery, who was two years her junior *anyway*, she would develop a high colour and abracadabra a healthy marriage out of her hat with two robust children, Dean and Jenna — proof that she and Jack Caffery were colleagues and friends, *and that was all*. The only person utterly convinced by her argument was Caffery himself. "Banana bread." She tapped the lid of the tin. "Me and Dean made it. I know it sounds a bit bonkers but you can stick it in the toaster, put some butter on it and, oh, God, even though I say it myself, it is to *die* for."

"Marilyn, thanks, but —"

"But you'll get your own breakfast? Something not so *sw*eeeet?"

He smiled. "I'm sorry."

"You do *know*, of course, that other people are falling all over themselves for my banana cake?"

"Marilyn, I don't doubt that for a moment."

"You wait, Jack." She lifted the tin on one palm like a waiter and turned for the door, her nose in the air. "One of these days I'll break you."

CHAPTER FOUR

(18 July)

Mrs Nersessian's house, with its modern leaded windows and carefully painted wagon-wheel on the front wall, gleamed like a polished stone. It took her several minutes to unlatch all the chains on the front door. Caffery realized that he must have had a vague image of the person who would be Carmel Peach's friend, and it wasn't Bela Nersessian: she was a short, red-haired woman — sepia skin, long earrings, ruched black blouse embellished with gold necklaces. As soon as she saw Caffery's warrant card she gripped his wrist with varnished fingernails and pulled him into the house.

"She's in the bedroom, the poor love, having some quiet time. Come on." She beckoned him. "Come with me."

They went upstairs, past framed family photographs, pictures of the Virgin Mary in mother-of-pearl frames, a glass chandelier pinging with cleanliness. Bela Nersessian went slowly, clutching the banister and turning slightly sideways in her tight knee-length skirt. Every few steps a new thought came to her and she would pause and turn to him. "Now, if I was the police I'd be searching those lakes in the park." Or: "I've had an idea. Before you leave we'll say a little prayer for Rory, Mr Caffery. Shall we do that?"

On the top landing Mrs Nersessian switched on a small crystal-based lamp, plumped up a yellow silk cushion on a small chair, then stood at the bedroom door, smoothing her blouse and taking a deep breath.

She knocked on the door. "Someone to see you, Carmel lovey." She pushed open the door and stuck her nose inside. "There you are, love. I've got someone to see you, OK?" She stepped back out of the room and stood on tiptoe to whisper in Caffery's ear: "Tell her I'm praying, darling, tell her we're all praying for Rory."

The bedroom smelt of perfume and smoke. It was full of pink satin — on the bed, the radiator, the dressing-table, like the inside of a jewellery box. It was at the back of the house: had the curtains been open the park would have been visible, but maybe the neat little WPC sitting on a pink chair near the window, her hands crossed on her lap, had worried about Carmel seeing the park, because they were firmly closed.

When the WPC saw Caffery she half stood, "Sir," and sat down, nodding at the bed. On the bed, facing away from the door, wearing a large T-shirt with a 1998 World Cup motif on the back and a pair of white leggings, lay Carmel Peach, a raw-skinned woman with thin limbs and chapped red arms. In front of her rested a packet of Superkings, a lighter and a crystal ashtray. He couldn't see her face but he could see that both her wrists were bandaged: Carmel Peach, everyone knew, had tried hard to pull her own hands off in order to escape from the handcuffs and reach her son.

He closed the door behind him and stood for a moment. *You've been here before, Jack, haven't you?* He remembered standing uselessly in the doorway while his mother lay on the bed and cried her heart out for Ewan. *And if she thinks about you at all it's only to wish that you'd piss off.*

"You're the CID, aren't you?" She didn't turn to look at him.

"Yes. I'm with AMIT. Do you feel a bit better now?"

She stared resolutely at the curtains. "Have you — you know?"

"Mrs Peach —"

She lifted her hands briefly as if to stop him speaking, then subsided. "Just tell it me straight."

"I'm sorry." He looked around the room, shaking his head for the benefit of the WPC, glad Carmel couldn't see his face. "I'm sorry. There's no news yet."

She didn't respond at first. Her bare feet stiffened briefly, but that was all. Then, just as he was about to continue, she suddenly, violently, jackknifed her body on the bed and hammered fists into her stomach, groaning and writhing, rucking the cover into pleats. The WPC stepped forward. "It's all right, Carmel love, it's all right." She gently caught Carmel's hands and stroked the backs of them with her thumbs. "There we go. There we go." Slowly she subsided. "There we go. We know you're upset, but you don't want to hurt yourself, too, do you, love?"

The WPC looked up at Caffery, who stood in the doorway, appalled, rooted to the spot. He should have stepped forward, should have grabbed Carmel's hands like that, but all he could do was remember — *stop thinking about it* — remember his mother biting her arms as the police searched Penderecki's house across the tracks, actually *chewing* her own arms to relieve what was inside. He realized he was as helpless now as he had been then to deal with female grief.

The WPC sat down and Carmel subsided. She seemed to be concentrating on her breathing. Then she took four deep breaths, wiped her forehead and shook her head. "And Alek? What about *Alek*?"

"I — he's — he's still at King's. They're doing everything they can for him."

"But they can't save him."

"Look, Carmel, I would be failing in my duty if I didn't advise you to expect the worst."

"Oh, just *shut up* — for fuck's sake, *shut up*, can't you?" She put her face in her hands. "Get the doctor back," she demanded. "Get him to give me something more. Look at me, for fuck's sake, I need something stronger than what he's given me."

"Mrs Peach, I know it's difficult for you. But it's important that you tell us everything you can remember. As soon as I've taken an initial statement from you I'll get your GP back —"

"No — *now*! *Get me something to make it stop*."

"Carmel, the doctor's given you something and we're doing everything we can." He took a step inside the room, looking for somewhere to sit, finding a pink cane chair with a teddy on it. He put the bear on the floor, propped up against the skirting-board, and sat down, his elbows on his knees, leaning forward to look at Carmel. "I've got fifteen of my own men out there, another twenty uniformed officers and I don't know how many volunteers. We're taking it very seriously, putting everything we've got into it. When we've gone through what you can remember I'm going to have an officer come over and talk to you — he's specially assigned to you, OK? He'll be available to you whenever you want."

"But I don't . . ." her body twisted with anguish ". . . I don't *remember* what happened." She dropped her face into her hands and began to sob softly. "*Oh, God, my little boy's gone and I don't even remember what happened*."

It was a long time since the Amateur Swimmers' Association had changed its code of conduct: in response to changing awareness of child abuse it now recommended that teachers minimized physical contact with children and taught lessons from the pool edge. Not all swimming-pools enforced the recommendations, and often the choice of whether to get in the water or not varied according to the teacher, but there was one teacher at the Brixton Recreation Centre who adhered rigidly to the recommendation. Relatively new to the pool, it hadn't escaped anyone's attention that Chris "Fish" Gummer always kept a distance from the children he taught. In fact, he sometimes appeared positively to *dislike* them.

"Almost as if he's nervous of them," the lifeguards would say to each other, watching him in his baggy red drawstring swimming-trunks, wearing his red bathing cap although he wouldn't get into the water (he insisted upon the cap, with its under-chin strap fastening, maybe because his hair was so thin that he looked bald from a distance). "You wonder why he puts himself through it."

They traded ideas for what Gummer reminded them of — a penguin, a fish, a flying bomb. Most of the names fitted, but Fish was probably the best: his smooth body with its rather small, triangular head, the ovoid weightiness in his middle, his legs big above the knee, tapering at the ankle, and then, comically tacked on to those slender ankles, overlarge feet, which he held turned out at forty-five degrees. The fine hair on his chest and legs slicked down to nothing when wet. "You must've got webbed feet," people told him. But he didn't: he examined them and found that his toes, instead of being flat and spatulate, were rather long and slender. But, fish or not, he made an unlikely swimming teacher. For one thing he was older than the other teachers.

"Probably a perve."

"Nah, he'd never've got the job."

They had had it drilled into them — *this post is exempt from section 4 (2) of the Rehabilitation of Offenders Act*. As far as the recreation centre personnel officers were concerned no criminal offence expired. Ever. It didn't matter how many years ago it had happened.

"Unless he *ain't got* a record," one of the lifeguards muttered. "Because he never got caught."

"Or cos he changed his name."

"He couldn't change his name if he had a record, could he?"

"Couldn't he?" One of the older lifeguards cracked his knuckles and stared out at Gummer, who stood on the poolside waiting for two of the girls to pull on their Rollo swim-belts. "Why not?"

At that the lifeguards all fell silent and turned to look at Gummer. He seemed particularly harried today. It was the turn of the "squids", the six- and seven-year-olds, and the two girls seemed to be having problems getting into their belts.

But Gummer wasn't about to crouch down and help. "You're all a bit slow today, aren't you? What's going on?"

Behind him one or two of the children whispered something. He turned. "What? What's got into you all?" No one spoke. There were more parents than usual today in the viewing gallery, he'd noticed, and some members of the class were absent. "Something's going on," he said, turning back to the two girls. "Isn't anyone going to tell me?"

"Rory," the taller of the two said suddenly. She was a solemn girl from Trinidad, whose hair was beaded in rows, and she wore a pink Spice Girls swimsuit. Her toenails were painted the same colour. "It's cos of Rory."

"Rory?" He raised his eyebrows. "What are you talking about?"

"Rory off Donegal Crescent."

"What about him? What happened to Rory?"

Neither girl spoke. The little one, a smaller, darker-skinned girl in a green two-piece, put her finger in her mouth. "We saw the police."

"And did the police tell you what happened?"

The two girls looked at each other, then back at him.

"No? No one told you what happened?"

"No." The bigger girl shook her head. "But we *know* what happened anyway."

"You *know* what happened? Well, that's very clever of you, isn't it?" He put his hands on his knees and bent a little, his eyes narrowed. He was conscious of being monitored from the viewing gallery — the parents were all sitting together with their wary, watchful expressions, little glittering eyes on him as if they suspected him of something. "Well? Come on, then, what happened?"

"It was the troll."

"Ah, yes." He had wondered when this would come up. He straightened, picked up a pile of frog floats, threw them into the pool and stopped for a minute to watch them bob off. He rubbed his hands on his T-shirt and turned back to the girls. "The troll."

The smaller girl looked down at her feet.

"Have you ever seen the troll?"

"No," said the taller girl.

"So how do you know all this? Have any of your friends seen the troll?"

She shrugged. She turned her toes inwards and tugged at the legs of her swimsuit, jiggling a little as if she wanted the toilet.

"Did you hear me? I said, have any of your friends ever seen the troll?"

She nodded, not meeting his eyes.

"Which friends have seen him?"

"Some of them," she said, looking away casually at the water, and he knew she was lying. "He lives in the trees in the park."

"Yes?"

"And he climbed up the drainpipe of that house. The drainpipe of Rory's house."

"I see."

"Climbed up the drainpipe and murdered them. Ate them in their beds."

At this the little girl in the green two-piece began to cry. Tears slipped over the lower lids and on to her knuckles.

"OK, OK." Fish straightened up, nervous now that there were tears. "I think we're jumping to conclusions a bit here. No one knows what happened." Anxious that the parents didn't see what was happening, he positioned himself so that the child was hidden from the gallery. "No one knows if it was the troll yet, do they? Do we? Eh? Do we?"

Eventually he got her to nod her agreement, but she didn't stop crying, her finger still stuck in her mouth. "Right." He turned and clapped his hands at the others. "Come on, nothing to get excited about. Let's have you in the pool. Take a float if you need one."

Later, walking home with his swimming kit in his battered red holdall, he passed four of the gates into the park and found that they were all closed, police notices propped in front of them. He continued on his way, unusually agitated, and when he got home he swallowed his pills immediately, washing them down with black coffee. Then he went to the window, his hands shaking.

A number of windows in Brixton had a view directly over the park. Some belonged to the twin towers at the north, some to the half-built houses on the Clock Tower Grove Estate, and some, like Gummer's, belonged to the council flats above the row of shops on Effra Road. He opened the window and put his head out tentatively. From here Donegal Crescent was almost a mile away and he couldn't see the police tape or the small gathering of journalists and onlookers at the Tulse Hill end of the park, but he did notice the quietness. On a summer's day like this the park was usually spotted with bright dresses and children, but today the great expanse of wood was silent, only the dull click-click of insects and the sound of a car radio coming from Effra Road. Beyond the treetops he got a glimpse, in the distance, of empty lawns stretching up to the top of the hill. He closed the window and drew the curtain.

It took Carmel a long time to stop crying. Caffery and the WPC had exchanged one embarrassed glance, then gone back to staring at separate patches of wallpaper until the Ativan began to work: something softer crept through Carmel's veins and she stopped crying. She reached over and patted the bed, feeling around for the Superkings. Slowly, falteringly, she lit a cigarette, pulled the ashtray towards her, and began to speak. "Even though I told them all this already? In the ambulance?"

"I'd like to hear it again, in case there's something we missed."

But it amounted to little more than a rehashing of the statement she'd given the divisional CID officer. There were few new clues to hang on to. She recalled feeling unwell after eating dinner and that she had sent Rory downstairs to play on the PlayStation with Alek before going to the bedroom to lie down. She had been concerned because they were planning to drive to Margate the following day and she didn't want to be ill. That was all she remembered until she woke up in the airing cupboard. There had been no noises, no one suspicious in the neighbourhood and, apart from the illness, nothing unusual about the few hours that led up to the attack. "We was supposed to be going on holiday the next day. That's why no one come for us. They must've thought we was away."

"You told the CID officer you heard something that sounded like an animal?"

"Yes. Breathing. Sniffing. Outside of the cupboard."

"When was this?"

"The first day, I think."

"How often did this happen?"

"Just that once."

"Well, um, do you think there was an animal in the house? Do you think the intruder brought a dog with him?"

She shook her head. "I never heard nothing else, no barking or nothing, and it weren't no dog. Not unless it was standing up on its, you know . . ." She tapped the backs of her calves. "Standing up on its back legs."

"What do you think it was?"

"I don't know. I ain't never heard nothing like it."

"Did you hear Rory or Alek at all in that time?"

"Rory." She squeezed her eyes closed and nodded. "Crying. He was in the kitchen."

"When was this?"

"Just before you lot come." The words dragged a little jerk out of her as if the effort hurt her. She tamped out her cigarette, lit another from the carton and started to cough. It took her a long time to regain her composure. She wiped her eyes, then her mouth, pushed her hair out of her eyes and said, "There was something I never told them last night."

Caffery looked up from his notes. "I'm sorry?" The WPC was looking at him in surprise, her eyebrows raised. "What did you say?"

"Something else."

"What was that?"

"I think he took photographs."

"*Photographs?*"

"I saw the flashbulb under the cupboard door. I could even hear it winding on. I'm sure that's what it was — photographs."

"What do you think he was photographing?"

"I don't know. I don't want to know." She started to shake again, rubbing her arms convulsively. "*It was so fucking horrible*. I was soft — so bleeding soft that I just sat there like a fucking frightened mouse for them three days. I never knew he was going to take Rory. If I'd of known what he was going to do . . ."

"You weren't a coward, Carmel. Just look what you did to your arms trying to get out. You tried as hard as anyone could have been expected —" Caffery stopped, suddenly self-conscious. *Don't — you'll only make things worse*. Quickly he found his attaché case on the floor. "Look, I know how difficult this is but we need you to sign something. It's not a statement, just a couple of release forms. We found a picture of Rory, a school picture, and we'd like your permission to reproduce it — to show people. And I've taken some of Rory's clothes and his schoolbooks."

"His clothes? Schoolbooks?"

"For the dogs. And —"

"And?"

And to scrape. For his own DNA so we have a hope of identifying him. Since, although I'm not going to say it, I think, Mrs Peach, that your son's probably already dead.

It was one of the hottest Julys London had seen and Caffery knew what could happen to a body in forty-eight hours of this heat. He knew that if Rory wasn't found before tomorrow morning there was no way he would allow a relative to identify him.

"And?" she repeated.

"And nothing. Just for the dogs. You can sign it now, if that's OK."

She nodded and he handed her the forms and a pen. "Mrs Peach?"

"What?" She signed the papers and held them limply over her shoulder without turning.

"I'm having trouble getting Rory's age. Some of the neighbours say nine." He took the papers and put them in his case. "Is that right?"

"No. That's not right."

"No?"

"No." She rolled over to look at him. For the first time he saw her face full on. Her eyes, he realized, looked dead, the way his mother's had after Ewan. "He's not nine until August. He's eight. Only eight."

Downstairs Caffery paused to thank Mrs Nersessian. "It's my pleasure, darling. Poor thing, don't even *ask* me to imagine what she's feeling."

The tiny living room was immaculately clean and choked with possessions — a silver punch bowl on the polished table, a collection of Steuben glass animals on the glass shelves. On the plastic-covered sofa a dark-eyed girl of about ten, in shorts and red-striped T-shirt stared mutely at Caffery. Mrs Nersessian clicked her fingers. "Annahid, go on. Get your little *dvor* upstairs. You can watch your videos but keep the sound down. Rory's mama's asleep." The child slowly peeled her thighs from the plastic and disappeared from the room.

Mrs Nersessian turned to Caffery and put her hand on his arm. "Nersessian. That's an Armenian name. Now, you don't meet an Armenian every day and you need to know before you come into an Armenian household that you got to be prepared to eat." She slipped into the kitchen and began fussing around, opening the fridge, getting her good crockery from the shelves. "I'm going to get you a little pistachio loukoum," she called through the door. "And some mint tea, and then we'll say a little prayer for Rory."

"No — I — I just came to thank you, Mrs Nersian —"

"Nersessian."

"Nersessian. I'll pass on the tea if that's OK, Mrs Nersessian. We're trying to beat the clock on this."

She reappeared in the doorway holding a tea-towel. "Come on, darling, you need to eat. Look at you — no fat on you. We all need to eat at a time like this — keep our spirits up."

"I promise I'll come back and have some tea with you — when we've found Rory."

"Rory." She pressed a hand over her heart. "Just the mention of his name! Poor soul. But God is protecting him. I feel it in my heart. God is watching him and — *Annahid!*" she said suddenly, her eyes fixing on the doorway behind him. "Annahid! I *said* —"

Caffery turned. "The troll did it." The little girl was standing in the doorway, addressing him directly, as vehement as a resistance messenger, her brown eyes huge and serious. "The *troll* climbed out of the trees and did it."

Mrs Nersessian made tut-tutting noises and shooed Annahid away, flicking the tea-towel at her. "Go on, go on." She turned to Caffery, her painted eyes half closed, pressing her hair lightly into place. "I'm sorry, Mr Caffery, I am truly sorry about that. The things the kiddywinks dream about, these days."

There are vortexes and whirlpools in Brixton like nowhere else in London. Hot, funky Caribbean blood finds a home under the austere ceilings of cool nineteenth-century houses, and since the nineties the new breed had been moving to town: the art crowd. Primarily white. Primarily trendy. They moved here for the local "colour" and then slowly, insidiously, pushed it off the streets. Gentrification writ big. On the station platform a statue of a *Windrush* boy, like a latterday Dick Whittington — bandanna around his neck, tiny bag at his feet — stood with arms folded, one foot bent back against the wall, ignored by the trendy new Brixtonites pushing and shoving to get on the train with their Gucci briefcases.

On this school summer holiday the streets were steaming. Lambeth Council cleaners had been through, hosing last night's jittery ravers back down into the underground station and the sun was burning the water off the pavement. Over the park another helicopter circled, sun glinting from it. A TV news team, drawn by the noises coming from South London, had cruised over to see if there was something to which it could turn its jaw. The team could look down and see the odd, piston-like movement of the search and investigation officers at work: the Police Search Advisory team moved in formation across the park, and other dark figures, detectives, radiated out through the surrounding streets.

Good morning, madam, sorry to bother you, I'm with the CID —

Is this about what was on the TV this morning? The little kiddie?

In and out of houses: down the front paths like morning rush-hour businessmen and back up the next path:

There was an incident last night. Do you remember where you were?

Never liked that park. See them trees over there? All sorts of things is coming out of them trees. It worry me some, know what I is saying?

The search team, with their red coats and black and yellow sticks, were professionals, but they all found something odd about the clump of wood around the ponds. It was high summer but there was a Bavarian darkness in the trees, too thick for London. They tried to keep it light — joked about it, swore that at any minute an allosaurus or something was going to come steaming out of the vegetation — but no one felt comfortable that day. In the ponds the frogmen did more safety checks on each other than they would ordinarily.

Caffery came out of the Nersessians', rolled a cigarette, and walked for a while along the park perimeter, watching. Woods: he didn't like them, hadn't liked them for almost a year now. It wasn't the sight of the trees, or the sound of the breeze manipulating the branches: it was the smell. Leaf mulch and damp bark. The smell could catapult him back eleven months in a breath — back to the attack on Rebecca, back to the day she wouldn't talk about, back to the wall that stood between them, and then the pressure in his chest would suddenly become so great he imagined that if he looked down he'd see his heart poking out through his ribs.

He turned his back on the trees and looked up at Arkaig and Herne Hill Towers. From a distance they looked proud, like Rhine castles above the trees, but closer up the land they stood in amounted to little more than a scrap of balding grass covered in dog shit. Used condoms and syringes decorated it and flyblown derelicts slept in the sun. A pod of AMIT detectives had been assigned there — as Caffery lit his cigarette he could see two of them moving along the balconies. He was about to head away, to the east, to join the house-to-house pod working on Effra Road, when something made him stop. The back of his neck prickled. He'd had the brief, unsettling sense that something was behind him. Heart thumping, he swung round. But there was nothing, only the search team moving silently through the park, insects hovering, traffic on Dulwich Road and a few fluffy white clouds low on the horizon. *Jesus, Jack* — he took a few puffs on the cigarette and pushed it through the grating of a drain — *you think the* team *is jumpy . . .*

It was a DC Logan of AMIT who visited Roland Klare at his flat in Arkaig Tower. Klare didn't like the police, didn't trust them, and this one seemed particularly dismissive of him: in fact, he seemed more interested in the view over Brockwell Park than in asking any questions. He stood at the window, right next to the Pentax in the biscuit tin, and looked down at the billowy treetops. "Nice view."

"Oh, yes, a very nice view."

"Well." DC Logan tapped his hands on the windowsill — *so close to the camera* — and turned, wrinkling his nose and looking suspiciously around the flat, taking in the piles of objects on the tables, the boxes all annotated and arranged one on top of the other.

Klare didn't avoid his eyes: he expected this reaction, knew quite well that his system would seem disordered to someone who didn't understand *why* he had to scavenge and curate like this. But it was all clean, no one could say it wasn't, and that almost excused the fact that sometimes even *he* lost track of what it all meant, where and why it had started. "Now, then," Logan sat down on the sofa, crossed his legs and pulled his jacket around his stomach, "this incident last night."

"Ye-es?"

Klare sat down too. He had decided that there was a way of answering the questions truthfully without giving away anything about the camera. He folded his hands in his lap, tried to stop his eyes flickering and admitted that, yes, he'd been in the park late last night but, no, he hadn't seen anything unusual. Logan asked him again, "Are you sure? Think carefully," and Klare did. He put his head back and closed his eyes. There wasn't anything unusual about the camera, he decided. Technically it wasn't *unusual*. Nor was there anything unusual about the gloves — anyone who kept half an eye open could see all sorts of flotsam and jetsam lying around the park. And the camera was worth money.

"No." He opened his eyes and shook his head decisively. "No, nothing unusual."

And Logan seemed to accept that.

Afterwards Klare stood in the window and watched him leave the building, no bigger than a microbe all that way down on the forecourt. When he was sure the detective had gone he drew the curtains in the living room, blotting out the sun and the fractured, dried-out park, picked up the camera and began in earnest to try to free the film. When he couldn't, upset by the visit and angry with the officer's cold disapproval, he sat down on the sofa, breathing hard, staring at his hands.

Meanwhile, down on Dulwich Road, Logan met the other officers with nothing to report. He held his hands up, as if to say "empty-handed". He hadn't even the whisper of a suspicion of how close he'd just come, close as a breath, to the only piece of evidence that could have closed the case for AMIT in hours.

CHAPTER FIVE

The artist's impression on the hoarding outside the Clock Tower Grove Estate, a Hummingbird Houses development overlooking the eastern flank of Brockwell Park, showed trees in blossom, blue skies. Professionals with suitcases walked along pavements bordered by shrubs and glass-globed street-lights. The skies were blue and there were no biscuit-brown machinery tracks on the roads, no windows marked with taped Xs. The girls in the marketing suite would protest — "It's not finished yet, not till autumn, three months to go" — and they'd direct any enquirer up a side entrance, along a brick herringboned street and into Clock Tower Walk, to a collection of four-storeyed terraced townhouses at the rear of the development, overlooking Brockwell Park: own back gardens, own garages, £295,000 a pop and completed three months ahead of schedule. An exclusive street for the middle-management classes who couldn't quite reach Dulwich village — even on financial tiptoe.

One family had already moved in, just in time for the summer holidays. Number five's railings and woodwork were painted glossy black and two small bay trees, topiaried into cones, stood on either side of the small flight of steps. On the building site a workman often sat on a pile of RSJs in his lunch hour and watched the blonde as she ferried her son back and forth in the lemon-yellow Daewoo. The workman looked after his body — at the moment he was on a high-protein diet — and whenever he needed inspiration he'd look at the blonde. She was very pretty, but in his opinion her weight spoiled her beauty. In fact, when he thought about it, the whole family could have done with dropping a few pounds. They didn't look healthy. The shiny hair, the sunbrushed skin, the good clothes — none of it could make up for those extra pounds, he'd think, as he munched his tuna and wholemeal sandwiches.

That July afternoon he had spent a good part of the day watching the search teams in and around the park, and had even given a statement to the plainclothes officer who had appeared on the building site. He was packing up to go home when he spotted a dark-haired man in his thirties on the doorstep of number five. The workman supposed he could have been another police officer, but looked more like a City type, with his well-cut hair and well-cut suit. The blonde answered the door.

"Hello." She had a tidy little face, a sweet crescent of pale skin under honey-blonde hair. She was wearing white trousers and a fisherman's striped T-shirt. An old black Labrador stood next to her. Caffery knew instantly that he had wandered off the track and into classier waters.

"Afternoon." He showed his warrant card. "Name's DI Jack Caffery."

"Like the beer?"

"Like the beer."

"Is it about the little boy?" She had very large, almost silvery eyes. He imagined if he stood any nearer he'd be able to see a perfect reflection of himself. "Little Rory?"

"Yes."

"You'd better come in, then." Bending over to take the old dog by its collar and turn it round, she beckoned Caffery in with the other hand. "Come through — kick the door closed. My son and I are making chocolate truffles. We're past the crucial point but you'll have to let me just clean up a bit." She paused in the hallway to open a cloakroom and switch on the extractor fan. "Sorry, there's a bit of a smell in here. Can you smell it?"

"No."

"My husband says it's my imagination."

"Women have a better sense of smell, you know."

"Ah, yes — all the better to detect a dirty nappy."

"Your husband here?"

"Still at work. Come through."

She led him to the back half of the house, a single huge space, divided into two areas by waist height cabinets. On the right an airy modern kitchen, light-filled: Scandinavian lines, skylights and raw wood, recessed lighting and heavy glass jars in rows. On the left a spacious family room with seagrass floors and sunlight streaming through huge clean windows. Designed so that one could cook a meal, hold a conversation and watch television all at the same time. Modern living.

"Oh, hi," Caffery said.

"Hi." In the kitchen a boy of eight or nine, slightly sloping eyes, nose rather pointed — like an elf's — and shortish hair sticking up from a tanned forehead as if he'd just come in from a beach volleyball match, stood to attention, hands at his sides, pretending he hadn't been doing something punishable while his mother's back was turned. He was wearing flip-flops and a T-shirt over blue swimming-trunks and had chocolate smeared around his mouth.

"Oh, yes, sorry about him — he's the hound." She smoothed back the hair from her son's forehead. "My little boy, Josh."

Caffery extended his hand. "Hi."

"It's OK," Josh said sombrely, shaking his hand. "I'm mad, not bad."

Caffery nodded. "Sometimes the mad ones are worse."

"And I'm Benedicte Church." She smiled sweetly and shook Caffery's hand. "Ben for short." She bent over her son, hands on his shoulders.

She was not the average middle-class housewife. She was enormously pretty, Caffery thought, with rather short legs and a round bottom. He imagined it would take a long time to tire of a bottom like that. He caught himself staring as she pulled her hair from her face and murmured to her son, "Tadpole, go and wash your face, OK? Then we can all have a chocolate."

Josh went into the cloakroom and when she could hear the tap running she dropped her chin and leaned a little closer to Caffery, her smile gone. "It's horrible, isn't it?" she whispered. "The TV's really vague. I mean, do *we* need to worry?"

"There's no harm in being aware."

"Heard the helicopter last night." She jerked her chin in the direction of the park. Only a few feet beyond the back-garden fence the trees started, as immediately thick and dark as if this was the dense heart of a forest. "Whenever I hear them looking for someone I always think of the Balcombe Street siege. Convinced the police are going to chase them through my front door and then we'll be kept hostage for days on end. But there you go." She smiled. "Paranoia can be a beautiful thing for the easily bored. Coffee?"

"Please."

"And I'll bring you a, uh . . ." She gestured at the tray of chocolates. "A truffle, if you can bear it." She poured coffee from a cafetière into two Isle of Arran mugs, spooned sugar into an earthenware pot and set it on a tray. "Go through and sit down. Make yourself at home."

He went into the family room. Here the walls were a fresh, cantaloupe colour, the sofas in pale, glazed linen — and other things told him this family was doing well — the gleaming wide-screen TV still with a piece of polystyrene packaging clinging to its shoulder. He sat down on one of the sofas facing out of the window. The dog, which had curled up in a patch of sun, blinked sleepily at him. Everywhere Pickfords boxes lay half unpacked.

"Just moved in?"

"Four days ago." She took milk from the fridge and filled a small glass jug. "The first ones on the estate. And I mean, how crazy is *this*? Sunday we're straight off to Cornwall for ten days."

"Nice."

"Absolutely *lovely*, if you haven't already been living out of boxes for weeks. This place was finished early so we went for it. And we couldn't cancel our holiday." Josh reappeared from the cloakroom and scampered over to the tray of chocolates. "We couldn't cancel Helston, could we, tadpole? The seals?"

"Nope." He stood on a stool and pulled the chocolates nearer. "Seals out of the sea."

The dog limped over to Caffery, looked up at him mournfully and rolled on to her back. "Hello." He began to scratch her, when something just above his field of vision, something in the woods, moved suddenly. He stared out of the window. For a moment he had thought he saw a shadow racing in there, but now whatever he'd seen was gone, an animal, a trick of the light, or one of the search team, and Benedicte was coming in with the coffee and he had to cool his imagination.

"Thanks." He took the cup and sat back, his eyes straying to the window. The trees were silent. Nothing out there. Nothing at all. "You're close to the park here," he said. "Very close."

"I know."

"Where did you move from?"

"Brixton."

"Brixton? I thought this *was* Brixton."

"I mean the centre — Coldharbour Lane. I don't know what we wanted to escape from most — the drugs or the trendies. But I don't really know Donegal Crescent and that side of the park." She stopped herself and looked back to the kitchen where Josh was using a knife to lever the chocolates from the baking tray. "Tadpole, bring that little saucer through and then you can go in the paddling-pool."

"'Snot a paddling-pool. It's a —"

"I know, I know. It's a secret location in the Pacific Ocean." She shot Caffery an amused look. "OK," she told Josh. "Bring the saucer through and you can go to Tracy Island."

"'Kay." Pleased, Josh slipped off the stool and padded through carrying a saucer with four newly dipped chocolate truffles, as shiny as if they were still wet.

"That's it." She settled down with her coffee. "Pass them round. Then you can go out."

"Thank you." Caffery took a chocolate.

"That's OK." Josh still had a smudge of brown on his chin and a crumbly fingerprint of drying chocolate on his thigh. He leaned forward a little, his face serious, his brows drawn together in adult concern. "You do know it's the troll, don't you?"

Caffery paused, the truffle halfway to his mouth. "*Sorry?*"

"Come on, brat." Benedicte pulled Josh by the T-shirt to where she sat. "Let me have a chocolate."

Josh dropped his head. "It's the troll," he murmured.

"Of course, darling." She took a chocolate and put it into her mouth, rolling her eyes in amusement at Caffery.

But Josh was suddenly determined. "The troll climbed in the window and stole that kid out of his bed." He put the saucer on the floor and stood, crunched up like a gnome, his face contorted, hands in front of his face like claws. Make-believe climbing. "Up the drainpipe, probably." He dropped his hands and looked seriously at his mother. "He eats kids, Mum, honest."

"Josh, really." Benedicte met Caffery's eyes, her face colouring with embarrassment. She leaned forward and slapped her son lightly on the legs. "Now, come on, enough of that. We don't want Mr Caffery to think you're a baby, do we? Go and put the saucer in the sink."

The troll.

The more Caffery tried to question Josh about it, the more outlandish and garbled the ideas got until they were back to one central fact: the troll lived in the woods and had a habit of eating kids. Benedicte Church was embarrassed that her son was taking a local kids' story as fact. "They just like to scare each other," she said. "They're so impressionable at this age."

At what age? he wanted to say. *At thirty-five, like me?* Because a picture of the troll had already begun to impress itself on the underside of his mind — spreading like a stain. At the end of the day, when he left Clock Tower Grove, he had an overpowering urge to get away from the park, with the sun running all over the horizon, the silhouettes of a tired and disillusioned search team dotted against it. A feeling was creeping up on him. He didn't know where it was coming from, and he didn't know how to put it into words. But that would come, he was sure of it. It would come.

"Troll?" he asked Souness later, in the SIO's office. "Does that mean anything to you? A troll?"

"Eh?" Souness ran the palm of her hand over her bristly number-two cut and frowned. She was back from the press interviews, a line of makeup on the collar of her blouse, and was sitting at her desk staring down at the screen of her new mobile, pressing buttons with her thumb, trying to make sense of it. "Eh?" She looked up at him. "What're you talking about?"

"The kids in Brixton were rabbiting on about a troll everywhere I went."

"The only troll I know is San Francisco slang — an old queen who likes gorgeous young meat. A tree jumper. A dirty, *ugly* old gay guy who only wants to have sex with cute young thangs."

"So it just means a nonce?"

"In my world, aye."

He sat, chin resting on his hand, and stared at his reflection superimposed over the long strings of London lights.

"You got the message about the photos?" he said after a while. "Carmel thought he took photos while he was there."

"Yeah." She looked up. "I've got some of the lads on to it already."

"If there are photos somewhere out there — shit." He shook his head.

"I know. Wouldn't you love to see them?"

"What do you think?" It was nearly midnight — they'd had to call in the teams. They'd found nothing. There was no sign of Rory in the park so Souness had extended the parameters to include every street that backed on to it. Tool sheds were searched, garages, empty property. Still no Rory. Every resident was questioned carefully but no one had seen anything. Rory Peach, it seemed, had disappeared in one of the most densely populated areas of the country and no one had seen a thing. Not a soul in Donegal Crescent had heard the glass shattering on the Friday evening; nor had anyone heard the intruder leaving the house. The media spent the day pestering AMIT for news but there was none. They knew about as much as they had this time last night. What kept drilling through Caffery's tired mind was a sentence an officer had said to his mother twenty-eight years ago: "*You'll have to accept that you may never know.*" Nor were any of the team taking it easily — an eight-year-old child had been separated from his family for the second night in a row: he'd already had to talk two of the younger ones out of a nose-dive depression.

"And funnily enough," Souness switched off the mobile and put it into her pocket, "I think I know exactly what's worrying ye."

Caffery — who had pushed back his chair and was considering unzipping the Nike holdall in which they kept their Scotch — straightened. He put his hands on the desk and paused, almost as if he hadn't heard. Then he looked at her sideways. "What?"

"What I mean is —" She leaned back in her chair and unpopped the top button of her trousers, getting her stomach comfortable for the first time that day. "What I mean is that I think it all sounds *a little bit too much like what happened to Ewan*." She raised her eyebrows. It wasn't a statement and she was neither smirking nor reproaching him. She was asking him to talk about it. "That's what I meant."

"OK." He held up his hand. "You can stop there." Any reference to Ewan always felt like something moving slyly around in the folds of his brain, digging fingers into the most private clefts. He rarely even said his brother's name — *and to hear someone else borrow it calmly like this, like it's a name no different from Brian, say, or Dave, or Alan or Gary, it's — Jesus, it's like finding a strange hair in your mouth*. "I suppose at this point I'm supposed to ask you how you know about it."

"Everyone knows."

"Great."

"Half of B team were at your party when Ivan Penderecki — when he, well, let's not go into *that* now, eh? But Paulina still gets little bits of intelligence on him coming through the paedo unit from time to time. Between getting her nails done and putting another zero on my Barclaycard statement, she did a bit of digging and, oooh, an interesting little fact pops up. Penderecki is linked to a twenty-five-year-old missing-persons case. And the name? Ewan Caffery. Just so happens that the name DI Jack Caffery is in every newspaper at the time and, well, it don't take much for a suspicious dyke to jump to conclusions." She bent over and scooped the bottle of Bell's from the holdall, opened it and dropped large doubles into each of two mugs. "Here." She pushed one across the desk and settled back. "I've known since before I started in AMIT. Before I even met ye."

"Well." Caffery slumped into the chair, pulling the Scotch towards him. "Welcome to my nightmare, DCI Souness. It's nice to know you've been enjoying it for so long."

"Ahh, now, ye see, you're being a bit of a wee girly about it, aren't ye? There ain't no law says you can't see this as genuine friendly concern, *D*eeetective Caffery."

"Yeah." He stared into the mug. There was a dried coffee rim halfway down.

"Och, come on, Jack, I'm trying to help. In my clumsy way."

"I know, look, I'm sorry. I get a bit . . ." He put a fist to his chest.

"A bit tight here about it, eh?" She downed her whisky and refilled her mug. "I know, I *do* know. But if you made an allegation against Penderecki?" She paused for a response. "Jack? Make an allegation, and the case'd be reviewed and someone *else* could stay up all night and worry about it."

He shook his head wearily. "Nah. That's OK."

"Been suggested before?"

"I've lost count of how many times. He's too clever. He'd turn it around and before you know it I'd be the one in the frame — malicious allegations, harassment, yadda-yadda."

"And not because you know you'd never be allowed near the case?"

"There is that, yes. That detail hasn't escaped my attention."

"You're a wee bampot, if you don't mind me saying."

"Thank you. I'm going to assume that's a compliment."

Souness smiled, a small smile. "I just don't want this Peach thing bollixing with ye more than it has to. Don't want it touching your personal life. That's my small concern."

Caffery tried to smile back. This was the time he should say it — that he probably shouldn't be on the case at all, that she was right, that already it was spilling over and getting out of control. Instead he wiped his forehead, finished his drink and said, "Ewan was nine, Rory is eight — I hadn't even made the connection." He stood, went to the door and called DC Logan into the SIO's room. Logan came in, raising an eyebrow when he saw them sitting together.

"Sorry." He coughed pointedly, as if he'd interrupted something.

"I want to add something to the intelligence search — you know how to use CRIS, don't you?"

"Sir."

"And tomorrow get the locals to go back into the collator's records for ten years with the same key word. 'Troll'. Find out if anyone knows anything about a nonce in Brockwell Park called the troll." He stopped. He'd only just seen it. Logan was trying to hide a smile. "Hey?" He put his face closer to Logan's. "What is it?"

"Nothing, sir." But before he dropped his eyes Caffery saw him glance briefly at Souness — at the top buttons of her shirt undone, at the opened bottle of Scotch. Caffery's tie was off and Souness's boots were on the floor. "Nothing," Logan said again, colouring, and turned away. "CRIS and the collators. Right away."

When Caffery closed the door and turned round, Souness had her elbows on her knees, her face dropped in her hands, and was laughing so hard her shoulders were shaking. "Can ye believe it?" She looked up, her face shiny. "Och, I love it — I *looove* it! I'm getting laid by the Met's pin-up boy." She wiped her face. "Look at me! *Diesel dyke* stamped all over me, but they still need a compass and map. It's like a giant panda walked into the room — they'd go, 'Yeah, looks like a giant panda, smells like a giant panda, but it can't be a giant panda, I mean what the fuck would a giant panda be doing here?' "

In spite of himself Caffery caught himself smiling. Later, he stopped her before she left the office: "Danni, thank you. I know I've made you late for Paulina, so thank you for talking to me."

* * *

Caffery's little Victorian cottage was quiet. He parked his battered old Jaguar carefully next to Rebecca's black VW Beetle and went inside, unknotting his tie. She was still awake in spite of the hour — there was warmth and noise coming from the living room at the back of the house and in the hall a pair of green metallic slingbacks, scuffed heels, lay toppled over, the words Miu Miu fading and worn on the inside. He paused, as he always did these days, wondering what mood she would be in, before he opened the door.

She was doing a shoulder stand on the sofa, giggling as she watched her bare toes wriggle. She wore khaki shorts and one of his grey T-shirts: a bottle of Blavod leaned drunkenly against the cushion and a cigarillo smouldered in the ashtray.

"Happy?"

"Oooops!" She dropped her legs with a bang and twisted round, grinning up at him. He saw with relief that she was calm. Flushed and tipsy but mellow.

"You look happy."

"Uh-huh." A CD played in the background — something smooth, Air or someone like it. "Drunk."

"You lush." He bent over and kissed her. "I've been calling you all day." He went into the kitchen, hung his jacket on the back of the door and got his Glenmorangie and a glass.

"I've been in Brixton with some Slade finalists. They think I'm God or something."

"Shameless." He pulled off his shoes and collapsed on the sofa, uncorking the whisky. "Egotistic little tart."

"I know." She coiled her hank of spice-coloured hair into a long snake, laid it over one shoulder, and clambered across to him. Good gymnast's legs she had — always lightly tanned, the colour of sesame oil. "Ouch," Souness once admitted, after half a bottle of Scotch. "She's the sort of woman you feel right here. In your groin."

"I saw someone I knew on the news." Rebecca rested her arms on his shoulders and kissed his neck. "Just from behind. I knew it was you from your backside. And because you looked pissed off, even from a distance."

He downed a glass, refilled it and linked his fingers through hers. In the last three days they hadn't had time together — he'd realized it that morning when the sound of one of the indexers crossing her legs in her fawn Pretty Pollys had popped a sweat on his forehead.

"You must be knackered."

"I've got a four-hour turnaround. Back to the office by five."

"It's a little kid, isn't it?"

"Mmmm. Yes." He held up her hand and studied her fingers. Her pearly clean nails against his. The thumb on his left hand was black, it was a bruise that wouldn't grow out. His own stigmata — injured the day Ewan went missing, never changing in twenty-five years. "Let's not talk about it, eh?"

"Why not?"

Why not? Because already Ewan was wilfully super-imposing himself over a picture of Rory Peach — *and you've spotted that, Becky, I know you've already spotted the resemblance and if we start, if I let you, we'll be talking about Ewan before I can put the brakes on, and then the mood will change and I'll say something about you, maybe, and Bliss, and . . .*

"Because I'm tired. I've had it all day."

"OK." She bit her lip and thought about this. "Well," she tried, working her fingers inside his shirt and smiling. "How about this? Are you horny?"

He sighed and put down his glass. "Of course."

She giggled. "Yeah, stupid question. I mean, when are you not?"

"I thought I was constantly pissed off?"

"No. You're constantly randy is what you are. Pissed off is what you do between having hard-ons."

"Come here." He pulled her astride his lap and worked his hands up her T-shirt. "Did you see *Time Out?*"

"I know." She began to unbutton his shirt, closing her eyes when he found her nipples and worked them between his thumb and forefinger. "How ace am I, then, eh?" she murmured dreamily, her head back. "Oh, God, that's nice. Did you read it, then?"

"Yes. I'm proud of you."

But he was lying. He shuffled down the sofa a few inches and moved his hands across her skin, like oil against his hard fingers, down the whole width of her pelvis, and the long fierce muscles of her stomach. Rebecca had told him that her body had changed since her artwork had taken off — she said her skin was smoother, her waist thinner; that she didn't get calluses on her feet any more and that these days she walked more slowly. But what Caffery saw was the opposite: a hardening, a quickening. And he knew it dated back to the assault. To Bliss.

Reflecting this switch came the new artwork, the sculptures. Before the assault Rebecca's work had been something quite different. Now the colours had disappeared and her work was sharper. Something in her had shifted, but she still wanted Jack and here he was, still hopelessly and helplessly attracted to her, in love with her in spite of how she had changed — she was the sweet weight in his heart and in his cock. Just the smell of one of her cigarillos in an ashtray could give him a hard-on.

He opened his eyes and looked up at her face above him, eyes closed, a calm, distant smile on her face. I should close the curtains, he thought distantly, looked at the dark window, and saw the white smudge of a face, a snout-like impression and the telltale frosting of excited breath on the panes —

"Shit!" He pulled Rebecca's T-shirt down.

"What?"

"Move it. Quick."

Rolling her away, he sprang to his feet, and slammed open the french windows. Penderecki had reached the foot of the garden, running for the back fence. Caffery sprinted the forty feet in seconds, but Penderecki was prepared: he had brought a green plastic milk crate that he used to hike himself over the back fence, and scurried away into the undergrowth of the railway cutting, leaving behind just the crate and the sound of his wheezing trailing in the air. Caffery, shoeless, shirt undone, picked up the crate and threw it after him.

"*Do that again and I will kill you*." He stood in the garden his mother had planted, watching the larval shape of the old man scuttling away through the undergrowth. "*I mean it* — I've got your *blood* in my *mouth*, Penderecki." He dropped his hands on the wire fence, letting his breathing slow, trying not to be drawn, trying to pull his anger back in. "I've got your blood."

It's just a new way of him disturbing the silt. Ignore it. Ignore it —

He dropped his head. Ignoring Penderecki was the hardest work he'd known. Sometimes his mere presence across the track felt like a telephone ringing in a neighbour's house on a quiet afternoon. The body reacted instinctually, made to respond, but the mind tugged it back — *Don't answer it, don't answer, not for you*. Penderecki, with his piercing gift for evil, was dishing out this kind of bait on a weekly basis: the odd phone call here, the odd scribbled note or letter, feeding Caffery a repertoire of theories about what had happened to Ewan. They were imaginative, they were varied, and he had learned to believe none of them.

Ewan had died instantly, hit by a train, the sheer velocity carrying his small body far away from the area the police searched; Ewan had survived but later starved to death in a caravan on an isolated farm where Penderecki had hidden him during the search of his house; Ewan had survived and lived as Penderecki's lover until he had suddenly, spontaneously stopped breathing one night; Ewan was alive and well and, having been so acclimatized, was now a paedophile himself, operating from Amsterdam . . . Any of the letters might have been the one to crack Caffery's will. It was his work to ignore them all.

Someone touched his shoulders. He started. "Rebecca." He shook his head. "I'm sorry." He was still shaking with anger.

"Not your fault. He's a little shit."

"He's baiting me."

"I know." She kissed his back. "He makes it difficult."

"Yeah, well." He felt in his trousers for his roll-ups. "He's always made it difficult."

She put her arms around his waist and they stood together in silence, staring into the darkness above the silent railway tracks. Watching the lights in Penderecki's house come on. Maybe, Caffery thought, he had decided to escalate the torment. In the last month there had been a sense of urgency coming across the railway track: it was only three days since the last letter had appeared on his doorstep:

> Dear Jack
> After 27 years it is now time to tell you the truth what happened with you're brother and you will know when I tell you that I am teling you the TRUTH, the most TRUTHFUL thing not because I am sorry for you no but because I have "remorse" and because you DESERVE to have the truth told you.

He was not in pain Jack and not scaired because he WANTED it. When I depuced him and when I told him to suck on my cock he did it because he WANTED it. He told me he would do anything for me, even would eat my doings if you know what I am saying because he loved me so much. This sounds crude to you and to me but it is the words of you're brother jack you're only brother and so I know you will see these words are SACRED and not think that I invented them. And anyway I should tell you the end came because it was an ACIDENT and no more than an ACIDENT and not because I wanted a bad thing for you're brother but because it was an ACIDENT. He is at peace now.
GOD BLESS US ALL.

And now this spying, this creeping around his garden. Caffery rolled a cigarette. He hated Penderecki for keeping up the pressure, hated him for the constant reminders. Rebecca kissed his back again and wandered away, over to the old beech at the foot of the garden. She pressed her palms against the trunk. "This is where the tree-house was, am I right?"

"Yes." He lowered his head and lit the cigarette.

"Then . . ." She rested her ear against the tree-trunk, as if listening for a pulse, and looked upwards, into the spreading branches. "How did you — oh, I see."

"Rebecca —"

But before he could stop her she was monkeying up the trunk using the iron hand-holds his father had nailed into it for his two sons. She crouched like a gnome in the elbow of a branch. Astonishing how a tree can cup a human body, he thought, looking up at her. Strange that we ever crawled down, traded the leaves and nooks for the wide uncertainties of the prairie. "Come on," she called. "It's great up here." He put the cigarette between his teeth and followed reluctantly, feeling the familiar irregularities of the iron loops against his palms. The night was clear, the sky sprinkled with stars. When he came level with Rebecca he leaned back against the branch, facing her, his feet braced against the trunk, the bark husky and warm against his soles. Behind her, above the houses, the green millennium laser on Greenwich Park sliced the great dome of black.

"Good, isn't it?"

"Maybe . . ."

He rarely came up here. Once a year, maybe, and not at all since Rebecca. He thought that she wouldn't want him sitting up here dwelling on everything. The view didn't change much. Still the long scar of the railway. Still Penderecki's house on the other side: unpainted for years, the guttering hanging so that the back of the house was coated in moss: as incongruous in the terrace of cared-for houses as the boarded-up house next to the Peaches'.

OK, he stopped himself, *no more connections like that. Rory isn't Ewan and Ewan isn't Rory. Get it straight*.

"Zeus was a baby in a tree." Rebecca dangled her feet over the edge and smiled. "He was hung in a cradle and fed by the bees. Stop thinking about him." She grabbed his hand suddenly. "Come on, stop it. I know you're thinking about Ewan."

Caffery didn't answer. He pulled his hand from her and looked across the railway cutting.

"Jesus." She shook her head and looked up at the stars. "Can't you see what's happening? Penderecki's got you so wound up that you carry it everywhere — the more he pushes the tighter you get. You're being eaten alive by it all, by Ewan, by that . . ." she nodded over the railway cutting, "that *pervert*."

"Not now, Rebecca —"

"I mean it. Look at you — a fucked-up, hunched-up, shrivelled-up *miserable* git coming through the door at night looking like he's been dragged backwards through Hades by his heels and *it's all because of Ewan*. You're *carrying* him, Jack, carrying him everywhere. The *smallest* thing makes you explode. And now you've got a case at work that's similar —"

"Rebecca —"

"And now you've got a case at work that's similar and God alone *knows* what'll happen. How will you control yourself? Someone'll get hurt — might even be you. You might even end up like Paul."

"That's enough." He held his hand up. "Enough." He knew where they were going. He knew that Paul Essex, the DS who had been part of the frantic hunt for Malcolm Bliss, stood for all Rebecca's fears about the job. Essex had died, on his back in a Kent forest, his blood soaking like bitumen into the ground, and all that Caffery had left of him was his driving licence. He'd removed it from Essex's wallet before handing it over to his parents. Maybe Rebecca imagined that was how he, Caffery, was going to end.

"He's got nothing to do with this."

"Yes, he has." She clicked her tongue against the roof of her mouth. "Because it might happen to you if you don't calm down — if you can't get Ewan off your back. *And* you know it. You *know* that if you get pushed on this it might even go as far as it did last time."

He looked up. "What? What *last time?*"

"Ah — that made you listen."

"What are you talking about?"

"He *knows* what I'm talking about." She smiled out into the darkness. "He knows to whom I allude."

"Becky —"

"Mark my words, Jack, you'll do it again. It's like a little thing growing in you, right about . . ." She put a finger on his chest. ". . . *there*. And it'll keep growing and growing, and if you don't get away from this house, if you don't get away from that sad old pervert over there, if you're stuck on a case that's pushing all your buttons, then *bam!*, you'll do it again and —"

"*Stop it.*" He pushed her hand away from his chest. "What the *fuck* are you talking about?"

"I know, Jack. I can see it in you. I know what happened in that wood."

He stared back at her, speechless. Scared to ask her what she knew. In case she said it: *I know you killed Bliss. I know it wasn't an accident like everyone thinks*. For a long time he was silent.

Rebecca tipped her head on one side. "Why won't you talk about it, Jack?"

"No, Rebecca," he said, pinching out the cigarette and dropping it out of the tree. His hands were shaking. "The real question is why *you* won't talk about it."

"Oh, no." She held up her hand. "We were talking about you."

"No. If we're going down this road then we talk about *everything* that happened. Those are the rules." He began to climb down out of the tree.

"Where are you going?"

"Inside. To have a run. To get away from you."

"Hey," she called, watching him walk back up the lawn in the moonlight, "one day you'll see I'm right."

CHAPTER SIX

(19 July)

In the morning, the note from Penderecki was skewered on his gate, wet with dew. Penderecki had taken the time to write more than was his habit and Caffery, who would ordinarily have crumpled it and binned it, stood in the street, attaché case in hand, and read.

Hello Jack.

Eerie reminders of the Yorkshire Ripper tape. It made Caffery shiver — only feet from his own home on a leafy summer day with joggers, the postman and the milkfloat creeping along the road towards him — as if someone had breathed on the back of his neck.

And now — I truly know YOUR name. To everything there is a season, and a time to every purpose under the heaven. The LORD and not YOU will call me, when it is HIS will and not YOU'RS and grant HIS healing, that the soul of His servent, at the hour of its departure from the body, may by the hands of His holy Angels be presented without spot unto Him. The sheep belong on GODS right, Jack. The goat's go to the LEFT. The sheep will receive heaven the goat's WILL receive hell. And from your ignorance YOU look into MY eyes and you think you see a goat. Dont you? You think I am a goat. But, GOD says the stripe of the goat is to look into the eyes of OTHER'S — (the GOOD and the PURE) and see itself looking back. THINK about it JACK.

Caffery got into the Jag and sat breathing in the smell of leather — already warm even this early in the morning. The stripe of the goat? A little something growing in him that would one day explode? Rebecca had shaken him up last night with her gloomy prognosis. He wondered if everyone could see it in his face. Could everyone see the word "killer" scrawled in his eyes? Was he so transparent? He rubbed his temples and started the car, adjusted the mirror and put it into gear.

In Brixton the day dragged. By late afternoon he was standing outside the Lido at the edge of Brockwell Park, drinking McDonald's coffee and smoking a roll-up. He was tired and immensely depressed. The blood on the trainer matched the DNA from Rory Peach's underwear, but there was still no sign of Rory. The search team had exhausted the possibilities in and around the park; they kept going but everyone knew that the current parameters were redundant. Rumours swept among the search teams every hour or so:

"They're sending us to Battersea, someone saw a lad like Rory down there, next to the river." Or. "There's a nonce over at Clapham who lives right above an empty factory, half of us are going to be sent over there." The operation was now costing twenty thousand pounds a day, but the reality was that none of the hundred or so calls that had come into the incident room had given Caffery and Souness any new leads. They were walking blind, and everyone knew it.

And then, at 5.30p.m., Souness had news. "Peach is going to make it." She came chugging along the road towards Caffery, waving her mobile in the air. "He's off the ventilator and they're letting us talk to him."

"I thought he was dying."

"I know. We're getting twenty minutes, so let's make it count."

Caffery let Souness drive his Jaguar. She did it with a wry, self-conscious smile on her sunburnt face. It wasn't a show car, nothing like the red two-seater BMW she had bought for Paulina ("She drives it like a typical bird, Jack, just like a bird. The rear-view mirror — it's not for checking the traffic behind, oh, no, no, no, no! It's for having a wee deek at your lippy. Bet you never knew that."). The upholstery in the back of the Jaguar was mended with Sellotape and both front wings were retouched fibreglass filler. It wasn't something he'd aspired to owning, it was just the only car he'd been able to afford ten years ago, but Souness treated it with a touching reverence all the way to Denmark Hill.

King's Hospital's face-lift was well under way: every conversation, every exchange was overlaid with the noise of construction. Inside the hospital it was a city — a law unto itself — with a Forbuoy's outlet, a travel agent, a bank and a post office. The corridors were polished to a squeak, and people moved with a Fritz Lang robotic ease, smooth and determined. The consultant, Mr Friendship, tall, in a blue shirt and patterned red tie, met them outside the Jack Steinberg Intensive Care Unit.

"He's off the Hickman line and the Gambro. I've kept him on a little pain relief — but I'm surprised, and very encouraged, by his response. He was hardly even dehydrated after three days without water. As a matter of fact, since we took him off ventilation" — he paused at the door and swiped his card — "he's done so well we've moved him to this progressive care section." He led them into the front of the unit, where five empty beds were ranged along the walls. "We're getting him set for a move to another ward or even discharge. Amazingly resilient. There you are." Alek Peach sat in profile near the window. "Strong as an ox, that one. Strong as an ox."

An ox indeed. If a bull had ever sat back on its haunches in a chair with a blue hospital blanket tucked over its lap it would have looked a little like Alek Peach. In spite of his defeated posture the real sense of Peach was of his *size*: his bones must have been massive, as dense as iron bars, to support that height and muscle. His dyed black hair was worn slightly long, he was dressed in checked green pyjamas, and under his chair was hooked a black "rebreath" rubber balloon and a catheter bag. He didn't respond when the two detectives approached.

Souness moved a chair to sit down and Caffery drew the pastel-green curtains around the bed. He cleared his throat. "Mr Peach. Are you sure you feel up to this?"

Peach turned slowly to them. His black Elvis side-burns were growing out and needed redyeing. When he tried to nod, his head seemed to droop, as if he was having problems holding up its enormous weight and it might flop forward on to his chest.

"Right." Caffery sat next to Souness, looking carefully at him. "First of all we're sorry about Rory, Mr Peach, very sorry. We're doing everything. Keeping positive."

Hearing Rory's name Peach squeezed his eyes closed and wiped his huge hand across his face, the thumb on the bridge of the nose, the palm covering his mouth. He sat like this for long seconds, not breathing. Then he dropped his hand and moved it in a convulsive circle on his chest, opening his eyes to stare at the ceiling.

Caffery glanced at Souness and said, "Alek, look, we won't take long, I promise. I know it's difficult for you but it would help if you could tell us anything you can remember — what he did while he was in the house, where he kept you, whether he left the house at any point."

Peach's hand stopped circling. His face tightened a little. He dropped his eyes and stared fixedly at the pulse-oximeter clip on his thumb, as if he was trying to focus his strength and will. Caffery and Souness waited expectantly, but Peach didn't speak for some time. They weren't going to get much for their twenty minutes. *Shit*. Caffery sat back and pressed a knuckle to his forehead. "Look, can't you even tell us how *old* he was? If he was white or black? *Anything?*"

Alek Peach turned to look at him. His eyes drooped, showing tired inner rims. He lifted his hand, shaky, bruised and swollen from IV needles, and pointed a finger at Caffery. His expression was ferocious, as if the ICU ward was his living room and Caffery was a stranger who had just swung in casually off the street and sat down on the sofa, feet on the coffee table.

"You." His chest shook, straining against the cotton pyjamas. "*You.*"

Caffery put a finger on his chest. "*Me?*"

"Yes, *you.*"

"What about me?"

"Your eyes. I don't like your eyes."

In the men's, Caffery stood on the toilet and stuffed a paper towel inside the ceiling smoke alarm. He locked the cubicle, rolled a cigarette, leaned his head against the wall and smoked slowly, only relaxing when he felt the welcome thump of nicotine against his heart. Instead of recognizing Peach's distress he had instantly grown angry at the hostility. His blood pressure had risen and he had shoved his feet out across the floor, preparing to spring up. It was only the cough and warning look from Souness that had straightened him out, prevented him slamming the door as he left the ward.

"Right," he muttered to the cubicle wall. "So Rebecca's nailed it. You are a fucked-up, hair-trigger little time-bomb." He flicked ash into the toilet pan and scratched the back of his hand. She couldn't have worked it better. As if everything was conspiring to back up her diagnosis of him. As if she'd paid them — Penderecki, Peach — to say it: "The stripe of the goat is to look into the eyes of other's and see itself looking back."

Your eyes. I don't like your eyes.

No one would ever know or guess just how far he had been pushed. They would never know how, in the hot centre of an estuary wood, panting and tangled in blood and wire, Malcolm Bliss had sworn to Caffery's face that he'd left Rebecca dead in a nearby house. "*I fucked her first, of course.*"

For that Caffery had killed him, a quick turn of the wrist. The barbed wire had punctured the carotid artery and irreparably damaged the jugular. "*Christ,*" he'd murmured to himself when he read the postmortem protocol. "*You must have tightened it harder than you thought.*" But that was all. He was still waiting, in a sort of numb suspension, a year later, for remorse to kick in. He thought he'd covered himself. He thought everyone believed Bliss's death had been an accident. He'd never guessed that people could look at him and see the killer, the liar, looking back out of the holes in his face.

No, *fuck it. You're letting her get to you*. He slung the cigarette in the toilet pan. If Rebecca wasn't ready to talk to him about what had happened last year —

talk to *him* and not to the press — then he wasn't going to let her run around excavating his feelings and making crazy connections between Ewan and his own inability to stay in control.

When Souness came out of the unit Caffery's heart sank. She was tight-lipped and sat in the passenger seat on the drive back to Shrivemoor in silence. From time to time she gingerly touched her face and scalp where the sun had burned them for two days in the park. They had hoped Peach would be able to tell them enough about the behaviour of the intruder for DS Quinn and the forensics team to focus on hot areas in the house, areas where the attacker had lingered, shedding hairs or fibres. But Souness's face said that hadn't happened. Neither spoke until they got to Shrivemoor.

"Not good news, I take it."

Souness sighed and dropped the bundle of papers on her desk. "No." She flopped into the chair, leaning back, her mouth open, her palms pressed against her burning cheeks. She stayed like this for a long time, staring at the ceiling, gathering her thoughts. Then she dropped forward, feet planted wide on the floor, elbows on knees, and looked at Caffery. "We're *sooooo* fucked, mate. So fucked."

"No leads?"

"Oh, we've got one lead — a great lead. The guy wore trainers, Peach *thinks*."

"He *thinks*?"

"Yeah." She nodded at his disappointment. "He's not sure what make, but he thought *maybe* they were cheap ones and suggested Hi-Tec."

"Hi-Tecs? Magic. As if we've never seen *that* on a witness statement before."

"Good, eh?" She scratched her chin. "I pushed him for all he could give me. He co-operated — I believe him. I don't think there's more." She swivelled the chair, fired up her PC and began to type up the report for Kryotos to enter in HOLMES:

> On the 14th July I was at home at number 30 Donegal Crescent. My son Rory and me were playing on the PlayStation in the basement. We were supposed to be going down to Margate the next day for a long weekend. No one else was in the room. I believed at that time that my wife, Carmel Peach, was upstairs, but I hadn't seen or heard from her for some time, so at about 7.30 (p.m.) I came upstairs to see where my wife was. I had not heard anything suspicious and all the doors were locked, the windows closed.
>
> I came into the hallway and turned to face the stairs at which point I believe I was hit from behind. Nothing was said —

Caffery, standing over Souness as she typed, pointed at the screen. "Didn't he hear the window breaking in the kitchen?"

"Says not."

"So this guy just drops into their hallway? Like Santa Claus?"

"That's how it sounds."

He frowned. He put his hand on the monitor and leaned over to read the rest of the statement:

> Nothing was said and from that point on I remember nothing until I woke up later with a headache and a sore throat. I do not know how long I had been unconscious. I was handcuffed to something and blindfolded and gagged. After a while I realized it was the radiators I was handcuffed to. I didn't know which room I was in, but I could hear my wife crying and it sounded as if she was in the landing which seemed to be above and behind me, so I guessed I was in the living room. And I recognized the carpet because it's new. I didn't know what time it was because it was dark, but when the sun came up I could see the light through the blindfold and I thought it was coming from the direction of the kitchen at the rear of the house. I stayed in this place for three days, during which time I did not see or hear my son, although I could hear my wife crying on and off. I do not know what happened to my son. I glimpsed the man once only under the bottom of the blindfold. I think he was very tall, even taller than I am maybe. I would say in his late twenties, maybe thirty, because he seemed strong and he must have been strong to have dragged me from the hallway into the living room. He was wearing a

pair of dirty white trainers, I couldn't see the make, but they looked like old Hi-Tecs or something. He had very large feet. I heard him moving up and down the wall and at one time he stayed in the corner of the room, crouched down — I could tell that from the sound of his breathing — like he was going to pounce, but he didn't. All I remember is that he sniffed a lot — as if he was smelling something. It's the way my wife is sometimes — she was always thinking she could smell something. On, I think, Monday morning I lost consciousness. Knowing my son I do not believe that he would have voluntarily left the house with anyone. I do not know the man who was in my house and there is no one that I know of who has any grudge against me or against my family.

"And that's it." Souness opened a new document and began the witness assessment attachment — her observations of Peach's state of mind, intelligence, ability with the English language, his emotional state (poor: Peach had been clearly confused during the interview, becoming tearful and agitated, particularly when his son was mentioned).

"What about the photos? The camera?"

"No." She shook her head. "Carmel must have imagined it — I asked him, he definitely doesn't remember photographs."

"He's sure."

"Oh, aye — I double-checked."

"Shit." While Souness typed, Caffery went to his desk. He sat down and picked off the Post-It notes Kryotos had stuck to his monitor. Messages: Rebecca had called, a few journalists wanted an interview, Kryotos wanted him to know she'd received the Quest Search disk from Registry, and that she had made a call to Missing Persons. After a period of forty-eight hours the Horseferry Road coroner's office would receive any unidentified bodies found in the Metropolitan area, but Caffery knew the call was a token gesture — futile: the whole of London was *burning* over Rory Peach — he wouldn't have made it as far as Missing Persons without someone speaking to Shrivemoor. He stuck this last Post-It to his finger and stared at it blankly. Where *was* Rory Peach? And were there photographs of the whole event somewhere? A camera flash. The sound of a wind-on mechanism. These weren't easy things to imagine. Had Carmel invented it? If not, and if Alek hadn't heard it in the living room, they must have been taken in the hallway. *What the fuck do you want with photographs of the poor bastards' hallway?*

He leaned back in his chair and sighed. He was out of ideas. "If we had just had some DNA we could start a screening locally."

Souness looked up. "Aye, and if we had a body we could get some DNA."

"So what's our next step?"

"Och, ye know the answer to that, Jack. More in-depth interviews with the Peaches, doctors allowing, get a victimology sketched out, widen the parameters, and — uh . . ." She paused. "Drop the area around the park —" Before she could hold up her hand Caffery had sucked breath in between his teeth. "I know, I know ye don't like it —"

"No, I *don't* like it — I still think he's in there. How could someone have left that park carrying a struggling kid and no one see him?"

"Maybe the bairn was walking."

"No one saw him. Anyway, none of Rory's clothes are missing. He would have been naked."

"Maybe the intruder brought his own clothes."

"Rory was bleeding, he was probably in shock — I just don't buy it."

"Well, he's not in the park now, is he?"

"No," Caffery admitted, ferreting under the desk for the holdall. He needed a drink. "Doesn't look that way." He held up a bottle of Scotch but Souness shook her head.

"Nah." She clicked, sending the report to the printer in the incident room, and stood, stretching, looking at her watch. "Nah, it's late. I need a kip."

She went into the incident room to distribute the statement in the team's pigeon-holes and for a few minutes Caffery was alone. He stood, holding the bottle, looking at his eyes reflected in the window, superimposed over the Croydon skyscrapers. What if Rebecca was right? What if people saw the naked teeth of a killer every time they looked at him?

"*A little thing inside you that just keeps growing and growing and if you don't get away from this house, if you're stuck on a case that's pushing all your buttons, then bam! you'll do it again.*"

He half filled a mug with Scotch, knocked it back and stared at his face, green tie unknotted and hanging loose around his neck.

It might go as far as it did last time —

She was wrong, he decided. She was making it up to get him away from the house. When Souness came back he turned and looked at her. "Danni?"

"Mmmm?"

"What do you think that was all about, before? You know, Peach giving me the old treatment about my eyes."

"Och — Christ knows." She shrugged and bent over the workstation, closing down the computer for the night. "Ye know how they get — he's probably got post-traumatic stress. Probably felt more comfortable talking to a woman, even an ugly old dyke like me." She straightened, pulled on her jacket, looked at him and smiled, clapping him on the back. "There's nothing wrong with your eyes, Jack, believe me. Ask any of the lassies in the team if there's anything wrong with your eyes and you'll get the answer." She coughed and straightened her back, running her palms down her lapels. "Except me, of course. I don't count."

CHAPTER SEVEN

He called Rebecca. The whole weight of the day was on him. "Let's just go home, cook something and go to bed . . ." But she was exuberant: she was in Brixton — she was at a private view at the Air Gallery on Coldharbour Lane — she wanted him to pick her up. OK, she agreed, they'd do some shopping in twenty-four-hour Tesco's, get some wild rice, some lamb, a bottle of something red and cook at home. But he could tell he was souring it for her. He could tell she wanted to stay at the party.

As he parked on Effra Road a herd of bright young things passed, bussed in by the score from West London and the home counties, moving through the street on their long, alien legs, heads back, faces lit like God's own converts as they moved through the darkness towards the lights in Brixton Central. Just as if they didn't know what had happened half a mile away in Brockwell Park. Just as if they had never heard of Rory Peach. He pocketed his keys and crossed Windrush Square into Coldharbour Lane, heading for the chief source of light, a great living column of heat and colour: the Air Gallery, lifting up into the night, a huge industrial space of textured concrete and galvanized steel. As he got nearer he could see Rebecca at the foot of the building, in the entrance, sipping a cocktail and looking at her watch.

He could remember a time when she would wait for him calmly, hands behind her back, the left foot resting lightly on the right. Now she stood with feet planted wide, dressed in a short leather jerkin, bubblegum-pink combat trousers, and, of course, her new accessory: her strange unhealthy energy, unravelling out into the night around her like a veil.

"Jack." She wormed a long brown arm under his jacket and pulled him nearer, standing on tiptoe for a kiss. Her nose was warm and her breath was sweet and orangy like Cointreau. He realized she was drunk. "I've just been speaking to someone from *The Times*, and Marc Quinn's in there — you know, the one with the frozen-blood head. He's in there and Ron Mue —"

"Great — shall we go?"

"And I told the guy from *The Times* I was doing more of my vaginas —"

"I'm sure he's made up about that." He tried to take the cocktail from her but she grinned and shook the glass at him, the crushed-strawberry-colour drink rattling like ice . . .

"*Diabolo*," she sang, curling her fingers at him. "It's a *Diiiii-aaabolo*. The *Devil*."

"Becky," he could feel irritation rising, "can we just get something to eat and head home —" He broke off. A Japanese woman in zipped PVC platform boots and a white vinyl raincoat had appeared from inside the crowded gallery bar and was staring at Rebecca.

Caffery was used to the shamanic appeal she had for strangers, but he didn't like it. He turned to the woman. "What?"

In reply she gave him a long, cold look, lifted a camera and before he realized what was happening had fired off two flashes. "Hey!" She slid back into the gallery bar and he caught Rebecca by the arm. "Right, come on — time to go." He took the drink from between her fingers and put it on the pavement outside the gallery. "Let's get some food."

She trotted along beside him, smiling and chattering about all the journalists she'd met. He walked fast; not listening to the details. Where had she got this hard gaiety of hers? The change in her had started like a sudden fever a month after the inquest. In the first few weeks, while she was back and forward from the hospital and he had been busy with tying up the case, there had been a strange lulled silence, a dreamy fermata in which Bliss's name wasn't mentioned. Then suddenly, overnight it seemed, Rebecca began talking. But not to him — to the press. To him she still wouldn't mention it directly.

"*Are you ever going to talk to me about it?*"

"*I already have. I gave you a statement, didn't I?*"

And off she went to bury herself in her mad art. Plaster casts of other women's genitals. It was as absurd as it was dispiriting. Sometimes he believed she could make her heart move in the opposite direction to her body, in a way his unsophisticated heart couldn't.

"You could have been a bit nicer," she said, as they walked around Tesco's. "You don't know who she was — she might have been with one of the papers."

"Or she might have been a ghoul."

"You don't understand." She lingered a little behind him, idly looking at the shelves, swinging her arms like a bored schoolgirl. "I have to be on display at these things — it's part of the game."

"Well, I'm not up for it." He walked ahead, not waiting for her, trying to get this over and done with, wanting to be out of Brixton as soon as possible, subconsciously scanning the other shoppers, wondering if Rory Peach's abductor might walk past him. He half expected someone to come up to him, point a finger, and say, "Why aren't you looking for him? What do you think you're *doing*, hanging around in the pasta section of Tesco's when Rory's still missing?" He threw some rice into the basket and continued up the aisle, Rebecca trailing behind. "I'm not up for another night of watching you talk to every dickhead with a mike and a pen."

"Ooooo-*wooh*," she trilled behind him. "Where's *this* coming from?"

He didn't answer. He walked a bit faster.

"Is it coming from the case we're working on?" she whispered, closing on him. "Does it all *remind* us of something we'd rather forget? Is that what the mood is?"

"Shall we change the subject?"

"Oh, Jack! I was *joking*." She got ahead of him, stopped to pull a bottle of red wine off the shelf and turned to him. "You should learn to lighten up a bit. You take everything so *seriously*."

"I mean it, Becky. Don't push it." He walked past her. "Unless you're after something, unless you *really* want to talk, *really* want to take the gloves off — and I don't think you do."

"Oooh!" She caught up and grinned up at him. "I *wonder* what you're talking about."

"It's not funny."

"I think I can decide what's funny and what isn't. After all —" She suddenly leaned back and lobbed the bottle into the air, her head back, watching the swish-swish-swish of light on the glass above her. The bottle twisted back down and she caught it, turned to him and smiled nicely. "— it was my assault."

"Jesus." He started to walk away, disgusted, but she caught up again, grinning at the side of his face, skipping along.

"You just can't stand the fact that I'm not traumatized and you are," she said. "I mean, what am I supposed to be grieving about? I lived, didn't I? I'm dealing with it."

"You call what you're doing with your work *dealing* with it? You call telling some jerk-off from the *Guardian* how it's 'informed' your art *dealing* with it? You've got a perverted sense, Rebecca, of what 'dealing' with it is."

"Oooh — perverted!" She scooted up ahead of him and turned, walking backwards up the aisle. "*Perr*-verted," she sang, whirling the bottle in the air again, almost missing it on its way down. A couple passed her warily, shrinking back a little against the shelves. "This guy, right." Rebecca stopped in Caffery's path, her face bright. Now he could read the print on her leather jerkin. Article 5 of the Alcatraz inmate regulations, stencilled in white: *You are entitled to food, clothing, shelter and medical attention. Anything else you get is a privilege*. "This guy says to his girlfriend, 'Let's have anal sex —' "

"Rebecca —"

"He says, 'Let's have anal sex.' And she says, 'Anal sex? Isn't that a bit perverted?' And he says —"

"Please — just stop it —"

"And he says, 'Perverted? *Perverted?* My, but that's a big word. Especially for a ten-year-old.' " She bent over, bottle clasped against her knee and shook with laughter. "*A ten-year-old!*"

"Yes, very good." He tried to get past her but she jumped from side to side, blocking his path.

"Oh, come on, Jack, read the dating manual. You're supposed to find my jokes funny. You're supposed to —"

"Will you just *think*!" He pushed a finger in her face and she shrank back a little, taken off-guard. "*Will you just fucking THINK, for once*." He put his face near hers, his voice low, stooping slightly so that no one else could hear. "Think about what it was like for *me* to find *you*, Rebecca, hanging, *hanging from a hook in the fucking ceiling*. I thought you were dead — he told me he'd fucked you and then killed you. How do you think that felt, eh?"

She blinked at him and with that small reaction something hardened in his chest. He slammed down the basket, bottles clinking, and walked away, feeling for his keys in his pocket. *She asked for it, she pushed me, she pushed me*. He took deep breaths, half expecting her to be bouncing along at his side, poking him, telling him to take a chill pill or something. He had wanted to push her, wanted more than anything to see her rattled, and when he paused at the exit and turned round he knew he'd succeeded.

She was standing motionless in the centre of the aisle under the vast fluorescent lights, a single, small figure, quite alone in the huge supermarket, her face quite blank. He took a few steps back down the aisle. "Becky?"

Her head jerked a fraction and her chin dropped but she didn't answer. When he took her hand it was cold. *So you've done it. Congratulations*.

Hating himself and hating her, he led her out of the store and across Brixton to the car. They drove in silence and at home she took a bottle of Blavod and a packet of cigarillos upstairs and went to bed without eating. They didn't speak another word to each other that night.

CHAPTER EIGHT

(20 July)

Reluctantly AMIT moved the search team from the park and extended their house-to-house parameters and witness-appeal campaign. DS Fiona Quinn went to Donegal Crescent. It was still sealed to allow the Specialist Crime Unit's chemicals to cook, but she went in and swept the corner of the room where Alek Peach's statement placed the intruder. Meanwhile Alek Peach discharged himself from hospital.

"*What?*"

First thing in the morning, his jacket still on, his hair wet, a cup of Kryotos's good coffee in his hand, Caffery stood in the SIO's doorway, disbelief on his face.

"Aye, this morning." Souness was sitting with one foot up on the other knee, using a screwdriver to pick a stone out of the sole of her cowboy boot. A pile of zoned search grids of Brixton generated from the MapInfo programme sat next to her on the desk. Her sunburn had turned a little brown overnight, making her ordinary eyes a starry, periwinkle blue. "He's definitely not dying — and even if he *was* he decided he was going to go a lot faster if he couldn't get a

Superking in his mouth. The consultant's got the right arse about it."

"So where is he now?"

"At the Nersessians'."

The family liaison officer had called Souness from there and told her about Alek Peach's tears: "Every inch of the sodding way from King's to Guernsey Grove." He had ignored Mrs Nersessian — standing with her arms wide open, a tragic look on her face — and had gone straight upstairs to where Carmel Peach was still lying on her side and had curled up on top of the coverlet, his arms around her. There they lay for an hour, neither speaking, chain-smoking together as if the fags were the glue in their marriage. And by the way, the officer, who had just consumed almost a pound of baklava and four Armenian demitasses, wanted to know, what was it that Mrs Nersessian owed the Peaches? If all she wanted was a captive audience for her vineleaf *mazzas*, wasn't she taking the Good Samaritan thing a little far?

Caffery listened to Souness in silence. He hadn't slept last night. Rebecca had lain next to him with her eyes closed, but he didn't believe she had slept either. He knew that she was seeing a ghostly image of herself — like a kite, a body distorted and re-angled. Dangling from a ceiling. He'd picked a scab off all the things she didn't want to talk about and she'd reacted as if he'd punched her in the face. He rubbed his eyes. "Danni."

"Mmmm?"

"I'm going to take the dog team into the park, just for a while."

"Eh?" She looked up. "What're ye talking about? We've finished in there."

"The human-remains dogs this time. We're not going to find him alive, are we?" He scratched the back of his neck. "I mean, not now."

"I'll ignore that, Jack. I don't want to hear ye talk like that again."

"I still want to go."

She looked at him for a long time. "When you get a bone between your teeth, Jack . . ." Then, shaking her head, she went back to the stone. She freed it, chucked it in the bin and brushed off her hands. "Go on, do what you like. Just make sure ye don't tell any of the hacks what those dogs are. I'll not have that in the papers."

In the incident room Marilyn Kryotos had arrived and had taken off her shoes as was her usual habit before the team arrived at the office. She was talking on the phone and Caffery paused for a moment on the other side of the desk, watching her. She looked up and winked, and he drew a question mark in the air. She finished the call and straightened, hands pressed in the small of her back. "Intelligence unit at Dulwich."

"Well?"

"This." She handed him the notes she had made. The search word "troll" had dragged up an old outstanding case. A violent sexual assault on an eleven-year-old Laotian boy, Champaluang Keoduangdy, in the dried-out boating-lake of Brockwell Park. "I'll try and track him down today, but in the meantime there's a DI at Brixton who was there in the eighties and might remember something."

"No one done for it?"

"Nope — and it's before the nonce register."

"Set up an appointment, will you, with the victim and with the DI."

In Brockwell Park the sun edged in increments up the sky behind that great druid tor, Arkaig Tower: its shadow raced down the park to collect at its feet. Two dog-handlers in blue shirts were climbing into forensic overalls next to the unit van. Caffery could see, on the passenger seat of the van, two SIRCHIE brand antiputrefaction masks. The dogs in the back were not the same ones that had been there for the last two days. These dogs were trained to search for dead bodies.

"You do know if we find him the dogs might, uh, destroy some evidence, don't you?" The sergeant was embarrassed. "We can't always stop them, they're hungry." There were pork trotters in a Dewhurst carrier-bag — three days overripe — for the dogs to blunt their hunger on if they were unable to find dead Rory Peach.

"Yes." Caffery rubbed his nose and looked across the trees. It was still there — that draw he felt to the park. He just couldn't give up on it yet. "Yes, I know."

They started near the van, pounding the earth with heavy metal probes. This was familiar ritual to the dogs — the noise told them why they were here. It opened the glands in their mouths and they moved in excited circles, blood-boltered, dripping saliva into the earth.

Caffery's hope rose a little as the dogs pushed noses into the holes made by the probes, crawled under bushes, and sniffed around the soft black edges of the lakes. But it is not only a helicopter's thermal imaging equipment that is hampered by hot weather: heat decreases a dog's sensitivity too, and an hour into the search they had found nothing. The officers were sweating in their forensic overalls and beginning to look despondent, but Caffery didn't call a halt. He was watching Texas, the larger of the two German shepherds. From time to time the dog lifted his head, distracted, and turned in a small fidgety circle.

"Come on, boy." The handler jerked the dog back to his task. "Over here."

But in the dog's odd lapses Caffery sensed something. Every square inch of the park had been searched — there had to be an angle he was missing: a light was being shone dead into his eyes and still he couldn't see it.

You're the one who thinks that he knows, thinks he has a special tap into the mind of the killer, and yet you can't see what happened here.

"*What's a troll, Danni?*"

"*A troll? A troll's just an old queer who likes gorgeous young meat. A tree jumper.*"

He thought about Rebecca the other night, squatting in the tree like a leprechaun. *Zeus was a baby in a tree.* He thought about the little boy in the Clock Tower Grove Estate pretending to climb a drainpipe. And then suddenly he had it. He was right — Rory was still in the park. And he thought he knew where.

* * *

At 12.30p.m. Hal Church came home for lunch from his furniture-design studio in Coldharbour Lane. He was a largish man — with his sleeves rolled up, sandy hair receding from a tanned forehead, he looked far more the broad-shouldered artisan than the designer.

Benedicte was in the kitchen unpacking Tesco's bags and Hal placed his hands on her hips, kissed the back of her neck then gently inched her sideways so that he could reach a bag of pretzels in the cupboard. Around their feet Josh jumped like a small cricket from bag to bag, opening them, pushing his nose in them.

"Mum, where's the Sunny Delight?"

"Sunny Delight." Hal put a hand to his forehead. "Oh, for Pete's sake. An orange kid. I'm going to have an orange kid."

"Da-aad!" Josh spun round on his heel, his hands over his face. "Don't mess wid my head."

"Hey, *wassup*, orange kid?"

Josh giggled, and came back at his father. "You come diss me and you is in some serious trouble, man."

"Josh," from the bag Ben pulled a ball of mozzarella, moving in its whey, and placed it on the worktop ready for the pizza she was going to make, "will you *stop* talking like that? It's not funny."

Josh dropped his head and made a face at his father.

"Josh. Come here." Hal bent over until his head was close to his son's. "You's pretty fly for a white boy," he whispered.

"*Word!*" Josh gave his father the Brixton salute. "Boyacasha."

"For heaven's sake, you two, just *can* it." Benedicte poked Hal in the belly. "Go on, let him have some juice, his knuckles've been scraping the ground all afternoon."

"Why don't you just get him a packet of Rothman's while you're at it? Josh? You will tell us when you want to go into detox, won't you, son?"

"Hey, Dad." Josh put the Sunny Delight on the kitchen top and stood on tiptoe to get a glass. "Mummy had to call the filth."

"The *police*, Josh, not the *filth*. Where *do* you pick these things up?"

"The police?" Hal looked at Ben, concerned. "How come?"

"We had to get the filth." Josh put the glass on the counter and used his teeth to open the bottle. "Because of someone tried to steal Smurf."

"*What?*"

"I'll tell you in a minute," Benedicte murmured, sliding her eyes meaningfully in their son's direction. "Josh, not your teeth, please. You never know when you might need your teeth." She took it from him and used her own teeth to tear off the plastic strip. "Now take your drink through, OK, peanut? If you're good we'll fill up the paddling-pool and get Tracy Island out."

"Ye — es!" Josh saluted, excited, and zoomed into the other room, almost spilling his drink as he went. "Virgil Tracy to control, launching Thunderbird Four pod NOW!" He threw himself at the sofa. "F-A-B!"

When he was settled in the family room, still within earshot but absorbed with the TV, Hal opened the pretzels, found a bottle of Hoegarden and turned back to Benedicte. He worked with linseed oil and maple, and the oils had coloured his palms so that his heart line was deeply, permanently ingrained. As faithful as a beach donkey, his family was everything to him: any real or perceived threat to them he felt like gunfire. "Well? What happened?"

"God, it was really creepy." She put the kettle on and pushed the hair out of her eyes, keeping them on Josh to make sure he wasn't listening. *The Simpsons* was starting and she could see him sitting on the sofa with his knees up, clutching the glass of orange juice to his mouth, eyes pinned on the screen. "Outside the ruddy camping shop on Brixton Hill, of all places. First thing this morning. I tied her outside because she was whingeing about being left in the car and I'm standing at the counter buying an icebox for Cornwall and I turn round and" — she waved her hand in the air — "and there's this bloke. Molesting her."

"Molesting her?" Hal chucked a handful of pretzels into his mouth. "What do you mean *molesting*?"

She put a finger to her mouth. "*Sexually*," she hissed. "He put his hand between her legs."

"*What?*"

"I know. I told you — creepy. He had her tail in one hand, held up like this — sort of like you'd hold up a . . . um, I don't know, like you'd hold up a cow's tail. You know, like the vets do. And he was bent over and staring, as if he was trying to, God, it's so disgusting, but like he was trying to *smell* her, or just sort of see up her, you know. So I — well, I shouted, and everyone in the shop's staring at me, but I thought, Well, I'm not going to let him get away with that —"

"Who was he?"

"He was a, uh, white guy, tall — he'd been in the shop behind me when I was buying all the stuff for Cornwall. I noticed him 'cause he had a hood on, and he was standing in the corner like he didn't want to be seen or something. I thought he was staring at me then, but he went out and I forgot about it and the next I know he's got Smurf's tail up in the air —"

"Bastard —"

"— and anyway, I thought, I'm not going to let him get away with that so I ran out of the shop and I'm shouting and screaming like some total nutter." Benedicte opened the fridge and rummaged for the milk. "But he went down Acre Lane and I'd let go of Josh so I had to go back and —"

"Jesus —"

"— and I called the police and told them, I mean, poor Smurf, deaf as a post and there she was having her *pounani* looked at like some common tramp."

"You're laughing."

"I'm not *laughing*. I called the police. Like we haven't seen enough of the police in the last few days. I had to call them, not that there's anything they can do." She stopped. She was frowning into the fridge.

"And?"

"Oh, for heaven's sake, look at this!" She slammed the door closed and turned towards the family room. "Josh!"

"What's he done?"

"He's been moving stuff around again. *Josh!*"

He looked up innocently. "Wha'?"

"Come here!"

"I've never heard anything so screwy." Hal tipped more pretzels into his mouth. "Looking up Smurf's bum."

Obediently Josh dropped off the sofa and came over into the kitchen. Benedicte bent to speak to him. "Have you been moving everything around in here?"

"No."

"Are you sure?"

"Ye-es."

"If you put the milk on the wire bits it tips over, I've told you." She looked inside the fridge again. "Well, if you haven't been doing it then I don't know who has. The fridge goblins, I suppose." She took the milk out and held it up to the light. "Oh, for God's sake."

"Eugh!" Hal made a face. "That is disgusting. I can smell it from here."

"God." She looked faint. "It smells like piss."

"Here — let me." He took it from her and, holding it at arm's length, went to the sink. Shaking his head, he turned on the waste-disposal, rinsed the bottle, put it in the bin and let the tap run until the disposal unit was clear. "Gurgh! When did you get it?"

"It's not past its sell-by date."

"Maybe the fridge is buggered." Hal opened it and looked dubiously at the dial. "I'll get on to it when we get back from Cornwall."

* * *

In the park Caffery took the young PC to one side. "This is going to sound like a stupid question."

"Try me."

"Is there any way of getting the dogs to search *up*?"

"Up?"

He nodded up into the trees. "In the branches."

"Sure."

"*Sure?*"

"Yeah — well." The PC rubbed his face, reddening slightly. "You know how it goes, aircrafts, y'know, come down, don't they? Sometimes, um, *things* get caught in trees." He looked upwards. "But why?"

"I dunno." Caffery turned to check that no one was listening. If he was wrong he didn't want to have to explain. "Look, it's just an idea. There's no harm, is there?"

"OK." The PC went to the van and found a light, galvanized-steel stick, about the size of a walking-stick with a green plastic handle. "Texas?" The shepherd's head snapped up and he watched with small quizzical eyes as the handler tapped the trunk of a chestnut tree. He tapped up in the branches and the dog understood. His head jerked forward and he trotted after the officer, tail lowered, nose pointing straight up into the leaves. Caffery followed a few yards behind.

They circled the park. It was 1p.m. when the dog stopped in front of a huge hornbeam dripping with caterpillars. He reared up on his hind legs, placed his paws against the tree-trunk, and there he stayed.

He was at the exact spot where Roland Klare had recovered the Pentax camera and pink gloves three days before.

CHAPTER NINE

Caffery, the exhibits officer and DS Fiona Quinn had a brief plan-of-action meeting with the pathologist, Harsha Krishnamurthi, in the coroner's office reception. Over dusty silk flower displays on formica tables they discussed how to cut up Rory Peach. Afterwards Caffery went into the men's and splashed water across his face.

When he had looked into the branches and seen how Rory had been tied his impulse had been to drive back to Brockley, walk straight into Penderecki's house, take him by his thinning hair, slam his face into a wall and kick him. Kick him until he stopped moving. The eight-year-old had been curled into a ball, fastened with rope, knees up to his chin, arms covering his head — from above he would have resembled something the size and shape of a car tyre. His fingernails had carved demilunes into his own cheek. If Rory had been any bigger they might have seen him earlier, if he'd been ten or eleven and not eight, maybe, Caffery thought, and then he thought that twenty-seven years ago no one had checked the trees along the railway track. No one had wondered about the trees. Even today he was stumbling over new ways Penderecki could have concealed Ewan during the police search of his house.

He wiped his face with a paper towel and went through, past the ante-room where bodies were stored in banks of lockers, ID tags slotted into holders on the doors, pink for a girl and blue for a boy — We are colour coded by our sex, he thought, not only at birth but in death too — and into the dissecting room. It was cool in here, as if it was winter. Mint-green tiles lined the walls, like an old-fashioned swimming-pool, and there it was — that familiar butcher's smell of old, mopped-around blood. Hoses lay under the tables, releasing small puddles of water on to the tiled floor. Two bodies, names written in black marker on each calf, had been pushed to one end of the room to make space, their belongings and toe-tags sitting on a separate gurney in yellow plastic hospital waste-bags. The bodies were split open: a heap of colours, blue paper towels crammed in the neck cavities, and a mortician in a green plastic apron and black wellingtons stood over one, lifting out a pile of intestines. He shook them, as if he was shaking washing coming from a bowl.

Rory Peach, once a boy who played football and stuck go-faster stripes on his bike, was now a circle wrapped in a white plastic sheet on the table in the centre of the tiled room. Around him stood three morticians arranged in an odd tableau. They didn't look up when Caffery appeared in the doorway. Morticians are a strange, silent group. Sometimes secretive, often cliquey, always down to earth: the real muscle behind the pathologist, they do most of the hard labour in an autopsy without raising an eyebrow. Caffery had never seen them behave the way they did that summer afternoon. It took him a moment, after they had broken off and gone in separate directions, collecting bowls, turning on hoses, to realize that he had just witnessed them paying respect. Oh, God, he thought, this isn't going to be easy.

Harsha Krishnamurthi came in. Tall, greying. All business. Fiddling with his new toy, a hands-free dictaphone with headset, he got it into position then briskly pulled away Rory Peach's sheet. Everyone in the mortuary stiffened slightly, as if they'd drawn a collective breath.

He was crunched into a croissant shape, almost like a sleeping cat, his hands wrapped over his head. He looked as if he was examining something on his chest. Brown parcel tape had been wrapped around his head, covering his mouth and eyes. He didn't smell, as if his flesh was too clean and young to smell, and his skin was smooth as if he'd just got out of a bath. Krishnamurthi cleared his throat, asked Caffery if this was the same body found in the tree in Brockwell Park. Caffery nodded: "It is." The formalities were over.

They removed the knots first. Krishnamurthi severed the rope with painstaking attention, more than two inches from the knot: the ligatures could be tested not only for DNA, but also by forensic knot analysts and he was careful to preserve their shape as he put them into an exhibits bag. The photographer moved around the table, working from every angle as the exhibits officer sealed and initialled the bag and put it on his trolley.

The process was repeated until all the ropes were removed and Rory looked quite different. He lay curled up, like a young spider in defence mode, deep swollen furrows made by the ropes on his arms, knees and ankles. Krishnamurthi gently tested the thin legs. When they uncurled obediently he hesitated, an odd look on his face. For a moment no one dared breathe. Krishnamurthi looked quickly up at the clock on the wall and carefully flexed Rory Peach's feet, then examined the boy's hands and face.

"There's — uh, yes." He flipped up his plastic visor and wiped his forehead on his sleeve. "There's rigor mortis present only in the face and upper torso. I'm . . . going to . . ." His pause was almost imperceptible. Only those with their antennae quivering, like Caffery, would have noticed the brief blush of emotion. Those flexible feet had started the pathologist thinking the unthinkable. "I'm going to take a liver temperature."

Caffery turned away. He had seen hundreds of post-mortems, most less recognizable as human beings than Rory was. He'd seen a forty-year-old man, reduced by faceless business associates to nothing but a one and a half stone cut of torso, rolling on the dissecting table. He'd seen a fifteen-year-old girl eaten by foxes from her eyes down to her shoulders. He didn't kid himself that he had a right to feel horror more deeply than anyone else but, like Krishnamurthi, he knew the mechanics of rigor — he knew what that stiffness in the facial muscles, what the flexibility in the feet said about Rory's death. He didn't want to think about it. For the first time in his life he had to step out of a post-mortem.

He was standing in reception, pressing Altoid mints into his mouth, rubbing his hands together hard, the smart of blood clearing his thoughts, when the door opened. Souness came in, brushing her jacket as if she'd walked through a cobweb.

"Fucking press all over me." She shuddered. "Talk about quick off the mark." She pushed the door closed behind her, pressing her foot on it to check that it was properly shut, turned and saw instantly that Caffery was trying to avoid her eyes, was trying hard to find somewhere to hide his attention. Her voice softened. "Ye all right?" She came a little bit nearer. He was slightly cyanosed around the mouth. "No, ye're not. Ye're crapping it, aren't ye?"

"I'm fine. Mint?"

"No thanks." She chewed her thumbnail, looked towards the dissecting room, and back at him. "Funny. I suppose if it was me I might be just a wee bit jealous."

"*Jealous?*"

"Rory's been found. He's dead, but at least he was found — Mum and Dad can start grieving now." She rested her hand affectionately on his arm. "And where does that leave ye, ye poor wee soul?"

Caffery didn't answer. He didn't dare speak or even reach into his pocket for cigarette papers in case his hands were shaking. He turned for the door to the autopsy suite. "I — uh — I think we've got a time of death. Just guessing from the rigor."

"And?"

"Uh — look, let's go back inside, shall we?"

Back in the dissecting room Krishnamurthi had moved on. He had taken nail cuttings, putting the scissors he used into the exhibits bag with the last cuttings and passing them all to the exhibits officer. He had removed the packing tape from Rory's face. DS Fiona Quinn was hopeful: in evidence bags on a separate gurney were five white fibres Krishnamurthi had removed from the ligature furrows on Rory's wrists with a strip of low-tack tape. She could run them through mass spectrometry and gas chromatography to find chemical composition and colour — hopefully match them to a suspect's clothing. Now Krishnamurthi was carefully breaking the rigor mortis in Rory's upper body and gently straightening him out on the table.

Caffery and Souness stood against the wall, Caffery sucking mints, Souness jiggling her finger in her ear as if she was embarrassed to be watching this.

Rory measured 127 centimetres from his left heel to his crown. He weighed 26.23 kilos. A Tanner scale reading would mark him down as slightly bigger than an average eight-year-old. A bloody paper towel with pale blue flowers around the edge had been scrunched against his shoulder and it clung there, pressed under his back when he was straightened.

Krishnamurthi, the photographer and the morticians moved around the table in a complex, calm ritual, each anticipating without word or signal when it was time to step in. Caffery and Souness watched in silence — they had the same two questions in their minds: was the paper towel hiding the source of the blood in the kitchen? And: had Rory Peach been sexually assaulted?

"I'm looking at an averagely nourished body of a child," Krishnamurthi said softly, into the headset. His voice echoed in the scrubbed-down room. "The face shows marked turgor, and what appears to be multiple aspects of Hippocratic facies, the ocular orbits are prominent, while the globes are sunken. Cheekbones and mandibles prominent. Mouth and nose appear . . ." He bent in and squinted at the child's face. ". . . dry. Crusted. Skin is tight to palpation so flag histology to look for hyperkalemia and I want sodium counts, anti-diuretic hormone levels and plasma volume."

"Harsha?"

Krishnamurthi looked up at Souness. "Yes, yes. When the microscopics are back I'll tell you more." Krishnamurthi had a reputation for denying the police the immediate answers they wanted. "And when I've looked at the organ capsules."

"What are you expecting?"

"Sticky, tacky capsules, maybe bleeding in the intestinal tract."

"Meaning?"

"I'll tell you when I've had a look." He narrowed his eyes at her, making a disapproving clicking noise in his throat. "OK?"

"Fair enough." Souness held up her hands. The last thing they needed was to alienate him. "That's fair enough."

"Right." Krishnamurthi bent nearer to look at Rory's throat. "There is a poorly defined mark overlying the larynx indicating some sort of — uh — occlusion of the carotid and jugular, some sort of ligature strangulation, but no petechiae in the eyes. Some scratch marks and bruising to the neck." He looked up at Souness. "But it's not the cause of death."

"Really?"

"Really."

Yes, really, Danni. Caffery looked at his shoes. *That's not how Rory died. I think I already know how he died*.

"I'd like later," Krishnamurthi continued, "to get some alternative light sources on these marks, photograph the area and see if we can see anything else. Right." He stepped back and allowed the mortician to turn Rory's body — expertly, efficiently, not looking at the child's face. The dissecting room was absolutely silent. Lying on his face the little lumps of Rory's spine protruded through the thin skin; the paper towel stayed stuck in place. Krishnamurthi didn't look at anyone as he peeled it away, dropping it in an evidence bag. He peered down at the wound on Rory's shoulder and after a breathless pause he stepped back and looked up.

"Yes," he said to the assembled team. "Yes. Someone have a word with the coroner. Need to have a dentist look at this."

Out in the high blue afternoon furnace Josh was in the paddling-pool in his Darth Maul trunks, his back to the woods, intense concentration on his face as he plunged Thunderbird Four to the bottom of the pool and let it bob back up to the surface. Sunlight flashed on the water, and over the fence in the park gnats hummed in the shade of the Spanish chestnuts.

Hal stood on the veranda with a cold bottle of Coke, staring at those trees. He could see flashes of white and blue out there where a police team had congregated on a small area — fluttering crime-scene tape had appeared, draped around bushes. They must have found something. He sipped his Coke thoughtfully — he had been so happy to be out of central Brixton, out of the cramped flat above an off-licence on the Front Line, but now Brixton's problems seemed to be chasing them up the hill.

The Front Line. At one time they had been proud of the cachet of the address, and life for them was Hoy Hoy cockroach traps under the sink, tuna and Scotch bonnet sandwiches in the Phoenix café, Hal forever tracking down and arguing revisionism with Darcus Howe. Life on the Front Line. He liked that — him and Ben frontiersmen, living down with the real people. They'd been there for the '95 Wayne Douglas riots — he had stood in the street, holding his doorkeys in one hand, library books in the other, and watched the Dogstar go up in flames. Whoomp! Up into the sky. And everyone looked out of their doors and windows to see burning, curling, crisp packets floating down from the clouds.

But with Josh it all changed. Responsibility kicked at them. The schizophrenics screaming, the muggings, the rich young clubgoers and the sinister followers of Louis Farrakhan — impossibly handsome black men in razor-sharp suits, standing on street corners with hands folded piously, terrifying plans darting behind their eyes — suddenly none of it was glamorous, it wasn't funny. One day Josh came screaming through the room with Buzz Lightyear: Buzz *en garde* with his scorching new weapon. A syringe, the words *Single Use Only For U 100 Insulin* printed on it. After that Hal decided to work himself lame to get his family out of central Brixton. But the lifebelt, when it came, was from Benedicte's family: an inheritance from her aunt in Norway had put them in this new house, just far enough out of the centre to keep them safe. There was lighting and security fencing, there was a bus ride separating them from the Fridge and life was, well, really rather cushiony.

"*Hal!*" From a window above him Benedicte was calling. He put the Coke bottle on the veranda. "Josh — stay there, OK?" He went inside, climbing the stairs two at a time. She was in the bedroom, standing at the foot of the bed.

"You OK?"

"Yeah." She was wearing a T-shirt, pink knickers and sheepskin slippers, as if she'd been in the middle of changing. One side of her hair was set in rollers, the other loose. "I'm OK, but look — look at the bed."

Hal could see that the whole length of her side of the bed was wet. As if Smurf had tottered up and down the bed peeing as she went. "Christ."

"Oh, God." Ben rubbed her face. "I'm sorry I yelled. I suppose it's not Smurf's fault. She's old." She sighed and began to remove the saturated duvet cover. "She gets on to the bed and she can't always get down quickly enough when she needs to."

He shook his head. "Should have seen her this morning. Dragging. Her back legs — you know. She started peeing before she'd even stopped walking. Walking along and peeing all down her legs. It's pathetic."

"She took her pills this morning but, oh, Hal, you know I still think we should get the name of a vet in Helston, just in case. Yeew — eee!" Ben puffed air from her mouth and slotted her hands under the pillow to pull back the sheets. "I thought my days of changing pissy sheets were over."

"It's probably all that excitement this morning."

"Oh, yeah, getting your bits examined by a total stranger makes you pee with excitement. Only a man could say that." She piled up the bed linen. "We're going to have to stop her coming up the stairs, Hal, OK? Keep her shut in the kitchen."

He sighed. "I suppose when we get back we're going to have to face it." He pressed two fingers to her temple and clicked a trigger with his thumb. "Poor old girl."

"Oh, for God's sake, please don't." She wiped her face on the shoulder of her T-shirt. She didn't think she could face losing Smurf. Secretly they hadn't expected her to survive this far — on her ID disc, after "My name is Smurf. If you find me please call . . .", their old telephone number was still given. They hadn't thought it was worth changing. Even so, Ben hadn't really accepted that the end was near. "Can't we think of something better to talk about?" She turned to the door, the bundle of sheets in her arms, and left the room.

It was a bite. An open red hole in the white flesh. As if Rory had been snapped at by a meat-eater. There were four or five less violent bites in the same area, but Krishnamurthi couldn't find any on the other places a male victim of rape is typically bitten: the axillae, the face and the scrotum. Only the shoulders. Bites to the shoulders — a method a rapist often uses to subdue his victim. And when Krishnamurthi did the anal swabs he found something else. "Yes." He cleared his throat and straightened up. "There's a contaminant."

No one spoke. Souness and Caffery exchanged a glance.

"Do you know what it is?"

"You can't tell just looking at it in this light — not until you get it in the lab — but I suppose we can hazard a guess."

Souness nodded. "I see." She looked at Caffery. He nodded tightly at her, put his hands in his pockets and turned back to watch Krishnamurthi working. Until the contaminant was identified they couldn't make assumptions. It could be anything.

The photographer fitted film into a Kodak 1-to-1 fingerprint camera and fished a pale-blue right-angled ruler from his kit. When Krishnamurthi stepped away he placed the ruler next to the wound and began to focus the camera. Souness and Caffery watched in silence, shoulder to shoulder at the edge of the autopsy suite, as the photographer recorded every bite on Rory

Peach's shoulders. He was finishing just as the odontologist arrived from King's.

Mr Ndizeye, BDS, PhD and Seventh Day Adventist, wore thick National Health glasses and a Hawaiian shirt under his white coat. His mouth was turned up at the corners like a clown's, as if he was permanently smiling. Sweat ran in rivulets down his polished mahogany forehead, as he inspected the wounds, made notes, and built up impression trays from dental boxing wax. The morticians exchanged glances behind his back.

"What do you think?" Souness asked. "Have you got enough to work with?"

"Yes, yes, yes." Ndizeye was waiting impatiently for his assistant to fill a gun with polysilicone. "They were slowly inflicted, some of these bites." He bent over, looked inside the wax tray moulded on to Rory's shoulder and moved his finger above it in a little stirring motion. "Radial abrasions, so the biter has had a bit of a suck while he's at it. Typical sadistic bites." He pulled a tissue from a back pocket and mopped his forehead to stop sweat dropping on to Rory's body. "I can see — um — upper left one, two, three, and upper right one, probably two." He looked up, his eyes magnified like fish behind the glasses, his clown mouth smiling. "Yes, I'm happy. I think we'll get a perfect cast from this."

After the post-mortem there were the alternative light source, ALS, photos to be taken. The science unit brought in their mobile blackout blinds and Souness and Caffery left, Souness to a press conference, and Caffery back to Shrivemoor to submit the results of the day's actions to Kryotos's ever-growing pile of documents. When he finally decided to call it a day, late in the night, he realized he hadn't eaten and was shaking. He got a takeaway in Crystal Palace and that stopped the shaking — but back at home he still had to pause in the doorway for a moment, promising himself not to let the case show in his face.

He needn't have worried. Rebecca wasn't in a mood to discuss his work.

She was lying on the sofa, dressed in caramel suede trousers and a short white sweater. She had a pink varnished nail in her mouth and was staring blankly at the TV screen. There was a pile of *Time Outs* on the table in front of her. She didn't look up when he came in — he had to be the first to speak: "How are you feeling?"

She glanced up at him vaguely, like someone looking at a window that has been left open, someone who can't be bothered to get up and shut it.

"My head hurts."

"Is that all?"

"Yes."

He dropped down on the sofa next to her, his arm around her. "I'm sorry about last night."

She didn't shrink from him or lose her temper. Instead she just shrugged and said nothing, and went on staring at the TV screen. He suddenly felt immensely sorry for what he had done the night before, pushing her face-down into memories she didn't want to address. He knew he'd have to move gently with her that night.

"Let's go upstairs," she said, much later. He followed her up the staircase, still baffled by her odd, silent aura and in the bedroom they hardly exchanged a word. It should have tipped him off — he should have seen the signs.

Rebecca liked Jack to go down on her. They'd established that early on in their relationship. "Actually it was the first night," she'd told her friends, "I didn't even have to ask him — it was a miracle." He would do it for hours if she wanted, her neatly turned legs hooked up and resting on his back. Sometimes she laughed because he insisted on keeping one foot off the bed or sofa, on the floor, as if he was ready to sprint off at a moment's notice. *What do you think's going to happen? A raid or something?* This evening she said nothing. She lifted her hips and let him roll down the suede trousers, resting her hands on his head, running her fingers through his hair, looking ruminatively at the ceiling. After she came he straightened, took off his shirt, wiped his face on it and was about to undo his trousers when Rebecca pushed herself past him and up off the bed. She picked up her clothes from the floor.

"Where you going?"

"To have a wash."

"What?"

"To *have* a *wash*."

She walked out of the room, pressing her heels into the boards, and he fell backwards on the bed, his hands over his face, his erection almost painful he had been so ready. *What the fuck is she doing?* He listened to the old water pipes creak, listened to her finish, leave the bathroom, go downstairs. She didn't return. The bedside clock ticked on and now his hard-on was dying. He groaned, dropped his hands from his face and lay there, staring at the ceiling, his head throbbing.

You've started something now, Jack. This is all about last night.

When she came back a few minutes later she was wearing his old towelling dressing-gown. She had brushed her hair and was carrying a glass of vodka and a lighted cigarillo. She stood at the small book-shelf in the bedroom, smoking and reading the titles calmly as if nothing odd had happened. He got up and rested his hands on her shoulders. "Look — last night — I —"

"Don't worry about it." She pulled away from him. "I'm going to bed now."

And that was it. He stood in the doorway, determined not to get angry as she put the cigarillo in the ashtray on the bedstand, crawled under the covers, levered her knees up and rested a book on them. Her tidy little face was illuminated from the bedside lamp. Serious and intent on the book as if he wasn't there. He knew there were things he should say. Things he should be able to say. But he was tired and full of the images of Rory's autopsy and he knew this was a bad time for them to start talking. "Right." He turned away and went straight into the back bedroom.

This was the room he'd shared with Ewan as a child — Ewan's room, he called it now. He found his trainers and pulled on jogging pants and a T-shirt. Ducking briefly to check the lights at Penderecki's over the railway, that habit he knew he would never slake, he put a doorkey on a piece of tape around his neck, went downstairs and slammed the door. He hadn't said goodbye to Rebecca.

As soon as he closed the front door she dropped the book on the floor and slumped down in the bed, staring at the ceiling. When the gate had closed and the street outside became quiet — only the occasional car going by, the headlights crossing the ceiling — she sat up, pulled the pillow from behind her head, lay back down on the bed and pressed the pillow across her face. *Oh, God, Jack, this is so screwed-up*. Using the weight of her forearms she held the pillow down against her nose and mouth and began to scream.

She screamed until her throat was sore and her head ached. Then she lay still with the pillow still resting across her face, muffling her breathing. The moisture in her breath wet the cotton, but otherwise her face was dry — she hadn't cried.

Running, which in his twenties had been a release of energy, in his thirties had become his way of letting his mind float free. It stopped his thoughts battering themselves against the walls and tonight the release was instant. He knew exactly what the deal was: he wanted Rebecca to talk about what had happened, and in return she wanted him to turn his back on Ewan — in fact, she'd like him to leave the house. In this she was exactly like the others, but only in this. Where everything else was concerned he found Rebecca utterly different — she held his attention more than any of the others, he loved her more, he fancied her more. Still he didn't want to have to choose. He ran, trying not to think about it, the doorkey banging on his chest, wrapping itself around his mother's St Christopher, out through the bad estates of Brockley — resolute little Brockley — row upon row of artisans' cottages pecked at by von Braun's *Vergeltung* doodlebugs. The view had changed since Ewan. Now Lewisham's neon monolith, the Citibank, the faulty C blinking and fizzing and popping like an ultraviolet fly-killer, filled the skyline. Around its feet, instead of wealthy city commuters, drugs dealers bought the airy six-bedroom houses in the avenues near Hillyfields and sometimes shot one another in the dead of night.

Caffery had bought the house he lived in from his parents in his early twenties. Once it had been called Serenity, but some wag in the sixties had got up a stepladder with a handful of quick-drying cement and changed it to Gethsemane. The first thing the Cafferys did was have the whole plaque chiselled out. "No need to bring agony here," his mother said. "Anyone who lives in a house with that name is going to be cursed." Her cure hadn't worked. Maybe she had left it too late.

He continued down the road, sweat darkening his T-shirt, taking a left at the end, and went on, past Nunhead cemetery, out on to the starlit Peckham Rye with its dark moving lakes and open spaces. He wondered suddenly about Brockwell Park, about Rory's killer, about connections. Was there a pool of tricks and skewed thoughts that every paedophile in London came to drink in? He'd read once, years ago, about the world's largest organism: a fungus, it lived underground and covered almost forty acres of Michigan. Sometimes he imagined the paedophile network to be a little like that fungus: every one of them living invisibly under society — *under our noses* — every one of them connected on some fleshy outcrop to every other. Penderecki was an old man, spent, his days of boys and prison sentences over, but he was part of that network and Caffery could guarantee that the old man knew someone, who knew someone, who knew someone who knew Rory Peach's killer. The number of degrees of separation he could only guess at — but he sensed it wouldn't be many.

He jogged back to Brockley, turning left across the railway bridge, letting his eyes skim along the tracks. The trees had still been in leaf when Ewan disappeared — it would have been easy, in the dead of night, to store a body in one of them, then take it down before the leaves fell. Not a good thing to think about. He crossed into Penderecki's road and jogged past the sunburst gates, the leaded stained-glass windows, the little enclosed porches with their wall baskets and shoes lined up in neat rows. The light was on in Penderecki's bathroom and Caffery paused — just for a moment — outside the house, looking up at that light with the fatal intensity of a moth. The frosted window made tinted diamonds of the light beyond, and it took him a moment to see that something was hanging just behind the glass — something long and coloured, a paper lantern, perhaps, the sort you might see in a student's bedsit. Not like Penderecki to decorate, or to flaunt something. Unless there was a reason. *You're probably meant to see it — it's the start of something new*. New torment.

He turned and began to retrace his footsteps back home, back to Gethsemane. There he took off his soaking shorts and T-shirt and stood in the shower, thinking of terraced houses and how claustrophobic they were. Then he lay next to Rebecca in the darkness, listening to her breathing.

CHAPTER TEN

(21 July)

The next morning Caffery found Kryotos in tears in the incident-room kitchen. He pulled her face against his chest and wrapped his arms around her. She cried harder, her shoulders shaking. The only time he'd ever seen Kryotos cry had been at Paul Essex's funeral. It felt strangely intimate.

"Don't let Danni see me, please."

"OK, OK, here." He kicked the door closed, not letting go of her. "What is it, Marilyn? Is it the kids?"

She shook her head and wiped her nose. "Danni just spoke to Quinn about . . ."

"About what?" He stroked her hair. "She spoke to Quinn about what?"

"The PM on Rory Peach." She pressed the heels of her hands against her face. "The photos are on your desk. Quinn wants all these tests — she wants you to call."

"What's upset you?"

"They think he was alive — in the tree. They think he was alive for two days up there. He tried to get out of the ropes —" She tore off a piece of kitchen roll and balled it up against her eyes. "I know it's stupid — I just can't help thinking about him fighting, just skinny little arms but he still *fought*."

Caffery stroked her hair and stared at the ceiling. Of course he'd known. He'd known it when Krishnamurthi had been unable to uncoil the small body. When he'd massaged the feet to see if he could flex them. When there was no smell. Had Rory been dead long enough for the rigor to have died away, he would have already been unidentifiable in this weather. As it was the boy had been smooth and perfect. The rigor hadn't even had time to reach his feet, he was so newly dead.

"Here." He pulled her against his chest. He could feel her warm breasts under the neat white blouse. He'd never been this close to Marilyn before — she smelt like a woman, she smelt of shampoo and baking and lipstick, and she smelt utterly different from Rebecca. He thought about last night, about Rebecca calmly leaving him in the bedroom, about him lying there on the bed with his useless erection, and, as if she sensed the shift, as if she was suddenly self-conscious about their closeness, Marilyn, with her face against his shirt, became still. She stopped shaking and breathed through her mouth. When she pulled away the tears had gone but she was red in the face and wouldn't meet his eyes. She went to sit at the computer terminal and as Caffery walked to the SIO's room he noticed that the back of her neck was flushed.

In the SIO's room, Souness, looking fresh in a Marks & Spencer's man's suit over an open-necked lilac shirt, was standing at the desk staring out of the window. She didn't speak when Caffery came in, just nodded at the blue and white Metropolitan Police Photographic Branch envelope on the desk. He put down his coffee, shook out the photos taken in the blue ALS light and called Fiona Quinn.

"How much do you know?" Quinn asked.

"Well, I guessed a lot yesterday," he said. "I guessed it took him some time to die."

"Krishnamurthi asked us if we could smell peardrops or nail varnish when he opened the body, yes?"

"Yeah — acetone."

"Ketosis." At the other end of the line Quinn shuffled some papers. "He was beginning to starve — his body was breaking down its fat, putting fatty acids into his bloodstream."

"And that killed him?" he said cautiously.

"No — no, it takes a long time to starve to death. We're doing shear rate tests and haematocrits — doesn't mean much to you, but his blood had got thicker. Remember Hippocratic facies?"

"Yup."

"That's the look you get from severe dehydration. He, well yes, he died of thirst."

Oh, Christ — Caffery sat down at his desk. *Oh, Christ, oh, Christ, oh, Christ* — It was true, then. He thought of the public fury about to land on the heads of the search team and the helicopter team — failing to find a child until it was too late.

"I was surprised he lasted as long as he did," Quinn said, "but Krishnamurthi reckons it *can* take quite a long time — the longest he'd heard of was a hospice death which took fifteen days — but at the other end it can take only hours, depending on the circumstance. You've only to drop about a fifth of your weight in fluids."

"What about kids?"

"Exactly — with kids it's more serious. They need more water for their weight than adults — plus Rory struggled through two hot days and really increased his use of water. You might ask yourself whether the killer gave him some water in those three days in the house. Maybe it's in Alek's statement?"

"No — nothing in the statement." Caffery fiddled with a paper-clip. Souness was standing with her hands on the desk, still staring out of the window, and he realized she'd already heard everything Quinn was saying. "Right," he said, trying to crank his thoughts forward. "Those bites? Do we know when they were inflicted?"

"Yeah, pretty late — probably about the time that he was taken from the house. That's where the blood on the skirting-board and his trainer came from."

"So he was put up the tree and left."

"That's what it looks like."

"No one came back to him?"

"Don't appear to have."

"Anything we can run for DNA?"

"Yes — you've got the photos, haven't you? You can see the toluidine blue that Krishnamurthi used — there was penetration, or an attempt at penetration. And that contaminant."

"Yes?"

"Semen."

Right. Caffery put a hand on his forehead. *Right. OK, it's definitely a paedo you're dealing with — you knew that anyway so it doesn't have to poleaxe you*. He glanced at Souness. She was still staring out of the window, so he found a pen and took a deep breath. "Good, that's, uh, right, good, we'll get some DNA?"

"Well, *maybe*."

"Maybe?"

"Well . . ." She was cautious. ". . . Rory was alive, see, and his body might have already broken down a lot of the sample. You know, if the victim is semiconscious, not moving around too much, sometimes we can still harvest DNA, even after a few days — but Rory was moving, and you do see it sometimes, the sample gets broken down and —"

"That's OK — do it anyway." He started to jot down details of the conversation. "And I don't want to wait two weeks for a slot like I did last time."

"If you get it premiumed it'll be faster."

"Ahem, Fiona, that *was* premiumed."

"God, I'm sorry. I can't always dictate what the lab'll do."

"Don't worry. I'll get the governor to rattle a few cages."

Even before Rory Peach the team had been at a low. Funds were constantly challenged, they were all overworked, there were eight "critical" racial harassment incidents outstanding, a four-year-old serial rape case, and the tyings up and collation of disclosure on five drugs shootings on their patch. Morale was low, and it was reflected in the tired way they dragged through the routine jobs: in the house-to-house inquiries DC Logan had only managed three houses in an entire day and Caffery knew that with Kryotos's workload none of the results would make it on to the HOLMES database. But they had to present a different face to the world.

At the press conference that morning Souness asked the assembled journalists and TV reporters to observe a minute's silence for Rory Peach. The country was gripped: the *News of the World* pawed the ground in the wings, gearing up for a new name-and-shame campaign. As if in divine judgement of the engine she had set rumbling, on Souness's way back to the incident room, sitting at traffic lights in the red BMW, the skies over South London cracked open and dropped hundreds of gallons of rainwater into the streets in minutes. A proper summer cloudburst: the streets looked as if they might be washed away.

At Shrivemoor Caffery was sitting at an open window watching the rain. He could smell earth and thought he wouldn't have blinked if he'd seen an uprooted palm floating along in the gutter in the street below. He closed the window and sat back at his desk, watching Kryotos through the open door. She seemed to have recovered and was bashing away at the HOLMES database. The tears in the kitchen had been a shock: he'd never known Kryotos lose perspective before. He'd always been a little envious of her — wondering why he couldn't keep a distance like that.

Suddenly, as if she could sense him watching her, Kryotos looked up. Their eyes met but this time she didn't look away embarrassed. Instead she seemed confused — as if Caffery's thoughts were strung out in a long banner above his head and she was reading them. She frowned, perplexed, and Caffery, uncomfortable with the sense that his naked brain was being watched, gave her a brief, efficient smile. He leaned over, kicked the door closed and went back to studying the ALS photos of Rory's neck.

"In the plus column, at least finding Rory means we've got some forensics." When Souness got back from the press conference she seemed to be making an effort to be positive. She brought through coffee and some of Kryotos's sticky, flaky pastries in a tin and shook the rain off her jacket, draping it on the back of her chair. "We've got those white fibres and as soon as Quinny's got us some DNA we can think about doing a mass screening."

"And what are your parameters going to be? Every white nonce in Brixton over five eleven?"

"I've got to show them something — we're three days and closing on the area interim report —" She stopped. "OK, Jack. Ye've got that look on your face again. Come on, what's on your mind?"

He shrugged. "He's going to do it again. Very soon."

"Ah, I wondered when this was going to start! My profiling baby getting out of his wee pram."

"Only this time he'll make sure he doesn't get disturbed and he'll complete his fantasy — whatever that was. It's a progression and he won't stop at the Peaches. He's juicing himself up for something more, I think he's probably chosen his next victims already."

"Oh, aye?" Souness pulled the chair back and sat down, folding her arms. "And where's all this coming from, if it's not a rude question?"

"We've got an ex-con."

"Oh, we have, have we?"

"Yes. He's got form and he's done time for it. Probably for the same thing or something similar." He took off his glasses. "I've told Marilyn to go into that Quest Search database and put any non-custodial sentences on the back-burner."

"Are ye going to explain?"

He pushed the photos towards her. "See?" No one had seen it or mentioned it in the morgue, and yet photographed under the blue alternative light source it was clear what had made the marks on Rory's neck. "See these?" Souness nodded. "Can you see these underlying marks? Here and here?"

"Aye, I can."

"Well?"

Souness tipped her chair forward and was silent for a moment, squinting at the photos with her head on one side. Her eyes moved rapidly across the odd marks, trying to shape them into something recognizable. When it came to her she dropped the chair back with a thud. "Jesus — of course, of course."

Roland Klare, who, like most Brixton residents, had been following the Donegal Crescent case on the television, now very much wanted to see the photographs that were stuck inside the Pentax. There was no question of taking the film to a chemist, even if he could get it out of the camera. But there was an alternative. When he got home that afternoon he consulted his notebook.

Yes! He'd been right. He'd been sure it was somewhere in the flat. He went into the bedroom and began pulling things aside.

Within an hour he had found it. It had been stored in a box of old Ladybird books: a large, slightly battered paperback, *Build Your Own Darkroom AT HOME!* On the cover there was a picture of a man in a white coat holding a piece of photographic paper by the corner, swilling it in a tank. Klare had discovered the book years ago on the platform at Loughborough Junction. Pleased with himself, he took it into the kitchen and wiped it clean, then made himself a drink and went into the living room. Outside it was dark and light at once: big clouds curled up from the distant horizon and shuffled across the sky, shooting sunlight down one moment, tipping out rain the next, but Roland Klare didn't notice. He got a pen and paper and settled on the sofa, his back to the window, and began to read.

CHAPTER ELEVEN

It was evening when Caffery found the time to visit DI Durham. He pointed the car against the rush, up over Beulah Hill where the drives were gravelled, the roads were wide as French boulevards, and horse chestnuts dropped red sap on to the pavements. In Norwood the buildings were a pace nearer the road, and by Brixton Water Lane the city had thoroughly meshed itself around him.

In central Brixton the traffic was already heavy. He parked in a turning off Acre Lane and wove through the cars, the thump-thump-thump of sub-woofers resonating against his stomach muscles. Amazing to think that this was less than a mile from Brockwell Park. Rory Peach, had he been able to sit up, would have been able to look down from his tree — *His tree? His* tree? *You make it sound as if he chose it* — and see these darkened stretches of decaying municipal pride. The person who had put Rory up that tree had form. Which meant that he had almost certainly made and developed connections in prison — segregated prison units were key cogs in paedophile networks, seeding beds for ideas and plans, where contacts and lifelong friendships were made. AMIT were going to concentrate one of their pods on moving through the nonce register and Kryotos's Quest Search results, speaking to convicted paedophiles in the Brixton area, trying to tap into that vast underground switchboard. He thought about those invisible connections, the creeping circuitry that linked every sick thing to every other sick thing. And inevitably, as it always did these days, his mind circled back to Penderecki.

Penderecki. He thought about him as he crossed to the police station. How long would it be before Penderecki was grilled? How many degrees of separation? And what if? What if . . .?

DI Durham was welcoming. He remembered the 1989 attack well. "Yeah — little Champ. Nasty." The office window was level to a street-light that came on red as they talked. Durham, in navy blue shirt and tartan tie, had been in Brixton fifteen years. He played with his double chin as he spoke, squeezing it and massaging it as if it had appeared overnight. "Dug that out for you." He slammed the filing cabinet and put the file in front of Caffery. "Is it the Peach thing, then? Is that what you're thinking?"

"I don't know yet." He opened the file. November 1989 and eleven-year-old Champaluang Keoduangdy had been attacked in Brockwell Park and so badly injured he had spent several days in hospital. "I was searching for a nonce called the troll and this case came up."

"That's right — it's all in there." Durham leaned over and picked out Champ's statement between thumb and forefinger. "That's what Champ called the guy who did him. A troll. Don't know why." He paused. Caffery had sat forward, hands flat on the desk and was staring at something in the file. "You all right there, son?"

He didn't answer. He felt as if something had landed claws first on his shoulders. This was the forensic medical examiner's report. The assault on Champ had indeed been violent: the attacker had almost ripped a chunk of flesh from the boy's shoulder. Caffery closed the file and looked up at Durham. He knew the colour had left his face. "He was *bitten*?"

"Didn't you know?"

"No —" he said faintly.

"Oh, yeah — took a great chunk out of his shoulder. Sometimes do see that with rape. Nasty."

"No other assault?"

"Just the piece of electric conduit — rammed up him so hard he was in intensive care for a week, poor little sod."

Caffery rubbed his temples. He could feel the beginnings of a lead. He took off his glasses and stared at a point just below Durham's chin. "Tell me something, have you heard about Rory Peach?"

"Heard what about him?"

"Same injury. Exactly the same. Shoulders bitten, a chunk almost taken out. Rape — rectal bleeding."

Durham didn't speak for a moment. His mouth, which was slightly twisted anyway, as if he doubted everything he saw, tightened further as he took in this new information. He coughed loudly, tapped his fingers on the desk for a few seconds and sat down opposite

Caffery. "Right, then." He pinched his double chin so hard it began to go red. "Right — I'll give the wife a call, tell her to put aside a plate for the microwave."

When Hal got home that night Smurf came into the hallway and rolled on to her back to please him, her belly pink and balding, the same colour as when she was a puppy. "Hello, old girl." He bent over and scratched the dog's chest, threw his wallet on to the window-sill and went into the TV room. He kissed Josh on the head, then got a beer from the fridge and stood watching Ben cook. Her eyes, an unusual almost metallic grey, seemed even brighter than usual tonight. The first present Hal ever bought her was a moonstone — the same colour as her eyes.

"Hal, are you sure you can't smell something?"

"Smell what?"

"I don't know, I can still smell something."

"Where?"

"In here." She walked into the hallway.

"What is it?" Hal followed her with his beer. "Is it a farty smell?"

"No. It's like really dirty clothes, you know, or like rubbish." She stood in the hallway, the dripping wooden spoon in her hand, and sniffed. Since they'd moved in she could smell everything much more intensely. At first she'd had an alarm bell that she might be pregnant again, but she was on the pill and she didn't have any other symptoms. Maybe she just wasn't used to the new environment.

"You sure there's not something we've forgotten to unpack?"

Benedicte shook her head. All the food had gone straight into the kitchen — she'd unpacked it herself. And, anyway, it had all been dry food, or tinned.

"Then you're imagining it." He put his arms round her waist. "You're going bonkers, old woman." He tried to push his hands up the old blue shirt she wore but she laughed.

"Stop it, you raddled old fool." She pulled away from him. "Come on — make me a glass of something while I do the dinner. Talk to me, tell me dirty stories while I'm washing the potatoes."

He made her a G and T and sat in the family room with Josh, watching her cutting up leeks. Upholstered like a mother almost from the start, sometimes Benedicte fretted about her weight — but he adored every inch of her, and the big, funny secret was that she loved sex as much as he did. They'd taken to it in their teens like kids to candy and had never gone elsewhere for it. *Look at us. No one would guess we're goers*. As a couple they were as untrendy as carpet slippers — and yet Hal believed that if there was a love story to be told it was theirs. He still got a faint sick feeling when he considered the possibility of losing her.

"It's Dad farting, that smell," Josh said after dinner. He stood in his slippers and opened the fridge on a late-night chocolate hunt. "He's always farting. He can fart at will."

"Don't be jealous."

"Ha-al — Jo-osh, for heaven's sake, some manners, please."

Hal put both hands on the worktop, bent over slightly, scrunched up his face and farted. Josh giggled, hand over his mouth.

"Oh — sorry," Hal apologized. "I didn't mean to do that."

Benedicte shook her head. "Yes, you did."

"No, really, I didn't."

"What did you mean, then?"

"I meant it to be much louder — I meant it to sound like . . . this."

Josh raced around the kitchen squealing with laughter and Ben turned away disgusted. "*Nul points* for presentation, Norway." She wrapped the remaining squares of chocolate and put them back in the fridge. "And *nul* for originality. And stop making faces behind my back."

Hal smiled. He could still make his wife laugh. As she took Josh to clean his teeth he poured coffee from the cafetière and went to stand at the back door. The kitchen opened on to a red-cedar patio, open runner steps leading into the square garden, which had been laid with heavy-duty grass, and a dog-ear picket fence seven feet high, so in their meagre, hard-won ten square metres of South London the Churches had total privacy. Maybe that would change when the neighbours moved in — maybe they'd lean out of the windows and watch him cutting the grass, watch Josh in the paddling-pool.

He looked up at the windows next door, still darkened, taped Xs still on the panes, his gaze drifting past them to where the giant megaliths Arkaig and Herne Hill Towers rose on the distant edge of the park — a sweet reminder that, for all their security fencing and magic-eye lighting, they still lived in Brixton. Hal shivered, suddenly conscious of the park's wolflike gaze coming from beyond the back fence and, as if the night had suddenly got cold, he went back inside, closing the door and locking it. He'd stopped liking the park after what had happened this week.

Caffery and Durham sat in the deserted office well into the night. From outside floated the otherworldly scream of sirens, the pulse of car stereos in dark alleys. The two men heard none of it. They were wrapped in a little pool of focus over the statements and reports in the Keoduangdy file. They studied the photofit of the attacker, they sent off requests for information about Champ's whereabouts, checked if he had a criminal record and searched for him on the electoral register. There were three Keoduangdys in Birmingham and a further two in East London but none with that first name. Still, they faxed Plaistow and Solihull and kept calling around. The night drew in around the building, but their light burned on.

Champ's attacker had never been found. Champ, who had been living on Coldharbour Lane at the time, hadn't got a good look at him and his explanation of what he had been doing in Brockwell Park was less than convincing. His statement was full of contradictions and half-facts.

"But one thing he was sure about," said Durham. "His attacker took photos of him, even after he fainted — he remembers a flash going off as he was coming round . . . oh, and something else." He scratched under his chin. "He kept asking him a weird question."

"What?"

"Do you like your daddy?"

"Do you like your *daddy*?"

"Uh-huh. Do you like your daddy? It's gay speak. Mind you, that's about all he was certain of. Not a good witness." Durham thought that the investigation had never got a good head of steam for the very reason that Champ was reluctant to talk. And that when he *did* talk he rambled, contradicted himself. That and the fact that he was Laotian. "Nobody *really* pulled their fingers out on it — half of them couldn't even pronounce his name. And it never happened again so it just sort of *slipped*. You know how it goes."

"Maybe he got put away for something else." Caffery took off his glasses and rubbed the lenses on his shirt sleeve. "Our Peach man's been inside."

Durham frowned, raised questioning eyebrows.

"The child had belt marks around his neck."

"Ah." Durham nodded. He knew what Caffery was talking about. A prison habit. For Durham, whose fourteen-year-old daughter lived horses and horsemanship, the practice that inmates had of subduing their rape victims with a belt around the neck always put him in mind of a halter — an unwilling horse snaffled into submission, muscular piston thighs squeezing its flanks. It was the first conclusion an investigating officer would come to, seeing telltale marks like that.

"You know, it's funny that you like the troll for the Peach case . . ." Durham tugged at his chin and watched Caffery put his glasses back on and go back to his notebook. ". . . because the first thing I thought about when I heard the whole Donegal Crescent thing was the Half Moon Lane photo hoax."

Caffery looked up. "The Half Moon . . . ?"

"Never heard of it?" Durham gave his wattle a reassuring squeeze. "No, why would you? It was twelve years ago. More. Nothing to do with Champ, just happened at the same time. Two Polaroids found in a council bin on Half Moon Lane."

"And?"

"Oh, it all blew over — it was just a prank. But at the time it really griefed us some, I can tell you. Got the locals running appeals all over the place. A poster outside all the stations — do you know this child? Could be in danger, etc."

"I don't remember it."

"Well, the father — we called him the father, we don't know for sure — the father and the kid, a little lad, were both tied up, naked. The posters were a shot in the dark — the boy's own mother wouldn't have recognized him from the photograph, they were so blurred — and if you ask me the quality was even worse after the secret squirrels had been at it. Image enhancement my arse. Not that I'd like that to go any further, you understand."

"You think it was a hoax?"

He shrugged. "I don't know for sure, but in the end we decided it had to've been a prank because no one ever came forward — no one was found, no one reported missing. The paedo unit at the Yard's got it on their books but here in Brixton we never heard anything more about it."

"Where did the photos go?"

"After the Denmark Hill lab, I suppose back here, but we clear our Book 66 out every year so they've probably gone for retention at Charlton or Cricklewood. I'll check the property vouchers if you want." Durham stood, pulling at his chin, looking at Caffery. Then he paused and, placing both hands on the table, leaned forward. "The reason it's funny is because it happened at the same time the Champ case was still active and when those photos came in I got a little *itch* on them. Know what I mean? I always wondered if it had anything to do with this troll character — with the guy who did Champ. You know, here." He tapped his chest with a biro. "In my giblets. Nothing to go on, of course, just that little itch."

CHAPTER TWELVE

At midnight, when Caffery finally got home, Rebecca did it again. This time it was in the kitchen. She had been sitting on the table, drinking vodka from a champagne glass, hardly speaking as he poured himself a drink — but when he drew the blind behind her, put his hands either side of her, when his jacket dropped open and he kissed her, she sweetly opened her legs and it happened all over again: she let him make her come, twice, and when he pushed himself up and undid his flies she sat up straight and turned her head away. "I'm sorry," she said, and slipped off the worktop, straightened her dress and left the room.

Caffery dropped forward, hands on the table. He took long, deep breaths and stared blankly down at the wet print she'd left on the table. *Don't lose your temper. Don't prove her right*. He waited until his pulse had slowed, then zipped up and followed her through to the living room where she sat silently watching the TV without the sound on.

"Rebecca."

"Mmmm?" She wasn't looking at him. "What?"

"I know why this is happening, Rebecca. I do know."

"Do you?"

"And you need to talk about it. You need to talk about what happened."

"I never *stop* talking about it."

"I don't mean *to the press*, I mean to *me*." Impatient now, he buckled up his belt. "Or just leave me be, Becky, just leave me be. Unless you want to give *me* a blowjob instead of giving one to the whole London art scene, then just leave me be."

For a moment she seemed to be about to say something but she changed her mind and dropped her hands on the sofa with an exasperated sigh. "*God!* What's got into you?"

"What do you *think*'s got into me? I'm standing here, *look* at me, a raging hard-on, and you" — he gestured at the TV — "you're watching the fucking television."

"Don't lecture me, Jack, when there's a few things of your own we don't exactly rip apart and put under the microscope."

"OK." He stopped her, holding up both hands in a gesture of surrender. "This is disintegrating." He turned to the door. "When you want to talk you know where I'll be."

"Where?"

"In the bathroom — having a wank."

He jerked himself off in the shower then pulled on his running gear and left the house without speaking, slamming the door behind him.

The night sky was the colour of sea. The deep blue that can sometimes be seen curled in the paw of a coral atoll. It was warm and someone's late-night music pounded out of a bedsit window and up into the starlit sky. Sweat dribbled into his eyes — he concentrated on making his heels hit the tarmac straight and tried not to think about Rebecca. But his mind kept orbiting back to it, back to the stalemate they were in. Neither of them was going to give way, that was clear, they'd just get harder and harder in their determination. *Shit, Rebecca*. He loved her, he had no question about it, had a real tenderness for her that was hard to heal, but from where he stood he couldn't see a way past these rigid battle-lines they stood in.

"Jack," Rebecca said suddenly, sitting up on the sofa and turning to the door. Her sudden sense of him was almost as if he'd walked in. "Jack, it's because" — she held her fists hard against her stomach — "it's because I'm wounded. Big bloody wound." She paused, open-mouthed, staring at the empty doorway — letting what she had just said sink in. Then her face crumpled and she laughed out loud at the stupid drama. "Oh, for Christ's sake. *I'm wounded!* Wounded? Poor, poor wounded Becky!" She jumped up, went into the kitchen for the champagne glass and came shimmying back into the living room, twisting her free hand in front of her face, a long-nailed Shiva dancing on the bare floor. "Wounded — you silly cow, wounded, *wounded*, wounded!" There was some grass she kept in an old Oxo cube box on the mantelpiece and she sang as she rolled a joint, sipping the vodka, her tongue getting numb and furry. She knelt down, put the glass on the floor, lit the spliff, took a few hits then suddenly rolled on to the floor, on her back, her hands over her eyes. "Oh, God, oh, God, oh, God."

They were in a hole. The pair of them, deep in a hole: Jack, with his determined tearing apart of himself over Ewan — it terrified her where that all might end — and then, on the opposite side of the battlefield, *she* stood, with her mouth healed over, her eyes shut. All Jack wanted was for her to sit and discuss it calmly, to flush it through, make it clean again. *I don't blame you, Jack, I don't blame you*. She wanted, really wanted, to tell him. But she couldn't, and that was where the wound was. In her memory. Because what Jack didn't know was that all the way through Joni's inquest, through him patiently taking her statement in the hospital room overlooking the dripping trees, through him gently prompting her when she dried, through her pretending to cry when the coroner asked her a question she didn't know the answer to — even when she alluded to it in the press — all along Rebecca had been telling a lie. The truth was something she hardly dared admit, even to herself. She dropped her hands to her sides and stared at the ceiling. The truth was that of the attack in the little Kent bungalow a year ago she could remember nothing.

The pavement was warm, it had trapped the day's heat. He had been going for half an hour when he became aware of his surroundings. This was Penderecki's street he was running down. He'd come here without thinking about it — drawn by some internal compass. He slowed to a jog, looking at the houses.

It was one of those peculiarly neat roads that bring with them the odd aroma of a seaside town, as if you might see Vacancies signs propped in front of the lace curtains. Penderecki's was halfway along it, flush with the others, but so luminous a landmark in Caffery's conscience that sometimes it seemed to him to protrude from the other houses, proud-bellied. He approached, feet curling down on to the pavement, and stopped outside, resting his hands on the gate, bending over for a moment, catching his breath, his sweat dripping in dark coins on the pavement.

He rocked back on his heels and looked up at the house. How long would it be before one of the team came knocking on this door asking about the troll? How long before Danni's girlfriend, Paulina, with her agile little mind and her databases, would point out the similarities between what had happened to Rory and what had happened two and a half decades ago to Ewan? Again he got that image, that slow spreading image of fingers reaching out under the soil. Of Penderecki touching fingers with the troll.

He straightened. Tonight something about Penderecki's house struck him as odd. The bathroom light was still on and the giant lantern, red and yellow and grey, was still hanging there. He thought it looked a little bigger. He stood for a moment, frowning, then slowly pushed open the gate.

He had never walked up Penderecki's path before — on the few occasions he had ventured to the house he had used the back route and travelled under darkness because Penderecki, being a criminal, knew his rights inside out and would have snapped restraining orders, *quia timet* orders, down on his head without blinking. The front garden was a mass of candyfloss-pink mallow, like crystallized sweets, thin as paper, gone native and seeming to move as if there was a breeze here. Long grasses brushed at his aching calves. At the bottom step he paused.

The front door still had its original leaded glass — a hill and a windmill, sun rays delineated in black. As he climbed the two steps he knew, he could hear them, the hum of them, the hum of wet bodies sucking and breeding, and then he could see them, individuals blackening the rays of the glass sunrise, and instantly he knew that whatever was hanging in Penderecki's bathroom, it wasn't a Chinese lantern.

What Rebecca did remember was this:

Night. She is in bed with Jack.

In the morning they wake up. It's raining.

After Jack has gone to work she has coffee and toast.

She notices Joni hasn't come home.

She phones around and discovers that Joni is at Bliss's flat.

She puts on old shorts and a T-shirt and begins the cycle journey to his flat.

Blank.

Blank.

Blank.

A flash of light and something — a knife? A hook?

Blank.

Blank.

Another light — a doctor shining it into her eyes.

Blank.

Just a little scratch — hold still, you won't feel a thing.

Blank.

Jack, in his hired mourning suit, bending over her hospital bed on his way to Essex's funeral.

Jack again. Taking her statement. When she passes her hand over her face, embarrassed to admit that she can't remember, he looks at her sympathetically and gives her a prompt — trying to make it easier on her.

Did you see Bliss take Joni?

Take her?

Into the hall where we found her.

Oh, yes, that. I — Yes, I saw that happen. He carried her.

From a distance Rebecca's most striking feature was her resilience: she wore it like a bright red winter coat — sometimes naturally and sometimes self-consciously. Always unmissably. She knew it could make her appear brittle, but she also knew *why* it was there. She'd had to grow it, like a new pelt, early in life, when she realized that her father would never be prised away from his obscure metaphysical apologias, and her mother would never be tricked down from the place she floated, doped and fat on imipramine. "The daughter of an English professor and a clinically depressed beauty", was how one journalist had summed her up. It took Rebecca a while to recognize that this was why she couldn't admit to the blank section of her memory: it was an admission that her tough little character was a lie, that she'd been left out of control for a while — without a skin, open to infection. She didn't think she'd ever be able to talk calmly about it. *How can you not remember?*

For a year now she'd kept a lid on it — until: *Think about what it was like for me to find you hanging, Rebecca, hanging from a hook in the fucking ceiling*. It was the first time she'd got a glimpse of what had happened that day in Kent and now she found she couldn't look at Jack's face above hers without the fear that Malcolm Bliss's would appear imposed over it. Something was on the move in her — something that wouldn't let her lie flat on her back without squirming, something that wouldn't let her sleep a night through. She rolled on to her front and began to get up — it was important to Rebecca, very important, that she didn't let anyone know the truth.

At home Rebecca was asleep. Or pretending to be. Two lipstick-stained cigarillo butts sat in an ashtray next to the bed on top of an article about the Turner Prize. Caffery changed into joggers, a sweatshirt and lightweight walking boots, got some tools from under the stairs and went into the back garden. He waded out through the undergrowth, past the green Express Dairies crate that Penderecki had used to stand on, through the nettles and submerged branches. The cutting was quiet, the last train gone, and down here, below the level of the city, there were cooler, clearer isotherms. Along the empty tracks the signals glowed green. Caffery crossed quickly, hearing the startled movements of an animal in the undergrowth. On the opposite side he found a fox path — *or maybe it's Penderecki's path* — leading straight to the garden.

The back of the house was silent and dark, the fence rotten with water. He moved quickly through the garden, his chest tightening as he got nearer. And now — why hadn't he watched more carefully? — he saw that along the metal frame of the broken old annexe flies gathered like clusters of hanging black fruit, rippling lazily.

He used his Swiss Army knife to gouge away the ancient putty of the kitchen window, flaking wood and paint on to his sweatshirt. Levering out the panel pins, he eased the pane from the frame and the stale trapped air inside the house came at him like a train. He could smell what was in the bathroom — the stench that stimulates the rarely stimulated root of humanness — the smell of opened human bowels, the smell of the dead sitting up in their graves and exhaling into the night. He could hear the flies — *No way, no fucking way, this can't be happening* — as he reached in, turned the key and opened the back door.

Quiet.

"Ivan?"

He stood there, counting to a hundred, waiting for a response.

"Ivan?"

He'd never addressed Penderecki by his first name before.

"Are you here?"

Still no reply. Only the pounding of his own blood in his ears. He stepped into the annexe.

Once — twenty years ago, before Penderecki had got wise to him and started locking the doors — Caffery had sneaked in here, and the surprise had been how ordinary the house was. Damp and fraying, but ordinary for that. Just an old man's house. Patterned carpets, a gas fire, a folded copy of the *Radio Times* next to the sofa. Milk in the fridge and a paper bag of sugar on the worktop. The home of a twice-convicted paedophile, and there was milk in the fridge, sugar on the worktop and a *Radio Times* in the lounge. Now, as he moved through the rooms, he was struck by how little it had changed. The house was smaller, the wallpaper yellower than he remembered, a strip of it hung from the ceiling above the stairwell and the carpet was shiny with dirt. A *Local Shopper* newspaper lay on the doormat with a pile of flyers from local restaurants, but apart from the flies it was all so unchanged it was like having his memory shaken out in front of his eyes.

On the small window-sill at the bottom of the stairs was the digital readout that he knew Penderecki used to monitor phone calls. On top of it sat a ripped-open brown envelope. No letter inside but the return address was the Oncology Unit, Lewisham Hospital. The first clue — he stuffed it into his pocket. *Oh, Jesus*, he thought, *oh, Jesus, let this not be happening*. He turned to the stairs, moving slowly, dead-fly husks crunching underfoot. Above him the living insects thrashed their wings in a single low note, in and out — as if the house was breathing with them.

All the doors on the landing were open, save the one into the bathroom. He could see the light coming from the crack under the door. The smell was denser here, and he had to lift the hem of the sweatshirt, exposing his stomach, to cover his face as he reached for the light-switch at the top of the stairs. The bulb pinged, died. *Shit*. Reaching inside one of the open doors, he found a switch and this time the light came on, throwing a rectangle of yellow out into the small landing. Quickly, breathing shallowly, he checked inside the doors. In two of the rooms there was nothing — just an empty Coke can and a few squares of carpet on the bare floorboards. In the third he discovered where Penderecki had been living.

The mattress was covered with stained nylon sheets, worn almost to transparency, a pile of newspapers next to the bed, a cup and an empty baked-beans can with a fork sticking out of it rested on top of the pile. There was only one decoration in the room — on the far wall: an Athena poster of two boys wearing straw hats, sitting on a wooden jetty, one with his arm draped around the other's shoulder. It was a photograph from the seventies — the sun had been a different colour three decades ago: softer and more yellow than a third-millennium sun. The two boys looked about the same age that Jack and Ewan had been when . . . He had to stop.

"*Shit, shit, shit — let's get this over with.*"

He pressed the sweatshirt into his nostrils, went back on to the landing, took a deep breath and tried the bathroom door.

It opened smoothly and there, in front of him, in the centre of the pale green bathroom, covered and moving with flies, hung Ivan Penderecki.

Somewhere someone was screaming. Benedicte fought up towards it, through hot layers of sleep, and sat up in the cool darkness of the bedroom, her pulse elevated, her skin damp.

"*Muuuuuum!*"

"*Josh?*" Sleepily she dropped out of bed and padded along the corridor. "Coming, tadpole." In his bedroom she flicked on the switch and stood in the doorway, blinking in the light. Josh was sitting against the bed-head, a pillow clutched to his chest. His feet were stretched rigid in front of him, his hair sticking up from his head as if electricity had passed through him. He was staring at a crack in the curtains.

"Mum — the troll —"

"It's all right, tadpole." Benedicte went straight over and pulled back the curtain. The garden was dark and silent, the window closed. Over the fence the outline of Brockwell Park was purple against the stars and in the distance the Crystal Palace transmitter lit up the sky. "Troll's not there, darling. Nothing there at all." She dropped the curtain and sat down on the edge of his bed, putting a hand on his hot little forehead. "It's Mummy's fault. I shouldn't have put you in these pyjamas, they're too warm." She tried to pull the flannel pyjama top up over his head. "You're wet through, I'll put you in a T-shirt —"

"No!" Josh jerked away from her, moving his head so that he could see past her to the window.

"Now, come on, darling, it's the middle of the night and Mummy just wants to get you out of these wet jammies so you can go back to sleep."

"*Nooo!*" He pulled his hands away. "He's watching me. *He was there*."

"Josh, I think you dreamed it — the troll couldn't get this high. You're all the way up in the air here, you're quite safe."

"You all right, peanut?" Hal was standing in the doorway blinking like a sleepy cat.

Benedicte turned. "Oh, Hal, I didn't mean to wake you up . . ."

"*That's OK*." He looked at his son — bolt upright in bed bracing the pillow against his chest. "What's up, peanut?"

"He thinks maybe he saw the troll —"

"Not *maybe*."

"He saw the troll at the window, you know, the one from the park."

"OK, ssh, ssh." Hal came to the bed and kissed his son's head. "Want me to go and check he's gone?"

Josh nodded.

"Ooooh." Hal went to the window, whistled softly and pressed his nose to the pane, looking down into the back garden. He pretended to squint and jiggle around, trying for a better view. After a while he stood back and smiled. "OK, all over. He's gone now."

"NOO-OOO!!" Josh began to cry. "*You can't see him like that*, he's hiding under the window. *You can't see him if you don't open the window.*"

Hal sighed, pulled back the curtains and unscrewed the window lock. He put his hands on the ledge and leaned out. The air was balmy, a delicious, palm-frondy night, and he could smell the rank green water of the four ponds in the park. The crackle of electricity came like cicadas from the building-site spotlights. He pantomimed looking carefully down at the garden. "Hmmm . . . Well, he's run away now — absolutely not here. Do you want to see?"

Josh wiped his nose on the sleeve of his pyjamas and blinked at the window.

"Want to see?"

He shook his head.

"OK." Hal pulled the window closed and was about to lock it, when Benedicte noticed him hesitate. He opened the window again and stretched his arm round, rubbing his fingers on the outside of the pane.

"Hal?"

He didn't answer. He frowned momentarily, then pulled the window closed, locking it carefully, drawing the curtains.

"There you are, tadpole — all gone. No trolls out there."

But Benedicte didn't like Hal's expression. Something was wrong. She leaned over quickly, pushing her face towards Josh. "Come on, tadpole. Kiss on the nose for Mummy?" But Josh turned on to his side, harrumphing like a girl, his little face knotted and angry. "OK — night-night, then, darling."

At the door she waited for Hal to blow Josh a kiss, then switched off the light, closed the door and beckoned Hal to follow her downstairs. In the kitchen she slipped bare feet into Hal's muddy trainers and took the torch into the garden. Hal followed in his slippers. "What?" he hissed. "What's up?"

She shone the torch around the garden, looking at the grass for any sign that someone had walked across it. "What did you see, Hal?"

"Eh?"

"Up there." She turned and shone the torch up the side of the house to Josh's window. "On the window?"

"Oh, nothing. Just a handprint."

Benedicte turned to him, her face white. "A *handprint*?"

"*Sssh*. I don't want to frighten him even more."

"Well, just a bloody moment," she hissed, "you're frightening *me* now." She went to the bottom of the wall and shone the torch into the flower-bed. "Josh thinks he saw something and now you tell me there was a handprint. I mean —"

"Ben," he looked up at the window, "it's twenty feet above the ground — someone would have to *float* up there."

She looked up and down the wall. Hal was right — someone would need a ladder and she couldn't see anything in the flower-beds. No footprints. Nothing disturbed down here.

"Come on, Ben." Hal was starting to feel cold in his pyjamas. "One of the workmen left it on the pane when he put it in."

She stood in the grass biting her lip, feeling stupid.

"It was one of the workmen, Ben, we haven't cleaned the windows on the outside. And anyway —"

"Anyway what?"

"It was upside down."

"What?"

"It was upside down so it must have been there before the pane went in."

Benedicte sighed. She hated these night fears of hers. She hated the park for being where it was, just over the fence, she even hated poor little Rory Peach for getting himself kidnapped and killed. She couldn't wait to get to Cornwall. She shone the torch around the little fenced garden. Josh's paddling-pool reflected the moonlight but nothing else stirred. *OK — fair enough, but don't blame me for being nervous*. Reluctantly she clicked off the torch and followed Hal back up the steps, locking the door behind her and pulling the little curtain. Hal was awake now, so he got a beer from the fridge and leaned on the kitchen worktop, looking at her.

"I do understand," he said suddenly. "I saw Alek Peach. In the park."

"Jesus." Benedicte rubbed her face and sat down on the sofa, blinking. "When?"

"When me and Josh walked Smurf this evening. I didn't tell you — I didn't want to upset you."

"What does he look like?"

“Terrible. I’ve seen him up there before, when I was walking Smurf.” As if she’d heard her name, Smurf, who had been asleep in the TV room, got up and came through, yawning, her claws clicking on the tiles, and Hal bent down to stroke her and rub her old, deaf ears. “Haven’t we, Smurfy, we’ve seen him before, haven’t we? I just didn’t recognize him from the newspapers.”

“What was he doing?”

“I don’t know. Wandering around where —” He straightened and drank half of his beer, an odd look on his face. “He was wandering around where his little boy was.”

“I’ve seen it,” she murmured, slightly embarrassed that she’d actually gone up there to look. Walking through the forest, it had been a shock suddenly to come upon a carpet of dying flowers. Purple paper, ribbons, cellophane, cards, teddy bears saturated with dew. Rory had been nearly nine, she remembered thinking, he’d have been horrified by the teddies. “I don’t know what they’ll do with all those flowers.”

“There are families out there, can you believe it? Making it into a day trip — kids wearing Kill the Paedos T-shirts.”

“I know. I know.” She shook her head. “Did Alek Peach see them?”

“Yeah — saw it all. He was just standing back, among the bushes, watching. You should have seen him staring at Josh — as if he was seeing a ghost.”

“Poor bastard.” She got up, came into the kitchen and put the torch in a drawer. “I can’t wait to go to Cornwall, Hal, I can’t wait to get out of Brixton for a few days." She kissed the side of his face. "Don't stay up all night."

At 4.30a.m. the sky over the houses in Brockley became baby-eye blue and only Venus was still shining. At the back window where Penderecki had stood so many times to watch Ewan and Jack playing in the tree-house across the railway track, Caffery sat on a chair half stiff with shock. Flies had come to sip his sweat and he hadn't stopped them.

For years he had wondered how he'd feel if Penderecki died — and this was it, the end of the possibility that one day he'd discover what had happened to Ewan. Here he was, living out his fear, and it felt like having the life squeezed from him.

When the first morning goods train rattled through the cutting at 5a.m. at last Caffery moved. He batted at the flies, and stood, letting the blood come slowly back into his legs, and went downstairs into the kitchen, his eyes smarting. He ran the tap, scooped some water on to his face, and set to work.

Somewhere in this house was the answer to his question. He went into the bathroom. The boom of noise and smell when he opened the door almost made him retch. Penderecki was rotted through. Underneath his feet a pool of matter had collected — crunchy with fly coating. He had to stand very still until the gag reflex worked itself out of his throat.

Penderecki had run the noose through a hole smashed in the plaster ceiling and over a joist — the small garden mallet he'd used lay on the floor, and the plaster in the bath showed that he hadn't taken much time in doing this. He had come in here with the tools he needed, bashed a hole in the ceiling, slung the rope up there and done the deed. The small bathroom stool was not kicked over.

Dropped in the toilet was a copy of Derek Humphry's *Final Exit: The Practicalities of Self-deliverance and Assisted Suicide for the Dying*. Sweatshirt over his mouth, Caffery leaned over and read. One paragraph had been scored through with a pencil — angrily: "If you consider God the master of your fate, then read no further. Seek the best pain management and arrange for hospice care." But he was familiar with the book's instructions and recognized that Penderecki had, at the last moment, abandoned his quasi faith in God and turned instead to Humphry: "Ice will stop the air in the polythene bag becoming hot and stuffy . . ."

On the floor was an empty ice tray, over Penderecki's head a plastic bag. In death his face had swollen to fill the bag, pressing moist against the polythene. A bottle of vodka lay next to the door and a plate of something that looked like chocolate Angel Delight: "Powder your chosen drugs and put them in your favourite pudding . . ."

There were no flies on the pudding. They were enjoying dabbling and squelching in Penderecki too much. Caffery checked he had left no footprints then closed the door and went to search the rest of the house.

Penderecki had come to England in the forties — "Probably something to do with the Yalta conference," Rebecca said sagely. She seemed to understand the demographic waves that had brought Penderecki to the plot of land on the other side of the railway tracks to the Cafferys. Penderecki had never married and seemed to have become fanatical about a religion to which he had been unable to cling at the end. His body had hung here for what? Three, maybe four days, without anyone noticing. Perhaps there was someone still in Poland — framed paper cuttings hung on the wall, the sort of folk art distant relatives might send, but apart from this Ivan Penderecki had almost no personal possessions. Nearly seventy and the only children in his life had belonged to other people.

Caffery was prepared to pull the walls down if he thought that he'd find the smallest hint of Ewan, but the house gave up nothing. He got into the loft where the air was warm and circled with dust, but apart from an abandoned wasps' nest hanging from the rafters there was nothing. In one of the bedrooms there was a pile of Hennes children's clothing catalogues — innocuous enough. Penderecki wasn't stupid — he'd known that with his police record a search warrant would be granted on the slimmest grounds. But apart from that small haul, Caffery found nothing.

In the hallway he pressed redial on the phone. The answerphone at the Lewisham Hospital Oncology Unit picked up. He dialled the number on the last caller ID digital display. Also the Oncology Unit. Someone at the hospital had rung three days ago. Since then no one had tried to contact Ivan Penderecki. And that was all.

Wherever Penderecki had hidden the little scrap of flesh and bone that had been Ewan, it wasn't in this house. The catalogues were only the tip — Caffery knew that. There was more. Somewhere. But then, of course, this was part of Penderecki's genius — his ability to hide things. Hide magazines and videos and photos and the body of a small boy.

CHAPTER THIRTEEN

(22 July)

At home he took off his clothes and put them straight in the washing-machine. He knew a lot about getting the smell of death out of clothes. Rebecca was still asleep. When she woke up she knew immediately that something was wrong. "Jack? What is it? Where've you been?"

He didn't answer. He sat on the bed in his boxer shorts and lit a roll-up. The sun was filtering through the curtains, making shapes on the ceiling.

"Oh, God." Rebecca rolled over on to her back and dropped her hands on her forehead. Overnight her eye makeup had smeared into panda rings. "It's about last night? Isn't it?"

He didn't answer. He didn't know what to say.

"Jack?" She sat up and put her hand on his arm. "I'm sorry — I can explain, I just . . ."

He smiled at her and cupped her face in a way that he knew must seem ridiculous. He didn't care. He was tired. "He's dead."

"Who's dead?"

"Penderecki."

"*Dead?*"

"He killed himself. He had cancer, I think. Hanged himself in the bathroom."

"Is that where you were all night?"

"Yes."

"Shit!" She dropped back against the pillow, blinking. For a moment his spirits rose — for a moment he thought she was as shocked as he was, he even wondered if she understood. But then she put her hand on her forehead, rolled her eyes down to meet his, and said: "So you've nothing to stay here for. You could just walk away from it all. Couldn't you?"

"No." He shook his head, understanding immediately that he was wrong, that he was still on his own. "I couldn't do that. I've got —" He looked out of the window. "I've got everything."

She sat up, took the cigarette from between his fingers and took a long drag from it. "You mean Ewan?"

He wasn't going to answer that.

"Oh," she sighed. "Yes, you do, you mean Ewan." He felt her tapping his shoulder and when he turned round she was holding out the cigarette to him. Not looking at him. "Penderecki's dead now but you're still not going to give up, are you?"

He didn't answer. He took the cigarette, dropped his head and looked down at his black thumbnail. She was right. It should be over. Penderecki was dead. Ewan wasn't in the house. There was nowhere else to turn. He should be able to give it all up. But he knew there was more. *There* has *to be. Maybe another place somewhere . . . A shed or a garage — maybe he rented a garage . . .*

Wearily he got to his feet, went into the bathroom and started to run a bath.

Now Roland Klare knew what he was doing. He had gone through the book and worked out the solution to the jammed camera. What he needed was a "changing bag" — a dark bag in which film could be worked on without being exposed to light. It had taken a while to gather the things he needed, but Klare was nothing if not resourceful: the basis of the bag was no more than a dirty black bomber jacket found in the clothing bank on Tulse Hill. He had cleaned it and painstakingly stapled it closed along the front, a double seam of staples so that no light would come through. It didn't look much, but he thought it would work.

Now he pulled the blind and sat on the sofa, the "bag" on his lap, and pushed the camera down one of the sleeves until it was in the main body of the jacket. Then he withdrew his hands, placed two broad rubber bands over the sleeves and pushed his hands back down them, making sure the bands rode up his wrists to seal the sleeves from light leaks. He found the camera, cradled it in his palms, and began to work.

Klare's hands were rather large and clumsy for this — he had to take it slowly, biting the inside of his lip his concentration was so intense, trying to keep his eyes focused on a spot on the blind so they didn't wander around as he worked. The release catch he found quite quickly. The back of the camera sprang away and he opened it, brushing his fingers tentatively over the interior. The film was in there: he could feel it, half finished, stalled in its cage. Careful not to touch the image, he patted around until his fingers found the cartridge. "Good." He sat forward a little in anticipation. It was a tiny gap into which he had to push his fingers just to get a grip on the top of the canister, and when he did get hold of it he found he could only turn it a quarter of a rotation at once. Today he was feeling unusually patient. He took a breath, closed his eyes and let his fingers work in the dark like a Braille reader's, his left hand feathering over the mechanism to check that the sprockets were turning, his right tirelessly winching on the canister.

It took Roland Klare, with his big hands like spades, over an hour to get the film wound on. By the time he had finished and could flip out the canister with his thumbnail, his fingers were throbbing. He pulled the camera out of the bag, testing the winder mechanism before he put it aside and this time, to his surprise, it jammed once then suddenly gave. He stared at it, amazed. He flicked it back and forward a few times in disbelief. Without the film inside, the camera was working perfectly smoothly. Maybe it wasn't as badly damaged as he had thought; maybe the way the film had been loaded was the culprit. Pleased that he wouldn't have to discard the Pentax after all, he put it back in the biscuit tin and turned his attention to the changing bag, giving it a little shake.

The film canister was safe in there, but now Klare saw he had come to a wall. He didn't know the next step in the process — he'd have to go back to the book. He sighed. He was tired, he needed a break, so he took the bag into the bedroom where it was dark, dropped it on the floor, went back into the living room and released the blind. The sun had climbed high in the sky over the park. He stood for a while, gazing out of the window at the sun-parched trees.

Caffery stood in a phone box in a side-street near the Shrivemoor offices, Souness and Paulina's red BMW gleaming in the sun a few yards away, and called Brockley station to report Penderecki's death anonymously: "My wife hasn't seen our elderly neighbour for a while — I wonder, could you . . ." And somehow that made him feel slightly better, somehow it released a small part of the infection. Still, he had to fight to keep his mind on the case, to stop it floating away to Brockley where dark shadows moved along the railway line.

Souness had gone for breakfast and the few early arrivals in the incident room were subdued. Things were not looking good. The golden hours in which a case is often solved were over. They could now define the Rory Peach case as a "sticker". From here on leads would decay, connections would be forgotten. What they needed desperately was DNA, but the lab hadn't come back to them yet.

Kryotos had been unable to track down Champaluang Keoduangdy. Instead she had put a blue and white envelope on Caffery's desk for when he came in. Now he took coffee into the SIO's room and shook out the envelope on to his desk. Two Polaroids in plastic ziplocks — blown-up copies attached — slid out. These were the photographs found in 1989 in a rubbish bin on Half Moon Lane. He'd been waiting for them, but now as he looked at them he found his mind wouldn't focus: it kept trying to saunter away, back across the railway track and into Penderecki's house, up the stairs, into the cupboards — *there has to be somewhere else, another hiding-place* —

"Stop it." He rolled a cigarette, digging his heels into the floor. He had to concentrate. He put on his glasses.

The first shot was of a young boy, maybe eight or nine. Caffery knew it was a boy for the simple reason that he was naked from the waist down — otherwise the child would have been sexless as his face was turned slightly away from the camera. He was white, very thin and it was clear from his posture that he'd been bound — that he'd been bound and tied to the white radiator he was sitting against. On the right of the frame was the edge of what appeared to be a melamine wardrobe and, taped to it, the side of a poster. At the edge of one of the copies an investigating officer from the eighties had circled an area on the floor and written in red the word "*foot?*". Caffery examined the object. It could have been a human foot — naked, five small flesh-coloured dabs. Toes? Quite slim and long — maybe women's toes? But no: looking at the second photograph he could see it wasn't a woman.

This photograph, taken from a slightly different angle, showed the bound figure of an adult male. He was no more than a crooked trapezoid of limbs, legs propped at an awkward, unnatural angle, all snapped up and odd-looking, his head on one side, facing away from the camera. His arms had been crossed over his chest and he had been bound with sheets and pillow-cases, like burial winding sheets. Behind him the wardrobe was in full view — the poster was a Teenage Mutant Ninja Turtles one — and beyond that was a blurred half-image of the small blond child. Above the boy's head, tantalizingly, the bottom edge of a window-frame. And that was all.

Dim old 1989. Caffery tried to stretch his mind back. He'd been doing his first board, getting a train to Luton, his girlfriend would have been — he felt into the dark well of memories — Melissa, maybe. Or Emma. She'd looked like Meg Tilly and he'd adored her for the mini-skirts and unfashionable clothes she wore. That year nearly seventy people died in the Loma Prieta earthquake in San Francisco, the Afghan war ended, the Berlin Wall came down, Champ Keoduangdy had been put into intensive care by a length of industrial conduit, and someone had dropped these photographs into a bin on Half Moon Lane.

Were they a hoax? If not a hoax then why had no one come forward? After twelve years someone *somewhere* would have said something. And if these two people had died — shackled to the radiator in a child's bedroom — why hadn't the bodies been discovered? He searched the photos for more clues, tracing his fingers across the swarms of pixels, darker here, lighter here. Were there enough similarities between this and the scene at the Peaches' house to link the cases? Maybe this was a staged scene — an image of the troll's fantasy. Maybe that was *him* lying on the floor trussed up — and that could be, what? A younger brother? The walls — magnolia; the wardrobe — MFI? There were a million other bedrooms like it . . .

Suddenly he thought of Carmel, of how convinced she'd been — convinced and embarrassed — that someone had been taking photographs in their house while they were tied up. And as he thought of it he had the sudden feeling that somewhere there was an obstacle, something stopping things flowing, something diverting him. A vague unease. A vague *itch*, DI Durham would say. Someone wasn't telling him everything.

He smoked half a packet of tobacco and drank four cups of instant coffee thinking about it, but by the time the morning meeting started he wasn't any wiser, he was just more exhausted. He still had the smell of Penderecki in his nostrils as he went into the incident room with his notes for the meeting.

Everyone in AMIT knew that at this point in the Peach case they could allow themselves to be put in a holding pattern, to be stalled by waiting for the DNA, or they could pursue other avenues. This meeting was to ready themselves for a day on the pavement: one pod was going out into Brixton with a liaison officer from the child protection team — they were going to talk to the kids, ask them about the mythic thing in the woods, their "troll", treat their stories seriously — another was going to help Kryotos to trace Champaluang Keoduangdy. A third team would spend the day with local child-sex offenders: they were going to push more holes into the already fractured South London paedophile networks, put a little careful pressure on the right pulse points, squeeze a little, until someone gave them a lead. It was for this reason that risk assessment officers of the Lambeth Sex Offenders Unit, and two members of Scotland Yard's paedophile unit had come down from Victoria. Souness's girlfriend Paulina, an intelligence officer for the unit, had used the opportunity to tag along.

It was strange to Caffery that only two people at the meeting that morning seemed to sense the tightness in him. One was Kryotos, with her unerring, almost *chemical* sense of him — she watched him carefully from her desk, not challenging him, just assessing. The other was Paulina, whom he had met only a handful of times.

She was wearing a modern powder-blue skirt suit and looked like a piece of bright porcelain sitting on the desk, coolly smoking a cigarette, checking out Souness's work environment with her bland aquamarine eyes. It seemed to Caffery that every time someone mentioned the paedophile networks Paulina would glance up at him — as if she knew how he had spent the night, as if she could sense what he was thinking. She had been the one to tell Souness about Caffery's connection with Penderecki, and he almost expected her to mention it now, to turn those unnerving eyes on him and say, "Maybe Mr Caffery can help us here — maybe he has contact with someone who could help."

Her focus on him seemed so acute that the moment the meeting broke up he made his excuses and went into the SIO's room, closing the door behind him.

The crows reminded Rebecca of a school of fish, the way they climbed up the air currents, twisting above the low roofs of Greenwich, turning to display their dark undersides and changing colour as one. She watched them from the table in her studio, a cup of coffee at her elbow, a cigarillo in the ashtray. She was cold.

This was the flat she had shared with Joni, until the attack. Until Joni's back had been broken by Malcolm Bliss and Rebecca had been . . . "Oh, God." She shuddered and picked up the cigarillo. She knew she should find a new place, get out of this flat, with the smells and memories, and the staircase leading up to Joni's room. But it was so *easy* just to go over to Jack's and let herself in: there was the sound of him showering in the morning, the smoky, urban smell of his suit when he came home in the evenings, sweat on his arms when he came back from his runs, his hard hot stomach against hers in the night. *Yeah — and his obsession, which is probably going to kill him*.

She sat back in her chair and stared around her. The shutters were open — flat white oblongs of light lay on the polished oak floors — and along the right-hand wall her sculptures were lined up on a trestle table, ready to be taken to the gallery next month. Like little men, or little towers. *Ridiculous. Jack's right — they're ridiculous*. On the left, stacked against the wall, her old paintings, the ones Jack liked, done before the attack.

The artwork seemed to have come from two different places, two different mothers. On the left the old. On the right the new. And between them, poking out of the ceiling in the centre of the room, glinting slyly and scattering a secretive glitter on the walls, a butcher's hook.

Rebecca had got up on to a stool and screwed it into the plaster the morning after Jack turned on her in Tesco's. Of course it wouldn't take any weight — certainly not the weight of a body — but she wanted it there: she thought it might help kick over the blank on her timeline. But so far it hadn't worked. So far the blank was still there — an *absence*, a space — a space with shape and weight and texture and it was directly *here*, under the hook, between the old paintings and the new. The attack. "How did you get from there to —" She clenched the cigarillo between her teeth and reached her arms up above her, trying to make a bridge, an electric charge to leap between the two. "From there to there." She tried to picture Malcolm Bliss — she must have been in the room with him in that little bungalow . . . and Joni must have been there too — but it felt like forcing a tired muscle, like trying to push her thoughts through a needle eye, and suddenly instead of Bliss she saw Dali's spindle-legged camels and the image of the bungalow slipped out of reach and she was left again with just the hook in the ceiling and nothing else.

Shit shit shit.

She pinched out the cigarillo and stood up. Her memory wouldn't make the jump here and now, so there was absolutely no reason to think it might when she and Jack were in bed. She was being ridiculous — ridiculous and childish. She ought to just toughen up. She pushed her hair off her face and tied it in a knot at the back of her neck. She was going to go over to Jack's tonight and they were going to start all over again.

CHAPTER FOURTEEN

The “barracudas” — the ten-year-olds, just the age they started to be trouble — were showing off. They made Fish Gummer uncomfortable.

“Can we do a trick now?”

“Yeah, let’s do that trick thing.”

“No, no.” He checked the big clock at the far end of the steamy pool. “I think we’re finished now — it’s gone half past.”

“Yeah, let’s do that.” A muscular Nigerian girl in a lemon-yellow swimsuit was jumping up and down excitedly. “Let’s do that thing where we swim through your legs.”

“Absolutely *not*.”

“The other teachers let us do it.”

“I don’t care.”

“You get in the pool and we swim through your legs —”

“Underwater —”

“Yeah — like mermaids —”

“No, I don’t think so.”

Three of them slithered towards him at the edge of the pool, their wet, glowing little faces smiling up at him. "We hold our breath like this —" A head disappeared under the water.

"Yes yes yes!" a girl in pink squealed, throwing an exuberant backward roll in the water.

"No!" He was getting anxious. The remaining two had reached the pool edge and were giggling uncontrollably.

"That's it," giggled another. "We all hold our breath." She pinched her nose and disappeared into the water.

"And you put your legs open — and we swim through them —"

Now he saw a little hand come out of the water, groping for his ankle. "No!" He wrenched his foot away and fumbled for the whistle on the tape around his neck, a look of rigid fear on his face. "Just STOP!" he said. "I said *no*. Absolutely no." The hand subsided and all the children flicked up their legs like dolphins and came to the surface, spluttering and shocked. They stared at him in stunned silence, getting their breath back, not knowing how to react.

Then, suddenly, at the back of the group, the Nigerian girl clamped her hand over her mouth and began to snicker. It spread quickly and soon they were all laughing. All of them looking at him and giggling. He wanted to turn and run into the changing room. Now they knew how to upset him, and he knew it wouldn't end here.

By the end of the day nothing was moving. The teams came back in dribs and drabs, dropping the completed

Actions forms into Kryotos's tray. They'd give verbal reports at the day's meeting, but Caffery, sitting in the SIO's room watching them through the glass, already knew from their faces that no one had any new leads. He sighed and sat back, lighting another cigarette. His stomach was tight — he hadn't eaten — and the day had been long and exhausting and dry. Champ's nickname for his attacker had passed into the local folklore, but none of the children could give the police more than the myth, nothing concrete. Caffery had Brixton send the photographs of Champ Keoduangdy's bite over to King's, hoping Ndizeye, the forensic odontologist, could establish if the person who had bitten Champ at the boating-lake more than twelve years ago was the same person who had inflicted the mark on Rory Peach. Ndizeye had completed Rory's casts — "An adult-sized arch and the incisors look smooth, so he's over twenty. Great clear casts. Teeth can be as individual as DNA, you know." But, no matter how individual the teeth were, Caffery knew that what they really needed was some DNA. And then at four thirty Kryotos came in with a smile on her face.

"Fiona Quinn on the line," she said, jabbing her finger at the phone. "The DNA's back."

He snatched up the phone and stood looking out of the window. "Fiona." He desperately needed to hear what she had to say. He wondered how his voice sounded. "How are you?"

"I'm OK, Jack, but I've got bad news. It's come back no profile."

"*No profile?*"

"No profile."

"Shit." He sat down again, deflated.

"But, Jack, at least eighty per cent of our samples come back this way, no or partial profile. It's really fragile, DNA."

"I know — you told me that already. I just thought . . ." He sighed. Without DNA they couldn't start a mass screening — all they had to work with were Ndizeye's casts. "Fuck, fuck, fuck. Haven't we got anything else to go on?"

"Well, I've had a look at that corner of the room Alek Peach was talking about in his statement —"

"And?"

"Nothing so far."

"The white fibres — from Rory's wounds?"

"Nothing yet. But that'll come. And we're still looking at his shoe, trying to see if there's anything on that. Then there's the stuff the biologists sprayed on the wall, the ninhydrin — in a couple of days we'll see how that's developed — but with the witness statements you got we're groping in the dark, to be honest. And even if his prints are all over the place there's no guarantee the ninhydrin will pick it up. Keep your fingers crossed your man is a meat-eater — if he's a veggie we won't get anything."

"OK, OK." He closed his eyes. His head was beginning to hurt as if he'd come off a drinking spree. "And absolutely *nothing* you can do with that semen sample?"

"Um — I'm not sure."

He opened his eyes. "I beg your pardon?"

"I said I can't say for sure."

"Jesus." He whistled between his teeth. "I don't believe this." In the incident room Souness and Paulina had come back. He could see Paulina's right foot where she was sitting, dangling in mid-air, with its expensive sandals and nails painted in shell pink tapping in a lazy rhythm. He turned away.

"Listen," he said to Quinn, "it's more than two days since the PM and now you turn round and tell me you can't —"

"There's no need to —"

"It's a good job we haven't got someone sitting here under arrest or we'd look a right bunch of tits."

"You're not listening."

"I *paid* to have it fucking *pre*miumed. If you think that means I was prepared to sit around for days and then get a phone call saying we might do it, we might not, we might just sit here and paint our nails —"

"Jack —"

"— then I wouldn't have bothered to pay through the nose. This fucking SGM, plus stuff you're all crowing about, two K a pop, why don't you just admit it's a great, infested, *steaming* pile of crap —"

"*Mr Caffery!*"

"*Wha-at?*"

They both stopped. Caffery locked his mouth and tapped his foot on the floor. He could almost see the pair of them, pawing the ground, red-eyed, snorting across London at each other. He knew he'd raised his voice and he sensed Kryotos was watching him from the incident room, and suddenly he saw himself through her eyes — volatile, unreasonable, sliding at a hundred miles an hour. He took a deep breath, leaned back, rapped on the desk with his knuckles, and said: "Yes, look, I'm sorry. What?"

"Have you heard of LCN? Low count number?"

"No."

"It can multiply the sample thirty-four times. It's only approved for major crime —"

"Then do it. You've got our lab cost code — it should have already been started."

"That's what I was trying to say. It has been. It's already been started."

The envelope was on the doormat when he came in. The conversation with Fiona Quinn had finished him for the day. He had lost his temper with her — *you just can't help proving Rebecca right, can you?* — and had left Shrivemoor early, knowing he should just go home and sleep. He drove to Sainsbury's where he bought four bottles of Pinot Grigio on sale, a bottle of Laphroaig, a carton of Coke bottles, milk and some Nurofen. Just before he left the shop he saw a bunch of sage green leaves mixed with peonies. He hesitated then bought two bunches. For Rebecca.

Now he picked up the letter and took it into the kitchen. He put it on the table, then stood for a moment and stared at it. It had a second-class stamp on it. It had been posted on Wednesday afternoon and was from Penderecki — he could tell from the writing. Maybe posting this had been the last thing he had ever done.

Caffery emptied the carrier-bags, stopping from time to time to go back to the table and look at the envelope. He carefully put one bottle of wine in the freezer, another in the fridge, looked through the cupboards for a vase, and when he couldn't find one took a plastic lemonade bottle from the bin, cut off the top, peeled away the label and filled it with water. He put the flowers in it, rested it on the window-ledge in the living room, rolled himself a spliff using the sensi that Rebecca kept in the Oxo tin, and then, when he could bear it no longer, he lit the joint, sat down at the table and opened the envelope.

It contained just one sheet of paper. There was no need for a note or explanation. The single sheet of paper told him everything he needed to know. It was a map.

CHAPTER FIFTEEN

It took Caffery about twenty minutes to understand exactly what the map represented. He sat at the kitchen table, next to the open window, turning the paper over and over in his hands, holding it up to the light. The little rectangle represented a building — "cottage" written next to it in Penderecki's distinctive hand. Caffery knew the slang for a public toilet — but the odd ladder rungs lying next to it? Steps? He turned the paper through ninety degrees, laying the ladder on its side. It was broken halfway along; a double-headed arrow joined the separated rungs, and scratched above the arrow: 10 – 140. The rungs to the right of the arrow were numbered: 141, 142, 143, 144, 145. He ran his fingers over the paper. Above rung number 145 was another arrow, at its head an X, circled twice.

He turned the paper through forty-five degrees, twisted it on its side and suddenly the meaning was blazing out at him. *Oh, fuck, of course. Of course*. He sat up, his heart pumping. The railway line — Penderecki's natural warren, he used it to come and go, he was as at home down there as the rats and the foxes. The lines on the map were sleepers. And if these lines represented the railway sleepers, then the rectangular box probably represented — *oh, shit, yes* — the unused public toilets just up the road from Brockley station? The X was one hundred and forty-five railway sleepers past the station.

"X marks the spot," he muttered, stubbing out the spliff. Penderecki could still jerk his strings — even past life he had the power. He found tools in the cupboard, a small camera in Ewan's room and took the backdoor key from above the lintel. "This had better not be a dead end, you old fucker, you old fucker."

The sun was sinking low over the roofs and in the back gardens along the rail cutting children shrieked, hung on climbing frames, chased each other in circles. Caffery used a fox track — two yards into the undergrowth, parallel to the railway — moving carefully, quietly, his head down: the Transport Police, who resented the "real" police, would be in hog heaven to find one of his kind wandering down the track. It was oddly silent down here. A sort of muffled, suspended silence. Occasionally the rails would hum and a train would race past, making the air thunder, and for a moment the cutting would hold its breath. But then the train would pass and the stillness would descend again, grass pollen floating to earth like duck-down.

He couldn't help thinking about Ewan as he walked along here, with the smell of the tracks after a day in the sun, metal and hot black engine oil. He thought of the two of them, racing up and down the cutting, playing cowboys and Indians, setting traps for each other. *Ewan — oh, Jesus*. He rubbed the sweat off his face with his T-shirt — he didn't want to imagine what he might find down the track.

He reached the public toilets — their graffitied backs staring out blankly over the track (*Tracii sucks cock — Shaz sucks pussy*), tiny windows, like gun slots in a pillbox, smashed and plugged with chipboard. Checking the map, he positioned himself with New Cross behind him, Honour Oak ahead, and began to count along the sleepers.

Fifteen, sixteen, seventeen —

Stepping over dead rats, dried toilet paper, sunbleached Coke cans.

Fifty, fifty-one, fifty-two — this had better not be a wind-up.

Outside Brockley station the land on either side of the railway lost its undergrowth and lay as flat as an alluvial plain, dusted with thistle and dock leaves, until about ten feet away from the railway line where the banks right-angled abruptly upward in great walls of vegetation, so deep and entwined that anything could live in there — capuchin monkeys, maybe, chattering and swinging on vines. Up ahead a footbridge, remote and spindly, like a bridge slung over a jungle gorge.

One hundred and forty-three, one hundred and forty-four, one hundred and forty —

The hundred and forty-fifth sleeper. He stopped. Dropped the hammer and stood, feet straddling the sleeper, facing at right angles away from the line, in the direction of the arrow on the map. Immediately he could see that someone had been here before. Someone had walked back and forward in a straight line between this sleeper and the foot of the bank — under tender new ivy shoots the vegetation was dead and trampled. *Just do it, don't stop to think*. He went to the bank and began tugging at the woodbine, tearing open a hole large enough to get into. Then he ducked inside.

It smelt of stinging nettles and dandelion, of fox dirt and oil, and it took a moment for his eyes to get used to the light. He stopped, wiping the sweat from his face, getting his bearings, and now he found he could straighten up in here. Someone had cleared a dome shape in the hanging undergrowth — in front of him was the bank, behind him curtains of ivy and bramble. *And down here? Down on the ground?* He crouched and found dried stems and root matter. He tore at it, tugging the meshwork away.

In spite of what he'd expected, in spite of the fact that he was prepared, when he saw what was under the roots his heart began to race. He didn't really believe what he was seeing. A small circle of ground, about two foot by three, had been disturbed within the year. Few plants had taken root there.

He sat down next to the circle, next to the turfed-over clumps of brown Eocene London clay, rested his hands on his ankles, and began to shake.

"You can see the balloon at Vauxhall." Ayo Adeyami went straight into the family room at the back of the house and knelt on Benedicte's sofa, opening the window and leaning out. "And look! The London Eye."

"I know." In the kitchen Benedicte pulled off her shoes and gave Smurf a bowl of water. They'd been for dinner at Pizza Express and afterwards had agreed to leave the men, Hal and Ayo's husband, Darren, in the pub "just for one pint". The two women had come back here with Josh and Smurf. Ayo was going to water Benedicte's plants while they were in Cornwall and she still hadn't seen the house.

She was enthralled. "It's brilliant! Absolutely brilliant."

"I know."

"No need to be smug."

"I know. Hey!" From the kitchen she leaned across the low units and spoke to Josh, who had already flung himself on the floor in the family room and was watching *The Simpsons*, his chin in his hands. "Hey, brat, keep the volume down, OK. Come on — we've got guests."

Josh grumbled about it. But he turned the sound down and dropped the control.

"Good." Benedicte got a bottle of Freixenet out of the fridge. "That fireplace," she said to Ayo, putting the bottle between her thighs and trying to prise out the cork. "That fireplace is Travatino limestone."

"Is it crap." Ayo looked over her shoulder and grinned. "It's cast concrete. Darren put one in our place."

"Yeah . . ." She scrunched up her face and wrestled with the champagne cork. "But most people'd believe me."

"Most people are soft." Ayo leaned further out of the window, smiling in the soft evening air. She was seven months pregnant and she carried it well: from behind she looked as slender as a teenager with her long limbs. Like a carving in a print dress, thought Benedicte, she would never get fat.

"There's something wrong in those towers," Ayo said. She was craning her neck to the left, to Arkaig Tower and Herne Hill Tower, the doomy twins at the bottom of the park. "They're evil."

"I know — great guardians of Brixton." The cork came away with a dull pop and she began to fill two crystal flutes. "Champagne?"

"Oh, Ben," Ayo pulled the window closed and turned to settle on the sofa, "I'm sure even *thinking* about champagne is bad for the baby."

"Come on. I took acid *and* Es when I was pregnant with Josh."

"See? *See?* I rest my case."

"It can't be as bad as all the crap at the hospital."

"Yeah — I got a lecture about it. No chemotherapy, no X-rays, no ribavirin." She stretched her feet out on the floor, dropping her chin on her chest. "God, I can't remember what my feet look like. Have you seen the size of these knockers? Darren thinks he's died and gone to heaven. Ah . . ." She took the drink from Benedicte and rested the glass on her bump, slyly watching Josh from half-closed eyes. "Ben?" she said innocently.

"Mmm?"

"You know with Josh?"

"Yeah?"

"Did he press on your bladder? Make you wee twenty times a night?"

"Mu-um." Josh half sat up. "Can you two *stop*?" He held his hand up and snapped it open and closed. "Yak yak yak yak yak."

Ayo nudged him with her foot. "Smarty-pants."

Josh giggled and rolled on to his back, play-kicking at her. "Yak yak yakety-yak."

"*Help!*" She struggled to get up, spilling champagne. "Help me, Ben, your sprog is attacking me."

"Hyperactive child. He should probably be on medication." Benedicte helped Ayo to her feet, out of the way of Josh. "Come and let me show my house off to you — come and see the room that's going to save my life."

The two women went up the stairs, clutching their champagne, giggling, Josh yelling insults after them. Smurf lolloped along behind, and this time Ben didn't send her back downstairs. "Be — en," Ayo hissed, the moment they got out of Josh's earshot. "Ben, what do you think about this business? You know, the little boy in the park."

"Oh — God." Ben switched on the light on the landing. "Screwy. I'm sort of glad we're traipsing out to shagging Cornwall." She'd been following it on TV. Two members of SERPASU, the South East Regional Police Air Support Unit, had resigned over the incident and the BBC had devoted five minutes to it at the head of the news. The worst thing, for Ben, was a piece of video taken from a helicopter. A news crew, filming the search in the park the day after the kidnap, had analysed the footage and discovered what they claimed was Rory Peach. A tiny patch of light curled in a tree.

They broadcast it with a circle imposed over the top so the viewer knew where to look. Benedicte had found it disgusting. "I don't want to think about it, to be honest. I've thought about it enough." She pushed her hair behind her ear and smiled at Ayo. "Come on, let's change the subject, OK? Now," she paused with her hand on the door and made a solemn face, "*this* is the room that is going to save my life." She opened the door. "Da-da!"

Ayo peered inside. The bedroom was no more than a box painted cream with blue curtains and a scalloped blue light shade in the centre of the ceiling. It smelt of paint and new carpets. "Ummm," she smiled, "nice."

"I know it's not *nice* exactly." Benedicte made a face and poked Ayo in the arm. "But it's the first time I've had somewhere I can go for some peace and quiet. Now," she closed the door and opened the next one, putting her hand inside the door to turn on the light, "the bathroom."

They both peered inside. Josh's trainers, which were covered in mud from the woods, had been hosed off and were upside down on the edge of the bath. But there was something else out of kilter in here. Benedicte stepped inside and saw that the floor, the little white pedestal mat under the toilet, and even a corner of the bath mat draped over the bath edge, were wet. She could smell it instantly — they'd been urinated on. "Jesus," she muttered, switching off the light and slamming the door. "Wait there, Ayo." She hurried down the stairs. "*Josh! JOSH!*"

In the TV room Josh looked up. He knew immediately from his mother's voice that he was in trouble. He moved an almost imperceptible fraction along the sofa away from her and Benedicte paused, momentarily ashamed that she could have that effect on her nine-year-old son. "Jo-*osh*."

"Yeah?" He was cautious.

"That mess upstairs."

He didn't answer.

"*Josh!* I'm *speaking* to you."

"What mess?"

"You know *what* mess. The one in the bathroom."

Josh's mouth dropped open and he half stood. "I never — I never went in there."

"Well, someone did. It wasn't Smurf — she's been with me all day and the door was closed."

"I never, Mum, honest. Honest."

"Oh, for heaven's sake." She got bleach, rubber gloves and a bowl from under the kitchen sink and slammed the cupboard door. "You'll have to learn, Josh, not to lie. It's important." She went upstairs to where Ayo was cleaning the mess up with a roll of Andrex. "He's turned into an absolute liar since we got here. It's like everything's gone haywire since we moved in."

"Maybe the house is cursed."

"Probably." Benedicte unhooked the carrier-bag from the bin under the sink and held it out for Ayo to dump the used tissue. "Probably built on ancient Navajo burial ground." She didn't smile when she said it.

* * *

The mosquitoes had landed a live one. They banked and throttled next to Caffery's ears, flying in formation between the thistle and ragwort, alighting on his hands and sucking eye-popping tubes of blood up into their proboscises. He slapped at them, flicked them, but they clung, drunken and bloated, in his sweat and wouldn't move as he crouched, scraping at the earth and root matter with the claw hammer. The sun had dropped sulkily into the roofs, throwing its last rays into the bitter green cutting.

Should have brought a torch, you dickhead.

Every step, every rock he turned, he recorded, straightening up to photograph his work, flooding the little cloister with artificial blue light, making himself blind briefly. Then, at 9.15p.m., after two hours of scraping and digging, he pushed the hammer once more into the soil and hit something unfamiliar. Something that didn't give like soil but slid and whispered. *Oh, shit, here we go*. Heart thumping, he threw aside the hammer and dropped forward on to his knees, scraping at the earth with his bare hands. In the dim twilight he saw a flash of plastic.

He stopped digging, rocking back a little on his heels, his chest tight — for a moment he thought he might vomit. He had to close his eyes and breathe carefully through his nose until the sensation went away.

CHAPTER SIXTEEN

It was a chequered blue laundry bag with plastic handles and it didn't contain Ewan Caffery's remains. Caffery carried it slung over his shoulder, back down the tracks, like a weary sailor carrying his kit on shore leave — it bumped on his back and left a grimy patch on his T-shirt. Night had come, the moon was out and he had to move slowly, feeling his way through the nettles with his feet. At his garden he fished inside his saturated T-shirt for the key on the tape. He was dragging, disappointed, but he wasn't going to give up. He knew that Penderecki had sent him to find this bag for a reason.

The house was cool: the french windows stood open, and he could smell cigarillo smoke, so he knew Rebecca was here. He didn't shout up to her or go upstairs to check the bedroom. He didn't want to speak to her at this moment.

Instead he went into the living room, swung the bag from over his shoulder and emptied out the contents. He stood, looking at what was on his floor for a few minutes, then went into the kitchen. The wine in the freezer was almost frozen; he rattled the huge chunk of ice, rinsed a glass, opened the bottle and poured. The glass immediately clouded with condensation and his fingers stuck to it when he touched it. He swallowed it whole, not tasting it, refilled his glass, lit the remains of the spliff he'd left in the ashtray, and went back into the living room, where he sat on the sofa, hands on his knees, staring blankly at what Penderecki had intended him to find.

By far the largest percentage of all child pornography is home-made — historically, little has been made for commercial distribution, and at one point or another Caffery had seen examples of it all. His time in Vice had been before the big split, before Obscene Publications, the "dirty squad", had become the dedicated paedophile unit and farmed its adult porn concerns out to Vice. In his day the responsibilities of the two units had often overlapped, and he had seen most of what lay on his living-room floor before.

Copies of *Magpie*, the magazine for the Paedophile Information Exchange network, a stack of Dutch, German and Danish magazines — *Boy Love World, Kinder Liebe, Spartacus, Piccolo*. Two scuffed copies of the book *Show Me*, three editions of the glossy Dutch publication *Paidika — The Journal of Paedophilia*, and NAMBLA bulletins from the early eighties. A pile of zip disks secured with an elastic band. Passwords for websites, and a photocopied list, a message splashed across the top: "*WARNING, WARNING WARNING!! If any of the usernames below try to join your chat room log off IMMEDIATELY*". At the bottom of the laundry bag, wrapped in Somerfield carrier-bags and taped with brown parcel tape, was a stack of unmarked videocassettes.

Spliff in his teeth he shook out the videos. He plugged the first into the VCU, found the remote control, started the tape and sat back on the sofa, holding a lighter to the joint. The screen flickered — he knew what to expect. It was years since he'd looked at child pornography, years since Vice, when he'd *had* to look at these images and had spent each night lying awake trying, like most officers new to the unit, to find a place in his head to put it all. Or, failing that, to build something around them. And the biggest fear — the fear they all had, but would never share — *what if, what if . . . oh, Christ, what if I'm aroused by it?* Tonight he knew what to expect, and it wasn't the pictures he was afraid of. His thumping heart was not for the children he was going to see bullied and tormented for the camera, his thumping heart was for the chance that he might see Ewan.

The tape rolled and the screen showed the scratching, the white flecks of magnetic interference. *Would you recognize him?* Nothing at the beginning. He sat forward with the remote control and skipped forward through the tape. The screen continued to flicker. On it went, on and on, with no image until, with a sudden creak, the tape butted up against the rollers. He'd come to the end. There was nothing on this tape. He ripped it out of the machine and plugged in a second one, started it, fast-forwarded it. Again he got all the way to the end and found no image.

"Jack?"

He looked up. "Go back to bed, Rebecca."

"What's going on?"

"Nothing — really. Go to bed."

But he'd piqued her interest. She was barefoot — wearing only a pair of his grey boxer shorts and a short-sleeved vest — and she padded into the room, trying to look over his shoulder. "What is it?"

"Really, Becky . . ." He stood up, holding out his hands, ushering her away from the stuff on the floor, from the video. "It's nothing. Go back to bed, eh? Go on."

She blew air out of her nose. "Will you come up too?"

"Yes," he said, without thinking. "I'll bring you a drink. I promise."

"OK." That quelled her. She turned obediently on her heel and went back up the stairs and Caffery sat for a moment staring at his hands, wondering what to do. Eventually he got up, got two fresh glasses of wine, and went upstairs. In the bedroom she was lying on the bed with her hands under her head. The lamp was on and her hair was loose, running down over one shoulder. She had taken off her vest and was smiling at him.

Right. He put the glasses down on the bedside table and sat at the foot of the bed. "Rebecca — look." He couldn't make the complex adjustment she wanted — not now. "I'm sorry."

"Sorry for what?" She rolled on to her front and walked towards him on all fours. She pressed her hands flat on his chest and kissed his shoulders, kissed the sweat-stained base of his neck.

"I'm busy downstairs."

"That's OK." She wrapped her arms round his neck. Her hair smelt of cigarillo smoke and something flowery — she pressed herself against him, her smooth breasts soft against his arm, and in spite of himself his heart dilated helplessly.

"Becky, please . . ." She buried her face in his neck and trailed her fingers down his stomach where the muscles fluttered weakly. She pushed her hand inside his trousers. He reached down and took her hand. Held it away from him "No. Not now . . ."

She sshed him and wriggled her hand out of his grip, put it back inside his shorts. "Becky."

"Ssh — it's all right."

She pulled her hand out of his trousers, sat up and rolled the shorts down to her knees, kicked them off her feet, and turned on one knee. She placed her hands flat on the bed and bent over in front of him on the bed — her back to him, her hips jacked up in the air. He stared at her, disbelieving, not knowing what to say or do. There was something so primitive about what he was doing — so crude. He stood, unbuttoned his trousers and dropped his shorts, kicked them aside and stood behind her. "Move down a bit." He dragged her hips towards him. She leaned forward to help, her chin touching the bed, reaching between her legs to guide him. "I won't last —"

"Ssh — it's OK."

He fell forward and kissed her back, her hair was in his mouth, he reached around to find her breasts, his heart expanding hard upward, got his cock inside her, wrapped his arms around her waist, then, suddenly, as clear as a bell on a cold day, he heard her say: "Stop."

He stopped, opened his eyes. She was staring up at him, looking up over her shoulder at him, her eyes wide and serious.

"*What?*" He trembled with the effort of not moving. "What's the matter?"

"Stop. I've changed my mind."

"You're joking?"

"No is no." She looked at his face. "Honestly, Jack — I mean it."

But it was too late. Something in his stomach, something that was close to opening anyway, broke. He grabbed her by the hair, wrenching her head back; and pushed himself into her as hard as he could, his heart pumping like a pile driver. "*Jack!*" She let out a sob and tried to crawl away across the bed but he held her. He knew her face was slamming into the bed and that there was blood — a line of blood in the corner of her mouth, he saw it but he couldn't stop. She was crying, tears running down her face, but he didn't stop. He didn't stop until he had come. Then he thrust her head back down, pulled out of her and padded into the bathroom where he stood in the shower, his head bent, one hand on the wall, the warm water pouring over his neck, and began to cry.

Carmel Peach hadn't been mistaken about the photographs taken in her house. They were currently on a roll of film, tucked inside a bag, a bag constructed from an old bomber jacket, and lying on the floor in Roland Klare's bedroom.

Klare had spent a long time going through the photography book, in great detail, making copious notes as he worked, listing the things he needed. Now, late in the night, he was consulting the list as he hunted through the rooms for the makings of a darkroom. He had already made his biggest find, earlier this evening: a cumbersome negative enlarger that had been stored for some months behind a pile of magazines. He had found it in a dustbin at the back of a photographer's suppliers in Balham — it was cracked and the timer was broken, but in Klare's world nothing, *nothing* was beyond rescue. Now the enlarger had been resurrected and was safely installed in the bedroom cupboard, the place that was going to serve as a darkroom. It was a big prize.

However, as he continued his hunt through the rooms, through the various boxes and corners of his flat, he was starting to see a problem. Klare collected things quickly, so quickly in fact that he frequently filled up a room within a matter of weeks, and periodically had to have a clear-out, taking everything from one room down to the dump and redistributing what remained in the flat in the cleared space. Sometimes he was careless, got himself agitated and ending up dumping things he hadn't meant to, and now he was starting to think he'd thrown away some of the things that he needed. Although he had a sealed plastic developing tank (this he'd got from the same bin as the enlarger, it looked like a tupperware container and was cracked but mendable — *make a note of that*

— *need some araldite*) — an old washing up bowl for washing the prints in, tape to light-seal the cupboard and plenty of discarded cat-litter trays that could serve as print-developing trays — although he had all this, when he ran an inventory against the list he realized there were still things missing: some print fixer, developer, stop bath, a safelight. As he stared at the list a nervous tic started in the corner of his eye. Stop bath — the book said he could make that from vinegar if necessary, but a safelight? A safelight, fixer and developer — these were things he could only get from a supplier. Face twitching with frustration, he wandered around the flat muttering to himself, checking and checking again that there'd been no mistake, that there weren't bottles hidden in some dark corner. But no — if he was going to get these photos developed he'd have to go down to Balham and maybe even spend some money.

Out of the living-room window the moon was bathing Brockwell Park in silver, but Roland Klare, immensely discouraged now, wasn't interested in the view. He drew the blind, dropped down on the sofa, clicked on the television and sat for several hours, staring at it blankly.

CHAPTER SEVENTEEN

(23 July)

He went to Shrivemoor. It was the only place to go. He was composed enough to put a suit in the car for the next day, to put the malt whisky into a carrier-bag on the back seat, and to pack most of Penderecki's stash away in the under-stairs cupboard. The video cassettes and the zip disks — those he took with him.

The offices were empty. He switched on all the fluorescents, rinsed a mug in the kitchen, filled it with the malt, and went into the SIO's room, where he sat and watched the snake of car headlights down below.

Well, Jack, now look at your pretty little CV . . .

That was rape. Wasn't it? Everything had been a green light until — No. He could turn it inside out, reinvent it, excuse it, but the hard fact remained — it had been rape. He had hurt her, her mouth had been bleeding. Maybe it meant she was right, and maybe that was what she wanted, to prove that he was out of control. He sighed and put his head in his hands. There were so many games to play. So many obstacles.

Caffery sat at his desk into the early hours of the morning, facing out of the window, letting himself get drunk on Laphroaig and London tap water while outside the city folded down for the night.

Hal Church got up early and dressed in blue jersey shorts and a T-shirt. "You look like a tourist," he told the mirror. "A middle-aged tourist." He went round the house locking all the windows, set up a lamp on a security timer on the first landing and put his AA card on the dashboard of the Daewoo. He stopped for a moment in the garage, the smell of new paint and varnish overlaid with petrol, the sunlight a crack of white under the roll-up garage doors, the back seat piled with the polystyrene icebox and Josh's old Pokémons. Here he was, an adult, his own child to take on holiday, a wife. He had the sudden aching sense that his life was whistling past him, stirring the hair on his arms it was going so fast. Where did time go — where did life go?

By eight the sun was hot in the back garden, the sky a still, absorbent blue, and Josh's paddling-pool had a thin scum of dead insects and grass floating on it. Hal turned it over to drain. "Come on, Smurf." He pulled the Labrador back by her collar, stopping her lapping the water from the grass. "Time for a walk, old girl."

When they got back Josh was in the kitchen eating Golden Grahams with a soup spoon. He was wearing his Obi-Wan Kenobi T-shirt, and Benedicte, dressed in a grey cord shirt of Hal's, capri pants and deck shoes, was opening a can of mandarins in syrup.

"Morning." He leaned over and kissed Josh on the head. His son grunted and went on eating. "Morning, darling." He kissed Benedicte's cheek. "Sleep well?"

"Yup." She plopped the segments into a glass bowl, hooked one up into her mouth, and shoved the bowl in front of Josh, who scowled at it. Hal hung up Smurf's lead on the back of the door and watched Benedicte out of the corner of his eye. She was upset about something, he could see — he watched her take her coffee cup to the fridge, smell the milk, frown, hold it up to the light, tilt it one way then another, then dribble some in her coffee and turn to face him. "Hal."

Here it comes, he thought. "Yes?"

"Hal, did you let Smurf upstairs again?"

"What?"

Benedicte sighed. She wasn't in a good mood and there was so much to be done before they could leave, and when she'd gone into the bathroom that morning she'd found something that had upset her.

"She got up to the top floor and pissed on my laundry basket." Hal and Josh looked at each other, Josh stifling a giggle, and that annoyed her. "It's not funny, you know. *You* can clean it up if she pisses on the bed again."

"Hang on. She was locked down here when I got up this morning." Hal was serious now. "Josh? You didn't let her out last night, did you?"

"Uh." Josh clicked the spoon against his teeth, thinking about this. "No." He shook his head. "I never. She must of got there herself."

"And that," Benedicte put the milk back in the fridge and went to the sink to rinse her fingers under the tap, "that is the smoking gun. Mr Hal Church, you stand accused."

Hal stuck his tongue out at her. "Well, I didn't do it, Miss Smart A-R-S-E." He went into the hallway and took the keys from the telephone table.

"Where are you going?"

"To cancel the newspapers." He turned and stuck out his tongue again. "And get away from *you*, you big girl."

Benedicte thumbed her nose back at him. "See if *I* care."

Hal checked that Josh couldn't see and quickly dropped his trousers, giving her a glimpse of his buttocks, then straightened and slammed the door behind him. Benedicte snorted loudly through her nose and Josh looked up.

"What?"

"Nothing." She smiled to herself and put the cafetière in the sink. *You know how to get round me, Hal, you bastard*. She banged around the kitchen a bit, emptying coffee grounds, putting ties on the cereal packs. Josh finished his mandarins and took Smurf into the family room to watch TV: *Honey I Shrunk the Kids*. Benedicte scooped a little water into her mouth from the tap — her tongue was burred this morning, heavy in her mouth. Then she looked up at the clock and suddenly realized it was even later than she thought.

"Oh, fuckety-fuck." She pushed hair out of her eyes. "Only an hour. Josh, go and clean your teeth, tadpole." She closed the back door and locked it. Over the fence the trees bristled with noise, a breeze rustling through the leaves, hissing like rain. God, but she hated that park. She turned to put the plates away, moving quickly. "Josh, come on." He was still on the floor in the family room, blackcurrant juice round his mouth, his usual cushion on his chest — *why does he need a cushion clutched to his chest just to concentrate on the TV? Watching* Ren and Stimpy . . . *Funny, I thought he was watching* Honey I Shrunk the Kids.

I'm going mad, she thought, it must be the stress. The moment Hal got back they'd have to get moving. "O-o-oh, Ha-*al*," she said aloud, to the closed front door. "Hurry up. We're going to be late, Hal."

" 'We're going to be late, Hal,' " Josh imitated from the sofa.

"Yeah, very funny." She put her hand to her head. "Josh, I thought I told you to . . ." But she couldn't remember what she'd told him to do — the colours on the TV were distracting her. They looked like they'd been blocked in by someone on PCP: the purples were the most saturated, like the juice of irises, the yellows the heartbreakingly pure yellow of pollen.

"The purplest purples," she murmured, leaning against the sink. "The blossomest blossom." Outside, in the glaring sun, the grass seemed to be swaying in slow motion. For a moment she thought she might be sick, and there was that awful thickness in her mouth again. And, now she thought about it, hadn't the coffee tasted odd? "Josh —" *Come on, Ben, get yourself together* — "Josh, Mummy's going to lie down, OK? Tell Daddy when he comes in."

"'Kay."

Maybe I'll just lie down here, on the floor, it looks soft enough.

She let a cup slide into the sink, the slow, silent explosion of brown over the stainless steel, and went into the toilet, banging her hip on the washbasin, holding out her hands to steady herself. The floor tiles seemed to lift up and melt into the wall and her mouth was so dry she had to scoop more water into it. *What's the matter with you?* Outside the bathroom something dark and huge scuttled across the hallway. She looked up.

"Smurf?"

No answer.

"*Josh?*"

But he wouldn't be able to hear. He was in the other room with the TV on. Instead of worrying she sat down on the floor, her head between her hands, wondering why her mouth was so furred. Something touched her shoulder.

Hal?

"I thought you said you wanted that room?"

Hal?

"Can't you go to the room?"

The room? What room? Why's he asking about a room?

"Come on." A bright light and now her armpits felt as if a vice had locked on to them. "Just leave me for a moment, Hal — I'll be all right." The back of her shoulders was hurting, and her spine too, as if she was being bounced on a hard wooden floor. The light was blinding and when she tried to speak her voice seemed to come from a thousand miles away. "Hal?" She couldn't speak — her tongue was so thick that it seemed to have blocked her mouth. "Whud uh —" She wanted to call to Josh but no sound came out and now she thought she could hear his pale, frightened sobs above the silly banging of her head. Bang bang bang. And her armpits were so sore.

"Don't let the troll get me, Mummy. *Mummmeeee!* Please!"

The troll? What —?

Then something was hanging over her. A face. The eyes glassy and folded.

"NNNNOOOOOOOO!!" she heard herself yell, and in that instant she was awake, somewhere with no sound or light, sitting upright, her voice ringing off empty walls.

Souness had a guilty secret when it came to the press: sometimes she practised. At night Paulina would sit cross-legged on the kitchen table in her nightie, a cup of Horlicks in one hand, and yell out the questions: "Superintendent Souness —" She enjoyed the role. Sometimes she held the handle of a tennis racquet to Souness's mouth. "What do you say to people who feel that Brockwell Park should have been better searched?"

Souness, in her pyjamas, hands on hips, would obediently rehearse her answers. Paulina was a disciplinarian: "*No!* You need to show more *emotion*. Convince me you mean it."

"*What?* You'll be wanting *tears* next. I'm nae crying in front of eight million viewers — I'm not a shagging *Yank*, you know . . ."

This morning the rehearsals had paid off: she'd put in a fine performance, no one knocked her off balance, and when she told the press she was optimistic about finding Rory's killer soon, she meant it. She almost felt like humming a tune as she came into the office at eleven. She was surprised, and a little pissed off, to find the SIO's room locked from the inside.

"Jack?"

She peered through the window and saw him in her seat, glasses on, his feet up on the desk, holding the remote control at the TV, which had been turned to face him. Caffery was very pale, his hair looked as if it hadn't been combed in weeks. Souness rapped at the window.

He looked up. Quickly he turned off the TV, took off his glasses and came to the door, unlocking it.

"Ye all right?"

"Yeah — no sleep again."

"Aye, and ye stink of booze. What're ye watching?"

"Nothing. Daytime soap."

"Daytime soap." She unhooked her pager from her belt, threw it on the desk and opened the window. "Will you be a wee sweetheart and not tell the team that?"

"Sure, sure." He sat down at the desk and started popping Altoid mints into his mouth.

Souness felt a sudden pang of worry for him — he looked utterly beaten. She bent over and ruffled his hair. "Sure you're still with us, Jack?"

"I'm sure."

"Anything to report?"

"Yeah — got some prints . . ." He rubbed his eyes, moved his jaw around, loosening himself up, and handed her a folder.

"Prints — Jesus." She took the folder and shook out the photos. "How come no one told me?"

"Relax, they're glove prints. The ninhydrin found them."

"Ninhydrin? Isn't that for latents?"

"Yeah, but he's got something on the tips of the gloves and the ninhydrin pulled up the amino acid in it so it could have been sweat — or he could've got food on them, meat or something. We were lucky — the unit were trying for the wallpaper but some of the aerosol got on the floor and that's where we got the print."

"If it was sweat —"

"Sorry." He shook his head. "Already been there. First thing I said. No DNA. Course, they're trying — like they're trying with the semen."

"So you don't hold out much hope?"

"On prints and DNA? No." He stretched and rested his elbow on the desk, positioning himself between Souness and the VCR. "But we do know the make of gloves — the pattern was hatched, criss-cross."

"Marigold?"

"Exactly."

"Carmel Peach?"

"Doesn't wear rubber gloves. Except for cleaning the toilet upstairs. Never brings them downstairs — and, anyway, she only buys Asda's own brand."

"So we know what to spin for if we find him."

"That's right."

The gloves responsible for the peculiar and distinctive cross-hatch pattern on the floor of the Peaches' kitchen had travelled a long way since they had been removed from the leaves in Brockwell Park then dumped by Roland Klare into a skip on the Railton Road. The skip had been picked up the following day — just before the POLSA team had extended the search parameters — and driven to a dumpsite in Gravesend, within sight of the river, where the rubber gloves lay under two blue plastic bags of building rubble, unremarkable and unnoticed, save by the rats.

Caffery was pleased when Souness went out for a coffee and he could be alone. He didn't want company — he was still aching from the Scotch — and he felt as if there was nothing but air and electricity between his ribcage and pelvis. He flipped the tape out of the video and locked it with the others in his filing cabinet. It had been blank, of course, like all the others. He knew he'd have to turn them in now. Penderecki's body had been removed from the house and Environmental Health had come in to clean up: Ewan's history was being wiped.

He sat down and dialled Rebecca's mobile. *We need to talk*, he thought, *we can go through what happened, talk our way back to each other*. But something stopped him. He lost his nerve and hung up before she could answer. He sat for a few moments, breathing slowly in and out, then picked up the phone again, changed his mind again, put the receiver back in the cradle and stood, angry with himself. He was supposed to be at work.

"Right." He went into the exhibits room to get the crime-scene photos of the Peaches' house, took them back to the SIO's room and sat for a long time staring at them. He placed them alongside the Half Moon Lane photographs, then got the photographs of the developed glove prints that Quinn had given him. The Peaches' kitchen floor, the place the prints had been developed, was of cushioned linoleum. Ordinarily the unit wouldn't have used ninhydrin on this surface — it was sheer fluke and luck that the chemical, sprayed from an aerosol, had drifted and developed a print in the last place they'd have looked. The lino was decorated with rose-covered trellises. Caffery stared at the grid those trellises made, trying to catch the tail of an idea, trying to remember what had bothered him when he'd looked at these photos, his mind locking and jerking and trying to circle back to Rebecca.

The light on the photographs faded and the room fell into shadow. He looked up. A cloud canopy had draped itself over Shrivemoor and before long rain was peppering the building. He turned: everyone in the incident room had stopped work and was staring up at the windows, awed by the weather's giant fist gripping the building. Kryotos was there, and Logan, sitting on their desks, clutching their mugs and gazing at the rain. Caffery took off his glasses, went to the doorway and nodded at Kryotos.

She put down her coffee and came over. "What's up?"

"Marilyn," he murmured, "you got any aspirin?"

"You look like you need it — stay there."

She went back to her desk and began rummaging in the drawers. An unnoticed window in the corner had been left open and the desk beneath was being sprinkled with the rain. He turned to go back into the SIO's room, scratching his neck with a ballpoint, when suddenly, as if someone had called his name from behind, he stopped. He turned slowly to stare at the opened window. When Kryotos found the aspirin and straightened up she saw that he had come back into the incident room and was standing in the corner, staring at the water-damaged paper.

"Ooops," she said, closing the window and looking through the papers. "Nothing serious — no lives lost. Here." She held out the pain-killers.

He took them from her, then put his hand on her arm and led her into the SIO's room, sitting her down opposite him. "Marilyn."

"What?"

"How many cloudbursts do you think we've had this week?"

"God knows. About a hundred."

"When was the really bad one? The one with the thunder?"

"The day before yesterday, you mean?"

"No — before that."

"Last weekend — it rained all weekend. And Monday."

"Monday too. Yeah, I remember." It had been an almost tropical storm. Afterwards London smelt of the sea. "The day we found Rory."

"That's right. Why?"

"Oh . . ." He chucked the tablets into his mouth and swallowed, rubbing his forehead, not certain himself. "Oh, nothing. Nothing."

Caffery went to Donegal Crescent to speak to the Gujarati shopkeeper who had raised the alarm. He asked for tobacco, then showed his card, "Remember me?" and started to ask questions. He wanted to know what had made the dog start barking.

"I told you, the dog saw something running away. From the back of the house."

"But you were walking in the opposite direction and you were more than a hundred yards away. That's good hearing by anyone's standard."

The man blinked a couple of times then turned and fumbled for the tobacco and even from the back Caffery could see he was trying to think what to say.

He tried again. "Maybe something made the dog turn round."

The shopkeeper turned back. He put the tobacco down and straightened the pile of *Evening Standards* on the counter, shaking his head. "You won't confuse me. You won't. I was walking away and the dog looked round."

"Why?"

"Maybe there was a noise."

"It must have been a loud noise. You were a good distance from the Peaches' house so it must have been louder than just the sound of someone running."

The shopkeeper nodded. "Something louder than that."

"Maybe it was glass breaking?"

"Maybe," he agreed. "Maybe something like that. I didn't hear it, but the dog did. And then he started barking. That's all."

"That . . ." Caffery found change in his pocket and paid for the tobacco. He might have smiled but the aspirin wasn't working yet. "That's what I thought." Now he knew what was bothering him.

Benedicte was in a room, the spare room on the first floor, *her* room — she recognized the curtains and the scalloped light shade and the smell of new carpet. Her heart was pounding so hard it seemed to be throwing her brain around her skull.

"Hal?"

Is there someone in here?

"*Hal?*"

No answer. She tried to sit up but the room jolted to one side, moving in a rolling, maritime gait and she toppled forward on to her face, slamming her shoulder on the floor, grazing a sheet of skin from her cheek. For a moment she lay panting, her eyes rolling around in her head.

"*HAA-A-L! Hal, for Christ's sake, Hal.*"

There was blood on her tongue. "HAL!" She tried to crawl towards the door, and realized something was stopping her. She whipped round, her heart hammering, and saw that her ankle was attached to the radiator by a silvery cuff. *Handcuffs? Someone's been in the house. It wasn't a dream. Someone's been in the house. That dark scuttling thing I saw* — And then, with a sick, sick rush she understood. *Oh, God*, a frantic thump in her stomach, *the Peach family*; the police detective — *No harm in being aware* — Josh screaming that there was a troll in the garden — *the Peach family — and that means . . .*

"Josh?" She jerked forward, clawing in the direction of the door, yanking at the handcuff. "JOSH! Oh, my God, *Josh — Hal!*" She wrenched her foot, shaking it, tugging it, jamming her free foot into the skirting-board and pushing back. "*Josh!*" And then, when she couldn't move from the radiator, she lost all sense of logic and began to throw her weight against the floor, volleying off it, ramming her fists blindly into the floor. "*JO-SH!!!*"

In the silvery brand-new millennium, where everything was freshly stamped and newly named, and no one went to sleep safe in the knowledge they'd have the same job title by morning, AMIT, which had once been known as the murder team, was under new management: now part of the Serious Crime Operations Group, their chain of command was direct from the Deputy Assistant Commissioner at Scotland Yard and every week Souness went up to Victoria for a meeting with him — "Prayers", she called it, for the reverent expressions the team leaders wore in the DAC's presence. And every week she had a lot to gripe about when she got back to Shrivemoor. Today she arrived only a few minutes after Caffery got back from Donegal Crescent. She came in carrying a pile of dockets, her mobile phone and a McDonald's coffee balanced on top. She put it all down on the desk and was starting on her gripe when she noticed how Caffery was watching her — tipped back in his chair, arms crossed, waiting for her to finish so he could speak. "Oh," she groaned, seeing his expression, "what now?"

"Doing anything tonight?"

"Uh . . ." She pulled off her jacket and plugged in the mobile to charge. "Let me see, do you mean *was* I doing anything before I saw the look you've got on your face?"

"Yeah." He nodded. "Uh-huh."

"I *was* taking Paulina to the fair on Blackheath."

"Will you come over to Donegal Crescent with me? I don't want to screw up things at home for you, but I think it's important."

"Uh . . ." She looked at him sideways, thinking about this, clicking her tongue and scratching her head. After a while she sighed and hitched up her waistband. "See me — ever the professional. Come on, then — let me go for a quick slash and call Paulina, then I'll be with you."

* * *

Benedicte lay exhausted and shivering, unable to believe that she was still breathing in and out. Tears ran off her face, into her hair, she had flung herself so hard against the floor and the radiator that she'd cut her arm — there was blood on the radiator, the walls, the carpet.

"Josh," she wept. "Hal?" Any number of awful eventualities she could brew up in a second — Josh already dead, Josh wedged into the branches of a tree, Josh ambushed by that creature of his imagination: the troll. "Stop it," she muttered, dropping her hand over her eyes. "There is no such thing as a troll . . . Just get yourself together."

But how did he get in? Is the front door open? The front door must be open — and Hal? What happened to you? But from the colour of the light beyond the curtain, the sulphured yellow of street-lamps, and the silence, Benedicte knew it was night. Although it had seemed like only a few moments of unconsciousness she had, in fact, been here all day. And if it was night, and if Hal still hadn't come to get her, she knew it was because he *couldn't* come to get her.

She wriggled on to her back and pushed her hand inside her capri pants, creeping them inside her knickers to feel herself. Normal. Not sticky or wet. She squeezed her inner thighs. No bruises, no pain. She touched the soft flesh around her armpits and found it was bruised. Aching. Someone had dragged her up here — all the way up the stairs. Now she remembered her shoulders banging on the hard floor — *is that what he did to Carmel Peach?*

"Hal?" She turned her face to the floor and cupped her hands around her mouth. "*Hal? Josh? Can you hear me?*"

Silence.

She pressed her ear to the carpet, straining to hear a flicker of her child in the house below. The same way she had once held her breath and waited to feel his movement in her womb — just a small movement would be enough.

"JOSH?"

Silence.

Oh, God — nothing but silence. She wiped her eyes. "*Josh!*" Her voice was hollow. She wailed like an abandoned child. "JOSH? HAL?"

Caffery, pulling off the main road and into Donegal Crescent, suddenly braked. He unwound the window and looked up into the evening sky.

"What was that?"

"What was *what*?"

"Didn't you hear something?"

Souness opened the window and put out her head. It was almost dark but kids were still out with their bikes, playing under the street-lights. "What was it?"

He shook his head. "I dunno." He listened again. But now all he could hear was the thump-thump-thump of speed garage from an open window on the main road, the children with the bikes shouting to each other and the distant peep-peep-peep of crickets in the park.

Your imagination's on fire —

"Jack?"

"No. I'm imagining things." He closed the window. "Nothing." He parked the old Jaguar next to a Lambeth Council dumpster, reached across Souness into the glove compartment, pulled out a flashlight and showed it to her. "In case the leccy's on a key."

"Aye, you should have been in the SAS, son."

The houses in Donegal Crescent were curiously somnolent — curtains drawn, windows closed, as if even on this hot night the residents were trying to close out the truth, pretend the witness-appeal signs weren't lined up the road. Number thirty was different from the others. It wasn't the blue-and-white police tape, it wasn't the fact that there was a couple standing, arm in arm, looking at it like solemn tourists paying respect at a military grave. It was the simple, bald fact of what had happened here. The Property Services Department had cleaned up, put a new lock on the door — the Met would try to claim the expenses from the Peaches' insurance if they had any — but the Peaches had not been back to the house, not even to pick up belongings, and now kids had graffitied the walls. On the left of the door, just above a purple hebe, two words were written in black spray: *TROLL'S HOUSE*.

When Souness, standing on the doorstep, saw the words she began to stamp her feet as if they were cold.

"What's the matter?"

"Uh — nothing." She rubbed her nose. "Really, I'm fine."

"You ready?"

"Of course. Of course I'm ready."

He broke the seal and used DS Quinn's padlock key. Neither of them spoke. The hallway was dark. To their left, in the living room, the dull glow of street-lights came through a gap in the curtains and lay in a faint stripe across the sofa. Caffery felt for the light switch, but it clicked up and down emptily. The light was dead and somewhere in the darkness ahead the key meter bleeped.

"Told you."

"Aye, you did."

He shone the torch into the hallway, playing the beam up the stairs and around the walls. *This is where it happened*. His neck prickled suddenly as if the air had moved and he had to resist the urge to shine the torch into the living room to check that they were alone in the house. The hallway was small, walls pale, decorated with two seascape prints, both knocked off centre. He was aware of his face momentarily reflected in the glass as he moved down the hallway to the kitchen, the torch playing in front of him.

The meter was next to the cooker. He pulled out the key, pushed it back in, and with a sudden *whump* and whir the house came alive. The fridge started, the light in the hallway came on and Souness appeared in the doorway blinking, disorientated, looking around this normal yellow-and-white kitchen with the toaster on the worktop and the opened packet of Coco-Pops on the fridge. The SSCU's fingerprint dust was everywhere — on the fridge, the door, the window frame; purplish puffs of ninhydrin on the wallpaper, silver nitrate on the cupboards. The scent of pine from the board on the window partly masked the smell of old blood. Souness and Caffery stood silently in the kitchen, their faces odd, embarrassed to be here, thinking of what the Peach family had gone through in this house.

Benedicte was shaking, exhausted from screaming, blinking at her cuffed foot in the navy canvas deck shoe. Now that she had stopped struggling, now that the room and the house were silent, she was aware of a new sound. A strained, rasping sound that she hadn't noticed in her panic. It was coming from the wardrobe . . .

Oh, Jesus, she shivered, *what the . . .?*

She crawled forward as far as the cuff would allow, then dropped on to her stomach and snaked her body forward, like a landed eel, moving in silence, just the hush and shush of the carpet against her trousers, until she could reach the bottom of the wardrobe door with her fingertips. She scrabbled at the door with her nails, straining forward until it swung open.

"Oh —" Something was propped inside the cupboard. One crabbed shape against the far wall. Benedicte recoiled, pushing herself back against the radiator. "*Smurf?*"

In the cupboard the dark thing moved a little.

"*Smurf?*"

The old Labrador struggled feebly to her feet, the air in her lungs whistling noisily, her claws tapping at the floor of the wardrobe. She came hobbling out, wheezing and whimpering, careful not to put weight on the right front paw. Benedicte saw instantly that the leg was swinging, like a pendulum, from a point above the knee. The Labrador limped across the room and dropped with a sigh into the curled crook of her body. *Oh, my God, Smurf, what's he done to you?* She raced her hands across the dog's coat, down the knobbly legs with their tired old tendons, the little horny dew claw at the back of the ankle, until she found the reflective glimmer of wet fur — a soft, hot area. The bone must have cracked, pierced the skin, and retracted — when she touched it Smurf whimpered and tried to pull away.

Broken. The bastard broke her leg.

Whoever had done this to an ancient animal like Smurf wouldn't be afraid of hurting Josh. "Oh, Smurf." She buried her face in the dear fur, the sweet doggy smell of leaves and forest mulch. "What's *happening* to us, Smurf, what's happening?" Smurf craned her head round, trying to lick the tears from Benedicte's face, and that small demonstration of faith, of dependency, gave her sudden courage.

"OK." Taking a deep breath, teeth chattering uncontrollably, she levered herself into a sitting position. "OK, Smurf. I'm going to get this fucker." She stroked the dog's head. "You see if I don't."

She jerked up her knee, tugging experimentally, wondering if she could pull hard enough to break the copper radiator pipe. But her ankle was already bloodied from pulling — and shiny, like inflamed gums — so she sat up in a crouch and inspected the handcuffs. Four delicate blind head screws — tiny, hardly bigger than match heads. Decisive now, she straightened up and pulled off Hal's cord shirt. She undid her bra, held it to her mouth and nibbled at the fabric on the inside until the underwiring poked through and she could get a grip on it.

Strong enough to kill him, the shit. I don't care how big he is.

She drew out the slender curve of wire and used her teeth to strip the protective plastic ends away. Then, with the sharp end, she dug at the handcuff screws. But the wire buckled and mashed the screw heads. "Shit, shit, shit. Don't give up." She turned her attention to the radiator, pulled off the plastic knob and was exploring the copper pipe when Smurf, although she had been deaf for months, sat up abruptly and growled softly at the door. A low, shaky growl.

Benedicte froze — crunched where she was in a runner's crouch, veins protruding on her hands. *What the* — ? Fear took a long, calm lick at her spine, and all her fine plans dissolved. Something was *sniffing* along the bottom of the door.

CHAPTER EIGHTEEN

"Where do we start?"

"OK — let's go through it." Caffery put his briefcase on the kitchen counter, pulled out his glasses and the crime-scene photographs. The room had been stripped by Quinn's team: large chunks of the lino had been excised, rectangular sections of the curtains had been removed and the skirting-board where Rory's blood had been found was still covered in amido black and stick-on number tags. Glasses on the draining-board had been dusted and a toasted-sandwich-maker that had been taken away to the lab had been returned, the cord coiled and taped to the lid.

They thought that it was here, in this room, that the bite had been inflicted on Rory Peach — the damage had been enough for the eight-year-old to drop blood on the floor. The paper towel had soaked up the rest. Caffery put on his glasses, looked briefly at the photos of the kitchen and handed them to Souness. He tried to imagine the scene — Rory struggling, Alek Peach, chained and exhausted, unable to move, or simply unconscious. Alek was not in the photographs but the impression and the stain he had left on the floor was.

"So he was lying like this." He stood at the intersection of the rooms, on the floor divider, and swung his hand along the mark. "Across the floor between the kitchen and the living room — chained here," he indicated the living-room radiator, "and here to this radiator."

Souness wrinkled her nose. "Is there food left in the fridge?"

"Eh?" He looked round and sniffed. "Oh, that, no — I think it's just . . ." Carmel, Rory and Alek Peach had all defecated on themselves at some point in the three days. They hadn't had a choice. DS Quinn had been surprised by the amount of urine Carmel produced — it had seeped out on to the landing carpet. "I think that's just — them."

Souness made a face and opened the fridge to check. Inside were a few flowers of mould, fingerprint dust on a plastic carton of *I Can't Believe It's Not Butter* and a jar of pickle in the door compartment. Otherwise it was empty. She closed the fridge and looked around the room, her mouth pulled down at the sides. "Is that really what the smell is? Those poor wee fuckers."

"Come here." Caffery went into the hallway and stood at the bottom of the stairs. Rory Peach's water-gun, covered in fingerprint dust, lay on the first step. "Right. This is where Alek Peach says he was attacked — so what do we think?" They both looked back down the hallway at the kitchen, then Souness turned to the living room.

"Here. Probably came from in here."

"I think so too — so let's say he's come from in there, from the living room, and attacked Peach from behind. No blood, but that might not be important — he might not have started bleeding straight off."

"What're ye getting at?"

"I don't know — just bear with me." He stood with his arms out at ninety degrees, one hand pointing down the hall to the kitchen, one pointing into the living room. "Now, before he attacked Alek, he had broken in through the back door and then he must have overpowered Carmel — must have done that first, and taken her all the way up here." He took the stairs two at a time, coins jangling in his pocket. Outside the airing cupboard he stopped. "Hospital says she was dragged up the stairs — so he did that and somehow or other got her tied up in here —"

"Christ — smells even worse up here."

"— and then he went back downstairs like this." They both went back down, Souness with her fingers under her nose. "And waited — we're guessing — here." He stood in the doorway of the living room and raised his eyebrows at Souness. "Right?"

"Aye, I'll go along with that."

Caffery raised his eyebrows. "Well?"

"Well what?"

"He did all of this in total silence?"

"Uh." Souness shook her head. "I'm not with you."

"OK, listen. Carmel's no help, right? She has no idea where she was attacked; the last thing she remembers is making supper. But as for Alek . . ." He went to the closed door next to the kitchen and rested his hand on it. The basement. "Now *Alek* remembers." He opened the door and went down two or three steps. "Alek was here with Rory. They were playing on the PlayStation — that's when he wondered where Carmel was." Souness followed him down the stairs, peering at the room. The walls were decorated with Deep South memorabilia, crossed pistols, longhorn belt buckles, a framed picture of Elvis. The carpet was deep pile, white, and in one corner was a mirrored bar, a photograph of a young Alek Peach next to a Las Vegas-style fruit machine, wearing a cowboy hat, smiling at the camera. Caffery went down the last few stairs and beckoned to Souness. "Come down — I want to try something. Here." He switched on the TV and the PlayStation and handed Souness the controls. "Quake any good to you?"

"You'd be surprised. I'm an expert."

"I'm not surprised. Put it on loud as you want — turn up the volume."

She sat down with the controller, shuffling to get comfortable in the velour chair. "And where are you away to, then?"

"Just keep at it."

He went upstairs, into the kitchen, the rumbling sound of the PlayStation with him all the way. He stood outside on the doorstep and did what he'd been planning to do all afternoon. Within seconds Souness appeared at the top of the stairs. "Ye all right?"

"Yeah."

"What happened?"

"Broke a bottle. Out here on the patio. The door was closed."

"I heard it."

"Exactly." He could feel a little pulse of excitement flicking at the side of his mouth. "So why didn't Peach hear this back door being broken into?"

"You're saying he's *lying*?"

"No — I believe him. I believe him *one hundred per cent* when he says he didn't hear that glass breaking on Friday night. Because . . ." He laid the crime-scene photos out on the worktop. ". . . because I think the glass broke on Monday."

"Duh — sorry, Jack, I'm not with ye."

"OK, OK." He handed her the photos and went to the back door. "Now the glass fell inwards onto the floor when the door was closed — see on the photos?"

"Aye."

"Which is why we all — even Quinny — assumed the offender did it breaking in. He smashed the glass, put his hand through and unlocked it. The door opens . . ." He pushed it open to demonstrate. "It opens outwards —"

"So the glass on the ground wouldn't have been disturbed."

"Exactly."

"But?"

He nodded. "*But* if that's what happened then Alek would have heard it — even from downstairs."

"So you think —"

"So I think it happened on *Monday* when the offender was *leaving*. Maybe it fell out when he slammed the door, or maybe Rory kicked it out in the struggle. It's the sound the shopkeeper's dog heard. Look," he tapped the first photo, "this is how the kitchen looked when we got here. Glass on the floor."

"Aye."

"There was a rainstorm on Monday morning — a cloudburst. If the window had already been smashed those curtains should've been damp, but they weren't. And that glass on the floor from the break-in — it hasn't been moved around, right?"

"Uh . . ." She squinted at it. "No — that's just fallen straight out. Just sat there, hasn't it?"

"So all the time he was moving around in here it didn't get moved? Not once?"

"Could he not have just avoided it? Walked round it?"

"Then how did he get his prints *under* the glass?"

Souness was silent. She rubbed her head until the skin under the colourless hair became pink. "Uh . . ."

"Look at this photo." He handed her the photo taken after the glass had been removed and the ninhydrin developed. He carefully counted the cross-hatched trellises on the lino. "There." He stood with his feet on either side of two faint brown stains just next to the door — the ninhydrin glove prints. This part of the floor had been under glass when the police arrived. "His prints were there before that window smashed." He leaned forward, tapping the photo to make the point. "He didn't come in through that back door."

"Then how? Everything else was battened down, Peach says all the doors were locked — the TSG had to use the sodding *Enforcer* to get in."

"Exactly." He took the photos from her and dropped them into his briefcase. "You know what I think?"

"What?"

"I think Peach let him in." He took his glasses off and looked at her. "I think Alek Peach knows *exactly* who did this to them."

The snuffling stopped as abruptly as it had started. Benedicte held her breath — *Think, Ben, think — What the — ?* Out of the hissing silence came the sound of water being poured on to the door. She rocketed back against the radiator.

Petrol — it's petrol —

The noise stopped and then she heard the long release of gas, or air. He was spraying something. *Hairspray? Something to start the fire?* Smurf growled softly, her fur pumped straight up along her spine and around her neck like a lizard ruff. Then in the hallway the thing, the troll, huge — *oh, Jesus, he sounds too heavy to be human* — turned and lumbered away, banging against the walls like a cornered sow, slithering and bumping down the stairs.

Then, quite suddenly, silence.

"Hal? JOSH!" *That breathing sounded like an animal. Not a human being . . .* "Josh!" She bawled so loudly that Smurf lifted her old, deaf head and howled along with her. "*JOSH!!!*"

When she couldn't scream any longer, and when there was no noise from downstairs, no exploding *whump* of fire, she dropped exhausted on to the floor, shaking uncontrollably. She rolled on to her side and pulled her fingernails along the marbled, transparent flesh on her inner arm, scratching and gouging, and trying not to think about what might happen to Josh.

Caffery stopped outside the Blacka Dread music shop on Coldharbour Lane to let Souness trot back down the road and pick them up some food from a takeaway. He smoked a cigarette while he waited, and watched the local pond-life — a white guy in a leather deerstalker hat was dealing on the corner next to the Joy clothes shop, and from the Ritzy came a trio of trendy young black guys in sharp fawn leather jackets, with bleached blond hair and goatees. They saw the dealer and subtly crossed away from him to the other side of the street. A girl on a cranky bike, her mirrored Indian skirt caught in the mudguard, shouted something to the dealer as she cycled by.

Caffery lit another cigarette and leaned back, suddenly realizing that he was opposite the deli Rebecca sometimes came to for mozzarella, still dripping in its muslin. Closed now, but he remembered her wandering with her bright, intrigued eyes among the loops of mountain salami, sea-green olive-oil bottles, dusty tins of something untranslatable: "Probably *merda d'artista*," she had whispered to Caffery, who had stood speechless, transfixed by a row of air-dried serrano hams hanging by the knuckles along the back of the shop: afraid that Rebecca would look up, scared of what she would make of those odd, dangling shapes. Now, from the car, he could see them, ghostly in the blue light of a fly-killer. He wished he had taken her by the arm then and said, "Do you ever think about how Bliss left you — suspended just like that, suspended like a piece of meat?"

"Oh, God — not this again." He rubbed his face wearily, wondering what she was thinking — wondering where she was. He knew she wasn't at home crying, scrubbing herself in the shower; he knew she wasn't shivering in a blanket in a medical examination room at the local station, dark rings around her eyes. He had a sudden picture of her looking over her shoulder at him, blood on her mouth, watching his face. What was she thinking? *Rapist?* Maybe she was happy he had been proved the foxy, unclean thing she said he was. Maybe there was no working back from that.

"Hey!" Souness was tapping on the window. "Will ye take that glaekit expression off your face and let me in the shagging car?" She was sweating from standing in the steamy takeaway. She'd got gungo pea soup in polystyrene cups and two Jamaican patties. "It's all I could find. Don't worry, it's all vegetarian — no billy goat in any of it."

They ate on the way back to Shrivemoor — Souness got soup on her tie and patty flakes all over her suit, but she didn't notice. She was still thinking about Alek Peach: "So why not just fess up and tell us who it was?" At Shrivemoor she swiped her card and they got into the lift. "It's his own wain, for Christ's sake."

"Guilt. Maybe he's into something — maybe with the business, maybe . . . I don't know, but maybe he's in so bad that this was a reprisal. He'd feel guilty, wouldn't he? Wouldn't he feel guilty if he'd done something that had brought this on to his family?"

"I don't know." She stared blankly at her fractured reflection in the aluminium lift walls. "He'd have to be well shitted up by whoever it is not to report them." She sighed. "But I'm with you — something's not adding up."

"Less and less is. He says he couldn't hear Rory the whole time he was tied up. Don't you think that's odd?"

"Hmmm . . ."

"If he couldn't hear Rory, how come Carmel *could*? She was," he reached up and knocked on the ceiling of the lift, "*upstairs* — and she could hear him crying. But Alek couldn't?"

"I did wonder." She looked at him sideways. "You think he's lying?"

"Look at the inconsistencies. The photographs Carmel heard being taken? The ones Alek knew nothing about? And this holiday thing? Luck? Or was it not such a coincidence after all? Maybe someone *knew* they were going on holiday, someone *knew* they wouldn't get disturbed." The lift doors opened and Caffery got out, walking backwards, looking at Souness. "Now I keep asking myself, how would a *stranger* know that they were going on holiday? Wouldn't it be more likely that it was someone they knew?"

"OK. OK." She swiped her card and they went into the deserted incident room. The monitors were dark and silent; Kryotos, as she did every day, had washed everyone's mugs and left them on a tray in the corner. Souness put her hands on the desk and leaned over towards him. "Jack. I think you're on to something. I don't know *what* but I think you've got a point . . ."

Benedicte lay on her back, exhausted, thirsty. She had felt through every inch of her prison, moving her body like a sidewinder, rubbing her elbows raw. She could reach the wardrobe but even at full stretch the door and the window fell more than a yard from her fingertips. She used every atom of energy trying to buckle the copper pipe — she had pulled so hard at the handcuff that her ankle had swollen and was almost enfolding the cuff, and the handcuff screws were ruined she'd jabbed at them so much with the wire.

It was dark, but she'd learned quickly how to estimate time. Trains, distant, on the other side of the park — she'd heard them once or twice before in Brixton: sometimes at night the sky lit up momentarily like white lightning from an electrical fault on the rail, and once, the June night that England had beaten Germany in the Eurocup, she'd heard the drivers blowing their horns at each other. Now the trains had a beautiful cadence in the quiet, they reminded her that people were out there, and the rhythm of them began to make sense. When they stopped she estimated it must be between twelve and one in the morning.

From downstairs she had heard nothing. Now she could smell the liquid she'd heard pouring on to the landing floor. It wasn't petrol, it was urine. He had come up here, stood *only a few feet away from the bathroom*, and pissed against the door. *The disgusting little shit*. Just be grateful, she told herself, that it wasn't petrol.

She sat up, began to unroll her buckled body. Urine. She had avoided that indignity until now — but she knew there was no point in holding on. "Gotta pee, Smurf." She had to stop herself apologizing to the dog. "It's got to be done."

She pulled her trousers and knickers down over the free foot and crumpled them around the bound ankle. With a pinched, contrapuntal squirm, she rotated herself so that she was crouching facing the radiator, holding on to it for balance, and crab-shuffled one leg sideways so she was as far from the shackled foot as possible. She held the trousers clear with one hand, feeling like crying as the carpet under her feet grew wet and warm. She hoped, *dear God*, she hoped they'd be out of here before she had to move her bowels.

Suddenly in the hallway downstairs something moved. The front door slammed. Benedicte stayed quite still, facing the radiator, trousers around one foot, hardly daring to breathe.

He's gone? *Then what about* . . .

"*Josh?*" Her voice rose frantically and, forgetting the mess under her on the floor, she hopped around like an injured animal, getting hopelessly, pathetically, tangled in her underwear. "HAL? JOSH? JOSH — GIVE ME

BACK MY SON! *JOSH!*" She hammered on the wall, screaming, bawling. And when no one answered she collapsed on the floor, on her back in her own urine, put her hands over her face and sobbed.

In the back of the cupboard in the incident-room kitchen Caffery found a dusty, forgotten bottle of Tesco's gin and some flat tonic water. He and Souness had spent an hour sitting at Kryotos's workstation, finishing off the Laphroaig and hashing through their next move. Bela Nersessian, they both agreed, was the person to speak to. They'd bring her to the office and start lightly, just casual inquiries into Alek Peach, his personal life, his business dealings if he had any. The family liaison officer set up the interview for the following day, and Caffery felt a small lift of spirit. Souness, too, was satisfied that they had a new direction. At 11p.m. she decided she was over for the night.

"Ye should do the same." She stood in the doorway with her jacket on, trying to scratch off the soup on her tie, spitting on her finger and rubbing fruitlessly at it. "You'll be no good to me, Jack, shagged out."

"Yup." He held a hand up. "I'm right behind you."

But he wasn't. He had no intention of going home. When she had gone he took Penderecki's cache from the lock-up filing cabinet, and sat with a mug of warm G and T at his elbow, staring out of the window, building houses from the videotapes. Several times he picked up the phone and put it down. Rebecca hadn't called and he didn't know how to approach it. *Dark fathoms under your feet, Jack*. At 11.30p.m. he pushed the tapes aside, swallowed the G and T, took off his glasses, and dialled her mobile.

She answered, sounding a little indistinct.

"Rebecca — where are you?"

"In bed."

"My place?"

"No. Mine." He pictured her dreamy and warm, one long brown arm stretched out across the pillow, her hair pulled above and behind in a long helix — serpentine, like a diving mermaid's. "I'm in my bed."

"Look —" He took a deep breath. "I'm sorry — Rebecca, I love you — I really — I —" He stared out at the lights of Croydon not knowing how to put it. *But this is as far as I can go. I can't give it up — I can't leave that house and you're something I don't understand any more*. "I'm sorry, Rebecca —"

"You're dumping me."

"No — I — look, I've tried very hard — I've tried hard, but something's happening to you — and I just seem to make it worse —"

"You are, you're dumping me, aren't you?"

He sighed. "What would you want me to do after last night? You couldn't go on with me after that — you don't want that."

"*Don't tell me what I want!*" Her voice rose. "How dare you tell me what I want? *I* don't know what I want so how can *you* possibly know?" She stopped. He could hear her breathing at the other end of the line, as if she was trying not to cry.

"Look . . ." He wound the phone cord around his finger and found himself saying, "If it would make you feel better, then report it. Tell them I raped you. Tell them what you said about Bliss too."

"*What?*"

"Report it." It would be suicide, the end of everything, if she did, but he suddenly realized he didn't much care any more. "Seriously — get it over with. I'm not going to fight."

"You're crazy —"

"No. I'll take the consequences." He paused. "Rebecca?"

"What?" Her voice was small, distant.

"I'm sorry. I really am."

"Yeah." She put the phone down.

Jesus. He sat motionless for a long time, staring at the dead receiver in his hand. Then he hung up and sat forward, rubbing his eyes, pulling his hands down his face. "Fuck fuck fuck." *What have you done? What have you done? How did it ever get this screwed up?* He'd had no indication, no reason to expect that the words were suddenly going to come out like that. *How does it feel?* he asked himself. *Does it feel good to self-destruct? Do you feel free?*

He sighed and pressed his fingers against his forehead. *It's all over, then, isn't it?* He couldn't sleep, he couldn't go home. He sat forward, and rolled a cigarette, staring out at the night as he smoked it. When he'd finished it, he stood, took the Half Moon Lane photos from the envelope on the window-sill, looked at them for a long time, then put them back into the envelope. Then he went into the incident room and detached Marilyn's zip drive from her computer, brought it back into the SIO's room and plugged it into his own PC. His hands were shaking as he took Penderecki's disks from the filing cabinet and sat down at his desk.

The zip disks were labelled from one to nine, and each one contained up to a hundred jpegs, harvested from Russian websites, from ever-moving newsgroups. Caffery had been on a day course to Hendon to learn how woefully ill-equipped the police were to do anything about tracking the posters of these photographs. The process of serving warrants on ISPs was lengthy and the perpetrators knew it — as soon as they felt the ground getting hot beneath their feet they'd move to another service provider. Among the files Caffery found saved newsgroup postings where users dealt passwords for sites, tips on masking ISP info, adverts for "cop software" "to tidy up your hard drive sectors for those awkward technical support visits . . .". He found the address of a safe mailbox to dump AVI and JPG files, the entire series of the notorious "kindergarten" photos, updated URLs for Russian "Lolita" websites, binary newsgroup postings with familiar filenames: FreshPetals.jpg, Buds.jpg, SweetAngel.jpg. That night he saw every type of child porn imaginable: some of the photos wouldn't have looked out of place in a high-gloss coffee-table book, beautiful, soft focus, blond children in T-shirts, shorts, bare-chested under dappled trees — but some of the files at the other end of the spectrum made his stomach turn, weathered to it though he was. He had to drink a little more G and T and press his palm flat on his stomach. Some of the photographs were so cropped it was impossible to tell the sex of the child.

He worked on, until he had a blister on his thumb pad from moving the mouse, imagining that he would find a clue in the corner of a photo — *for fuck's sake, what are you expecting to see?* And then, very suddenly, he sat back and released the mouse. It was 1.30 a.m., the traffic noises outside had long died away, and the building was quiet. He turned slowly, an odd sensation racing across him, to look at the videocassettes. Something had occurred to him. He had just realized why there were no pictures on them.

Quickly he went into the exhibits room and got latex gloves from the evidence grab bag — when he handed the tapes over he didn't want the unit thinking he'd jumped into them like a nonce — filled up his mug and switched off all the lights in the incident room. *But it's classic nonce behaviour, Jack, just think how this would look, sad old Jack with his booze and his smutty vids.* Back in the office he found the old Swiss Army knife in his jacket pocket, pulled up a chair and positioned the Anglepoise over the desk.

Rebecca was sitting in her studio with the curtains open, holding a vodka and orange and staring at her solitary reflection in the dark window a few feet away. Beyond it the lights in Canary Wharf were on, and the other great citadels of Docklands blazed in the sky, but she hardly saw them. She was trembling. "Right —

right. OK — fine," she said. "You didn't expect this — but that's OK, just keep calm, keep it in perspective." She downed the drink in two straight gulps and looked at her hands. They were still shaking. "For heaven's sake, calm down — it's not the end of the world." She went into the kitchen, sat at the table and filled her glass. Vodka: the secret drink — the alcoholic's drink. Her mother's drink. It's supposed not to smell. But Rebecca could smell it. She had learned the smell of it at her mother's breast: as a baby she had tangled the smell of vodka with the smell of milk — for years alcohol on her mother's breath could make her salivate.

She swallowed the drink, made a face, and looked down into the empty glass, peering at the line of orange pulp. *Just get on with it — maybe you and Jack, maybe you weren't ever supposed to . . .* She stood, almost lost her balance, recovered and took the glass to the sink, rinsed it out, and poured another drink, marvelling at the way the juice dropped into the clear, oily vodka. Yes, that looked good. And it tasted good — it tasted so good that she swallowed it whole and quickly poured another. Through the door she could see the stupid little sculptures lined up in the studio. "Your work!" she said out loud, holding up the glass, toasting them. *They make the place look like a bloody sex shop*. She should smash them all to pieces — *a grand gesture — an artistic gesture*. Yes! She finished the drink, put the glass down, and walked decisively, in a perfect straight line, to the studio, only swaying once, pleased at how sober she was. But by the time she'd got to the door she'd forgotten what she was going to do. She stood there for a moment, her hands on the doorposts, trying to remember where she was headed and, when she couldn't remember, turned, shaking her head — *silly cow* — went back to the kitchen table and picked up the vodka bottle. She'd had a lot already, she thought, holding the bottle up to the light, and she supposed she really shouldn't have another. *But this is different*, she told herself, *quite different*.

She took the next drink into the bathroom, a little unsteady now that the vodka was taking effect, and stood in front of the mirror. "Cheers," she said to her reflection. "Here's to you and Jack." She downed the vodka in three swallows, banging the glass carelessly against her teeth. *I will survive*, she thought, feeling immediately sick and closing her eyes, resting her hand on the sink, taking deep breaths. What? Did you really want to end up hitched to a *cop*? Coffee mornings with the other wives, whingeing about the hours you spend on your own, and maybe, if you're lucky, a couple of brandies with your husband in the golf-club bar on a Sunday? When she looked up the room had stopped swaying and her own stupid face was staring back at her. "Oh, just go away." She flapped her hand at the mirror. "Go away." She bent over the sink to rinse out the glass, but there must have been something on her fingers, because now the glass was slipping out of her grip and although she made a grab for it her fingers didn't seem to be working properly, and instead of catching it she just knocked it sideways against the tap. It rebounded and shattered in the sink.

She stood for a moment staring at it, the noise still moving around her skull. *Shit, Becky, you're drunk.* She went into the kitchen and made a drink in a fresh glass. *You need to be careful with the vodka*. She didn't want a hangover, so after this one she was going to stop. *The fridge*, she thought, distractedly, *why is the fridge so loud?* And then she thought, *You must clear up the glass, or you'll cut yourself.* She put the drink down, determined to stop with the vodka now — *now, before you do something stupid* — got newspaper from under the sink to put the glass in, and hurried back into the bathroom, quick, too quick, sliding on something, and before she had time to realize what was happening she was on the floor, on her bottom on the floor, the newspaper still clutched in her hand.

She sat there for a moment, blinking at the wall like a doll with moving eyelids, wondering if she was going to laugh about it. She should laugh about it. She should laugh about it and then she should get up, but she didn't have the energy and the room was spinning. *Get up, Becky, get up*.

She roused herself, groping upwards for the towel rail, pulling herself up off the floor, head still whirling. She was going to clear up the glass and then have a Horlicks and go to bed and she'd be OK, but the towel rail came away in her hand, snowing plaster down and dropping her back on to the floor, her head banging on the bath. And there she stopped, propped up against the bath, one leg tucked under her body, her hair all over her face, and began to sob.

* * *

It had been one of the Russian "Lolita" websites that did it. The name *Lolita*. From his time in Vice he remembered a seized set of the infamous Rodox/Colour Climax Lolita videos. For Lolita 1–12 the Dutch dealers had been careful to export the videotape cracked out of its casing so it didn't X-ray as a cassette and arouse the suspicions of customs or post-office workers. Mainstream porn often came into the country like this. But Caffery wondered if Penderecki had gone one step further.

Hunched over the videos like an East End jeweller, cigarette in his mouth, glasses all the way down his nose, carefully he unscrewed the plastic casing. The shell cracked — he opened it cautiously, like a precious book, lifting out the white plastic spools. He put the cigarette in the ashtray and gently pressed the tape between his lips, soft-biting it. When he opened his mouth the tape had stuck to the top lip. This was exactly what he'd betted on: the mylar coating was on the inside. The tape had been taken off its spool, flipped over and rewound.

He dug in the Swiss Army knife, released the little white clip from the spool and flipped the tape over. It took him twenty minutes to respool it, a roll-up wedged between his teeth, the G and T dwindling in the mug. *And this stray end in here — on this spool*. He inserted it in the casing and tightened up the little screws. He pushed the tape in the VCR and aimed the remote control at it.

"There isn't much that's surprising in kiddie porn," one of the "dirty squad" had told him in the eighties.

"Once you get over the fact that it's kids, then it's not all that much different from adult porn. Of course, getting over the fact that it's kids is the trick. If you can't do that you're buggered. Pardon the expression."

Caffery prepared himself, sat himself down and waited for the feelings, the panic, the sadness, to come at him. And they did: as he watched the videotapes all the feelings came back, only this time they were duller. And this time he found himself irritated by them. *There you go*, he thought throwing down the Army knife, *you're almost resigned to it*.

Where did all these children come from, he wondered. Where were they now? This small blonde girl he was looking at, she could have only been about three foot tall, standing in front of a pink and gold painted dressing-table, scalloped ankle socks on, her hair in bunches. *Who was she?* Where was she now? What had they said to convince her that it was right and good to smile and hold her legs open for the camera?

He sat through poorly lit scenes in trailers, hotel bedrooms, one on a balcony in broad sunlight — flags on a golf course visible in the distance. Slowly he began to realize exactly what he'd stumbled on to: these videos weren't porn for Penderecki's personal use, they were more serious than that. They were first-generation tapes, he was sure of it: the quality and the manner in which they had been stored suggested they were master tapes. Caffery thought that he'd come smack bang to the coal-face of a paedophile ring. This was their payload, stored by Penderecki next to the railway track.

"Fuck."

He stood up, windmilling his arms, trying to get rid of the crick in his neck. He lit another cigarette and paced the office, smoking and staring at the screen. What he should do at this point was call the paedophile unit. What he *should* do was call Souness at home, wake her up, get Paulina on the phone. But Penderecki had sent him these tapes for a reason. He put out the cigarette and went into the incident room, locked the door to the passageway and came back to the office. The tapes were staying with him, he decided, until he knew what message — or what torment — Penderecki intended him to get from them.

Eleven twenty-minute tapes. Almost four hours. They seemed to constitute only five different episodes, some spanning more than three tapes, and he sensed from the quality and changing clothes styles that the sessions had taken place over ten or more years. He worked into the night, letting one play as he respooled the next. A one-man assembly line: spooling, watching, spooling, watching.

By 6 a.m. he had watched all the tapes and there was only one that he wanted to see again. It was possibly the most shocking of the tapes, for the simple reason that the abuser who leaned on the creaking fake leather sofa to unzip and fellate a boy of, Caffery guessed, about eleven, was a woman. She had been in four other tapes, but this one was the one he pushed back into the VCR and rewound.

When Benedicte could cry no longer she lay on the floor, on her back, in a straight line next to the radiator so that her ankle wasn't bent, and imagined she was still a child, her mother's face above hers, downy and warm as the underside of a wing, smiling as she bent over for a goodnight kiss. She thought about Josh, little Josh, when he was a baby, so new that part of her had been jealous that she would never be so new again. And Hal picking Josh up and holding him above his head and waggling him, his fat little legs wiggling with delight as if he could swim through the air. Nights when he had a fever, Hal rolling a glass over the rash terrified that meningitis would come and steal him away. They'd always known there were black holes in the world: Sarah Payne; Jason Swift; a little boy knocked over by a truck in Camberwell; another falling from a fourteen-storey high-rise. She thought of him sprawled out in front of the telly, picking a scab on his knee, and all she could think was how much she wanted to take his socks off and kiss his little toes. He could walk all over the house in his muddy boots, he could scribble on the walls, put footballs through every window in the house, steal her life, shout abuse at her — if only she could see him again just once. If only she could smell his hair again. Just once.

A little before dawn Benedicte fell asleep in spite of herself, a fevered, infected sleep with lights in her brain and voices careening around her skull.

In Croydon the bottom of the sky, jagged between the skyscrapers, had brightened to a cool opal. It was nearly 6a.m. and downstairs the TSG Tannoy blurted commands through the building. No one would come into the incident room for another two hours. Caffery was watching the video again, aimlessly doodling on a scrap of headed Met notepaper. The woman weighed — he'd squinted and tried to guess when he first saw her enter the frame — maybe fifteen, sixteen stone? She had a flat boxer's nose, flaky skin, dark glossy hair and was dressed in a black camisole and satin mules. The boy glanced up occasionally at the camera, as if to say, "Am I doing it right?" and the brunette made obscene little *moues* as she lightly scratched the inside of his thigh with her scarlet and black nail designs. At the beginning of the tape she came into the room and sat on the sofa, and for a moment she passed close enough to the camera for a tattoo on the top of her arm to come into focus: a heart behind prison bars. Caffery absently scratched the image into the doodle.

It wasn't just the woman's appearance and the slack, rather blank way she was abusing the child on the sofa that had struck him: it was the astonishing carelessness with her identity. Maybe because these tapes were intended to be edited a surprising number of them revealed clues about the abuser — ordinarily any adult taking part in a film like this would be at pains to keep their face hidden. Identifying peculiarities would be covered, sheets hung over bookcases, labels cut out of any clothes the children wore — most pictures that made it to the internet had identifying features airbrushed out with graphics software. Not so in these tapes. He got glimpses of faces, records, CD titles — of this tattoo. In three of the videos he could actually hear muttered conversations off-camera, men speaking, commenting on the action, muttering about what they could do to the child on screen. Caffery could even hear names in the conversations: *Stoney, Rollo, Yatesy*. He carefully noted down everything.

There was no audio on the tapes of the brunette, but in this one there were plenty of visual clues to work with. Behind the peeling, fake-leather sofa was a veneer display cabinet, lighted from above, and he could see decorative glasses, a pile of duty-free Silk Cut boxes, a photograph in a gold frame. But more importantly, and more unbelievably, there was a single, blatant identifier in the earliest part of the tape. Caffery paused the tape and rewound. Played. The woman stood and crossed the room. He rewound. She crossed the room backwards, sinking on to the sofa and crossing her legs. Stop. Play. She uncrossed her legs, stood and crossed the room. Stop. Rewind. Back to the sofa. Stop. Play. Back and forward. Eventually he froze the tape where he wanted it.

As she crossed the room she passed, briefly, a window. The swishglide curtains were slightly open, and although it could only have been ten frames or so, less than half a second, Caffery had glimpsed a distinctive yellow flare. He leaned forward now, staring intently at the screen, and put the ageing VCR on to frame-by-frame, letting the brunette move jerkily forward until the yellow was clear. He paused the tape. He tore the top sheet of paper from the pad and found a pen. His pulse was racing. Now that the tape had stopped he could see exactly what that yellow splash was. Outside the window of the room someone had parked a car. For two frames the number-plate, although at an angle, was legible. He scribbled the number down and went into the incident room.

The PNC2 computer could fit a name to an index number in seconds. By 6.05a.m. he knew who owned the car, and Phoenix, PNC2's newly attached database, had told him a lot about the owner. Things were starting to make sense. He pushed his chair away from the terminal, rolled it across the incident room to the tray marked "Receiver In" next to Kryotos's workstation, and picked up the sheaf of returned Actions forms for Kryotos to type into HOLMES. He wanted to know if during the day the paedophile unit had detailed any of the team to speak to one Carl Lamb of Thetford, Norfolk.

CHAPTER NINETEEN

(24 July)

The hallway was quiet. Not silent: on the landing the electric security timer trundled through its increments, but otherwise the hall was quiet. Not a creak of board or a shift of air. At 6.30 a.m. the timer clicked through and the lamp on the landing switched off. Builders' sand had been trodden into the stair carpet and someone had been spray-painting on the walls. Visible from the hallway were the letters **HAZA** — painted in red. To anyone mounting the stairs the final letters were visible at the bend in the staircase, across the front of the spare bedroom door: **RD**. The entire graffiti read **HAZARD**. Next to it was the cross and circle symbol representing the female.

Caffery left Shrivemoor before anyone arrived and took all of Penderecki's tapes home. The black Beetle with the lime interior wasn't outside, and when he checked in all the rooms he found himself almost disappointed to see that Rebecca hadn't defied him and wasn't sitting up in his bed smoking a cigarillo. The sheets had been changed, she had washed the old ones and left them in the dryer. Apart from that she had left almost no sign of herself. "That's what you asked for," he murmured, "and that's what you got."

He wrapped the videos in two plastic bags, secured them with tape, pushed them to the darkest corner under the stairs, and locked the door. He showered, slept a deep, jetlaggy sleep for two hours — on the sofa, the bedroom smelt of Rebecca — and just before 10a.m. drank coffee and got into the car. It was a hot day — he wore a short-sleeved shirt and shades and kept the window open. He knew he looked like a gubernatorial security guard in a southern state, Texas maybe.

Carl Lamb had died within the last month. Judging by his criminal and prison record his death had left the world a safer place, but one thing the authorities had never picked up about him was that he had been a nonce. There was no intelligence linking him to Penderecki, and his criminal record had been for breaking and entering, GBH, ABH, aggravated vehicle theft and a string of credit-card frauds. But when Caffery checked where and when he'd done time he discovered that he'd been in Ashworth at the same time as Penderecki. The stray ends were beginning to come together. Penderecki had meant Caffery to take this journey.

There was a sister still alive, Tracey Lamb, aged forty-two. She had a minor criminal record, had done little bits of time here and there. Caffery wondered, as he drove through Suffolk, through quiet villages coiled with climbing roses, past white weather-boarded dovecotes, cakes of saltlick glittering in the sun, he wondered if Tracey Lamb had a tattoo on her right arm.

The roads grew emptier as he reached the poorer end of Suffolk, the north, where it bled into Norfolk. Here the population lived in isolated farmhouses or in crumbling ribbon developments, and the only signs that he wasn't alone on this planet were burnt-out cars on the verges and the occasional ghost filling station with rusted petrol pumps on weed-covered forecourts. This was Iceni territory, blood and isolation in the air, as if Boudicca herself was shadowing him through her land. *You could do anything out here and no one would know.*

Rebecca's face came to him once, but it was OK, he found he could push her away. He could push her out on either side, out into the slipstream of the Jag, and off into the fields that stretched away from the car into the shimmer of midday.

He almost missed the turning in the trees. It was on a deserted, heat-cracked road, marked by a rusting sign, "4×4 tyres" hanging from a post. He had to brake and reverse up, then swing the Jag into the grassed-over drive. The ground was rutted, and tangled trees on either side created a natural alley. He was aware of things squatting out in the nettles: piles of breezeblocks, old abandoned caravans and chassis, a rusted shipping container as tall as a man standing up straight in the trees. After a hundred yards or so he stopped the car — safer to continue on foot, safer to let the grass muffle his footsteps — and climbed out. He was immediately struck by the quiet: the only sound was the distant mosquito whine of a jet from Honnington RAF base.

Another hundred yards on and he found himself at the edge of a clearing shielded from the rest of Norfolk by a ring of towering sycamores. Nothing moved. On his right stood a corrugated iron hangar, the words "Sports Cars" in chipped paint on the lintel, the doors open to reveal the decomposing remains of a business of sorts — a crumbling engine hoist, rusting Elf oil cans and a pile of Land-Rover roofs. Beyond the hangar, across weed-blistered tarmac, he could see the pebble-dashed walls of a house, square like a nuclear bunker, nettles growing up to the windows. And now that he listened he realized that somewhere a TV was playing. He took a few steps forward and saw, parked against the house — *Jesus fucking Christ* — the Fiat from the video. A sheet of chicken wire lay up against it; it was covered in nettles, the springs in the seat lolled out like spent jack-in-the-boxes, but it was so ridiculously *exactly* the same car it almost made him feel he was walking into a set-up. The video, then, would have been shot from inside that window. He inched a little closer.

The curtains were drawn and he had to get very close to see through the crack. The light from the TV flickered on the walls. It was gloomy inside but he knew instantly that he was looking at the room from the video. Full of furniture, the walls decorated with cheaply framed oils, a gilt-covered starburst clock, four 200-packs of imported Rothman's on the book-shelf. *This is it — this is it*. And then he saw her.

A woman, huge, sitting on the sofa in the shaded room, blue light playing across her face. She wore pale nylon knickers and an ageing bra. Her legs were too enormous to close — the whorled fat on the insides of her thighs forced them out in a stubby foreshortened V. Her blonde hair, worn with a fringe, was pulled severely back on top of her head and secured there with a black band, revealing small gold earrings. Next to her sat a mug, an ashtray and a packet of Silk Cuts. *Is that her? The hair's different*. The woman in the video had been a brunette. *A wig then — in the video she must have worn a wig*. At that moment she put down her cigarette in the ashtray, lifted a small polystyrene cup to her mouth, spat a glob of brown sputum into it, wiped her mouth, rested the cup on her belly, picked up her cigarette and went back to the TV. As she settled back he saw a tattoo on her arm and a little bolt of hope went through him. He was meant to be here.

The back door was locked, so he went round to the front. The paint was peeling and there was a disposable barbecue on the porch, full of rainwater and flies. He looked through the window and could see the blonde through the door at the end of the corridor, her legs bathed in blue TV light. He knocked on the window.

In the living room her legs jerked as if she'd been shot. She bolted upright, things falling on to the floor, and he saw her big blank face turn wildly to the door. He took a step back, took off his sunglasses and waited. Soon he could hear her breathing on the other side of the door.

"Who the fuck's that?"

"Tracey?"

"I said who the fuck is it?"

"Jack Caffery."

"*Who?*"

"Jack Caffery."

"Never heard of you." The chain was drawn across and the latch was unhooked and now the door opened a crack and her big face appeared in the gap in the door, pale eyes blinking in the sun. "Who the fuck are you, then?" She had pulled on a flimsy pink gown. In spite of the nicotine-stained blonde hair, this was definitely the woman from the video. She had the teeth of an old rabbit. "What d'you want, then? I'm not buying nothing."

"Are you on your own? Is there anyone else here?"

"What the fuck's that to you?"

"Caffery," he said. "Jack Caffery."

"Am I supposed to know what the fuck you're talking about?"

"Ivan Penderecki sent me."

Her face changed. "Eh?"

"Ivan Penderecki. You know who I mean. A friend of your brother's."

At that she took keys from a hook, took the chain off the door and stepped outside, closing the door behind her and tying the gown closer. "Don't give me all that. He never did send you."

"No, you're right. He never did because he's dead. I found out about your brother from the videos Penderecki was keeping for you."

Tracey Lamb's mouth opened a little. She stood with her feet apart, her big ham arms crossed under her breasts, her mouth slack and nasty. "Who *are* you?"

"Detective Inspector Jack Caffery. Metropolitan Police."

He knew she'd bolt when he said it and he was ready. He stepped straight forward and put his hands on either side of her as she scrabbled to get the keys in the front door.

"*What?*" she screamed, frustrated. "*Get off of me!*"

"Stand still, I want to talk to you."

"*I'm not talking to the fucking filth.*"

"Stand still, Tracey!" She abandoned the attempt to get into the house and instead launched sideways, breaking past his arms and charging along the side of the house. But he mirrored her, his hands out, herding her back towards the wall. "I mean it, Tracey. *Keep still.*"

"Fuck off. Keep a-fucking-way from me." She put her head down. He saw she was preparing to aim a knee at his groin and he stepped sideways, quick as a *torero*, getting her right hand behind her back.

"No no no. *Never* kick a man in the balls."

"*Oww!*" Tracey Lamb had been arrested before and was "hold-wise". She tried to lock her arm at the elbow but Caffery caught her by the hair, repositioned his feet and grabbed her arm, twisting it behind her back before she could lock it. "*Owww!*"

"Yes — OK, OK. Try not to struggle, Tracey. It just makes you look even more suss."

"Get your fucking hands off me." She struggled and kicked and twisted, and clamped her hand over his, trying to loosen his grip. "You touched my *tits*!" she screamed. There was no one to hear her, but this was kneejerk con behaviour. Even during the arrest they began plotting for the lawsuit they'd serve on the Met. "Touched my fucking tits —"

"Yeah, c'mon, c'mon." He hesitated a moment, looking around at the clearing. *Where now? Where shall I take her?* The car. "Come on." He dragged her back down the little drive, his hand bleeding where she'd clawed at it. A crow or a rook screamed above them and took flight from one of the huge rustling trees. At the car he pushed her roughly into the passenger seat and locked the door. She scrambled to the driver's side, but he was there already, opening the door and getting in, pushing her into the seat. "Back — back. Or do you want cuffing?"

"You bastard."

"I mean it, I'll cuff you."

"You fucker." She puffed her breath out in a sigh and fell back in the seat.

"Good. Now . . ." He started the engine and turned the air on full. He hadn't broken a sweat but Lamb was red-faced and puffing. "Don't try to get out. Just behave yourself."

"*Don't* talk to me like that." She sat forward in the seat shaking a bitten, nicotine-stained finger at him. "I don't care who you are, don't talk to me like that. Filth!" She sat back in the seat, breathing hard. "Should've fucking known to look at you you were filth.

Evil fucking eyes. Typical filth to go round hitting women, that's real filth behaviour."

"Just calm down, OK?" He reached across her and she flinched. "Relax." He unhooked the seat-belt. "I'm not going to touch you."

As he pulled the seat-belt across her huge body Lamb dropped her chin and sank teeth into his arm.

"*Fuck, Jesus.*" She had him in a vice grip. He grabbed her by the hair and jerked her head back, shaking her like a dog. "*Let go*. Come on, let fucking go, you *shit*house." She gave a little gasp and released her grip and he sat back, pulled his hand away, examining the grey marks, pinpoints of blood under the skin. "You spiteful little slag."

He drove her to a layby on the A134, opposite a graffitied power substation in the centre of an overgrown field. He parked the Jag so the passenger door was hard up against a hedgerow, switched off the engine and turned to her.

"Look, first let me give you a little straightener, OK?" He got tobacco from the glove compartment and began to roll a cigarette. "I don't know why TO9 haven't got a file on you, but I can promise you that when they do they'll find you so *tasty* they'll crow it from the rooftops. You'd be looking at, what? Something between seven and ten? But for now they don't know — and guess who can keep it that way?"

"I'm not a snout if that's what you're getting at." The gold earrings clung precariously to the bottom of a long slash in her earlobes, stretched by years of heavy jewellery. He was sure he could see a tiny flash of sky and trees through them every time she moved her head. "If that's what you've come here for. Not a fucking snout."

"I'd like you to tell me if any of your brother's fucked-up and twisted pals had a habit of biting. Hmm? Someone in Brixton who likes biting little boys?" He sealed the Rizla and lit the cigarette, pointing it at Tracey. "It's got serious now, Tracey, really serious. I want some names — I want to know all the names of Carl's friends."

"You're fucking joking, aren't you? I'm not rolling over — go fuck yourself."

"You specialize in juves, don't you? You and Carl were part of a paedo ring. I've seen the videos."

"They were faked, ya stupid cunt. Faked."

"Yes, well, first off, you're lying. But let's just say for the sake of argument that this is your excuse, then welcome, Tracey, to the land of the pseudo photo — the Home Office is one step ahead of you and we can do you for pseudo photos too, although I've never heard anyone, even those with twice your nous, try to use that as an excuse for a video, so ten out of ten for originality."

"I haven't done nothing."

"You're a liar —"

"I'm *not*! It was me brother's thing. All them vids were his — I never even knew —"

"Even so, you *are* a fucking liar — I recognize you." Caffery put his cigarette in the ashtray and inspected the mark on his arm, squeezing it, seeing if it would bleed. "You had a wig on, but you made a boy who looked, to my untutored eye, about eleven . . ." He paused and looked up from his arm. "Actually, you know, I could be wrong, maybe he was even younger — just goes to show I can't tell kids' ages very well. Anyway, you made him go down on you, didn't you?" He dropped his arm and looked her square in the eye. "You know, the video with you on the sofa. Little boy of about eleven having his cock sucked. And there were three others."

"Don't you start trying to grief me now." She rubbed her chest. "I've got a bad chest. Doctor says stress could be dangerous."

"Don't threaten me. You're not Cynthia Jarrett. Nobody's going to give a flying fuck if you keel over, except for a couple of sad old nonces."

"There wasn't no harm in what I did." Her face was growing redder. "He wanted it, that lad. He *wanted it*. Couldn't you tell? You don't get a fucking lob-on if yer don't wannit."

"Tracey, he was only a *kid*. Legally he can't make a decision at that age — and you shouldn't have put him in a position where he had to —"

"You're stressing me." The phlegm was rattling in her throat. "You're really stressing me." She moved her tongue around and began to lean over between her knees.

"Don't you dare spit in my fucking car!"

"I'll suffocate if I can't."

"Oh, for *Christ's* sake."

He leaned over, undid the passenger window and pushed her head out. She hawked phlegm into the hedgerow and it landed on an opened cow-parsley umbrella at shoulder height. "Charming." He pulled her back into the car and pushed her against the seat. She sat back, blinking, and suddenly dropped her face into her hands and began to sob self-pityingly.

"Oh, Jesus." He sighed.

"What are you going to do to me?" Her nose began to run. "What're you going to *do*?"

Caffery stared out of the window at the cars going by on the A134. Tracey Lamb was depressing him.

"Don't shop me — please don't. I don't want to go away again."

"You won't if you help me."

"*But I don't know any of them who was biters — I don't!*"

"Not good enough. Not fucking good enough."

"*It's true.*" Tracey started crying even louder.

"Oh, for Christ's sake." He rolled his eyes skywards. "Here — have a fag, for fuck's sake."

She wiped her nose and watched him roll a cigarette. She took it, let him light it and smoked for a few minutes until she was in control again. He watched her carefully, knowing that all he'd said so far was subterfuge, that he should cut to the chase. He rested his elbow on the steering-wheel and turned full on to her.

"Look," he said, "be straight with me — don't you recognize my name?"

"What name?"

"Caffery."

She shook her head. Her nose was still running.

"But you've heard of the boy across the railway tracks?" That got her attention. She opened her mouth a little and looked at him. "You know about the boy across the railway tracks, don't you? Penderecki told you, didn't he?"

"Uh —"

"What happened, Tracey? Eh? What happened?"

"I — uh —" Her eyes had changed. They flickered uncertainly and he knew he was getting somewhere.

"Come on — where did Penderecki put him?"

"Why d'you want to know?"

"Doesn't matter *why*." Caffery put his index fingers on his temples as if she tired him immensely. "What matters is what happens to *you* if you *don't tell me*."

Her eyes travelled back and forward across his face as if she was working something around in her head, and slowly her expression changed. "Here," she said eventually, a suspicious little glint in her eyes, "I thought you was asking about a biter. That's what you said — someone who bites little boys."

"Well, now I'm not. Now I'm asking about the boy on the railway tracks."

"How comes you're here on yer own?"

"I'm the only one who knows."

"Are you arresting me?"

"I will if you want."

"No, you won't." Her eyes glittered like fake gems. She'd sussed him. "This ain't official, is it?" She smiled, her lips pulled back from the yellow rabbit's teeth.

"You're working for someone. There's some gelt in it. You're in with someone."

"Just give me the truth."

"The truth? The real truth?"

"Yes."

She didn't answer. They stared at each other for a long time. Then Tracey raised her eyebrows and grinned.

"*What?*"

"I don't know. I don't know what happened to him."

"Oh, Jesus." He shook his head and dropped his face into his hands. "Stop dicking with me," he said wearily. "I mean it, Tracey, no more fucking bullshit. I want to know where they put him."

"I don't know — seriously, I don't. All I know is that Ivan wouldn't tell me brother and that's all. I swear I don't know."

CHAPTER TWENTY

Caffery sat back, exhausted. He lit another cigarette and smoked it without speaking. *Fuck this*. He believed she didn't know anything about Rory's killer — but he was sure she knew more than she was letting on about Ewan. Was he going to let himself be suckered in again, sniff along blindly like a desperate, hungry dog? *I think you will*. He imagined Rebecca smiling in amusement, smoking a cigarillo and coolly assessing his behaviour. *Penderecki's gone but you still like being jerked around when it comes to Ewan*.

No, he thought, fuck it, no. He chucked the cigarette out of the window, started the car and nosed it forward a few feet. "I'll come back." He reached across Tracey and opened the door. "When you've had time to think about it."

She looked dubiously down at the stinging nettles pushing though the cracks in the hot tarmac. "I'm not getting out here in me drawers. Can't you drive me back to the house?"

"No." He unsnapped her seat-belt and shoved her. "Go on — get out."

She jerked forward. "Oi, ya cunt. What d'you think you're doing —"

"Go on. Fuck off."

"You cunt!" Tracey Lamb got out of the car, squealing, "You *cunt*!"

"Yeah." He closed the door. "OK, see you later." She was in her underwear and a see-through wrap, barefoot in a layby two miles from her house, but he didn't care. *Fuck her*. He accelerated away, his hands shaking on the steering-wheel. He followed the A12 into London and straight into the City, where he turned south, setting the car for Shrivemoor. He was going to go straight back and tell Souness about Penderecki's cache and then he was going to go home and sleep. Sleep — it sounded like a long drink from a cold well.

The Jaguar was almost empty so he pulled into the petrol station opposite Shrivemoor to fill up. It was hot: overhead the sun was steady at the midday position, shrinking the grass in the front gardens, making the drains sweat. He stared out absently at the street as the car filled, conscious of the way he'd just lived out Rebecca's diagnosis of him — all through the time in the car with Tracey Lamb he'd wanted to push those rabbit's teeth down her throat. He sighed and replaced the nozzle, locking the petrol cap. He was tired of it all. He was tired of knocking himself out for a child he didn't know — and suddenly he didn't care if they caught Rory Peach's killer, he didn't even care if there was another family, tied up somewhere, their own child naked and terrified.

He went into the kiosk to pay, bought a truffle ice-cream for Kryotos, and was crossing the forecourt, the tarmac hot underfoot, when someone came trotting over from the direction of Shrivemoor. "Mr Caffery."

Instinctively he left his hand where it was, on his breast pocket, closed over his wallet. A very tall man — with pale, almost alabaster skin and fine blond hair in a neat baby curl — stopped a few feet away on the edge of the forecourt. He was dressed in a pop-button cord shirt and matching fawn cords and was holding an old Argos carrier-bag containing a few belongings. "You are DI Caffery." He put his hand up to shield his eyes. "I saw you in Brixton."

"Have we met?"

"No. I was interviewed by one of your men. He gave me your name."

"And you are?"

"Name's Gummer. I'm, uh —" He looked over his shoulder. "I've got a few things I'd like to discuss about the Peach case."

"Uh." Caffery didn't move for a moment. He supposed he should shake Gummer's hand, but there was something about him that said Gummer was more interested in giving Caffery a lecture on the allocation of man-hours than passing on any information. He looked like someone who had a theory. Or maybe he was a journalist, giving him an act. "It might be easier if you made an appointment."

"Maybe we could have . . ." He waved vaguely down the street in the direction of the shops. "I could buy you coffee. They wouldn't let me into the station — made me wait out in the sun."

"They probably would rather you called first."

“S’pose so.” Gummer began to tuck in his shirt, and now Caffery could see a slight stoop in his posture, as if he was afraid he had shown too much of himself, too much spirit in that brave, rash sprint across the tarmac.

Suddenly Caffery felt a little sorry for him. He dropped his hand from his wallet. “Look, what did you want to talk about?”

“I just said — the Peach family. You know. The ones in Donegal Crescent?” He crossed his hands over his chest and gave an odd little dip at the waist, as if his hands had been bound across his chest like a pharaoh. “You know, the ones who got tied up.”

“Yes, surprisingly, I do know.”

“I’ve got a theory.”

Ah. I was right. I’ve got you sussed. “Look, Mr Gummer, maybe an appointment would be better — do it officially.” He turned to go but Gummer stepped in front of him.

“No.”

“We can make an appointment now.”

“No — come and have coffee with me.”

“If it’s so important why don’t you just tell me? Now.”

“I’d rather you had coffee with me.”

“I’d rather you made an appointment.”

“OK. OK.” Gummer dropped his eyes and stared at his greying, unlaced trainers, shifting from one foot to the other as if getting up his courage. His face was becoming red. “Has — um — has anyone said anything to you about a bogeyman? A troll?”

That got Caffery's interest. "Where've you heard that?"

"It was in the paper. A little boy got *raped* by him in the park."

"I see," he said cautiously. "And when was this?"

"Long time ago. His name was Champaluang Keoduangdy."

"Did you know him?"

"No. I read about it."

"You remember his name? It's a difficult name to remember."

"I learned it. I was living in Brixton then. It was the troll who did that, you know." His neck was red now, bright red. He seemed to be blushing all over.

"Is this what your kids have told you?"

"No, no. Not *my* kids . . ." He put his hands in his pockets and shuffled his feet a bit more. "I haven't — uh — I haven't got any."

"Got any?"

"Any kids."

"Then who told you about the troll?"

"The kids I teach — at the swimming-pool. The little ones are always talking about it. And . . ." He looked up and met Caffery's eyes. "And I wondered what the police knew about it."

"But we're talking about kids' fantasy lives. What's it got to do with the Peaches?"

"They're not stupid, children. If they talk about a troll in the woods, about a troll watching them in bed, maybe you should listen to them. Whoever it was who raped Champaluang wasn't a figment of someone's imagination."

"That's true." Caffery put his hand under the ice-cream, afraid it would drip. "Mr Gummer, these children you teach, have any of them actually *seen* him? The troll? Have you heard any of them say they've seen him or been approached by him?"

"Just because they haven't doesn't mean you can *dismiss* it. You should be exploring every avenue."

"Yes. That's what we're —"

"And something else," Gummer interrupted, agitated now. "I read the Peaches were going on holiday — is that true?"

"If you read it then it must be true."

"Well, then," he said, "maybe we should ask ourselves if *that* is relevant information."

"I think it would have crossed the mind of any investigating officer. If he was doing his job. Wouldn't it?"

"If he was doing his job, yes . . ." Gummer met Caffery's eyes defiantly, leaving the sentence to hang there between them.

Caffery sighed. He was tiring of this jousting session out in the midday sun. "Look." He held up the ice-cream. "It's melting. I should go."

Gummer shifted his weight from foot to foot and back again, the corduroys folding and pleating around his feet. "You police, you won't take any help —"

"I'm sorry."

"You're all as bad as each other." He rolled the carrier-bag and its contents into a little ball. "*You*'ve all got your theories but anyone else comes along you've got to be the kings of the castle, haven't you? Won't listen to anyone else."

"Mr Gummer, that's not true —"

"No wonder no one never reports anything to you." He began to shuffle away. "No wonder — kings of the castle."

Caffery stood in the hot sun and watched Gummer's shambolic progress across the tarmac. He waited until he had disappeared around the corner then sighed and turned back to the Jaguar.

Bela Nersessian was in the downstairs lobby waiting for the lift, breathing heavily. She was wearing a sequinned low-necked sweater and tight black leggings, and had three bags of shopping gathered around her feet. Caffery had forgotten she was coming today.

"Bela," he said.

"Afternoon, darling." She held a hand out for the ice-cream. "I'll take that and . . ." She nodded at the shopping. ". . . if you wouldn't mind."

"Go on, then." He handed her the ice-cream, picked up the shopping and they got into the lift, Bela clutching his arm for support. "I'm yours for as long as you want me — Annahid's gone to the cinema with her daddy." When the doors closed she took a handkerchief from her gold-chained handbag and mopped the back of her neck, plunged it into her sweater and dabbed her armpits, her cleavage. She smiled at Caffery. "Sorry, darling, just need to make myself presentable."

Souness met them at the lift doors. She was worried by Caffery's drawn face. "Are ye all right, Jack?" she whispered, as they led Bela into the SIO's room. "Ye look like ye're going to throw up."

"Yeah. I'll tell you later." He took the ice-cream through to Kryotos then joined Souness in the SIO's room. Settled now, all attention on her, Mrs Nersessian was in her element. She reached inside one of her bags and found a long packet of Dottato figs and two packets of Garibaldi biscuits.

"Good figs." She peered at them, pressing a varnished nail into the soft flesh. "Yes, perfect. The fig is the poor man's food, Mr Caffery, full of calcium, good for your bowels too — you have clean bowels you have a clean mind, you can think straight. And you are going to need that, straight thinking, I hardly need remind you — here." She spread the biscuits across the desk, smiling encouragingly at Caffery. "Come on, now — what's the matter with you that you're so thin? Your wife doesn't feed you?"

"Mrs Nersessian —"

"Call me Bela, darling. I might be a mother but I'm not an old woman yet, and *you*, darling"— she leaned over and rested a hand on Souness's wrist — "darling, call me a busybody but has your husband ever mentioned your weight? Not that I think there's anything wrong with it, some men like something to hold on to, don't they —"

"Bela," Caffery interrupted, "we'd like to talk about Alek."

"Ah, yes!" She turned to him, gold jewellery jingling. "Now *there*'s another one needs to eat a bit more — you should see him. All he does all day is walk — all day long wandering around the park. Poor man, poor man, what that family's had to endure." She pressed her hands together in a gesture of supplication and rolled her eyes to the ceiling. "God protect us all from what they've had to live through." She dropped her hands and leaned over the food on the desk, scooping a plump fig into her mouth and chewing for a long time, smiling at Caffery over moving teeth. "Course, if I was the police I'd have let them down a bit easier than you did. I'd have broken it to them more gentle. I'm not criticizing you, of course."

"Bela, let's talk about Carmel. How's Carmel?"

"Your man's been round, talking to her, but she just stares at the wall."

"We heard. Does she speak to you?"

"Only to Annahid." She pressed another fig into her mouth, and bent over, her face close to the fruit, inspecting them for the next candidate. "Cries a bit with Annahid, but maybe that's good."

Souness shifted in her seat. "Bela, about Alek, he hasn't worked for a while, has he?"

She looked up as if Souness had suddenly leaned over and slapped her. "The man's *grieving*." She stared at her, her mouth open. "He hasn't time to worry about *work* — he's just lost his son."

"I think the Chief Inspector means *before* —"

"Before? Oh . . ." She patted the top of her lip where a line of sweat had started. "Oh, that. Well, he used to have a disco, see, a mobile disco, and, oh, he loves his records and America — he loves America, dreams he's going to live there, reckons he looks like Presley with all that black hair of his. The biggest dream of his life was to take Rory to Graceland. Of course, you can understand all the fuss, you can understand why the family never approved of him marrying Carmel in the first place, but *I* never held anything against him. Nor Carmel." She waggled a box of Garibaldi biscuits under Caffery's nose. "Come on, darling. Make me happy."

"Thank you." He took a biscuit, the last thing he wanted, and rested it on the rim of his coffee mug. "You were saying, about Alek's work, his disco . . ."

"I'm not saying he was the hardest working man, and then there *was* all that trouble, which makes it more difficult for him, but let's not go into that — they're not a traditional family, see, her being an *odar*, not that I'm saying I hold *that* against him."

"I'm sorry, you said an *oh-dah*?"

"An *odar*. A foreigner — not one of us."

"One of you?"

"Not an *Armenian*."

"But Alek Peach *is*?"

"Oh, yes." She blinked. "Not a traditional one, of course, but he is one. Oh, I know, I know . . ." She touched Caffery's arm with her long gold nails. "He's got blue eyes — lots of us have got blue eyes, just like you, darling. Everyone thinks we're Iranian, but we're not. Look at me." She pulled off her tortoiseshell glasses and blinked at him. "See? See?"

"Yes, I see."

"Blue, and what's interesting is . . ." She replaced her glasses. "What's interesting is our great-grandfathers, mine and Alek's, they were best friends. Fought together against the Turks — died together too. Our grandparents were sent to Paris and —"

"But Peach — that's not an —"

"An Armenian name? No. Of course not. That's what I'm saying — he's not traditional, he's ashamed of his heritage is what I think."

"He changed his name?" Caffery could feel Souness's eyes on him, could feel her interest spiking out into the room. "Anglicized it?"

"Only his second name. Not Alek, of course, he kept that because it didn't sound —"

"And his real name? What was Alek's real name?"

"Oh, you won't be able to pronounce it." She flipped out one jewelled hand dismissively. "If you can't manage Nersessian you *certainly* won't be able to do Pechickjian."

When Caffery left Tracey Lamb on the A134 she had no choice but to walk the mile or so home. *Like a cunt in me drawers*. It was a pale blue day and the distant finger of steam from the sugar factory in Bury St Edmunds was visible above the trees. Few cars passed, the tarmac was hot under her bare feet, and she passed only one phone box, a little brindled dog sniffing around it. But even if she had 20p to call a cab she didn't have any cash at home to pay the cabbie. Since Carl's death things at the house had got bad. There were only four cartons of Silk Cut left, the Datsun was low on petrol and the dole cheque couldn't even begin to cover everything. And now, it seemed, the Bill were on to her.

Tracey had no one to ask about DI Caffery's visit — the person she would usually have turned to was gone now, her brother Carl. She and Carl had clung together for the thirty years after their parents' deaths in a way that some called unhealthy. They had so many things in common — "Even got the same teeth capped." Carl would grin and pull up his front lip for anyone who would listen. He'd lost his in Belmarsh, and Tracey, well, he had to admit he'd taken hers out for her one St Patrick's Day. Carl had lots of "friends". Tracey knew all about his "friends" — she'd met one or two of them when she'd done the videos.

She paused for a moment on the roadside, bent over and dragged brown phlegm out of her throat, spitting it into the ferns. A car went by and hooted loudly. In the back window she saw faces laughing at her. She put her hands on her knees, straightened painfully, and looked up the baking road to where it disappeared into a point on the hazy horizon. She couldn't let herself be fucked around like this — when she got home she would find Carl's book and call his friends, ask them what to do next. She didn't like talking to them — some of them were insane, even Carl admitted that. Some of them would do it with anything and anyone: "Some of them'd do it with the exhaust pipe of an old Cortina," Carl would laugh. "It'd have to be a good-looking Cortina, of course." But she had to do something.

She hobbled on in the heat, her feet hurting. Apart from the occasional passing car she hadn't seen anyone for over an hour, only a grey-haired old man in overalls, scavenging around the disused industrial poly-tunnels near West Farm. She turned off towards Barnham, past the derelict military houses, bricked-up windows and plywood on the doors, past an abandoned hangar. She was making slow progress — she had to stop every few minutes to catch her breath and bring up some phlegm. Tracey's lungs had never been right, not from the start.

"Nothing to do with the sixty a day, is it, Trace?" Carl would grin when she bent over her little polystyrene cup and hawked gobbets of phlegm into it. "Nothing to do with that."

"Fuck off." She'd give him the V-sign and Carl would laugh and they'd both go back to staring at the TV. She missed him, God love him. *I miss you, Carl*.

By the time she got to the little track that cut across farmland, along the top of the disused quarry, and on to the garage, her feet were bleeding. The garage was a long way from the road, but she kept going, limping now. Every now and then a military jet from Honnington would blast its way across the sky, splitting the air open, disappearing in seconds into the horizon, but otherwise the countryside around her was quiet, quiet and very still in the sun. She knew it so well now, these fields, that fence, that path. Carl had been renting the garage and the house since their parents died when he was nineteen and Tracey was thirteen. She understood his business. She understood all about the pile of smashed car windows, the stolen chassis stamps and the dodgy MOT embosser. There was always a stripped-down car up on blocks in the garage, a pile of moody numberplates in the kitchen and a Transit van or an old Ford parked under a tarp out the back — Carl would let her have a peek then drop the tarp and put his fingers to his mouth: "*Never say nothing about this car, all right, girl? Just pretend you ain't seen it*." Every now and then a car would come in that needed "valeting". "Urgent valet job": Carl would jump like a whippet at those words and would work all night on some anonymous Discovery or Bronco, the electric lights in the garage blazing out across the countryside. And he collected people, too, the same way he collected scrap metal: they'd come and go, day and night, through the little breezeblock house, carrying car stereos and carrier-bags full of duty-frees. Tracey had grown up with the sound of Harleys zooming up and down the driveway. There was always someone around, someone sleeping in the bath, someone curled up in a grubby sleeping-bag in the garage, an ever-changing string of boys who came and went, helping Carl with the resprays (and other things too, she was sure of that). The Borstal Boys, she called them, because they always seemed to be on the run from the borstal. "And that's something else to stay schtum about, Trace, all right?" Everyone in Carl's circle had done time at some point or another — and that included the "biter" that DI Caffery had been asking about.

"He was a weird one, him," said Carl. "Always reckoned women were dirty. You should have seen him, he had to put on rubber gloves before he touched any of the boys in case they'd been near a woman." He lived in Brixton and although DI Caffery hadn't said *where* the little boy had been bitten, Tracey had a suspicion it might have been on the shoulders. But in any case her predator instinct told her that actually it wasn't the "biter" Caffery was most interested in at all — in his questions about him she sensed a cover of some sort — and it was only when he began asking about Penderecki's boy that she thought he was getting to what really interested him.

Penderecki's boy. Although Tracey knew what the shifty old Polack had done to the child, she had never been told who the boy was, neither his name nor where he'd come from. But, from the way Carl had built a mile-high wall of silence around the subject, she had always guessed it was because the boy meant something to someone important. She guessed there was money in it somewhere. And maybe, she thought, that was why Caffery was so interested.

She stopped. She wasn't far now. She could see the sun glinting off Carl's abandoned vehicles on the edge of the quarry: an old Triumph, a moss-covered caravan, a picked-clean Ford. Only another ten minutes to the garage, but she stood quite still, the pain in her feet forgotten, hardly registering the clutch of pheasants that rose screeching from the trees. Something was emerging from the dank, unexercised walls of Tracey Lamb's brain. Something about DI Caffery. Maybe, she thought, maybe he wasn't the beginning of her problems after all. Maybe he was the solution.

⋆ ⋆ ⋆

Roland Klare had spent the morning making notes, considering short-cuts, finding new ways of looking at it, and had finally worked out what he needed: a few sheets of print paper, a litre can of fixer, and some Kodak D76 powder. The photography book was clear: it warned him that he might damage the film if he didn't use a professional safelight, but he had decided to take the gamble anyway and added a twenty-five-watt red lightbulb to his list. He had turned out his pockets and drawers and old cider bottles full of coins, and had got together thirty pounds, all of which he put into a dustbin liner, twisted up and slung over his shoulder.

It was heavy, all that change, and it took him a long time to get to the bus stop. On the bus the other passengers gave him strange looks, sitting at the back with the dustbin liner squat at his feet. But Klare was used to people moving seats to get away from him, and today he sat quietly, his eyes wandering patiently around in his head, until the bus reached Balham.

He got off just outside the photographer's shop, the shop whose dustbins he routinely purged, and before he even thought of going into the front he slipped up the road and around the back. He put down the bag of coins, pulled over an old crate and stood on it, up on tiptoe so he could peer down into the big dumpster. His heart sank. It had been emptied recently. There was nothing in there except an old cardboard Jaffa oranges box. He climbed down off the crate, wiping his hands, resigned now, picked up the bag full of coins and trudged round to the front of the shop.

CHAPTER TWENTY-ONE

Neither Caffery nor Souness could believe what the computer was telling them. They sat for a long time, chairs a few feet apart, staring at the screen in silence. They had gone into the Police National Computer and come back with a CRO number — a criminal records office number — for Alek Pechickjian. Indecent assault on a minor. Sentenced in 1984 to two years.

"No." Caffery shook his head. "Nah — I can't believe it. Just because he's got a record, doesn't mean —"

"For indecent assault? Of a minor?"

"Jesus — Jesus." He put his head in his hands, his mind racing. The first of Peach's offences was pre-1985 and not back-record converted — they had e-mailed the records office for the microfiche to be couriered down — but Peach's second offence, a nominal term for a pub brawl in which a seventeen-year-old's eye had been popped out, had started at the end of 1989, shortly after the assault on Champ and the Half Moon Lane hoax. Caffery stared at the screen in disbelief. All the odd loose ends in Peach's account of the events at number thirty Donegal Crescent — his denial of photographs being taken, his denial that he'd heard

Rory at all in those few days, the fact that his wife and son were dehydrated and he wasn't — all the drifting question marks seemed to be settling silently around Caffery.

He got up and took the photofit of Champ's attacker from the file. Then he took all the crimescene photographs and spread them out on the desk. "What do you think?"

Souness leaned over the photofit and shook her head. "I dunno. What do you think?"

"I don't know either." He turned it one way then the other. "Could be, could be." He picked up the crimescene photos. "That thump he took on the back of the head, d'you think he could have . . ." They both leaned forward and looked at the mark that Alek Pechickjian, Alek Peach, had left.

"If he manacled that end first . . ." Souness pointed to the photo. "And then the hands — ye know, Jack, he could actually've done it . . ."

"No, no, no. Hang on." Caffery pushed his chair back. They had asked Bela Nersessian to leave for a moment and she was in the incident room with Kryotos; he could see her red hair bobbing up and down, as if she'd like to get a look through the window. He leaned closer to Souness and lowered his voice. "No, look. What are we saying? That he ran out the back when the shopkeeper knocked on the door? Climbed up that tree, dumped Rory, got *back* to the house and tied himself up — *all* before the police could . . ."

His voice trailed away — Souness was nodding. The shopkeeper had gone all the way back to his shop to raise the alarm and in that period Peach had had more than enough time. Quite enough to make it look as if he'd been attacked. Caffery and Souness had both heard of this sort of scene staging — the manic writing on the wall, that was a popular one. And they had both seen enough to know that people can, if they put their minds to it, push themselves into unimaginable positions, inflict unimaginable injury on themselves. Caffery was thinking not only of autoerotic deaths — sad souls wrapped in tent bags, in rubber masks, faces obscured by used underwear, manacled on pulleys to the ceiling — but of others which could have so easily been mistaken for murder: he had once seen a suicide who had pulled out his own intestines and snipped them into pieces with sewing scissors, another who had set fire to herself in the locked boot of a car. He knew too well how murder can masquerade as suicide and how suicide can masquerade as murder.

"'Do you like your daddy . . .?'" he said quietly.

"Eh?"

"Champaluang Keoduangdy. That's what his attacker said. 'Do you like your daddy?'"

"What?"

"That's right." He sat up, his blood stirring. Suddenly his day trip to Norfolk, the tangle he and Rebecca were in, it all began to sting a little less.

"Hang on." Souness pulled over the photos and peered at them, her mouth pressed in a little doubting bud. "He was half dead when they found him."

"But he snapped back, didn't he? Snapped right back." Caffery pushed his chair back. "Proper little Lazarus — the consultant was popping veins he was so surprised."

"He'd pissed and shat all over himself — that's some good play-acting."

"Probably thinking of Gordon Wardell."

"What?"

"Don't you remember?" Caffery took his glasses off. "One of the things that tipped them off was that Wardell never pissed himself in all the time he was tied up. That's how they guessed he'd done his wife. If that wasn't all over the papers, Danni, from Brixton to Birmingham, I'll buy you dinner."

She sighed. Shook her head. "It's not in my nature to say this, Jack, but I think you're right." She stood and hitched up her jeans. "So what do we do?"

"I'd like some DNA. Wouldn't you?"

"How long is that going to take?"

"Fuck knows." Caffery got to his feet. "Anyway. We've got another way."

Souness stayed in the incident room to arrange an emergency briefing for the team and Caffery accompanied Bela back to Guernsey Grove. He was so wired and ready to see Alek Peach again, to reassess him in this new light, that when Souness stopped him on his way to the lift, dropping her head and turning slightly so that Bela couldn't hear, and murmured, "Ye were going to tell me something, Jack? Ye had something to say?" he shook his head. "No, that was — that was nothing. Really. Nothing."

He was back in the saddle. He wanted to know if, after everything, Peach had been squatting — complacent like a toad — right under their noses. It took him out of himself, made him forget everything. He wasn't tired any more.

Explaining to Bela without giving the game away wasn't easy: "Our forensic team have discovered some toothmarks on some food in the Peaches' kitchen — it's normal to get the victims to give us a cast of their own teeth, just in case they left the imprint."

"Well, I don't suppose he's here." She let him into her antiseptic house, her bracelets jangling, her face set. "He was off again this morning, crack of dawn."

"That's OK." He put his head around the living-room door. It was quiet, just the gold-plated carriage clock in the display cabinet starting up its chime. "If he's not here I'll wait."

"See if he's in the garden, darling." She hung her handbag behind the door. "And I'm going to bring you a little *soorj* — a little demitasse — keep your spirits up."

"That's OK, Bela — thanks, but I'll pass." He went into the kitchen. Strings of walnuts, steeped in sugar, hung like wood-carved mobiles above the sink. He unlocked the back door and stood on the little concrete patio, blinking in the sunlight. The garden was neat, the sunken fitting for the carousel clothesdryer dead centre in the little square of grass. Annahid's pink Barbie bike was in position up against a newly creosoted tool shed, but otherwise the garden was empty. He closed the door, locked it again and went into the kitchen where Bela was boiling the kettle. “Thanks anyway.”

“Are you sure?”

“Sure I’m sure. We’re trying to beat the clock on this.”

“You need fattening up. I know they’ll all say you look fashionable, but fashionable doesn’t mean healthy.” Bela followed him up the stairs, breathing heavily behind him. When she realized he was going to the top floor she plucked at his sleeve. “You’re not going to disturb Carmel, darling? I don’t think you should, she doesn’t need to be reminded. It’s not my business, but really you should have more tact . . .”

But Caffery went ahead and opened the door. The room was filled with smoke and sunshine. Carmel lay on the bed, cigarettes and ashtray next to her, body facing the window, head rolled backwards over her shoulder to see who was at the door. Beyond her, staring out at the garden, a cigarette between the fingers that hung out of the opened window, was Alek Peach, dressed in a nylon Arsenal shirt and stonewash jeans.

Caffery hadn’t known what to expect. Alek Peach must have anticipated what was coming, he must have heard him downstairs, but he appeared calm and took his time turning round. He took one last drag on the cigarette, crushed it in a pile of dog ends on the window-sill, and stood slowly. His big face was redder, more blood-infused than Caffery remembered, but his eyes hadn’t lost that hollow, guarded look. If he was surprised to see Detective Inspector Caffery, standing in the door, slightly breathless as if excited, he didn't show it.

Smurf was limping in a confused circle, panting and whimpering, trying to get comfortable, the old claws making little fricative picks at the carpet. Her leg was oozing a clear sticky fluid and she had relieved herself twice in the corner of the room. Benedicte guessed now that she was searching for water. *Me too, Smurf, me too*. She lay on her back, letting the trains mark off the hours, running her sore swollen tongue along the inside of her mouth. She had licked her lips so often that now she could feel the tender raised outline of them. For a moment yesterday she'd believed they were safe — some time in the morning the doorbell had rung.

YES! Her heart had leaped into her mouth. "*I'm here, HERE!*"

Keys in the lock.

Keys?

The front door opened and, with a horrible lurch of despair and panic, she understood her mistake. She heard his feet on the stairs, racing up — then the furious pounding on the door. She curled back against the radiator, hands wrapped around her head. Surrendering.

And he'd done the same thing several times that day, coming and going, using the front door. Slamming it as he left and ringing the doorbell on his return to reassure himself the coast was clear, that no one had arrived to spoil the party. Benedicte knew he was using her keys — she could hear him in the hallway fiddling with the key-ring: those irritating Space Invaders sound effects that Josh loved, starship bleeps, rapid fire echoing in the quiet. Every time the troll came back Benedicte curled into a silent, shivering ball. She wasn't going to let him know a thing — wasn't going to let him know if she was dead or alive. And every time he was out she rolled on to her stomach and yelled encouragement through the floor, praying they could hear.

The trains told her that this time the troll had been gone for more than four hours. What if he wasn't coming back? That meant it could all be over already — and Josh could be . . .

What about the Cornwall cottage agency? Wouldn't they raise the alarm? A construction worker might notice the troll coming and going or Ayo might decide to come over early. Maybe someone would look through the garage window and spot the Daewoo in the garage all ready to go, their packed lunches festering in the heat, popping the lids on the Tupperware.

Smurf stopped her incessant wandering and lay down in the corner, deflated, her head on the good paw. The wound was beginning to smell, and Benedicte had seen bluebottles trying to land on it so she'd torn the sleeve off Hal's shirt and tied it around the area. But still the flies came, drawn by the scent. It broke Ben's heart — she knew that even if they were saved now Smurf might not survive this assault on her system — she was too old, far too old.

"It's all right, Smurf, old girl . . ." she murmured. "Not long now, I promise."

In the car Peach didn't stop complaining. He'd been sick that morning and he really didn't feel like going anywhere — the excuses kept coming. Caffery didn't say a word all the way to Denmark Hill.

Dr Ndizeye was waiting for them outside King's Dental School, smiling and sweating. Visible under the open medical coat, he wore a T-shirt bearing the logo "Programme Alimentaire Mondiale" in blue.

"Mr Peach." He took Peach's hand from his side and shook it. "Come with me." He took them to the small office that doubled as a tutorial room in his role as consultant dental pathologist. It was comfortable, slightly cluttered. A modern, computerized dentist's chair stood in the centre of the room, and on the window-sill an antique goniometer gathered dust. There were few pictures on the walls: some X-rays of skulls, a studio portrait of a smiling American (Robert S. Folkenberg said the gold plaque) and a photo of a woman and two girls in church clothes. A silent nurse in a blue shift was laying out a series of trays on a paper towel.

"It's a beautiful day," Ndizeye said opening the window. "But then, He maketh His sun to rise on the evil and the good, on the just and the unjust." His eyes seemed to look simultaneously in opposite directions behind the thick glasses, his clown mouth seemed to be smiling and Caffery had to tell himself that Ndizeye wasn't aiming that comment at him. As Peach lay down on the dentist's chair, staring at the ceiling, his hands resting at his sides while the nurse velcroed a bib around his neck, Caffery found an aluminium chair and sat with his back to the window, sucking Altoid mints, watching in silence while Ndizeye worked.

"I'll get an impression first, and then we'll get bite-wing X-rays and an orthopantogram." Ndizeye circled his hand around his head. "A look at the whole lot. OK?"

Alek nodded. He hadn't spoken a word since they had arrived. His face was red, as if fevered, but he patiently allowed Ndizeye to try the stainless-steel impression trays for size. "Right." Ndizeye rinsed the last, largest tray. "That's a U14 so I think we'll go for three scoops. You're a big man, Mr Peach."

The nurse mixed the pale pink alginate with warm water, a smell of something like violets and warm plastic coming from the mixing bowl. Ndizeye folded the mixture into the upper impression tray. "Right, let's just lift these lips up." He caught Peach's lips on his fingers and carefully seated the tray, allowing bubbles to escape and the tray to settle neatly into the sulcus, the fissure between the cheek and the gum. "And just keep still." He began to time it, counting off the seconds on his wristwatch. "Only takes a minute."

But after only 30 seconds Peach rolled on to his side, his face sweating, groping for the tray, saliva spilling on to his lips. "I'm going to . . ."

"Keep still." Ndizeye tried to keep Peach upright. "Big breaths through the nose."

"I'm going to puke —" He rolled himself off the chair and put his hands out, stumbling forward, the tray falling on the floor, his trainers slipping in the alginate.

Ndizeye leaned over and tapped the sink. "Here, over here, not on the floor, please."

"Here." Caffery stood, grabbed his arm and jerked him towards the sink. "In there." Peach barely made it before a thin brown coffee-like fluid came up. He stood at the sink, his body heaving, mucus coming from his nose.

Ndizeye laughed. He pulled paper towels from a dispenser on the wall and wiped the sweat from his face. "Don't worry — it gets some people like that. I'll spray a little surface anaesthetic on the back of your mouth while we do the lower tray."

"I don't think I'm well." Peach clutched the sink and looked up, a rope of saliva depending from his bottom lip. His face was brilliant red, the veins around his eyes startling blue in contrast. "I don't think —"

"Here." Caffery hooked him under the arm and helped him back to the chair. He pressed a mouthwash cup and a paper towel into his hand. "Get yourself cleaned up."

"I'm not well."

"We can see that."

"I think I'm going to wait till you feel a bit better," Ndizeye said, tearing another paper towel and going over to the sink. "Yes. We'll wait till you feel better."

Peach's eyes were closed. He rolled his head slowly from side to side, having trouble finding a comfortable position for it. He patted his mouth with the towel and sipped the water, then folded his hands across his chest, his hands tucked lightly under his armpits.

"OK?"

He nodded weakly.

"Feeling better?"

"I think so."

Ndizeye wiped the sides of the sink and ran the tap to clear it. He paused, looking dubiously at the brown fluid in the sink. "Mr Peach? How's your stomach? Have you got pain?"

Peach nodded. His eyes were small in the bright face.

"Do you mind if I feel your abdomen?"

Peach didn't speak as Ndizeye gently pressed it. Caffery could see that the skin was taut, the stomach rigid, like a drum.

"What is it?"

"Do you take ibuprofen, Mr Peach?" Ndizeye leaned near to his face. "Do you take any anti-inflammatories?"

He shook his head again, groaning softly, his eyes flickering. Ndizeye reached for Peach's hands. "Hot," he said. "Right." He kneed a button on the base of the chair and the platform reclined flat. "I think we should get someone up here to have a look at you."

One of the photos of the "outstanding suspects" on the wall of the paedophile unit on the third floor of Scotland Yard showed a woman in half profile, from the waist up, sitting next to a red curtain. An overweight brunette, she was wearing a black bra and her flesh was so dimpled that in the harsh overhead light she looked as if she had taken a dose of grapeshot across her belly.

No one knew her name. The photograph was a still taken from a video the unit had discovered in the early nineties. The film had been scoured and put through the usual enhancement processes, but apart from two cans of John Smith and an empty glass on the bedside table, the only identifying sign was the distinctive tattoo. A heart behind prison bars. The enhancement unit at Denmark Hill froze and blew up a frame where the woman had leaned sufficiently close to the camera for both the tattoo and her face to be in shot, and the photo had been there on the wall ever since Paulina had joined the unit — "I'm so used to these faces now," she had once told Souness, "that if I walked past one of them in Waitrose I probably wouldn't even notice."

When she came up to AMIT's offices that evening the woman on the video was the last thing on Paulina's mind. What she wanted to know was why Danni was in this foul mood. She walked around the incident room picking up papers, barking instructions, and already they were twenty minutes late for the table booked at Frederick's. When Paulina saw she wasn't going to make Danni move any faster by sitting there and glaring, she wandered away into the SIO's room and sat in Caffery's empty chair, head bent over as she used her index finger to push back the cuticles on her nails, lazily swivelling the chair round and round.

Souness found her there twenty minutes later. "I'm sorry, baby." She stood behind the chair and leaned over to kiss the top of her head. "I'm sorry."

Paulina looked up. "You want to cancel, don't you?"

"Our chief suspect's just been taken back into Intensive Care. I'll take you at the weekend — how about that?"

"Oh." She shrugged. "I don't suppose we'll get another reservation till next week. But whatever . . ."

Souness didn't reflect that she'd got away unusually lightly. She didn't know that Paulina would have taken it a lot worse had she not become quite intrigued in the time she'd been left alone in the office — quite fascinated, in fact — by an unusual little doodle she'd seen on Jack Caffery's desk.

CHAPTER TWENTY-TWO

(25 July)

The darkroom, the little cupboard in his bedroom, was ready, and now he closed the door, sealed it with tape, switched on the red lightbulb, and got himself comfortable: seated on a stool, the canister inside the bag on his knees, the book propped open on the enlarger easel in front of him.

The photograph in the book showed a woman's hand using a specialized tool for removing the top of the canister — Klare's coins hadn't stretched that far, "But you could use a bottle-opener," the shop assistant had said, eyeing him suspiciously. "A bottle-opener will do the trick." And the assistant had been right — the bottle-opener worked perfectly, snapping the lid off in one, and now the film was ready to be transferred into the little plastic developing tank.

Klare withdrew the bottle-opener from the bag, dropped it on the floor, wetted his thumb and turned the pages to the next section. Tongue between his teeth, slightly hunched over the book, he followed the instructions minutely, cutting the film leader then, with his right hand, introducing the developing tank into the bag. He replaced the rubber bands on the jacket sleeves, opened the tank and finally, after a lot of fumbling, fed the film on to the spindle in the centre. He pressed the button to let the spindle take up the film, closed the tank, one on top after another, so it was tight and safe, and pulled it out of the jacket.

"There!" He stood, put the tank on the easel, and went into the living room to mix up the Kodak D76 powder.

Smurf was snoring in an unhealthy way and bluebottles flocked around the wound on her leg. Where had they all come from, Benedicte wondered. From nowhere it seemed, magically secreted by the walls, the carpet, the curtains. From time to time when the dog stopped snoring Benedicte could hear how silent the house was beneath them, nothing on the move down there, not a creak or murmur, only the faint helicopter buzz of the flies, and the incremental change of temperature as another summer's day ticked by.

But something was different. Benedicte felt it rather than knew it. The troll hadn't come back last night. She didn't dare to imagine what that might mean for Josh.

There must, she decided later, be a brain chemistry linked to full-blooded, angry desperation, because suddenly she started to feel strong. Something odd and preternatural descended on her — a cool, pearly calm. Her spine felt harder now that she knew she was going to die — and she made a decision to see her child and husband one last time. Whatever had been done to them she wanted to see them, see their eyes.

She examined the handcuff again, jerking on it. She ran her fingers around the copper piping — there were stories sometimes in the *National Enquirer* about lumberjacks carrying their own arms across miles of hickory and balsam forest. Maybe she should hack off her foot — the papers said that Carmel Peach had nearly severed her hand trying to get out of the handcuffs. *My God, is she a better mother than I am because she almost pulled her own hand off?*

She sat back and looked around the room. Featureless. She palmed her way along the skirting-board, trawling for telephone wire and when she found nothing she sat, her hands pressed against the radiator, coaxing her tired, desperate brain. Could she get under the floorboards? Maybe find a joint in the piping? Slide the cuffs off the end of it?

"If it kills me," she muttered. "If it kills me."

"Not again," the nurses whispered to each other, exchanging glances when Alek Peach was brought into ICU. The endoscopy staff thought they could see a stress ulcer down there — Mr Friendship, the consultant, knew a stress ulcer instantly, they were a common problem in Intensive Care: shock could starve the intestines and stomach wall of blood, but although patients were routinely prescribed cimetidine, occasionally one boomeranged back and turned up a few days after discharge "hosing blood", as Friendship put it. Endoscopy had shot a dose of adrenaline into Peach's ulcer, to try to stem the blood loss, but it looked as if it had already developed into peritonitis — potentially fatal if they couldn't pump him with enough antibiotics. This time Friendship wasn't taking any chances: the press were interested enough as it was and he intended to guard Alek Peach's life like Cerberus.

Ayo Adeyami hadn't been on duty when he was admitted. She arrived this morning fresh from two days off — after all the champagne she'd drunk with Ben she'd only had the energy to lie around on the sofa and feel the baby move inside her. She hadn't expected to come back to a ward in chaos. Police officers were at both entrances and all the nurses were twitchy. One of the juniors, the one who drove Ayo mad sometimes with her speculating and gossip, naturally had a story about the Peaches. This time even Ayo had to admit it was worth listening to. When the ward had settled a little they sat in the nurses' coffee room, drinking machine coffee and eating a family-size bag of cheesy footballs, the windows open, a delicious breeze shifting calmly across them. In the hallway outside, an armed officer, in full body armour, sat discreetly next to the door.

"Well, listen, OK?" The nurse turned to face Ayo, crimping one hand casually at the side of her face to shield her mouth from the police officer. "My sister, yeah?" she mouthed, orange-painted lips moving with precision.

"Yeah."

"Well, she's a medical secretary and guess who she works for?"

"I dunno."

"For *their* doctor. The Peaches' doctor."

Ayo, who in spite of her reservations spied the makings of a prime piece of gossip, glanced at the door-way then turned her body round, getting her stomach comfortable by wedging it sideways against the chair back. She pulled her eyebrows down and moved a bit closer, mirroring the nurse's hand gesture. "Ree-uh-lly?"

"Yes, really. And, anyway, she took a call from the mum about a month ago. She was in tears, said she wanted to see the doctor, that her hubby had hit the little boy because —"

"God." Ayo looked nervously around herself, trying not to lick her lips. "That wasn't in the papers."

"I *know*. She wanted to see the doctor because the little boy had been pissing on things. You know, really weird, like on the carpets and stuff."

"An *eight*-year-old?"

"Uh-huh." The nurse licked her fingers and used it to press a curl against her cheek. She flashed a smile across at the officer as if they were talking about nothing more important than *Friends* or *The X Files*, then turned back to Ayo and covered her mouth again. "Never kept her appointment and the next they heard Dad's in hospital and the boy's — well, you know . . ."

"That's *screwy*."

"Isn't it?"

"Creepy." Ayo tapped her teeth, thinking about a child peeing on a bed. Just like Ben's old dog had done. Just like Josh had done in the bathroom.

"So you think that's why they're here now?"

"You watch, I think we'll know soon enough."

* * *

Rebecca was cold. It was bright outside her flat, the top of the Greenwich roofs all rusty-coloured against the blue, but this wasn't a weather cold: it was a different cold, a cold inside her, like stone. She stood in the kitchen unloading shopping-bags — three cartons of orange juice, milk, two bottles of vodka and a ready-made meal, chicken and tarragon. She knew she needed to eat — she had been drunk all yesterday, hadn't eaten and had slept for just three hours, waking with the sun, her skin damp, her hair matted. The flat had been a mess — some time in the night she'd broken another glass, in the studio this time, and there were rolled-up edges of Rizla packets everywhere. No food in the kitchen, only a year-old bottle of Bailey's, curdled in the heat on the window-sill. Her brain had been swooshing around so much that she'd had to take a deep breath, get her keys, and venture out to get paracetamol. Now she put her hand on her head and stared at the groceries. No paracetamol. She had gone out intending to get paracetamol but had come back with vodka.

Oh, God. She didn't think she could face going out into the sun again so instead of pain-killers she found a dusty glass in the back of the cupboard, rinsed it, opened one of the bottles of Smirnoff and poured herself a weak vodka and orange. Just to soothe her head and send her off to sleep again — she wasn't going to get drunk but, *God, it's so difficult to sleep when the sun is up*. She sniffed the drink, turned the glass around, and tasted it. After the first sip it didn't taste bitter — it tasted sweet. She rolled up her shirt-sleeves and took the drink into her studio to close the shutters and that felt better. Now all of Greenwich couldn't look in and see how transparent and substanceless she was. The sunlight had found a way in from the kitchen, so she went back in there and closed the blinds, stopping to refill her glass on the way.

"Jack," she muttered, walking unsteadily back into the studio. "Oh, God, Jack —"

In the relatives' room at King's Hospital ICU, Caffery woke up with a jolt, as if someone had said his name. He lay there for a while blinking, trying to piece together why he was here. Last night Souness had come over to the unit and together they had tried a little pressure on Mr Friendship. But for health professionals the police come a long way down the chain of priority, and the answer was: no, not yet. "There's a life to be saved — whatever it is can wait until he's stabilized."

So Souness went home with Paulina, and Caffery spent another night away from home, sleeping on a banquette in the relatives' room, waiting for news. The relatives' room could have been Gatwick airport for all the makeshift sleeping arrangements. Except for the tears. A woman with a massive brain haemorrhage had come on to the ward in the night, and her husband, unable to bear his wife's almost dead face on the pillow, sat in a corner on his own, staring at the floor, not moving. He hardly seemed to notice the baby in the car seat on the floor next to him, who cried and made faces and curled its little fists and didn't have any idea how wildly its future was pivoting in the neighbouring ward.

Blinking, Caffery sat up and rubbed his face. His neck was sore from sleeping on the banquette. He went straight to the main doors of the intensive care unit, straightening his shirt, flattening his hair back with his palm. Time to get moving. The armed officer let him in, but the manager inside the unit was ferociously tall, heavily pregnant and quite determined that Caffery was not to trouble her patient.

"I'm sorry, sir, Mr Friendship talked to you about this last night. He says he'll let you have access to the patient when he's ready, but until then I've been told not to let you inside. You can wait here with the officer."

"Look, I was the one with Mr Peach when he got ill. I'll only be a moment."

"Mr Friendship said he's sorry. Not for the time being." She nodded to the PC sitting in an alcove just inside the door. "You've been allowed him."

"Fine, fine. I don't suppose if I said please . . ."

"No — really." She smiled. "I'm sorry. Honestly, I'm sorry."

"It's OK." He scratched the back of his neck and looked around the small area where the officer was posted. "I suppose I couldn't just sit here for a bit? In case there's any change."

"There won't be."

"Well, OK, but maybe if I could."

"I can't stop you, but nothing's going to change until Mr Friendship says it's changed."

"OK." He took off his jacket and sat down opposite the uniformed officer, stretching out his legs, watching the manager walk away with her small, clipped steps. From the storeroom a nurse, unpacking a box of ventilator tubes, watched him, her eyes big and unblinking. The armed officer nodded at Caffery but neither of them spoke. Eventually the nurse took the endotrachial tube and went back to her patient, and presently the unit manager reappeared, wandering over to where Caffery sat. She leaned against the wall, her arms crossed. "Why the urgency, then?"

He half stood, thinking she'd changed her mind. "We just want to speak to him about what happened."

"It was terrible, wasn't it?"

"Terrible," Caffery agreed. "And God forbid it should happen to someone else."

"Oh, crumbs — don't say stuff like that."

"These people don't stop at one. There's too much fun in it."

"Stop it. You're not being serious, are you?"

"As serious as a heart-attack."

She frowned. "We don't use expressions like that here."

"I'm sorry." He straightened and came to stand next to her, looking at the name on the staff badge hanging around her neck. "Sorry. Didn't mean to offend, Ayo."

She smiled and half put her hand over the badge, slightly embarrassed, slightly flattered. For the first time in months she wished she hadn't got this football up her sweater. "That's OK. It was horrible how it happened, wasn't it?"

"Yes." He scratched the back of his neck and leaned a little closer. "And he's very clever — whoever it was who attacked that little boy was very clever. And I'm sure that if I spoke to Mr Peach now I'd get that final" — he made a quick fist — ". . . that final bit of the puzzle. Anyway," he rapped his knuckles on the wall and looked around him, "do you, uh, mind if I use the gents'?"

"Back through the door, first on the right." She gestured down the corridor.

"Thanks."

In the gents' Caffery closed the door and counted to five. Then he turned around and went straight back to Intensive Care, buzzing urgently on the door. Ayo opened it.

"Is that one of your patients?"

"What?"

"On the floor in the gents'. He's got a drip with him, I thought . . ."

Ayo dithered, confused, not certain what to do.

"He's just inside the door. Do you want me to call someone?"

"The consultant!" She hurried down the corridor, her nametag swinging wildly on its chain. "455 for an air call."

"Will do." He waited till she was through the doors, then nodded at the uniformed officer and slipped inside the unit.

The carpet came away quickly — like Elastoplast coming away from skin — the tacks pop-pop-pop-pop-popping. She scrabbled away the underlay, dropped down and pressed her ear to the naked floorboards. Silence. For a moment she lay there, comforted by the texture of the wood — the lovely grained surface, the outdoorsy Canadian smell of forest and rain. But she had to keep going. She took a deep breath and sat up, looking at the area she had cleared.

The grip rod, the little wooden strip with tacks in it, was nailed into the boards so she leaned over, found the wiring from her bra and slotted the end under the rod, sliding it down as far as it would go. "Hey, Smurf," she muttered. "Look at Wonder Woman." She took off her shirt, double-wrapped it around her hands and pulled on the wire. The grip rod creaked, rose quickly and broke away from the floor.

"Good."

Quickly she rolled over and looked at it. Projecting from the strip of wood, like renewable shark's teeth, a gully of sharp tacks. A tool. And if not a tool, then a weapon. She shuffled forward on her bottom, bending her knees up so that she was as close as possible to the radiator, and jammed the strip against the copper pipe, moving it back and forward — a makeshift saw — back and forward, back and forward. She wasn't going to sit here and die. She was going to get water and then she was going to get out. Simple as that.

The intensive care unit was quiet, only the soft bleeping of the monitors, the occasional sucking noise of a nurse testing a mouth aspirator against her hand. There were eighteen beds ranged around the room and the nurses, in their blue theatre scrubs and soft white mules, moved calmly among them. There was no fluster, no panic. Caffery felt as if he was watching them through a plate-glass window. No one questioned him as he walked along the ward and when one of the nurses turned to him briefly, her fair eyebrows raised slightly, he thought the game was up — thought she'd point, challenge him, call her colleagues — but all she did was smile and continue along, rolling a portable drip stand in front of her.

Alek Peach was in a private room with two beds. Caffery checked through the window and entered, closing the door quietly behind him. The curtains were drawn around one bed and in the other lay Peach, on his back, his eyes closed, his arms flat on the covers. Catheters snaked from his chest and arms, up and out to an array of bags suspended above the bed: some were clear and contained drugs, some were garish, multicoloured "Nutrison" feeding bags. At least one was feeding him blood. Coloured lights flickered along the bank of monitors, the electrocardiogram, the pulse-oximeter, leaping and dancing.

Caffery closed the curtains around the bed, went to Peach's side, rested both fists on the side of the bed and bent until his mouth was next to his ear: "It's time you were straight with me, Alek."

Peach's eyes fluttered. His head moved and a small groan escaped him.

"I don't give a shit if you're not well enough to talk to me, I don't give a shit."

Above the bed the heart monitor began to stammer. Somewhere, in some distant nurses' station, Caffery could hear it trigger an alarm. He moved even closer until he felt he was almost inside Peach's ear. "If it's you and you've got someone else you're going to tell me who. I don't care if *you* die but I'm *not* going to let it happen to someone else."

Peach's face suddenly changed. He licked his lips with a pale tongue. He blinked once or twice then snapped his eyes open, rolling them sideways. Caffery almost took a step back, there was such anger, such empty, unthought-through malice in those eyes. Then Peach's mouth began to move. His voice was whispery — too low to be heard above the machines.

"What? Say it again, you little shit."

A nurse, summoned from the coffee room by the monitor alarms, appeared, shocked-faced, at a gap in the curtains. "Sir! Please, we have to ask you to leave —" In the ward outside someone was shouting about getting Security. "Sir — *please*!" But Peach's mouth was still moving, and Caffery bent nearer, straining to hear what he was saying.

"What? Say it again."

Just as the unit manager arrived, just as Caffery knew he was going to be thrown out, Peach opened his mouth one more time and this time was loud enough to hear: "*Fuck you*," he was saying. "*Fuck you*."

The slit in the pipe was weeping, not even a trickle, more a slow, barely perceptible ballooning — a single drop seemed to take several minutes to form. Nevertheless Benedicte fastened her mouth to it and sucked. It was only enough to wet her tongue and leave its metallic taste in her mouth, but she pressed her cracked lips to it with the desperation of a baby, forming a vacuum, and slowly, painfully drew another weak drop on to her tongue. She pushed her body nearer, hugging the radiator with one arm, working it, working it, but after twenty minutes, and less than a thimbleful of water, she was exhausted. She dropped on her back panting. "Oh, shit."

It took a long time to get her breath back. When she had, she brought Smurf to the pipe and tried to encourage her to drink, but the Labrador just turned her head away and sighed. "OK, Smurf, you stay there." It hadn't been much water, but Ben felt stronger, knowing what she'd achieved. "Won't be long now."

She turned her attention back to the boards. In the planks between her hands there was a join, a knot hole on the inner edge of one. She could widen it enough to get her fingers in. And if that didn't work she'd already made up her mind: she was going to use the grip rod to saw through her ankle. The thought didn't even make her feel ill.

The incident room was buzzing. The team was rested, and now they had new leads they were ready to roll. Caffery had been home for a shower and a change of clothes — no sign, he noticed, that Rebecca had been there. Now he was refreshed, feeling clean under his arms and in his hair. He was determined to speak to Peach again, get some space, get a little leverage going.

If Mr Friendship wouldn't listen to him, maybe he'd listen to Souness.

He arrived in the incident room just as Kryotos's phone was ringing. She leaned over, and hooked up the receiver on one finger. "Yup?" She tucked it between her chin and her shoulder, and put both hands on the desk, staring down at a pile of forms as she listened. Caffery came and stood next to her, looking at her face. "For you," she mouthed.

"OK. In my office."

She put the call through. In the SIO's office he nodded at Souness and caught up the phone.

"DI."

"Jack," Fiona Quinn was breathless, "wanted you to be the first to know. That DNA's come back."

"Jesus." He closed the door and pulled the chair up to the desk, his heart pounding. "And?"

"And we got a full male profile. *Full*. Came up as bright as the Oxford Street Christmas lights."

Caffery clicked his fingers frantically at Souness. She looked up in surprise. "*What?*"

"*DNA*," he mouthed, his hand over the receiver.

She used her heels to rodeo the chair over to his desk. She sat close to him, trying to overhear the conversation. He almost had to keep her from grabbing the phone.

"What've we got, Fiona?"

"You're not going to believe it."

"I might. Try me."

* * *

The sky over Brockwell Park was a calm, pearly blue, only a few clouds strung along the horizon, as if they were heavier than the blue colour and had sunk down to the edges. Roland Klare could have seen the sky through his window, but at the moment he wasn't interested in patterns in the sky: he was further back in the flat, in the cupboard, bathed in red light, tongue between his teeth as he cut the negatives and placed the first in the enlarger.

He knew he was getting close and had to stop his knee from jerking in a nervous tic as he moved the lamphouse up and down, trying to get the print to fit on the paper. He adjusted the focus, switched off the red bulb and flicked on the enlarger light. A triangle of white flooded down on to the paper, perfect against the blackness of the cupboard — just as it appeared in the book. The timer was broken but Klare was ready — he had read somewhere that the word "photography" equalled one second, so he sat on the stool, staring down at the paper, his hands between his knees, and muttered the words out loud: "One photography, two photography, three photography." When the twenty seconds he'd calculated were up he switched off the enlarger light and, illuminated only by the red safelight, carried the paper over to the litter tray where he'd prepared the developing solution. He stood over it, swirling the paper around, keeping count in his head, peering down at the magical picture creeping across the paper.

"A hundred and two photography, a hundred and three photography, a hundred and —" He stopped counting. The print was taking shape. It was still blurry, and it was too dark in this light to see properly, so he quickly splashed around some stop-bath and fixer — hardly able to keep still as he waited for the allotted time — then carried the dripping print into the kitchen, ran it under the tap and peered at it. The picture was a little hazy, either from the damaged enlarger or maybe because the original hadn't been properly focused. Heart thumping now, Klare took it to the living room window and held it up to the sunlight.

CHAPTER TWENTY-THREE

The ward had settled now and was quiet, the only noise the whir of syringe drivers, the occasional equipment alarm. It was a warm day and the window in the nurses' room was open a crack, the curtains lifting as a mild summer breeze moved through the ward. Ten minutes before lunch one of the staff slipped silently along the ward. She stopped outside the private room, as if something had just struck her, and stood for a moment, one foot stretched out slightly behind the other, then turned the handle and went in, closing the door behind her. Less than a minute later the door opened and the same woman came out. She headed quickly away from the room, her body stiffer than before, her pace suddenly abrupt.

Ayo thought herself a good nurse: a nurse of the critically ill, she rarely had a problem finding the human vibration in everyone, never had any problem reaching under the wires and tubes and finding the warm pulsing soul. But when she had pushed the door open and looked at Alek Peach lying on the bed — *well, Alek Peach was like no one I've ever seen . . .* It was as if there was a shell lying on the bed, an empty husk. He breathed, his heart moved, his vital functions were good, sound — but the warmth had gone from him. It had all leaked away.

Ayo wondered where her compassion had gone. When he'd opened one eye and fixed it on her she'd instinctively taken a hurried step backwards. He frightened her. Quickly, before he could speak, she had left the room, and now, as she marched up the ward, she decided she was going to ask Detective Inspector Caffery what he wanted with Peach, exactly why they needed an armed officer at the end of the ward, why he had lied to her just to get into the private room. The police usually only mounted a guard if the patient was the victim of a drugs feud and needed protection. Or if he was a suspect.

That thought made her stop and turn to look back to Peach's room. Beyond the glass door a shadow moved. It was just a nurse in there, changing drips, but still it made Ayo stiffen. *Bloody hell, Ayo, apologize to that detective — say you're sorry about the business this morning, that you had to take orders from above, and then maybe you should tell him about your mad brain and how it's run away with ideas*.

Yes — that would give her something to tell Benedicte when she got back: "*I only went and told the bloody police, didn't I?*" She could picture it: the Churches, exhausted from the journey, pulling up in the driveway, the car covered in sand, looking up and seeing their front door kicked in, police tape all over the place. "*I'm so embarrassed, Ben, but I'd found out something weird, I found out that Rory Peach had been peeing on things in the house — you know, like Josh did. God, Ben, I'm such a drama queen — I'm sorry.*"

She tried to shake it off, clear her mind — *For God's sake, girl, get a grip, your poor child is going to have a wild woman for a mother* — but she couldn't escape the feeling that Peach's eyes were following her, could reach her, even out here.

The photograph Roland Klare was holding up to the window showed a man having intercourse with a boy. In fact, the man was *forcing* intercourse on a young boy — that was clear from the child's expression, and from his posture. The man's face was blurred, slightly tilted on one side, but it was a face that Roland Klare had seen a lot of recently. It had been all over the news this week. It was Alek Peach's face.

At that moment, hundreds of feet below, a policeman on his beat walked along the front of Arkaig Tower and, suddenly nervous, Klare closed the curtains. He couldn't be seen all the way up here in the sky, he knew that, but nevertheless he felt safer taking the photograph to the sofa, where he sat and stared at it, his heart pounding.

The team was amazed. The DNA found on Rory belonged to his father, Alek. And there was more: the fibres that had fluoresced under the Crimescope light in Rory's wounds had been identified. They had come from the T-shirt Peach had been wearing during the supposed attack on his family. Although he had claimed not to have seen or heard his son the entire time they were kept in the house, somehow fibres from his T-shirt had got underneath the ropes binding his son. And now that the team was starting to ask questions about him they had weeded out a couple of people who had always wondered — *just a suspicion, mind* — whether Mr Peach hadn't been in the habit of clouting Rory once in a while.

"The clanging of things falling into place is deafening." Souness was at her computer, firing off e-mails, sucking on a can of Dr Pepper. She looked up at Caffery standing in the doorway of the SIO's room. "What? You got nothing better to do than stand around wi' a gob on?"

"Danni." He closed the door and came in. "Look —"

"Oh, God," she sighed, "I know you so well — you want something, don't you?"

"I want you to speak to that knobshine down at King's for me. Friendship. He won't give me the time of day, won't let me speak to Peach."

"Don't worry about that, Jack. Give Alek time to get better, then we'll come down on him." But she saw that wasn't going to be enough for him, so she pushed away the keyboard, leaned back in her chair, her hands folded across her stomach. "Jack? You've not *arrested* him, have you? Before he went into hospital?"

"No."

"So the detention clock's not on? None of this counts towards our thirty-six?"

"None of it."

"He's under guard and not going anywhere?"

"That's right."

She opened her hands. "Then what's up? Why the urgency? Let the consultant take his own sweet time."

"Oh, God . . ." He fell into his seat and rubbed his eyes. "Look — I don't know *how* I know, but I promise you it's not that simple." He sat forward, steepling his hands and pointing them at her. "I am so sure he's got someone else, Danni. Once he's safe inside a house, got everyone safe and gagged, he can come and go as he likes —"

"Jack —"

"— and if he's got someone else then how long do you think they'd survive? Four days? In this weather, without any injuries, five days if they were *very fucking lucky*." He got up and put his hand on the door. "Now please, *please* speak to that arsehole at King's."

Benedicte worked, sawing with the grip rod, growing sicker and shakier by the minute. She didn't care how much sound she made now that she knew the troll had gone. Hair-fine pieces of wood peeled away, then larger, curly pieces. Every few minutes she had to stop and get her breath back, sitting with her legs splayed on either side of the area she was working at. Then she'd topple on to her side and fasten her mouth to the radiator pipe, sucking as much water as she could into her parched mouth. She was getting weak, but she wasn't going to give up.

It took almost three hours for her to scour a line about half a centimetre deep. A fragment of wood had come away — it was only the size of a sugar cube, but it had left a two-finger hole in the plank. She dropped the tack strip and inched the bra wiring into the hole, pushing it so it poked back up through the knot hole and created a handle. She sat on the floor, her feet planted against the wall, giving her something to strain against, gripped both ends of the wire and pulled. The blood vessels in her head ballooned with the effort: *Can your veins pop?* she thought. *Can they just burst?*

London was melting. The earth in Brockwell Park was cracking, long open sores in the ground, and in Brixton market girls sashayed down the street dressed only in denim shorts and seersucker bikini tops, hair tied into bunches with pink ribbon. On the edge of the steaming swimming-pool Fish Gummer was tired. Ever since he'd had the encounter with DI Caffery he'd been irritable. *That's the last time I'll ever speak to the police*. Today's class was the "otters", the eight-to nine-year-olds. He stopped and narrowed his eyes at them lined up on the water's edge, standing with arms at their sides like penguins in multicoloured arm-floats. "Well? Who's missing?"

The children all bent forward to look up and down the row.

"Josh." One of the boys gave him a toothless grin.

Josh Church was new to the class. He'd come only twice, dropped at the door from a big yellow car. "Well? Have any of you seen him? Any of you live near him?"

The children all looked at each other and shrugged. Josh was so new that no one had got to know him that well. None of them cared whether he was there or not.

"All right." He blew his whistle. "Get yourselves a float if you need it, and get into the water."

DC Logan stood in the incident-room doorway, coffee cup in his hand, examining his tie as if he suspected he'd spilled something on it. When Caffery stopped next to him, he dropped it and looked up guiltily: "All right?"

"How many houses did you do on the house-to-house?"

"Uh — I — well, y'know, I tried to do them thoroughly."

"Right —" Caffery put his hands in his pockets and stood a little closer, murmuring into Logan's ear. "I've just had your overtime sheets in, and checked them next to the number of statements you took this week and there's a problem . . ." He dropped his chin and raised his eyebrows.

Logan knew what he was saying. He lowered his eyes.

"It's OK, you can make up for it," Caffery murmured. "I've got a little job for you." He checked over his shoulder. Danni had her feet on the desk and was speaking into the phone. "There's a Mapinfo sheet and instructions in my pigeon-hole. You will knock on twenty doors before the sun goes down. Just so you know."

Logan stood, hands limp at his side, until Caffery had gone. Then he straightened his tie and looked over at Kryotos: "What the *fuck*'s got into him?" he mouthed.

Kryotos shrugged and turned away.

"Here we go." It had taken almost five hours but at last Ben felt the wood crack between her hands. She scrabbled at it, her fingers bleeding now, and slowly enough of the board splintered for her to see into the space under the floor. She put her head down and peered in. The cavity was about ten inches deep, warm with incubated air. Pipes and wires zoomed in from the side of the house and snaked away from her into the darkness. It didn't smell musty or spidery, instead it smelt of new wood and mastic. She sat up and pulled away the remainder of the plank then pushed her face back into the hole.

Now what? Close to her eyes was a round electrical junction box screwed to a joist, tentacles of white cable exiting north, south, east, west, like a tiny octopus. One of the leads docked with the top of a black cylinder standing proud of the plasterboard. It took Ben a few moments to recognize that she was looking at the metal sheath of a light fitting — the recessed lighting in the kitchen — somewhat bigger than a beaker, inverted and pushed up through a circular hole.

My God — this type of fitting, she was *sure*, was simply pushed up from below into the plasterboard, nothing holding it up, no screws or nails. She recalled Darren, Ayo's husband, pulling one out to work on it in their kitchen in Kennington — she remembered seeing it dangling from its cord.

She lay on her belly and cupped her hand over the top of the lamp, pressing it down. It moved with a long, soft, sucking sound — like jelly from a mould — and dropped out of sight, the wires catching the weight, daylight flooding into the space from below. Ben sucked in a breath. The light swung under the ceiling like a pendulum, the wires banging against the sides of the hole, and when nothing happened, when no one charged up the stairs and slammed into the door, she felt brave enough to get her face into the hole and see what was going on down there.

She lay down on her front, her arms out in front of her like an obedient schoolgirl in a diving lesson, *fingers pressed together, children*, and thought of Josh running out of the swimming-pool from his new lessons and jumping into the car: "Mum, what's a aquadynamic?" The plasterboard ceiling cracked suddenly under her weight. She recoiled, horrified, pulling her head out, her hair catching on nails so that she came out backwards with a snarled crown. "Oh Jesus oh Jesus oh Jesus —"

She crouched there for a moment, panting, expecting the ceiling to collapse. But when it didn't her heart slowed a little. She pushed her hair from her eyes and slowly, carefully, bent down again. This time she was more cautious. She spread her hands across the floor like a gecko, and slowly wormed her face into the airless space, stealthy as a hunting cat, until she could see into the circle vacated by the light fitting.

It was bright down there, bright and open. And ten feet below her, in the kitchen beneath, Hal lay on the floor. On his back, his face almost directly beneath the hole.

Oh my God —

His feet were up, at an odd angle, both ankles individually cuffed to the big oven handle; his hands had been stretched above his head and fastened by electric flex to the squat feet of the washing-machine. His shorts had been removed and put back on with both legs forced into one leg opening, secured with the orange and blue bungee cords from the Daewoo roof-rack, and his mouth was covered with a piece of brown parcel tape. A large stain, a corona of his own filth, surrounded him. Now Ben realized she could hear him snoring, as if he had simply got bored with the whole thing. As if he'd eaten Christmas dinner and drifted off in front of *The Wizard of Oz*.

She manoeuvred her face so her mouth was at the opening and whispered softly: "*Hal?*"

Parallel to Brixton Hill, along the route of the old river Effra, consigned to the underworld since the last century, ran Effra Road, a hill that linked the lower, fashionably self-conscious slopes of Brixton with the poor council estates at the Streatham end. On this, one of the hottest days of the year, DC Logan was climbing the hill with slow deliberation, cooking in his own sweat. The sun had heated up the earth until the paving stones lifted at odd angles. In front gardens cats slept under bushes, twitching their ears at the midday insects. *Jesus*, he thought, *what I could do to a cold Red Stripe is criminal*.

Up ahead on the left was the new housing development, Clock Tower Grove — he could see the hoarding and the flags — and beyond them a concrete joist swaying in the claws of a crane. There were some bigger houses at the back overlooking the park. He supposed he'd have to go and find out if any of the places were finished, if anyone had moved in yet. He wiped the sweat from his forehead. There were eighteen more addresses to make that day — he wasn't going to hang around at any of them. If no one answered the door he was out of there.

Meanwhile, in number five, Clock Tower Walk, Hal opened his eyes and thought he was seeing an angel. A sweet geometry — her face in a circular frame. At first the eyes, those eyes like mirrors, seemed to take up the whole of the room.

Benedicte?

"*Hal*," she whispered.

And then he thought, for the first time, that maybe they had a chance. He tried to jerk his head up in reply but he had been bound so he couldn't move. Tears slid from his eyes.

"Hal," she murmured, her voice faint and sick. "*Josh?* Is he . . .?"

He moved his eyes sideways, showing her the direction.

She pulled back from the hole and tried to reposition herself to get the angle right so she could see into the family room. She could feel the uneven temperature of the air, she could smell her own breath in the tiny space. As if all her tension and sickness had been converted to chemicals and breathed out through her lungs. She pushed her face into the hole until her flesh and eyeball bulged down into the room. Her eyes clicked open and closed. Rotated and froze.

Fastened to the radiator in the family room, curled up like a little fern, his knees pulled up under his chin, was Josh. Although he was grey and washed out his expression was calm, his eyes fixed, concentrating on trying to unpick the rope that bound him to the radiator. On the wrist he had already freed were deep furrows, shiny and red, and there was a rash on his mouth where a tape had been.

"*Josh?*" Softly at first, because she couldn't believe she wasn't seeing a mirage. Then: "JOSH!"

He didn't react immediately, just remained staring at the ropes. It took him a while to break his trance, then his eyes rolled towards her, blinking.

"Josh!"

"M-mummy?"

Her child had changed. His head was thin, his eyes huge. He looked like Hal — like a tiny twenty-year-old Hal with veins standing up on his forehead and hands. Poor progeric child — he reached a hand up to her, not saying anything, just reaching it out in the air, the palm towards her, as if he was trying to feel her face. Check it was real. Then he dropped his hand, turned away from her and started pulling on the rope.

"*Josh!*"

"Daddy's not well," he whispered, not looking up. "He can't talk."

"I know, darling. Have you had something to drink?"

He shook his head.

"No?"

"A little bit." He wouldn't look at her. He's already a little man, she thought, already being the big little man.

"Do you feel all right, baby? How's your tummy?"

"Feels funny. I'm thirsty, Mummy."

"That's OK, we'll get you something to drink."

"I never meant to, Mummy, I had to go wee-wee on myself, I'm sorry."

"Oh, sweetheart, that's OK. Don't worry." Upstairs, with her bleeding fingers and her exhausted mind, she wanted to cry. This little boy, whom she had thought would be the casualty, was sitting up and getting on with it. He had nearly undone the rope. Instead of sobbing and despairing, like she had, he had been determinedly and silently getting on with escaping. "The nasty man's gone now."

Josh nodded. "He's gone. He's been horrid and the police are going to beat him up and put him in prison and kill him."

"Did you hear Mummy calling?"

"Yes — I couldn't say nothing because I had a thing on my mouth."

"Don't worry about that, sweetheart. I love you."

"Me too."

"What are you doing down there?"

"Getting out of the rope. I'll come and I'll get you." He was quiet for a moment. Then without looking at her, "Mummy?"

"Yes?"

"Maybe he killed Smurfy." His chin trembled. "Cos I — cos I don't know where Smurf is."

"Oh, Josh —" Benedicte's throat was tight. "You are such a — such a good, such a clever . . . *brave*, brave little boy. Don't worry about Smurf, peanut, she's with me. She's feeling a little bit poorly but she's up here and she can't wait to see you. She sends you her love and a big lick on the face." She paused because now she could see that his fingers were bleeding. "Josh, I love you, darling, Mummy loves you so, so much —"

In the hallway the doorbell rang. Josh's head snapped up, staring in horror at the door and Ben froze. *No!* She couldn't believe it.

"Josh," she hissed. "Quick now. Come on now, baby, move it now —" Beneath her Hal jerked frantically and noiselessly on the floor and Ben's voice rose hysterically: "*Come on, Josh. MOVE IT*. Just MOVE!!"

He pulled frantically at the rope, tugging and pulling, biting it, the blood from his fingers staining his mouth. His teeth were strong but the rope was embedded.

"*Quickly!*"

He pulled harder, eyes on the door, preparing for the menace to hurtle down the hallway. Then Benedicte saw her little boy make a decision.

"*No!*" she screamed. Another crack ricocheted along the plasterboard. "*No! Josh, RUN, Josh, please RUN*."

But he couldn't have freed himself in time. So he took the brown parcel tape from the floor and pressed it to his mouth, smoothing it down with the flat of his palms, swivelling his little body round, pressing the rope behind him and turning so he sat with his back to the radiator. Ben's heart squirmed. "God, *no*." She began to weep, long silver threads falling out of the ceiling and landing next to Hal's face. "No!"

And then the doorbell rang again.

Everyone froze. Ben stopped crying and Hal stopped thrashing on the floor. Josh's eyes flew to his mother. The troll never rang more than once. For a long time no one dared to breathe. The bell rang yet again and in the hallway the letterbox clanged.

"Hello?" A man's voice. "Hello-oh?"

The police — maybe Ayo's sent someone — maybe . . . Benedicte opened her mouth to call out, but something stopped her, a survival instinct, maybe, a survival instinct older than her own cells. *No, it's a trick — it's him. It must be him.* In the family room Josh was scrabbling at the rope again. "Josh, don't say anything, don't move," she hissed. "Keep quiet." He obeyed her, kept quite still, and in the silence she could hear her heart thudding. *It's OK*, she told herself. *If it is the police they'll see something's wrong — they'll know something's wrong and they'll come and find us, I'm not giving myself away if it's him —*

The doorbell rang once more. She sucked in a breath, biting her lip, the look in her eyes keeping Josh pinned where he was. The sound of the bell hung in the silence. To anyone on the garden path at the front of the Churches' deluxe polished oak door, with double glazing and thermal seals, the house would have appeared quite uninhabited.

Souness came in, placed both hands on the desk and leaned forward. "Right."

"OK." Caffery threw his pen down on the desk. "Lecture?"

She nodded. "Lecture. I got through to the consultant. We had a wee slanging match about my DI."

"Great."

"Jack, *what* were ye thinking?" She pulled up her chair and sat down. "Can you imagine the field day Peach's brief'll have?"

"I don't care, Danni, I've got to speak to him. He's got someone else. I *know* it."

She closed her eyes, pursed her mouth and shook her head. "Jack, you're *squeezing* me. I've spoken to the gov and what he's saying is clear: you've got your man, put the resources into closing it, put your energy into being ready for the interviews when Peach is well enough. We've got another critical incident come in this morning, they want this Peckham rapist *off* the back-burner and we just haven't got the manpower, Jack, for what, in the cold light of day, is a domestic incident, we haven't got —"

"Maybe I shouldn't be on the case anyway."

"Don't talk nonsense —"

"Maybe I've lost my perspective."

"Oh, please, cut the melodrama —" She stopped. Caffery had stood up. "Jack? Ye've to try to see it from my point of view."

"I'd love to, Danni," he picked up his keys, his cigarettes and put them into his pocket, "but to be honest I don't know if I could get my head that far up my own arse."

Souness shot to her feet. "Don't ye speak to me like that." She lifted her finger to him, her lips a dry, angry pink. "I did nothing to merit that — I'll discipline ye for it."

"Thank you." He stood, pushed some papers into a drawer and locked it. Pressed pens into the pen tidy and pushed his chair firmly under the desk so that it lined up perfectly. Suddenly his taste for the job had turned. "I think I'll go now. Since there's nothing else to be done but sit around with our feet up and wait for Peach to get better."

"Go on, then, fuck off home." She rubbed her head until it was hot. She was furious. "The rest should do you some good."

But when Caffery turned to the door Kryotos was standing there holding a green message form. "What?"

"Call from the hospital."

"That's OK, Marilyn." Souness reached past Caffery and took the form. "I got through to them on another line."

"No — I mean, not the hospital, I mean the sergeant. On the ward. It's Alek Peach. They want one of you. Urgently."

"Josh —" The house was silent and Benedicte's heart rate had slowed. But now she was seized with the idea that she'd been wrong. "Josh, listen — can you get out of that rope?"

He nodded and redoubled his efforts, gnawing at the nylon with his teeth.

"OK, darling, OK, listen. When you're free just go straight into the hall and open the front door. Into the hall and open the door." Josh looked from his father to his mother, his eyes huge with fear. "Go on, darling. I promise you it's OK. Just *hurry*."

With one last tug of the rope he freed himself. He was up, staggering a little, his leg muscles cramped, shooting out a hand to steady himself, but he was up. He held out his thin arms in front of him, as if it was dark, and pattered over to the kitchen sink, turning on the tap and putting his mouth under it to drink. Benedicte could almost *smell* how cold the water was. When he straightened, panting, water dripping from his chin, she whispered to him, "Good boy, now go and open the door."

But Josh pulled a glass down from the cupboard, filled it with water, and knelt down next to Hal. He pulled the packing tape from his father's mouth, rested the lip of the glass against Hal's lips, tipping water into his mouth. Hal bucked a little, almost choked, then greedily swallowed the water, his Adam's apple moving madly. Benedicte watched, impatient, resisting the urge to tell Josh to hurry. He was sitting next to Hal, as expert as a nurse, running a hand over his forehead and pouring more water into his mouth. "You next, Mummy," he said.

"OK, baby — but first go to the door, OK, go to the door — there might be someone out there to help us."

"OK." He put the glass on the floor and stood, unsteady on his feet, looking down once at Hal, who was thrashing his head from side to side, his mouth moving, trying to speak. Josh turned to the hallway, using the kitchen cabinets to keep his balance, jolting his way to the door. Benedicte could just see the bottom of his feet and his reflection in the laminate flooring. Tiny, thin little boy. He reached up, fumbled with the catch, and opened the front door.

She stayed there, her eye bulging down from the ceiling like the silent dome of a CCTV camera clicking on and off. There were no sounds from the hallway for several minutes. She imagined him opening the door and simply stepping out into a summer's day, bluebirds maybe, carrying a ribbon in their beaks, flying over the park.

The door slammed and she could see the reflection coming back. One tall, with heavy dark hair, one her son, being led back into the room — the familiar ease of an older brother guiding a small boy through a shopping centre. Except that Josh was crying silently.

She should have stayed, should have pushed through the ceiling, should have torn away her own skin before she let someone hurt Josh, but instinct sent her squirming back up through the hole, whimpering like a child, pulling the dangling light fitting behind her like a trap-door spider. Her ankle twisted, pain shot up her leg, but she didn't scream.

She knew that figure — she knew exactly whose it was. And now everything made sense.

Caffery left the Jaguar in the car park, forgot to pay and display, and raced into the building. He took the stairs two at a time, the squeal of his shoes on the shiny lino making orderlies pushing wheelchairs stop and stare.

He ran. Ahead of him, at the end of the long, polished corridor, the door to the ICU flew open. A nurse came out, pressing a crumpled paper towel against the bib of her uniform. As he got closer to her he could see darkness on the towel and when they passed each other he saw it was blood that was mashed into her bib.

The door opened again and this time the police officer came out, his face pale, blood on his hands. "In there." He nodded. Caffery pushed past him into the unit.

The window in the nurses' room was open, a soft breeze playing through the ward. In Peach's small annexe curtains had been pulled around his bed, and two nurses, faces set, busied themselves, silently mopping the floor and the walls. The curtain, lit from within like a vast, stretched Hallowe'en lantern, had a huge peacock-tail stain in the centre, a great, plumed splatter of blood, almost the size of a human. And beneath the bed — on the floor where the nurses mopped — shiny and rubbery as black PVC, more blood flattened out towards Caffery's feet.

Two miles away in Brixton DC Logan was enjoying that Red Stripe in the Prince of Wales. The marketing girls at Clock Tower Grove had been funny with him, stared at the sweat marks under his arms, so he'd given up and come back down the hill. He could fake the report, he decided. Jack Caffery, it was well known in

AMIT, had gone off the rails recently: probably his head done in by his nutty girlfriend with her trick pelvis and weed habits. DI Jack Caffery was crazy. Everyone knew he was letting loose in all directions, giving everyone both barrels for no reason. And Logan had not liked the sly threats Caffery'd made about his overtime. *Young Turk, my arse*, Logan thought, going to the bar for a refill.

CHAPTER TWENTY-FOUR

In Norfolk the forest at the top of the quarry was quiet, only the ghostly pitter-patter of rain on the leaves. Every ten minutes or so a car went by on the road half a mile away. Some had their headlights on although it was midday. Tracey Lamb lit a cigarette and leaned back against the rusty old Datsun, staring at the cars. She felt confident, pleased with herself. When she got home yesterday she had taken Carl's "book" and sat in his bedroom, on his bed — *that bed was his pride and joy* — black and silver lacquer with mirrors set in the headboard, and started calling his friends. None of them seemed to know about Penderecki's death — as if they cared — and when she told them about the visit from DI Caffery they all went into a panicking freefall.

"*Jesus Christ, Tracey!* Don't bring your shit to my doorstep."

"It's not just *my* shit —"

And then horrified realizations at the end of the line. "Tracey? *Tracey, whose fucking phone is this?* Don't tell me you're calling on your own phone?"

"Why?"

"Oh, you stupid fucking slag, you're even stupider than I thought —" And down went the phone. By the time she'd got to the end of the book the bush telegraph had been humming and the phones had all been taken off the hook. She had sat there smoking, among Carl's barbells, the weight-lifting belts and his DVD collection. She'd wanted to cry. The gates were closing and she'd been left outside. Penniless.

Well, fuck you all, she'd decided — *fuck every last one of you, you bunch of perverts*. She should have given them all up to Caffery — the arseholes.

Now she wiped her face, threw the cigarette into the undergrowth, straightened and coughed up a little phlegm. Here the grass and ferns stood high and thick and undisturbed; this was the little clearing Carl had used for dumping dodgy vehicles. At the far end, past the dead cars and among the wild poppies and storksbill, so far over it was almost in danger of falling into the quarry, was the caravan. It was old — the rain was turning it green in places and the scratched acrylic windows were thick with condensation. Peeling letters on the side were a reminder of Carl's attempts to start a hot-dog stand. The business hadn't taken off, but the sign was still there — she could see a faded stencilled price list, "Hot Dog — 15p", and the nailed-up hatch he'd cut in the side. The Borstal Boys used to live in the caravan when they stayed. They always seemed to be drunk on White Lightning cider and puking up into the quarry. Carl, who could always find work for an extra pair of hands, had liked having them around, especially in the late seventies when he had somehow wangled the licence to pick up wrecks from car accidents. "Cut and shunt", they called it, and most of the write-offs somehow found it back on to the streets with a little help from the Borstal Boys: resprays, welding, fibreglass filling, *get rid of those etched windows*. Carl would pay them in duty-free cigarettes and gin from his beer runs to Calais, or he'd give them the car radios to fence if they could stop the bereaved parents claiming them. How many times had Tracey witnessed one of the Borstal Boys standing in the garage explaining to a couple why they couldn't have the radio from their dead son's car: "The radio's not in a very pretty state, as it happens, probably best left well alone — eh?" And if they persisted: "I never wanted to say this but you can't 'ave the radio cos there's claret all over it — and something worse clogging up the tape deck." That would usually end the argument.

They'd cut up cars like abattoir animals — using every spare piece. Carl really had a way with him — the only thing he hadn't been able to out-think was the cancer. He got it, like a present, for his forty-eighth birthday.

"*It's cancer of the sixty Capstan a day, love. It's the same way your mother went — it'll be the way you'll go too. Family tradition*." He'd always been rat-thin, but when he died Carl was even thinner — like something from a concentration camp, she thought. And as soon as he'd gone the others lost interest and drifted away, and the wind came in off the fens and blew through the garage at night and made the corrugated iron rattle.

Now Tracey found her keys and got back into the old Datsun. She was hot in spite of the rain and immediately the windows steamed up. She put the radio on, turned the car round and drove off along the top of the quarry, the car jerking and lurching in the potholes. Wet ferns and nettles slapped down on the windscreen and behind her the caravan's little curtained window got smaller and smaller until it had disappeared in the dripping forest.

She had a plan, and had just taken the first steps towards making it a reality. She knew that there was nothing left for her here — Carl's death had left her high and dry: she didn't know how she was going to make next month's rent — she didn't even know how much it was, or whether Carl had a deal with the landlord. Christ, she didn't even know *who* the landlord was. *You always kept me away from the money, Carl, didn't you?* But she had some ideas. Once, twenty years ago, Carl had gone to Fuengirola — he knew people out there and had some business to deal with. It was the only time he'd been out of England, and he'd come back with stories of drinking cocktails on yachts and a postcard of a little village that looked in the sun like sugar cubes stuck to the edge of the mountain. It looked like heaven up there — so close to the sky, and the olive trees and the bright flowers hanging over the walls, blazing like gypsy scarves. Tracey Lamb felt sure she could be happy there. And she thought that the key to that happiness, the money to make it a reality, might come from DI Caffery's need to discover what had happened to Penderecki's boy.

Ayo came out from the curtains holding a bedpan full of plastic line clamps and bloodied towels.

"Oh!" She put her hand on her chest. "You made me jump."

The good-looking detective again — the one she'd imagined blabbing her mad ideas to. About Ben and Hal and how Josh was peeing on things. Maybe she'd tell him, make him laugh, show him there were no hard feelings.

"What's happened? What's going on?"

"Eh? Oh . . ." She looked back to where Alek Peach lay groaning softly. "He got agitated, coming out of sedation. Pulled his radial artery line out — it looks worse than it is."

"The blood?"

"We were giving him blood when he pulled it out. Most of that," she nodded to the floor, "is from the bag, not from him. He's in no danger."

"Right." He started towards the bed. "I'll talk to him now."

"Uh —" Ayo skilfully put herself in his way. "I'm sorry. Mr Friendship still hasn't given me the all-clear."

"Mr Friendship is more interested in pissing me off than anything."

"Maybe you should talk to *him* about that." She held up her hand to guide him out of the door. When he didn't move she dropped her head to one side. "Look, I'm sorry, and I really mean that. I'm sorry. If it was up to me . . ."

"Ayo, listen," he hissed. "It was *him*. He did it. He killed his son."

Ayo closed her mouth. *So he is a suspect — they should have warned us.*

"Come on, Ayo . . ."

"Look." She closed her eyes and held up her hand. "Thank you for telling me, but I'm sorry, you know, I have to not *care* what you *think* he's done."

"Oh, for Christ's sake. You crappy fucking do-gooders."

Her eyes snapped open. "There's no need for that."

"I know." He looked around the room, helpless, frustrated. "But you're just proving that really you don't give a shit. I mean, did you *read* the newspapers about Rory? Did you read what that man in there *did? To his own son?*"

Ayo swallowed, her blood pressure rising. "I've already explained my — *our* — position, so . . ." She pressed her hand to her belly. The baby was kicking, as if it was angry on her behalf. ". . . so if you'd be good enough to leave now, please — please just respect us, OK? Or I'll have to call Security."

"Thanks, Ayo," he said. "Thanks for the generosity of spirit." He opened the door to leave. "I'll remember it."

"And don't come back until we call you," she yelled down the ward after him, "which could be several days."

Afterwards her hands were trembling. She put down the bedpan and went into the nurses' station where she sat, breathing carefully, waiting for her heart to stop thumping. One of the junior nurses was concerned. "Hey? You OK?"

"God — I dunno. I think so." Ayo put her head back and breathed in through her nose. Her pulse was racing, she felt nauseous — she supposed it must be some form of panic-attack. The nurse, seeing her clammy face, her shaking hands, came in and put the kettle on.

"I'm going to make you some camomile tea. Can't have you stressed in your condition, can we, Mother?"

"God, thanks — you're a lamb." Ayo settled back, rolling the top of her tights down and cupping her hands around her stomach. A Braxton Hicks came and went, but she breathed her way through it. For God's sake — he only raised his voice to you and look at the state you're in — you're all set to go into premature labour over it. This poor, poor child, she thought for the thousandth time, a neurotic for a mother — how *will* it cope?

"I'm sorry if I jumped the gun." The armed guard stood a little outside the ICU, embarrassed, shuffling from foot to foot. "All we heard were the alarms, and the nurses getting aerated — thought you should be here."

"It's OK." Caffery's mobile was ringing. "Really — call me any time. Especially call me" — he fished in his pocket for the phone, hit the OK button, and used his thumb to cover the speaker — "especially call me when the lovely Mr Friendship gives us a clear, OK?" He nodded briefly, and turned away, speaking into the phone. "Yeah? DI?"

"It's me. I've heard something."

He hesitated, trying to place the voice. When he had it he raised his hand to the armed officer and headed off down the corridor. “Tracey,” he said, as soon as he was out of earshot. “Say that again.”

“I heard something that might be useful to you. Something about what we talked about.”

“Nah — that’s OK, we managed on our own, after all.”

At the other end Tracey paused for a moment. “I’m not talking about Brixton,” she said. “I’m talking about that boy of Penderecki’s.”

Benedicte remained where she had shrunk, eyes pricking and bright with fear. She had meant to be a warrior, meant to save her family. Instead she had scuttled back and lain on the floor, panting, weeping in the sour darkness, a hopeless lump bubbling away. *A shitty little curled-up coward on the floor*. If she was rolled on to her back she would remain locked in this position, like a brittle bluebottle, dead from terror. *Pathetic*.

And all she could think was: *He is a monster. Josh was right — a monster*.

Thick red lips, white hairless skin. Like Snow White, his dark hair was so luxuriant and shiny it almost didn’t look real — like a shampoo advert. His trainers were scuffed and dirty and the red nylon Adidas sweatpants were stained. She could imagine cloven hoofs and thick-haired legs under those trousers. And he was wearing pink rubber gloves. Benedicte knew exactly when she’d seen him before. It had been one morning in the camping shop on Brixton Hill. He had been behind her one minute, back turned to them as if he didn't want to be seen, hood pulled smartly over his face — the next she knew he was outside, holding up Smurf's tail to examine her. Now she thought about it she could convince herself that it had been Josh he was trying not to be seen by. Did Josh know him? Or was it just that Josh was the main focus of his interest? Suddenly her blood ran cold. *The Peaches, they were supposed to be going on holiday too*. Had he heard her talking to the assistant about the holiday in Cornwall? She tried to remember what she had said in the shop. Something about a long car journey, and — Oh, Jesus, yes — he would have overheard her talking about it — she'd even told the shopkeeper *when* they were leaving for Cornwall. Maybe he'd followed them home, been watching ever since, and in that case it was all her fault.

Suddenly Smurf, who was lying next to her, lifted her head and began to howl, a high-pitched pained squeal, the sound that comes when the pain is deeper than skin and muscle.

"Sssh . . ." Benedicte tried to hush her, stroked her, tried to coax her to the copper pipe to drink, but Smurf turned away and dropped her head on the floor. Ben sat back and began to pray. *Oh, Ayo, Ayo — please, God, come early — realize something's wrong — please*.

Caffery drove through the afternoon lanes. It had been raining in Suffolk, but now the sun was out, shining through the pollarded willows and making a patchwork of the road. Through tree tunnels he went, past horse farms, pleached maple corridors and low spreading ornamental junipers on perfect lawns. His hands were damp. *Rebecca is right — you are so desperate to get fucked around that you just jump to it. Leave your backbone at the door, Jack, why don't you?* Tracey Lamb, that bundle of selfish impulse wrapped in a human skin, had only to put her hand behind her back, look him in the eye and say, "Guess what I've got in my hand," and she'd got him — by the nose. The smallest crumb, the smallest possibility that she could tell him something about Ewan, and he was prepared to risk everything.

For a moment, just outside Bury St Edmunds, he got the sudden impression he'd picked up a tail. The flash of sunlight on a windscreen, a grille glinting in the rear-view, a red car, low, like a sports car. It had been with him for miles. He adjusted the mirror, wondering if he was being touched. *What would the rubber heelers want with you?* And before he even finished the thought the answer came to him: Of course.

Rebecca had talked.

Jesus fucking Christ, Rebecca, you did it, you've talked — she'd given them chapter and verse on what he'd done to her and what he'd done to Malcolm Bliss. Heart pounding now, suddenly panicked, he jammed his foot on the accelerator, leaned across the front seat, flipped open the glove compartment and dragged out the map. The road slipped away under the wheels of the Jaguar and the speedo crept up past seventy, eighty. From a driving course at Hendon he knew plenty of surveillance-avoidance techniques, but most of them depended on local knowledge, so he flipped open the map on the steering-wheel, steadying the car with the pressure of his knees and raced through the pages. He found the Thetford page and jabbed a finger down to anchor it, shooting a look in the mirror.

No! His hand drifted from the map. He couldn't believe it. The car had melted into the distance. He was alone on the road.

"Shit." He held the car steady, staring in the rear-view mirror to make sure he wasn't imagining it. Nothing. Just a silent road stretching out behind. He fumbled around for his mobile, holding it up, jabbing at it with his thumb to check he hadn't got a message — if something was happening Souness would have warned him, given him a head start, he was sure. But there was no message icon and the road behind was deserted. He'd imagined it. Imagined the whole thing. *If that doesn't make you sit up and take notice . . .*

"Right." He dropped the phone on the passenger seat, pushed the map aside, and let the car continue for two miles in silence, the blood pounding in his head. He was strung out, he decided, looking at the way his hands were shaking. When he got back to London he was going to tell Souness and Paulina all about it. Because Lamb was just spinning him a line. He knew in his heart that was all she was doing. *Don't get your hopes up*.

He told himself this so many times as he drove into Norfolk — past abandoned, boarded-up houses on deserted roads, past rubbish tips and derelict industrial greenhouses — that by the time he found Lamb sitting on the step outside the back door smoking a cigarette, dressed in pale leggings, high-heeled yellow sandals and a Shania Twain T-shirt, he had convinced himself not to listen to anything she said.

"Tracey," he said. "What do you want?"

She took a drag on the cigarette, looked up at him through the smoke and smiled. "You want some tea?"

"Not really, no."

"OK." She nodded. She had watched him climb out of the car, his shirt blinding white in the sun, and waited for him to cross from the garage. Yes. She'd been right. She could see it in his face. And as he approached, taking off his sunglasses, she saw him glance, just once, over his shoulder at the road behind him. And that little gesture told her everything: *He shouldn't be here — he knows that. He's just as bent as I thought. I was right — this is going to be easy.* "Who are you working for?"

He put his keys in his pocket and nodded into the house. "Can you turn the music down?"

"I said *who* are you working for?"

He sighed. "I'm not working *for* anyone. I'm Bill. I told you that."

"Then this lad — this kid that Penderecki done — who is so interested in him?"

"Just me."

"You're a liar." She took another drag on the cigarette and pointed it at him. "I know your type — there's gelt in it, isn't there? I don't know who that lad was, or anything, but you know what I think? *I* think someone really, *really* wants to know. And when someone *really* wants to know there's always gelt in it somewhere." She wiped her hands on the dirty leggings, pushed the ironweed hair behind her ear and made a face. She summoned phlegm into her throat and hawked it on to the ground. "Five K."

"*What?*"

"Five K and I'll tell you —"

"*Five grand?* Do I look like a —"

"I mean it — five K and I'll tell you exactly what happened."

"Piss off, Tracey. You're a liar. And I don't have to pay, *Tracey*, to force information out of you. I'm all that's standing between you and the dirty squad and I won't hesitate —"

"Oh, no." She gave him a slow smile. "You'll pay me."

"I fucking won't." He looked up at the sky and began feeling in his pocket for his keys. "You're full of crap."

"I'm your informant. You're supposed to register me. Have you?"

"Of course I have."

"*You*'re the liar." She smiled. "I know your sort — you're *worse* than my sort because you're legal. Much worse."

"Don't threaten me, Tracey —"

"Five K — and I'll *show* you what happened."

"Uh-uh." He turned to go. "You're in a sit com now, Tracey."

"*Listen!*"

"No way." He started towards the car, holding up his hand to dismiss her. "No fucking way."

"You'd be really, really surprised what I found out me brother knew all along." She jumped up, determined he shouldn't go. This was her one-way ticket sauntering away across the sunny forecourt. "You'd be surprised what happened to Penderecki's boy and what I can tell you about him." Caffery was walking faster now and she hurried after him, her arms extended, her feet in the yellow high heels pecking the ground like a wading bird. "Look, I'm not fucking with you — why would I?" The phlegm rattled away in her throat. "I can show you exactly what happened to him. Not *tell* you, I'll *show* you."

"Tracey." Caffery stopped and held up his finger warningly. "Cut the bullshit, Tracey. I mean it!" A flock of crows took to the air from the trees behind him, startling her by the way those wings darkened the sky so quickly — as if the crows wanted to emphasize his words. "I'm going straight back to London," he said, "and I'm going to hand the whole thing over to the Yard and don't fucking ring me again with your fairy-tales."

"But —"

"But nothing." He swung the keys on his finger and turned for the car, leaving her standing next to the rusted old Fiat.

"Fuck," she muttered after a while, deflated. The Jaguar reversed up the drive and she stood, watching the flock of crows bank away against the blue sky. When they had disappeared behind the trees she turned and limped back to the house.

* * *

Afterwards she sat on the doorstep, staring out at the hangar, at the rusting old engines, and the old Landrover roofs tangled in woodbine. She had almost forgotten she was holding a cigarette. It was only when it burnt her fingers that she dropped it. She scowled, leaned over, pulling her hair back from her face, and let a globe of granular phlegm drop directly on top of the burning butt. She was scuffing the phlegm with her shoe, so she didn't slide on it in the morning, when she heard wheels on the gravel. She looked up, suddenly nervous.

"Oh, fuck." She got to her feet, wheezing, sliding the locks on the door and hurrying back inside the house. *Maybe he meant it — maybe here come the mates —* She had got halfway down the corridor when she heard the voice ahead of her.

"Tracey!"

That made her stop — just by the kitchen door, her heart knocking against her throat. She swallowed. Rested her bitten nails on the doorpost and leaned cautiously back into the hallway. He was standing motionless in the sunlit front doorway, his hands in his pockets, his face tight. A wasp had got into the house and was banging itself on the ceiling. "What?" she called. "What do you want?"

"Three grand."

"What?"

"I said three grand — I'll give you three."

Roland Klare could have told the police that they needed to be looking for someone more than just Alek

Peach. Oh, yes, he could tell them that in one sentence. He knelt on the sofa, his nose and hands pressed against the window, one knee jerking up and down nervously, and stared out at the lovely trees and dried-up lawns of Brockwell Park. The photographs hanging in a row in his darkroom clearly showed Alek Peach raping his son. But the same images made something else quite clear: they made it clear that Alek Peach hadn't been the only person in the house at the time. They made it clear that someone else had been involved — the someone who was holding the camera.

Klare made a little clicking noise in his mouth and tapped at the window, wondering what to do next. "Hmmhm, yes," he muttered. "Hmm." He pushed himself away from the glass and turned back to the big, well lit living room, rubbing his hands nervously.

CHAPTER TWENTY-FIVE

Caffery got back to Shrivemoor just after 6p.m. and as he parked he saw Kryotos, dressed in a cream jacket, climbing into her husband's car. He crossed the road. "Anything happened?" he asked, both hands on the roof, looking up the road to check that no cars were coming in this lane. "Logan back?"

"Been and gone, photocopied some Actions and left them in your pigeon-hole — nothing doing."

"Shit." He bent down, looked into the car and nodded at Kryotos's husband. "Pardon my language."

"No problem."

"There're some messages for you," Kryotos said, putting on her seat-belt and eyeing Caffery cautiously. He had that run-ragged look about his eyes again. "That dentist, he called, wants to talk to you, and someone called Gummer, oh and West End Central have found Champ Keodua-wotsit for you, if you still want to see him."

"Peach?"

"No change." She nodded up at the incident-room windows where the sunlight bounced off the silver anti-blast film. "Danni's still up there."

"Shit."

"I know. She's not in the best mood."

"OK." He straightened up and knocked on the car roof. "Right, thanks, Marilyn. See you tomorrow."

The incident room was empty and Danni was in the SIO's room filling in her duty sheets for the month. Next to her was an open bottle of Glenfiddich — an oiler courtesy of a Sunday tabloid journalist doing an article on geographical profiling: Caffery and Souness had talked her through the Rossmo/Barwell stuff and she'd squeezed three articles out of it.

"Danni?"

She looked up. "Oh," she muttered. "You." She went back to her work.

He stood awkwardly in the doorway, watching her, not certain whether to leave or stay. When she seemed determined not to speak to him he sat down at his desk, hands folded on his stomach, and stared out of the window in silence. Before long Souness caved in.

"Right." She signed off the form, threw her pen on the desk and sat back in her chair. "Spit it out."

"OK . . ." He put his hands flat on the desk and looked out of the window for a moment, thinking how to approach this. "I —" He turned to her. "Look — about this morning."

"Yes?"

"I'm sorry."

She pursed her mouth, looking at him suspiciously with her narrow, blue eyes.

"It was out of all proportion," he continued. "I'm finding this case, y'know, not great, for the reasons you know all about — and I suppose I haven't been sleeping." He shrugged. "Just means I'm sorry."

Her mouth remained in its sour little bud knot. "I see." She picked up the pen and tapped it on the desk, up-ending it, tapping, staring at the desk. She seemed about to say something, then changed her mind and rubbed her head. She stretched her arms in the air and looked out of the window. "Oh, fuck," she muttered. "I suppose I'll have to forgive ye."

"Oh," he sighed, "well thanks, you know, thanks for the build-up."

"That's OK." She put her finger in her ear and jiggled it ferociously, looking sideways at him. " 'I don't think I could get my head that far up my own arse.' Could ye not have come up wi' something a wee bit better than that?"

"Next time, I'll try."

"You do that," she said, swivelling her chair round to face him, her hands clasped on her stomach. "Anyway — have ye seen this?" She shook her belly up and down. "See that? I'm losing weight." She looked up at him, her face serious. "And didn't you say something about owing me dinner?"

"Did I?"

"Yes, you did — if you were wrong about Gordon Wardell being all over the newspapers you'd buy me dinner."

"Was I wrong?"

"Doesn't matter. I'm your boss."

"I was right, then."

"Maybe."

* * *

"In the end I had to forgive ye, Jack, I've got no transport today — Paulina took the Beemer." They didn't discuss where to go. They just got into the Jaguar and drove to Brixton as if it was the most natural place on earth, as if they were being drawn by the imprisoned river Effra along its route. On its fringes, where the mystifying eye-dust of nightclub and art house hadn't permeated, Brixton was still dangerous and lonely. Here, shrivelled men in mud-stained tracksuits and straw hats, tinsel flowers on the brims, rolled their eyes at the stars and the lamp-posts and mouthed madness to the moon. Here street-lights had been taken out by BB guns from the estates, and the only illumination was cold cubes of ultraviolet in the shops, installed to stop addicts cranking up in the doorways by making their own arm veins invisible. In central Brixton the real nightlife hadn't woken up yet — it was too early: the Bug bar, the Fridge, Mass were all silent. It wouldn't be until midnight that central Brixton turned into little Ibiza — traffic jams at midnight and Balearic beat bunnies standing up through car sunroofs waving at the world. Still, as they parked on Coldharbour Lane, Caffery was glad of the comparative light and warmth.

He stopped at a cashpoint: "Just for forty quid or so."

"I'd get more than that if I were you. I'm nae a cheap date, y'know." Souness stood with her hands in her pockets, her back to him, and tried to outstare the beggar with the baby who sat under the cashpoint. Caffery checked his balance. That figure he'd given Tracey Lamb hadn't come out of nowhere — he'd had good reason: he knew how far the bank would extend his overdraft at short notice. Three thousand pounds. *What could three grand buy you?* No matter how many times he reminded himself — *she's a liar, she's a washed-up old con* — his hopeful heart, his *pathetically* hopeful heart, kept up the pestering: *what if what if what if* . . .

"Right." He pocketed the money, checked around to make sure no one was watching, and nodded towards Coldharbour Lane. "Dinner, then?"

The *Windrush* population, who had once laid claim to these few streets, had largely been pushed out of central Brixton and into the narrow capillaries around. There were few true black pubs left — few places one could walk into on a Saturday afternoon and see young men playing dominoes, screaming, slapping their thighs, flipping open their mobiles to relay twists in the game to absent friends. Most of Coldharbour Lane catered to the new population, and Caffery and Souness chose a place near the square, the Satay Bar, with its mirrors and bird-of-paradise flowers in towering glass vases. They ordered Malay kebabs with rice cubes and two Singha beers, and sat at a tiny table next to the window. Souness sat comfortably, her jacket unbuttoned, her pager resting on the table between them.

"I like it here." She leaned forward a little and peered out of the window. "This road is so fucking trendy that if you sit still long enough, in your wee cave, once in a while a bit of A-list totty breaks cover. Saw Caprice out there once, I'm sure it was her, wearing these . . ." She sucked breath in through closed teeth and chopped her hands at the top of her thighs. ". . . these red shorts, right up to here, and who's that one with the big tits? She gets fat like me now and then. You know. Big mouth."

"Dunno."

Souness smiled wryly and picked up a kebab. "First sign of depression that."

"What?"

"Losing interest in sex."

"I haven't lost interest in sex."

"Oh, aye." She pointed at him with the kebab. "The day you die'll be the day *you* lose interest in sex, Jack Caffery."

"I'm just . . ." He unrolled his knife and fork and pulled his plate towards him. He looked at the food for a minute, then leaned forward, elbows on either side of the plate. "You've been in the force, Danni, what? Fifteen, sixteen years?"

"And the rest — I know I've the face of a wee angel, but my thirty's only nine years away."

"So — remember back to when you joined. Do you remember what was in your head?"

"Oh, aye. I was excited. Came straight out — the moment I got into Hendon I came out. *But*," she said, emphasizing the word with a little jab of the kebab, "I never used it, Jack. Even when the world changed and I could've used it, I never did." She put the food in her mouth, chewed. "Of course, that doesn't mean I never kissed a little ass. No. Nor kissed a little pussy neither."

"And you still love it?"

"Kissing pussy?"

He smiled. "The force."

"Aye. I still love it. Every minute of it."

"And you never feel you got in for the wrong reason?"

"No." She forked rice cubes into her mouth and looked around the restaurant, chewing hard, focusing her eyes on a point somewhere above his head. "But, then, nothing happened to me like what happened to you when you were a wain."

At that Caffery cleared his throat and sat back a little, looking down at his food. He knew Souness was waiting for him to pick up the baton. Suddenly he wasn't very hungry. "You know, don't you . . ." He looked up at her. ". . . you know I only joined the force because I had some fucked-up idea I was going to find Ew —" He paused. "Find my brother."

"Aye, it doesn't take a genius to see that."

He sat forward. "But, Danni, I can't disentangle it. I get a case like Rory Peach and suddenly I'm ten years old again, fists up and wanting to take them all on — wanting to bare-knuckle fight."

"So ye get angry from time to time. What of it?"

"What of it?" He pulled out his tobacco and quickly rolled a cigarette. "What of it? Well," he said, holding a lighter to the cigarette, "well, one day it's going to go too far, I can see it. One day someone's going to push me and I'll do something I can't go back on." He dragged on the cigarette and held the smoke in his lungs, head back, eyes closed. Then he let out the smoke and rested the cigarette in the ashtray. "It's all about perspective — that's what they'd call it, isn't it, perspective? Look at what I did at the hospital — look at the way I laid into you, trying to batter it into you that there's someone —"

"Ah, wait," Souness said. "I know what you're going to say."

"Do you?"

"Yes." She dipped the meat in peanut sauce and ripped a piece off the skewer with her teeth. "Aye, and I've been thinking about it too. You think there's still someone out there. Another family."

"Yes. I told you, I'm a dog with a bone."

"'s OK, Jack," she said, chewing hard. "I've spoken to the gov about it — I can give you two of the outside team. Do whatever you want with them — just bring them back with a smile on their faces. OK?"

He stared at her. "You're feeding me."

"No. No, I'm not. I think ye might just have a point. Now instead of sitting there with your mouth open like an eejit say thank you."

He shook his head. "OK," he said. "OK — thanks, Danni — thanks."

"It's nothing. Now, put *that* out" — she jabbed the skewer at his cigarette — "and just get on with your food. You look like a proper meal would kill you at the moment."

He stubbed out the cigarette, but when he pulled his plate towards him he found he still couldn't concentrate on the food. "What went on in that house, Danni?" he said after a while. "What the fuck went on in there?"

She used a fork to push the rest of the meat off the skewer into the sauce. "It's simple. Rory Peach got raped. By his father. It happens, you know."

"Then what was going on in that family?"

"I don't know." She forked some beef into her mouth and chewed. "I often wonder what it'd be like to rape. It's one of those things women wonder about — not to be raped, but to be the one who rapes. Not very PC for an old dyke, is it?" She took a swig of Singha and wiped her mouth. "I had a conversation once with this rapist, and you know what he said? He said — and I can remember every word, because it was then that I knew that whatever I did, however much I strapped my chest down and cut my hair, I'd never really understand what it feels like to be a guy — he said" — she sat forward and looked Jack in the eye — "he said: 'It's like your heart is sticking out, it's like you're biting down so hard on leather that your jaw cracks, it's like the hard-on to end all hard-ons, it's like having your soul dragged out through your dick.' " Souness sat back, stabbing her fork into the meat. "Pretty loony tunes, eh?" She stopped. Caffery had stood up. "Hey, where ye going?"

"Do you want another drink?"

"Yeah." She was bewildered. "Yeah, go on then, another beer." She put the food into her mouth and chewed as she watched him go to the bar, wondering what she'd said. Something was definitely a bit tangled in Caffery — there was no doubt about it. Sometimes he had the eyes of a lion on a lead. When he got back with the drinks he was quiet.

"Jack — what is it? Come on, talk to me."

"I think I'll call Rebecca."

"Aye, Rebecca. How is she?"

"She's fine."

"Good. Well, send her my love, then." She leaned over and took his plate. "You're not wanting this, are ye?"

"No — go ahead."

She scraped what he hadn't eaten on to her plate, and started to fork her way through it. The meal finished early and Caffery found he didn't need the extra money he'd got from the cashpoint.

On the phone Rebecca's voice was indistinct. "Jack — where am I — I mean, God," she took a breath, "I'm sorry, I mean *where* are *you*?"

"Are you all right?"

"I'm — I dunno — drunk, I think. I think I'm lost, Jack."

"Where are you?"

"At the — y'know, at the gallery."

"The same one I got you from before?"

"I think so."

"I'm only over the road. Wait for me."

The Satay Bar was only a hundred yards from the Air Gallery. He went inside, his tired eyes smarting in the smoke, and wove through the bar, past hanging aluminium panels, cast resin columns, tungsten pin-pricks of lights, not meeting the cool, otherworldly gazes of all the modern faces in the semi-darkness.

When he eventually found Rebecca, on the first floor, he stood for a moment and stared, as if he was seeing into another world.

A fully lit glass cabinet displayed models of pathology specimens in coloured fluid. In front of it, on matching chairs, sat four girls with pale East European faces and geometric haircuts. They wore intent expressions and were leaning forward listening to the man who sat on the red plastic sofa opposite them. He was tall and stricken-looking in a black poloneck, and Caffery recognized him as a journalist from a late-night Channel 4 show.

"Like Michelangelo's blocked windows in the Medici library these are vaginas that go nowhere," he was saying, biting with precision on the ends of his words. "They invert the natural order of a phallocentric society; they create the organic, the *organ like*, where a male-obsessed perspective thinks there should be a space. They are saying, '*Look!* Look at the tribalness, *look* at the *vagina*-ness — do not ignore it!' "

Rebecca sat next to him as he talked about her work. She was folded into the crease of the sofa, dressed in a T-shirt and a dragonfly-blue skirt. Her chin was down on her chest, her hands were loosely wrapped around an open bottle of absinthe resting on her bare knees and, although no one seemed to have noticed, she was fast asleep.

"Becky." Caffery put himself between the small audience and the sofa and held a hand out to her. "C'mon, Becky."

The journalist stopped talking and turned to look at him: "Yes?" He pressed a hand on his chest and lowered his chin. "Did you want to ask something?"

Caffery bent down to see Rebecca's face. "Rebecca?" She didn't stir. She'd had her hair cut since he'd last seen her. It stood in wild tufts around her little smudged face. Two clumps of black eyeliner had collected in the corners of her eyes and she looked like nothing so much as a casualty at a teenagers' drinking party. A little drunken pixie. "Becky — come on." He took her hand, peeling the fingers from the bottle, and she stirred a little.

"Uh?" She looked up and her eyes zigzagged across his face. "*Jack?*" Her breath was sour.

"Come on." He took the bottle from her hands and put it on the table. "Let's go." He draped her hand over his shoulder, and bent down to put his arm round her waist.

"She going?" the journalist asked mildly.

"Yes."

He shrugged and turned back to the women. "Now, Cornelius Kolig, for example, might take a different approach to the issue of sexual abuse . . ."

The women uncrossed and crossed their legs with the absolute symmetry of a dance troupe and leaned forward, ignoring Rebecca, eyes fixed on the journalist, ready to suck up his words.

"You bunch of pricks," she said suddenly, pushing herself away from Caffery. "Can't you see it's all bollocks?" She plucked the bottle of absinthe from the table and waved it around wildly. The liquid moved like melted emeralds in the lights, sloshing out on to the floor, and the girls looked up in surprise. "It's all a *huge joke* — don't you get it? The joke is on *you*." She stopped for a moment, swaying slightly as if she was surprised to find herself standing up. "You — you —" She took a step back and almost lost her balance, putting out her hand to steady herself. "*Oh* —" She stopped suddenly, breathing hard, looking helplessly around her. "Jack?"

"Yeah, come on."

"I want to go . . ." She slumped slightly and began to cry. "I want to go home."

He managed to get her out of the club without attracting attention. Outside, when the night air hit her, she reacted slowly, raising dead-weight hands to rub her arms but she allowed him to bundle her into the passenger seat of the Jaguar and fasten the seatbelt across her. "I want to go home."

"I know." He propped her up and pushed her hands inside the car, where they remained, on her lap, her head slumped against the window as he drove in silence through Dulwich, glancing at her from time to time, wondering how she had let herself become a sideshow like this. Rebecca had a long, vibrant survival streak in her — it was the first thing he'd noticed about her, the thing that most repelled and most attracted him. It was incredible to see her so demoted, so helpless, so needful. Her face in the car headlights was a little grey, her mouth bluish.

They stopped at lights in Dulwich, outside a white weatherboarded villa — they could have been in a

Pennsylvanian Amish village, not South London — and he put out a hand to touch her head, to stroke the sturdy little tufts of hair. "Rebecca? How you doing?"

She opened her eyes and when she saw him she gave him a muzzy little smile. "Hi, Jack," she murmured. "I love you."

He smiled. "You all right?" Her mouth was a dusty purple shade. "You OK?"

"No." She dropped her hands. She was shivering. "Not really."

"What's the matter?" She fumbled for the door, her feet rucking up the rubber mat on the floor. "Becky?" But before he could pull into the kerb she stuck her head out of the door and vomited on to the tarmac, her body shaking, tears coming up.

"Oh, Jesus, Becky." Caffery rubbed her back with one hand, his eye on the traffic in the rear-view, looking for a space to pull over. She was shuddering and crying, wiping her mouth with one hand and trying to close the door with the other.

"I'm sorry, I'm sorry —"

"All right, just a moment, just a moment . . ."

The lights changed and he cut across traffic to pull the car on to the kerb. She dropped back into her seat, sobbing, her hand to her mouth, mascara running down her cheeks. He couldn't remember the last time he'd seen her cry.

"Come here, come here —" He tried to pull her to him but she pushed him away.

"No — don't touch me, I'm disgusting."

"*Becky?*"

"I took some heroin — I took some smack."

"Some *what*?"

"Some smack."

"Oh, for God's sake." He sighed, dropped back in the seat, raising his eyes to the ceiling. "When?"

"I don't know. I don't know — maybe a few hours ago . . ."

"*Why?*"

"I . . ." She rolled her eyes to him and now he wondered why he hadn't recognized that glazed smacked-up look before. "I wanted to try it."

"Do you have to try *everything*? Every fucking thing?"

She wiped her mouth and didn't answer. The traffic was slowing down to see what was happening — to see if there was an argument. He leaned over and pulled her door closed so that the interior light didn't give the passers-by a stage-lit show. "Is this the first time?"

She nodded.

"OK." He shoved the Jag into gear. "I'm not going to lecture you. Let's get you home."

In Brockley he got her cleaned up and made her drink tea. She sat like a child in bed wearing one of his shirts, her hands wrapped round the mug, a pale, numb look on her face.

"I'm getting a doctor."

"No. I'm OK." She stared into the bottom of the mug. "I feel better now. Will you . . ." She didn't look up at him. ". . . will you come to bed?"

He stood in the doorway, his hands on the doorposts, and shook his head.

"No?"

"No."

"I see." She was silent for a while, as if moving this new resolve of his around in her head. Then suddenly she let go of the mug and put her face in her hands. The mug rolled off the bed and shattered on the wooden floor. "Oh, *Jack,*" she sobbed, "I'm *lost* —"

"OK, OK." He sat on the bed and rubbed her back.

"*I'm lost*. I used to know where I was, but I just — I just *don't know any more* —" She cried so hard she seemed to be crying for everything — for every small disappointment, for everything she had ever lost. Tears boiled down her cheeks.

"Becky . . ." He put his arms around her and kissed her head. ". . . you can't go on like this."

"I know." Her shoulders were shaking and her neck had grown hot. She shook her head. "I know."

"What are you going to do about it?"

"I don't know — I —" She rubbed her eyes and took deep breaths, trying to control herself.

"Rebecca?" He dipped his head to look at her face. "What are you going to do?"

She wiped the tears off her cheeks. Her breathing was getting steadier.

"Well?"

"Uh." She turned her head away. "I'm going to — I don't know, I'm going to tell the truth, I suppose."

"OK —"

"No, I mean really *tell the truth*." She raised her hands, then dropped them again. "Jack."

"What?"

"I've been — I've been lying. A bit," she stumbled. "No — not a bit, a lot. Jack, I've been lying to you — all the way along I've lied and now I'm so sorry and it's because I lied that we've got like this and it's all my fault and I'm —"

"Hey — ssh, come on, calm down, what have you been lying about?"

"You'll hate me —"

"What have you been lying about?"

"About Malcolm."

"What about him?"

She took a deep breath and squeezed her eyes closed, speaking into the air as if reciting a hard-remembered poem. "I don't remember what happened, Jack. The last thing I remember is getting on my bike to go to Malcolm's — and that's all until you were going to Paul's funeral." Silence. She opened her eyes and looked at him. "Jack — I know I've fucked up and I'm sorry — I just thought — oh, I don't know — I thought there was something wrong with me if I didn't remember — or — or —"

He dropped his hand from around her shoulder and sat for a long time in silence. So this was what it had all been about. He thought about the statement in the hospital, he thought about the inquest, about her dead flatmate's body lying in the hallway, about Rebecca, hanging in the kitchen. And then he realized that what she had just done was to take a step towards him.

"Is that what it's all been about? The sex?"

"I got scared, I must've thought I might suddenly remember while we were — oh, fuck." She jammed knuckles into her eyes. "I know it's stupid —"

"Because I've been trying to make you think about it?"

She nodded, her bottom lip twisted under her teeth. All her eye makeup was down on her face, the eyelashes quite soft and naked.

"You didn't report it, did you?"

"Of course not — you didn't really think . . .?"

"Bloody hell, Rebecca." He pulled her closer, pressing his face into her lopped-off hair. "Bloody hell."

CHAPTER TWENTY-SIX

(26 July)

"Yes, hello?" A woman's voice on the answerphone in the hallway, the sound echoing through the house. Upstairs, stretched out on the floor next to the radiator, Benedicte jerked awake, pawing blindly towards the sound.

"Hello, this is a message for Mr and Mrs Church. I hope I've got the right number, my name is Lea and I'm calling from the Helston Cottage Agency, and, um, we were expecting you at Lupin Cottage in Constantine on Sunday, and I'm just calling because we haven't heard from you and we're just checking that everything's OK. And, um, what it is, Mr Church, what it is, is because we haven't had a, you know, an official cancellation we're going to have to, I'm sorry to say, we might have to charge you for Lupin Cottage if we don't hear from you and you might lose your deposit — so, well, maybe you've been delayed, but do give me a call and let me know. Right." She paused for a moment. "Right. That's all. So goodbye now."

"*No!*"

"Oh, and it's about nine a.m. on Thursday. I might try to give you another call at the weekend just to make sure everything's OK. Thank you."

The receiver clunked down, the tape whirred, a series of clicks and the ageing answerphone rewound the tape.

"Fuck you, fuck you, fuck *you*." Benedicte sprang forward, roaring at the door. "*I'll kill you*." She hammered on the floor with her broken-up hands. "You fucking BITCH! You and your fucking deposit, you shitty BITCH. *Hal! — Josh! Can you hear me? Can you hear me? I love you so much, I love you so much . . .*"

Tracey Lamb's mood was good. *Cooking*, she told herself, *you're cooking now*. She put her hair in rollers, big pink rollers that glistened like sugar sponge. When it was set she didn't brush it out. She sprayed a little mist in it, pulled on wellington boots and, carrying a cup of tea, a bucket full of bits and pieces, keys, and with her sputum cup in the pocket of her cardigan, she left the house by the back door, thinking about sangria and cheap, strong cigarettes. She was singing to herself.

She took the Datsun up to the quarry and parked it facing into the trees. An anorectic brindled dog was sitting in the undergrowth staring up at the caravan.

"Go on!" She kicked at the dog and it slipped back into the hedgerow, its legs so bent that its stomach almost dragged the ground. "That's it, go on. Git." She put the mug of tea on the bonnet of a rusting old Ford Sierra and fished in her pockets for the keys. Carl had always told her to lie about what she was keeping in the caravan, but Carl was dead now and she no longer had a reason to obey him.

Caffery and Rebecca slept together in an exhausted knot on his bed, her face resting on his hand so that he could feel it twitch and move as she dreamed. She had kept on her underwear and T-shirt, and although he had his arm around her he tried to keep it unsexual, tried to keep a segment of air between their bodies. In the morning he pulled out his arm carefully and got up without waking her. He showered, shaved carefully, dressed in a well-cut Italian suit, the legacy of an ex-girlfriend, put on a grey Versace tie and began to move his mood round to bargaining with the bank manager.

When he went downstairs Rebecca had woken and was walking around the kitchen in jeans, making coffee, diminutive as a young boy with her new haircut. When she saw him in the suit she whistled. "My God, you're so gorgeous."

He smiled.

"Where are you going?"

"Just the office." He straightened the tie and poured some coffee. She looked rested. In fact, considering last night, she looked incredibly well. For a moment he felt hopeful for them, as he sat at the table with his coffee and watched her moving around, opening the fridge; for a moment he thought it could all be easy, but then he thought, *Maybe it's just the heroin — don't they say that about heroin? At first it makes you look just great . . .* and then he thought about where he was going today and how by rights he should cancel it, how by rights he should make an effort in return for what she'd done, and the whole thing made his mood crash so quickly that he got an instant headache. He downed his coffee, stood and kissed her quickly on the forehead. "I'm just going to the office."

When he'd gone Rebecca went into the garden and lay on her back in the grass. It was a perfect day — so blue, just a few clouds running Grand Nationals across the sky. She lay in silence, waiting to find out how she felt about it all. She'd done it. She'd taken steps, big, big steps. She'd stuck her finger up at one of London's biggest art critics and now she supposed she should start unpicking it, wondered about making amends. But she couldn't convince herself she'd done the wrong thing: every time she tried to be strict with herself and give it serious consideration, her thoughts floated away, like a bubble from one of those silly children's games. Maybe it was the heroin — *maybe that's why the junkies put up with puking for the first few rounds, just to get this numbness for a while*. Shouldn't it have worn off by now? She had the sense that something very important had happened, that she'd been spun round to face in the right direction, and that she should be feeling very scared and very exhilarated. But then she thought about Jack, nuzzling a kiss in her new-cut hair — *Jack, you didn't get angry, you didn't tell me to leave* — and she knew that it was OK and that, after all, she could be quite calm. When she dropped her hands over her face she found, oddly, that she was smiling.

* * *

The brain is something like a blancmange on a stem, floating perilously around the skull in a protective whey. Its tissue cannot be compressed without damage, nor can it survive even short periods without oxygen. Thus there are many ways to damage this sensitive, unfathomable organ: it can be pushed against the skull by a leak of blood or a tumour, it can be starved of blood by trauma or stroke, it can be twisted and whipped around inside the skull so quickly that its connective tissues are sheared, it can be forced downwards through swelling and bleeding until it is almost pressed out through the hole at the base of the skull, or it can be shaken up like a plastic snowstorm and hurled against the skull. If a young child were to be thrown backwards on to a concrete floor, for example, there is a chance that his brain, responding to suction forces and the laws of acceleration and deceleration, would be thrown backwards and then *forward* from the impact site, where it would be grazed and ripped on the jagged interior of the skull diametrically opposite. This peculiar phenomenon is a "contrecoup" injury and it is exactly the injury that Ivan Penderecki inflicted on the small boy he had imprisoned in a chilly Nissen hut on the Romney Marshes.

Carl Lamb, by a peculiar quirk of fate, saw the whole thing. It was a cold October night in the 1970s and he was standing at the window of the hut, smoking a cigarette, waiting for the big Polish man to finish with the child so that he could have his turn. A struggle started, and when the child fell Lamb knew immediately that something was wrong — there was no blood, but there *was* something sinister about the way the boy's eyes dilated, the way he became suddenly limp.

"Oh, fuck," he said, chucking the cigarette out of the window and starting to panic. "Fuck — what're we going to do?"

But in Penderecki's eyes it wasn't what *they* were going to do, it was what *Carl* was going to do. *He* was going to be the one to deal with it, to dispose of the child. Carl was young, still in his early twenties, and still a little in awe of Ivan Penderecki, who in those days was the mogul of the ring. So he obeyed without argument, gathering up the broken, still pulsing thing from the floor, expecting that within minutes he'd be holding a dead body. A body he'd have to find a hole for. On the long drive home, with the child on the back seat twitching under a blanket, he passed reservoirs and lakes and even drove under the big river Thames, which snaked under the moonlight out to the estuary. He should have stopped and launched him there and then, but somehow he didn't have the juice for it. He'd done a lot in his short life — but he'd never got rid of a body before. Something, maybe cowardice, maybe an overpowering sense of the significance of what had happened, made him keep driving.

Back in Norfolk he put the boy on the sofa, got a beer, put some music on and sat down in the armchair to watch him die, wondering how he was going to dispose of him, wondering if he could cut up a body without puking. Minutes turned to hours, the boy's face swelled monstrously, hours turned to days and he breathed on, a glittering string of saliva connecting him to the pillow. His right arm and leg drew up on themselves like a bird's claws, but by the third day, when Carl put a hand on his shoulder and shook him, he sat bolt upright and vomited down his mustard yellow T-shirt.

"Fucking animal." Tracey, still a teenager in those days, was furious with this intrusion. She stomped out of the house and went to stand next to the hangar, lighting a Marlboro and turning her back angrily on the house. Carl ignored her. He paced the room looking at the boy, wondering if he could kill him here and now. He should just drive him out to the motorway, he decided, and dump him on the hard shoulder — but he didn't know how much he remembered of the night in the Nissen hut, who he could finger. Maybe he should just drive him down to London and dump him on Penderecki, but Penderecki was still an intimidating prospect. So he was stuck. He examined the child, trying to decide if he would be worth something to someone. The right side of his face was ruined, swollen and drawn downwards as if melted. He dribbled constantly. Basically he was useless. Over the next few days Carl made up his mind countless times that he was going to do it — he was going to kill him. But countless times he found he didn't have the courage. And then, suddenly, something put an end to all his indecision. Suddenly Carl noticed that the boy was changing.

It was a slow process, but gradually, miraculously, the paralysis in his face began to correct itself and the dribbling stopped. He still grimaced and jerked, his head zagging back and forward like a baby trying to get out of a high chair, and when, a month or so later, he got up and tried to walk, his right foot pointed down like a horse hoof, but somehow Carl found all that easy to overlook. New possibilities were opening up to him.

The change in Carl's attitude didn't escape Tracey's attention. She was glad. He had stopped being surly and losing his temper every five minutes. One night she heard noises coming from the bathroom, noises that echoed around the dark house, animal screams and the thudding of a body being battered against the cast-iron bathtub. When she tiptoed upstairs she met Carl coming out of the bathroom, a grim look on his face. He was sweating, he didn't meet her eye, and she knew, without knowing how, that from now on the boy was going to be Carl's special friend.

And she was right. When he got boozed at the weekends Carl would come down the stairs in a T-shirt and Y-fronts, a fag in his teeth, down to the living room where she and the boy watched TV on a Saturday. He never spoke, he didn't snap his fingers or beckon or anything, he'd just switch on the light so they'd both look up and he'd stand there until the boy got up and limped out of the room. Tracey would turn up the volume on the TV and smoke a bit faster on those nights, trying not to think about what was going on upstairs. For days after these episodes the boy would go off into long periods of non-communication — he would sit in the corner rocking, a blanket over his head, a steady whinnying coming from his mouth.

"Just make out like it's our brother," Carl said. "Say he was born like that, OK? And we'll call him something else — call him, I don't know, call him Steven." And so it was established — Steven was his name, he was their idiot brother. The Borstal Boys liked to beat "Steven" up: Tracey often found him lying on his side in the hangar, rocking and whimpering amid the engine oil, and after a few years Carl also lost his taste for him. Steven had started smoking on the sly and tearing photos of Debbie Harry and Jilly Johnson out of the *News of the World* to Sellotape on the wall. One morning Carl had woken up and found the pile of part-worn tyres in the garage burnt to a cinder from one of Steven's carelessly dropped cigarettes. He'd cracked the boy's nose open for that. He didn't have a child's body any more and was showing signs of growing up and now Carl prowled the house losing his temper every five minutes, if not with him then with anything he encountered: with Tracey, with the cars in the garage, with the Borstal Boys. Steven was a young teenager now, an overgrown child in cancer-shop trousers whom Carl didn't fancy and didn't have the ingenuity or energy to get rid of. He started locking him in his room at night with a slop bucket and nothing else. "It's for your own good, you little fucker."

Tracey was pleased — at last it seemed that Steven had reached the end of his useful life. But then one day, by chance, Carl discovered that Steven had been doing the work of the Borstal Boys. While they sat back with their plastic bottles of cider and watched, it was Steven who was lugging the piles of car windows etched with vehicle identification numbers into the trees to smash. It was Steven who was doing the work with the angle-grinder, removing chassis numbers or cutting panels out. It was Steven who was growing bigger and more muscular and skilled around the garage. He couldn't string a sentence together but he could weld a plate over a chassis number in seconds. A light seemed to come on in Carl's head. If Steven could do the Borstal Boys' jobs then, "What the fuck am I doing wasting me gin and Silk Cuts?" Before long he had set him to work — he became a little grease monkey, filling and beating and grinding and "I don't even have to find him a mask for the resprays," Carl said. "He don't know any better. Absolutely pukka." Now any Borstal Boy who couldn't help Carl in the bedroom was redundant, and the caravan stood empty for long periods of time.

Then suddenly, out of the blue, Steven said Penderecki's name. That really made Carl sit up and pay attention: "What d'you say?" He glared at him from over the *News of the World*. "What was that?"

"AhhhBan."

"Whassat?" Carl looked up at his sister, standing there biting her nails and pulling a face. "Whatsee say?"

"I don't fucking know, do I?"

"Iibaaan."

"Fuck me." Carl crumpled the newspaper and jumped up. "He said Ivan. Didn't you? Didn't you say Ivan?"

"Unnng!" Steven tugged his head back and his hands jerked up under his chin. "Ung."

"What's Ivan?" Tracey said. "His name?"

"Nah — that's Penderecki's name, isn't it?"

"Uh-hh." He jerked his head back, his claw hand flailing under his chin. He had odd, wandering irises, which skittered across the top of his eyes like wind-blown leaves across a lake.

"Say it again. Who broke your head, eh?" Silence. "Come on, you stupid little shit, who done your head? Was it Penderecki?"

Silence.

"Come on — was it Penderecki what broke your head?"

A sudden jerking and rolling of his eyes. "Ung!"

"Who?"

"BBeMBe — rrrrr-kki —"

"That's it!" Carl was amazed. "And who helped you? Eh? Who helped you after? Was it me? Was it Carl?"

"Ung — *ung*!" He jerked his head and rolled his eyes. That meant yes. Carl sat down on the sofa with an odd look of revelation in his eyes.

"That Polish piece of shit!" He slammed his fist into his palm and Tracey shrank back a little, not sure what was coming next. "I've got him, that piece of shit."

The way Carl explained it to her, that Penderecki was getting old, slowly drying up, becoming inactive, losing all interest in little boys and forgetting he had anything at all between his legs, that there was some leverage to be had here, that he, Carl, could drop hints about what really happened to the boy and soon have Penderecki eating out of his hands, it all made sense to Tracey in a way. He'd have a place to crash in London whenever he needed it, he'd have Penderecki's contacts if he wanted them, he'd have a second place to stash his collection of tapes if things got dodgy at the garage.

"Or if I have to go away for some reason. He'll guard them with his fucking life if he knows what's good for him." Carl was in a good mood now. "So, Tracey, you ain't to talk about who Steven is, right? If Ivan ever turns up here for some reason, don't you never let on — if there's talking to be done it'll be me does it."

So Steven became part of the house and they got used to him wandering around. He had a favourite hat — a knitted Manchester United bobble hat that he wore pulled down over his forehead: "Bobah", he called it, no one knew why. If he was separated from Bobah he would cry — so when she was feeling spiteful Tracey hid it from him until she had managed to get him curled up on the kitchen floor in tears. Afterwards he never seemed to bear any resentment towards her, he seemed to forget about it almost as quickly as it had happened. In fact, Tracey realized that he didn't have much of a memory for anything that had happened since he came to Norfolk. He craved chocolate and got fat on Caramel bars; over the years he had crushes on Madonna, Kylie Minogue and Britney Spears. When Carl wasn't around Tracey tormented Steven. She made him clean the house, and would sit on the sofa painting her toes, listening to him in the hallway, ringing out each task he did: "Duh — ddinnn, now," he'd warble. That meant dusting. "Hooooberiinnnn" (Hoovering) or simply: "Kerneaninnn, now" (cleaning).

"What do you put up with him for? He's a fucking *mong*. Why you hanging on to him?"

"Tracey, it's none of your fucking business."

But she thought it was her business — she was savvy enough to know that Carl wasn't telling her something about the boy. She felt sure that there was something else about Steven. Maybe Steven meant something to someone important — and if she knew anything about Carl there was probably money involved somewhere along the line.

And so it went. When Carl died Tracey was left to deal with "her brother". She'd entertained some ideas about approaching Penderecki — she turned the idea around for hours as she sat watching *Ricki Lake* and marching through her supply of Silk Cut. But then DI Caffery had knocked on the door and everything had fallen into place. Now she saw why Carl had clung to the boy — there *was* money involved. Just what she'd always thought. She wasn't the slow-thinking mule Carl said she was, after all.

The first thing she decided to do was find somewhere to put Steven — she didn't want Caffery coming back and finding him pottering around the house clutching a duster and grinning idiotically. So yesterday she had put him in the Datsun — "Look, you can bring Bobah too" — and taken him out to the caravan at the top of the quarry. "Later I'll bring Britney."

"Bwidney —"

"I'll bring her over too. I promise."

And she did. She brought all of his Britney posters and his one Britney tape and the Walkman Carl had given him four Christmases ago, and settled him down with some Caramel bars and Cokes, padlocked the caravan and stood outside in the rain, smoking a cigarette and watching the cars go by on the road with their headlights on, thinking that she was very brave and very clever. And today, back at the caravan, on the day that Caffery was due to come up the A12 with the money, she was feeling even braver. It was sunny and clear. She paused briefly outside the caravan to spit on the ground. She had to find a way of establishing that "Steven" was indeed the same boy Caffery wanted. Inside he was warbling along to a song — "Ooopsh, ah did id ug-ed." *Britney fucking Spears*. The only tape he had and he never seemed to tire of listening to it. Over and over again, and still he didn't know the words. She unlocked the padlock and went in. The curtains were wet with condensation and the caravan stank of mildew.

"Listen, Steven." She put down the bucket and sat on the bunk next to him, lifting one of his earphones. "Steven . . ."

He grinned at her, flopping his head back and forward. "Traith —"

She smiled, trying to look patient. "Look." She took the headphones off and rested them on the bed, switching the Sony to the off position. "I've got something I want to ask you. OK?"

He paused for a moment thinking about this, his eyes skittering around, his hands moving one over the other.

"I said *OK*?"

He seemed to focus. He nodded hard, so hard that his heels knocked against the floor. "'Kay."

"Good. Now listen. Do you remember the name of the bloke in London?"

Steven stopped nodding. He made a little choking sound and his eyes wandered away and came to rest on Britney Spears, pasted up on the back of the door: Britney lying back on a yellow pickup truck in a red and white cheerleader outfit.

"Steven?"

He bobbed his head up and down and now she saw he was mouthing something. She bent closer.

"What's that? What you saying?" He put his finger up his nose. "No, come on, don't do that." She snatched his hand away. "Now, come on, you used to know it, you little shit — come on, the man what broke your head?"

He frowned suddenly and his eyes glazed over. He tipped his chin back and flapped his face towards the windows as if he was laughing. But he wasn't laughing. He was nodding.

"You remember?"

"Uuuungh."

"What's his name?"

"AahhhBaaan . . ."

"Ivan? Is that what you said? Ivan?"

"Ungh." He jerked his head up and down, eager to please.

"Good. Now if someone asks you, 'Who did this to you?' you say, 'Ivan, Ivan Penderecki.' "

"Aaaahh-Baannn Bemmb-bbbemmb —" He looked as if he was going to weep with the effort of getting the words out. "Aaah-Bann. Bember — Ahhbann Bemmberedddih!"

It was good enough. Tracey sat back, satisfied, and lit a cigarette. She felt confident now — very confident. Britney Spears, in jeans and a pale blue T-shirt, smiled sideways at them out of a hot day in Times Square.

From the Jaguar parked outside the bank in Lewisham Caffery called Souness: "I'm not going to make it this morning. I'm sorry, I'm — I don't know, food poisoning from last night or something."

"Oh, Jesus, Jack." The two DCs she'd assigned to him were waiting in the office. "They're sitting here like a pair of wee bairns waiting for their daddy to come and tell them what to do."

"OK, OK — put them on." He spoke for ten minutes to one of the DCs, giving him the door-to-door parameters he wanted them to cover — Logan had already done the west of the park and he wanted the two DCs to start on the east side. Afterwards he spoke to Kryotos, asking her to contact Champaluang Keoduangdy and arrange a late lunch meeting.

"I thought you were dying?"

"Marilyn, please, I just need a little rest."

"OK, I'm with you, I won't say a dickie bird."

"The phone'll be off the hook so if you need me use my mobile."

"Will do. Oh, and Jack?"

"What?"

"The dentist. From King's. Remember?" She paused. "He called *again*, Jack. Can you *please* — ?"

"Yeah, yeah. OK. Leave it with me."

After the call he took off his tie and put it into his pocket. He had felt like a catalogue plate sitting there with the bank manager. But he'd got the money — it was in a brown banker's envelope in his breast pocket — he had his bargaining tool. *Pathetic, so obsessed that you'll pay more than a month's salary for the ramblings of a washed-up old con and then lie about it to everyone*. After this, he made a promise to himself: after today he was going to put it all behind him. He pointed the Jaguar towards Norfolk, opening the window, keeping the radio off. If nothing happened today it was going to end: he was going to hand it all over to the paedo unit and tell Rebecca she'd got what she wanted and that the Ewan story was over. But as he drove he couldn't help catching sight of his eyes in the rear-view mirror and all he could see in them was hope — as if he really expected to pull the car up at Lamb's and see Ewan saunter around the corner of the house, out into the sunlight, still wearing his shorts and little mustard T-shirt.

And now think what you're really *going to see*.

An old child's shoe, or a fragment of bone probably. Three thousand pounds and the prize would be delivered with a saintly relic's ceremony. *I hold in my hand a genuine piece of the True Cross*. Or another animal carcass, green with burial. He knew he was going to be screwed around with — he just wished he could get rid of that bubble of hope in his chest.

* * *

Tracey Lamb knew the moment she got through the door. She didn't see them, and they'd been clever, hiding their car, but she knew. She dropped the bucket and turned to bolt. A uniformed arm came out, pushing the warrant into her face. "Miss Tracey Lamb?"

"*You never fucking asked to come in my house!*" She thrust away the hand and swivelled so that she could look back up the hallway and see the extent of it. "*You never fucking asked.*"

"Didn't have to, Miss Lamb. You weren't here."

"No! You *cunts*!"

Everywhere the house was being clawed at. They were walking around in their shirt-sleeves, ignoring her wails, in and out of the rooms, snapping on their latex gloves. At the top of the stairs she could see a step-ladder placed in the attic access panel, and a woman's elegant ankles in tan high heels, cut off just below knee height. She could hear someone walking around up there and see the flash of a torch.

"*Get out of my fucking attic!*" she yelled up the stairs.

An officer put both hands on her shoulders. "Miss Lamb, I think you'd be better off just letting us get on with it."

"You fuckers — oh, God —" She knew she couldn't fight this. *Caffery — that bastard — that fucking-shit-for-brains piece of filth*. She sank to the floor, her hands in her hair. "You fuckers."

The woman in the attic came carefully down the steps and passed an old blue shoebox, covered in cobwebs, to the PC at the foot of the ladder. He turned and carried it down the stairs.

Lamb saw him coming towards her and was furious. "Don't you dare take my things." She grabbed hold of his leg. "Give me back my things — give me that."

"Yow!" The PC tried to wrench away his leg, holding the shoebox in the air out of her reach, but Tracey clung on. "Get off — get her off me, someone!"

"Miss Lamb," another officer said. "That contains evidence."

"I know what it fucking *contains*. It's my bollocking shoebox —"

"Get her off me —"

With unexpected speed Lamb jumped up and swung out her arm, catching the PC enough of a blow for the box to tumble to the floor. "Jesus, you *cow* —" The contents spilled out, slithering along the floor. For a moment everyone fell quiet, staring at the images among their feet. Even Lamb was momentarily shocked by what she saw. She stood over them, her body curled forward, her knees half bent, her face white as if she had been about to fall to her knees.

"Tracey, let's make this as easy as —"

"FUCK OFF."

There were thirty or so photographs — the old type of print with a small white border around them, the images grainy. They showed a tiny blonde girl of about six sitting on a garden bench. In some of the photos she wore hotpants with bib and braces, a bunny rabbit embroidered on the bib. Her hair had been back-combed and given a shoulder-length sixties flip, like an adult. In some shots she was pictured playing with a beach ball; in others the bib was peeled down and she was proudly baring her thin white chest, her head tilted on one side for the camera. In two photographs, which had fallen near the back door, between the feet of an embarrassed officer, one slightly covering the other, the same little girl was on a bed. She was straddling the face of a grown man. No hotpants in this one. No knickers.

"*No!*" Lamb fell forward, landing face down on the photographs. "No — they're mine, don't take them, *please*!" She moved her arms compulsively up and down — like an exhausted swimmer trying to stay afloat, gathering the images under her body, one wellington boot coming adrift.

"Come on, Miss Lamb." The silence in the hallway broke, and someone put a hand on her shoulder. "Get up. And pull your skirt down too — you're showing the world what you've got."

"*Get*the*fuck*awayfromme —" She batted the hand away. "*Let go*."

The PC, afraid Lamb might roll on to her back and kick at him — worse, that he'd see more of what was under her skirt — backed away a touch, looking up at his colleagues for help.

"Miss Lamb," a WPC tried, "that's crucial evidence you've got there. If you don't let me near it I'll have to arrest you. Can't you see what's happening to that poor little girl there?"

Tracey Lamb, lying like a frog on the floor with all her limbs moving at once, became still at this sentence.

The two officers exchanged glances, wondering at this sudden hiatus. Then Lamb rolled on to her side and covered her face, her chest convulsing, tears making mirrors of her red cheeks.

"Miss Lamb, you have to get up — have you seen —"

"Yes, I *have* seen, I *do* know," she wailed. "Of course *I've seen*. Who do you think she *is*, you cunts? Eh? That 'poor little girl' — *just who do you think she is*?"

They had to drag her, one on either side, out of the house and over to the car, past the rusting oil containers, the old ivy-covered engine hoist. The arresting officer had just spent a day at Hendon learning the Quik-kuf arrest technique. By the time Caffery arrived at 11 a.m. the PC was using a ballpoint to close the double-locking pins of the handcuffs and Tracey Lamb was under arrest.

It took until lunchtime for the MG 1-16 forms to be filled in and signed so that Tracey Lamb could be officially charged with the indecent assault of the boy in the video. The interviewing officers — members of the paedophile unit down from Scotland Yard — had brought the video with them. They'd had it for ten years and had been looking for her all that time. A wig, they told her, didn't make much difference in identifying her. After she'd been charged they agreed with the custody officer that she could be bailed.

Outside, on the trimmed lawn in front of the police station, she lit a cigarette and stood for a moment, ignoring the council workers coming in and out of their offices for sandwiches, and gazed up over the unfinished stump of the cathedral tower, out to the clouds moving in ranks across the sky. *Shit*. She couldn't believe it — just couldn't believe it. They'd warned her that there might be other charges under the Obscene Publications Act, which "might arise in the course of our investigation", but the duty brief, Kelly Alvarez, a little Mexican-looking woman in a navy suit with a grubby lifeboat sticker on the lapel, told her it wasn't as bad as she thought. They only had one tape, and the photos taken of her as a child would help establish "the enormous influence your father and later your brother exerted over you. Don't worry, Tracey, we might, if we're lucky, get away with a non-custodial."

But she couldn't accept it. She'd been hauled in before, of course, done her own bits of time here and there, but what really slaughtered her was the money. When the unit had dragged her out of the house and into the panda car she'd caught sight of Caffery standing just inside the trees, watching, a stuck sort of look on his face. Now she didn't know what to think.

"How did they find me?" she wanted to know. "Who fitted me up?"

Alvarez shrugged. "They've had the video for years."

"But how did they know it was me?"

"I'll find out — I promise. Now, don't worry about this, Tracey — it's not the end of the world."

"Of course it's not," she muttered to herself now, walking away from the station, down the sunny Bury streets. *Like a bag lady in your wellingtons*. "Not the end of the fucking world."

She paused, the cigarette halfway to her mouth. A familiar car. Just crouching like a cat at the corner of the road. Quickly she turned on her heel and walked in the opposite direction, pulling the collar of the T-shirt higher as if it might make her invisible.

Caffery had seen her coming out of the turning ahead and started the car. He was wired, so alert his eyes hurt — in those few hours that Lamb had spent in the police station everything had come into focus: now he understood the tail on the country lane yesterday. Souness's red BMW. Rebecca hadn't gone to the police, it was all down to bottle-blonde Paulina — infant-blue eyes and a pedigree car. An intelligence officer for the paedo unit, in the incident room she had latched on to him instantly. She must have heard about Penderecki's death, must have been watching him. Souness hadn't said anything about it over dinner last night. *She must have known — she knew that Paulina had taken the car — so what was all that trust and love and tolerance shit last night?* Now he was in the business of waiting for the other boot to fall, waiting to get the first sinister hint that Souness or the paedophile unit were talking to the CIB — *Let's count your breaches of the discipline code, shall we? Corrupt practice, abuse of authority*. He knew the whole thing was about to crash around him — and now he just had time to give it one last shot.

He put the car into gear and slid along next to Lamb before she could turn into a side-street. He opened the passenger window. "Tracey."

She ignored him, kept on walking, and he had to edge the Jaguar forward, one hand on the steering-wheel, leaning across the passenger seat: "*Tracey* — listen — this wasn't mine — I swear — I didn't have anything to do with it." He held his hand over the envelope in his breast pocket to stop it falling out on the seat. "The money's here. It's right here."

"Bit fucking late now, isn't it?"

"No — we can still talk." He looked up at her. "We can still talk."

She stopped. She tucked her bottom lip under her long teeth and bent a little, trying to see what was inside his pocket. So intent, so fascinated, she had the wet mouth of a dog running a scent line. He'd got her by the nose.

She took a step closer and slowly he opened his hand away from the pocket to show her. *That's it, that's the way — just a little nearer . . .* Reflected in the car's wing mirror someone walked across the lawn from the courthouse and Caffery registered it momentarily, a passing flash of anxiety that he might be seen with Lamb, and that momentary lapse cost him the day. When he looked back the line had broken. She'd seen the simple flicker of his attention and followed his eye, seen what he was looking at, and lost her faith. She took a step back, glancing up at the courthouse, her eyes darting back and forward.

"Tracey —"

"What?"

"Come on — talk to me."

"No. There's nothing to tell. I was lying." She was backing away now.

"*Shit.*" He slammed his fist on the steering-wheel and put the car in gear. "*Tracey.*"

"There's nothing to tell." She set her face and walked away. He had to shoot the car forward to keep up with her.

"Tracey!"

"I mean it — I was lying. You're not stupid, you knew I was lying." She took a last puff on the cigarette. She didn't want to stop to tread on the butt so she threw it through the opened window of the Jaguar, crossed her arms resolutely across her breasts and turned into the abbey grounds where the car couldn't follow.

CHAPTER TWENTY-SEVEN

He didn't let it touch him — he didn't let it get to him. He did what he'd said he was going to do and put a line under it. He had already wasted enough of the morning. Cigarette between his teeth he put his tie back on, checking in the mirror, put on his sunglasses, and grappled his mobile out of his jacket. What was Souness doing right now? Sitting in the SIO's office, counting off the minutes, waiting for him to come through the door, waiting to ask him the questions about Tracey Lamb and Norfolk. It was time to get it all out into the open.

"Well?"

"Well what, Jack?"

"Have you got something to tell me?"

"About *what*? Your lads aren't back — they were going to call you direct, weren't they?"

"Anything else?"

"Jack, listen, son. I hate to be a pain in the arse, but I've got the DAC e-mailing me, the borough fucking commander on the line and, oh, just one or two reports to get ready for the case review, so with all due respect . . ."

He sat back in his seat, staring at the alley of beech trees that marched off towards the abbey. She didn't know. Souness didn't know. What the fuck was —

"*Jack?* I don't want to hang up on ye, son, but —"

"OK, Danni. I'm sorry. Put me through to Marilyn, will you?"

Kryotos agreed to contact Champ and reschedule the meeting. Champ was in the West End — he wanted lunch and if Caffery could make it for two thirty they could meet in Soho. So he pointed the car down the M11: Canary Wharf on his horizon for nearly an hour as he closed on London. He got to Soho for two fifteen, parked in one of the expensive local car parks, went into a branch of his bank and paid the three thousand straight back into his account, then walked calmly down to Shaftesbury Avenue.

Champ was only twenty-four but he already owned an electrical retail shop in the streets behind Chinatown. "I do know which way is up, you see. I make it here with my Laotian name because nearly all my blood is Chinese." He'd had acne at some point in the past, but his hair was neat and gelled, and he was well turned-out in a slate grey Armani suit and immaculate leather shoes. "I get left alone as long as I'm quiet. I understand the *guanchi*, see." The boys sunbathing in Soho Square lifted their heads to watch him and Caffery walk by.

They went to a good, honest Italian in Dean Street: hand-painted Amalfi plates on the walls, bottles of Strega and Amaretto in a rack above the heads of the kitchen staff. Caffery had fish and sat with his back to the window watching Champ twisting up the *spaghetti alle vongole*. He leaned forward as he ate to avoid getting tomato sauce on his suit.

"When it happened they all came up out of nowhere, all the do-gooders trying to help me. I just kept quiet. I was working, you see."

"Working?"

"When it happened. He was a punter."

"A *punter*?" Caffery wondered if the PNC had made a mistake. "But you were only —"

"*Almost* twelve, and it wasn't my first." He pushed some spaghetti into his mouth and pointed the fork at Caffery. "You probably want me to say I was harmed by it, don't you? By the men? But some of them had more time for me than my own mother. I was in care for a year when I was two." He chewed and swallowed. "They found me in my cot with half a pound of shit in my nappy, me just lying there not moving or crying, even." He twirled more pasta on his fork and pushed it into his mouth. "She was, and still is, a slag, my mother." Chewing, not taking his eyes off Caffery he reached inside his suit pocket and drew out a scrap of paper. "Fished this out for you." It was a crumpled, faded small ad. "That's how he found me."

> I am an 18-year-old who had an accident which has left me looking only 10. Call . . .

Caffery pushed the paper back across the table. "You were eleven and you were advertising?"

"I was a clever little Asian monkey even then. Our minds are quick, you know, skip through the gaps that GI Joe can't get through. Look where I am today — you know why? Because I never got a junk habit like everyone else. It was Mr and Mrs Bombita in those woods, believe me, businessman's specials — meth, the lot. But me, I saved my money." He waggled the fork at Caffery. "Told you I'm mostly Chinese meat."

"He asked you about your daddy."

Champ snorted. "Yeah. I'd forgotten that. That's the first thing he said, when he phoned, he asked me did I like my daddy. I didn't get it at the time — now I know it's just, y'know, normal gay talk."

"And he took photographs of you?"

"I didn't show the camera my face, but what weirded me out was that I'm sure he took photos of me after I was down — after I fainted. I remember the flash going off." He mopped his plate with some bread and shrugged as if he hadn't given the incident much thought. "Believe me, before that night I thought I knew what weird was — some of them liked you to do such shit you wouldn't believe. There were the ones who liked yellow — you know what that is, don't you?"

"Uh — yeah."

"And brown and fawn and red — y'know, fisting. Hey, you're the police, nothing I can say is going to shock you, right?"

Caffery looked down at the fish on his plate. "That's right."

"But this was one sicko, weird from here to next week. First he's telling me he's going to watch over me.

He said he would come and look down at me, that he'd like to watch me in my bed."

"What do you think he was talking about?"

"No idea. Probably just his mad-speak — and, anyway, he's fiddling around with me down there as he's saying it and I'm like, 'Hey hang on, you better put something on — this is not barebacking times no more. You put something on.' But when I turned to check he hardly had nothing to put a rubber on anyway. Tiny, *tiny* little pecker like . . ." He held his thumb and finger apart. ". . . like that. Never seen nothing like it — Midget Dick, the Angry Inch — and he hadn't even got a hard-on. Couldn't get himself up. Course, turns out he had better ideas than that." Champ forced the bread into the corner of his mouth. "When he rammed that thing up my arse I fainted."

Caffery put his hands on either side of his plate and looked down for a moment. His black nail looked purplish against the yellow check tablecloth. "They never caught him."

"Nope. He never did it again. Stopped — just like that. And I never saw him again. I called him the troll, cos he was so big and so fucking *ugly*, man. I told the other boys — I mean the meat-rack boys — and the name just got handed down, like a legend. Later the other kids, you know, the straight little kids from the estates, they used to talk about the troll in the woods, play these games and run around and scream and work themselves up and shit."

"We think we've got him."

Champ didn't stop chewing. He scooped some tiny pieces of clam on to a piece of bread and pushed it into his mouth. "I guessed that when you called. Who've you got?"

"I've got a photo. Do you think you'd remember him?"

"Yeah — I'd remember him. Plain as day. Black hair — he weren't a black guy, he was white but he had this black hair — shiny" — he held his hand up next to his head — "like mine. And he was huge — I reckon about six and a half feet — but he was young, you know. He can't have been more than sixteen."

"*Sixteen?* You told the police in his twenties."

"Well, yeah, I was only eleven — he seemed really old. But I s'pose he can't have been all *that* much older than me."

Caffery didn't speak for a while. He sat with his mouth slightly open, staring blankly at the cups resting on the cappuccino machine, a clean white napkin spread across them. Champ continued to chew, watching him. After a while he sat forward and said: "Problem?"

Caffery closed his mouth and dropped his chin. "No, no. No problem." He pushed away his plate and felt under the table for his briefcase. "I'll show you the picture then, if you think you'll remember."

"I'll never forget him, the troll." He leaned over, looked at Peach's photograph and shook his head. "Nope. Not him."

"You sure?"

"Sure I'm sure." He put his fork down and patted his mouth with the napkin. "Right — dessert?"

"What's this fucking mess you've made?" Tracey Lamb was furious. While she'd been at the police station Steven had tried to get out of the caravan — he'd thrown himself around, putting a long crack in one of the acrylic windows and upsetting his slop bucket. Now he sat on the bunk bed rocking himself, his head in his hands. "I wasn't gone *that* long." She splashed around some Dettol from under the sink, then grabbed his hand and pulled him to his feet. "Was I — eh, you little fuck? I wasn't gone that long." She shook his arm roughly. "So what the fuck's all *this* about?"

"Traaaytheee —" His bottom lip stuck out. He looked as if he was going to cry.

"Oh, stop it, for fuck's sake." She shoved a cloth in his hand and pulled him down on to his knees. "There, wipe it up. Go on, clean it up, you filthy little shit."

He started to move the cloth across the floor and Tracey dropped down on the bunk lighting a cigarette, watching him. On the way back from the police station she had been turning the problem of Steven over and over in her mind. When she was arrested her first thought had been that Caffery had set her up, that she'd been wrong about him, that he wasn't bent, wasn't working for someone. But during the questioning, as she calmed down and thought it through, she started to wonder if maybe she was mistaken. She sensed that Caffery was just as cautious of the dirty squad as she was. When he came down yesterday he'd been as nervous as a horse — he had spent half the time looking over his shoulder as if he knew someone might turn up at any minute. *He was* cacking *it*. And during the arrest that morning he hadn't wanted to show himself — he had taken one look at the area cars and melted away into the trees before any of the officers saw him. He hadn't expected it — because, she decided, *because he is as bent as you thought. And afterwards, outside the nick. What* was *that in his top pocket if it wasn't the gelt?*

Kelly Alvarez had promised to tell Tracey how the unit had tracked her down. Maybe Scotland Yard had already been on to her, and maybe loose-cannon Caffery had discovered she was about to be done and used the opportunity to get in a little ahead of the pack. Maybe he really did want Steven. She started to feel better. *You might still be in for that three K, Trace*. She decided to call him tomorrow straight after the Narey hearing and try to suss him out again. She chucked the cigarette in the sink. Whatever Caffery's true nature, she knew that the person on his hands and knees in front of her was far more important to him than that pervert in Brixton, with his insane photographs and hygiene obsessions.

The barracudas. Named after fish, but not real fish: real fish would die in the chlorinated water. "The water tastes funny because of the chlorine," Gummer would tell the new children. "And chlorine is there for a *purpose* see? And what does it do? It *protects* us. It protects us against germs and other nasty things that get into the water. Very important."

But the barracudas didn't need to be told about chlorine — the barracudas knew far too much already. They were at that dangerous age. All the instructors were trained, not only in their own responsibilities towards the children but also to be on the look-out for any signs of abuse — and Gummer knew that children in their swimsuits attracted more than their fair share of inappropriate interest. Once, a man had paid the spectator's fee to get into the building, gone into the gallery and had stood there blatantly taking photographs of the barracudas swimming around. Gummer didn't raise the alarm, instead he stood on the pool edge and waved his hands warningly until he'd scampered away. Gummer was relieved — he didn't want the police coming and questioning him about the incident and making *him* start thinking about the wrong things. They'd see it in his face. *Safer not to be questioned at all*. So the mysterious cameraman had gone off with his cache of photographs — scot free.

Photographs —

Gummer, standing now on the pool edge in his T-shirt and bathing cap, was thinking about the photos he had in his flat — a nine-year-old boy, beautiful, *so beautiful*. He had them displayed in a back bedroom, pasted on the walls. No one would ask questions about them — there was no one to see them, no one ever came into his flat, nor would they ever. He let his mind wander off and tinker with the subject, and the first image he got was of Rory Peach. A boy, naked, arms crossed over his chest. Tied to a radiator. That bit, the bit about the radiator, hadn't actually been in the newspapers, but he knew it was reality. Then Gummer thought about another set of photos. *Where were they? In someone's house? Maybe displayed somewhere?* He wondered for the hundredth time if the police would find them . . .

"Look at me — I'm a mermaid!"

Gummer stiffened. The barracudas, especially the girls, were always getting too close for comfort. If one of them brushed against him it made his flesh crawl.

"Can we do that thing now?" They were jumping up and down in the shallows, one or two climbing out of the water, pushing themselves on to their bellies on the pool edge and kicking their legs out. "Want to do that trick now."

"No, I don't think so."

"Yes!" In the pool a little girl spiked out her arms and legs into a star. "I stand like this and then you have to swim through my legs."

"No, we don't do that in this class." The children coming out of the pool were making him nervous, too many of them and too fast, like penguins flinging themselves at a rock. And when he got nervous his head got red all the way across the top to the bony bit at the base of his skull, and down his neck and into the tops of his arms. "I think we should all get back into the pool."

"And we swim through your legs." They knew his weak spot and were prodding at it now — standing on the pool side, squirming around his legs like fat tadpoles, tugging at his hands, trying to get him into the water, teasing him, brushing him. "And after that you swim through ours."

"No — definitely not —"

"We're all mermaids. Look —"

"Let go!" Gummer was starting to shake. He'd taken his pills that morning, but there was still that bloating tension in him, waiting to burst out. He wanted to cry. The girls were *swarming* around him now, stirring the hairs on his skin. He couldn't bear them to touch him — it was so important that they didn't touch him. It was no good it was no good — he was going to —

"STOP!"

His voice echoed around the pool. The lifeguards and the spectators in the gallery all looked up. "*Just stop it now!*" A blast on his whistle and one or two heads, slick heads like young seals, popped up in the water, shocked and sobered. "*When I say no I mean no*." The children next to him backed away, surprised. He was trembling, bright red, his whole face the colour of his rubber bathing cap. This time none of the children laughed. "Right." He gestured to the changing rooms. "Lesson's cancelled for today. You've proved you can't follow the rules so the lesson's cancelled."

It was getting late but there was nowhere to park in King's car park, and Caffery had to take the Jaguar almost halfway to Brixton before he found a side-road to leave it in. Souness still hadn't paged him. Walking to the hospital, twice he broke into a jog — as if he might silence his mind. *Hyper hyper hyper* — a hothouse of images and voices, making connections where none should be. *Peach, Alek Peach, it wasn't you ten years ago, but it* was *you with Rory. What's happening? Are you copying someone?* It didn't make sense. He felt like striking his forehead. Exasperated and tired, he stopped in the main corridor to get a cup of vending-machine coffee.

"Mr Caffery."

He looked up. Ndizeye stood a few yards along the hallway, body turned slightly away as if he had been crossing the corridor and stopped when he'd noticed Caffery. He was holding a stack of X-rays under his arm and his glasses had slipped down his sweaty nose.

"Mr Ndizeye." *Shit — I haven't returned his calls*. He straightened up. "I'm sorry — I've been meaning to — uh — I just . . ." He tailed off, looking down at the empty styrofoam cup in his hand, embarrassed. "How's the family?"

"Yes. Very well. My family's my blessing." He pushed the glasses up his nose and crossed the corridor to watch Caffery adjust the plastic cup under the nozzle.

When he didn't say anything and didn't move, and when Caffery could feel the clown face smiling at him, he let go of the cup and straightened. "Did you want me to — did you want to talk about the case? You can just submit your expenses to our office manager."

"That's OK, I've done it."

"Good, good."

"Well," Ndizeye leaned back slightly, clutching the X-rays to his round stomach, "it's not going too well for you I suppose."

"You can say that again."

"Is there anyone else you're interested in? Anyone else you'd like me to have a look at."

"Maybe if something comes up on another case, then yes, but we've got the corroborative evidence with the DNA. I mean, I'm sure prosecution will be wanting to see you in court, of course, but that won't be for some time."

Ndizeye frowned and leaned up against the coffee machine. "Corroborative evidence?"

"DNA. We got DNA proving that Peach was the motherfucker who did his own son — sorry if that's offensive."

"Mr *Peach*?" Ndizeye blinked behind his thick spectacles. "Then who on earth bit him?"

"I'm sorry?"

"I said who on earth bit Rory? It was the same person who bit that young lad in the park, but it wasn't Alek Peach."

"*What?*"

"I'm sorry, I thought that's what you meant. His cast. Doesn't match the bite."

"His cast? But I thought . . ."

"Oh — it's not perfect, he moved too soon. But I got enough. Oh yes. Whoever it was bit Rory it certainly wasn't Alek Peach."

It was an odd sunset — as if the earth was tilting sideways, or the solar wind had lost track and was mixing pink light from another galaxy. Caffery cruised slowly round Brixton, as conscientious as a kerb-crawler, looking at the lights in the houses, wondering, just wondering. He parked on Dulwich Road and walked across the park, listening to the wind howl and chase things through the trees.

Number thirty had been released as a crime scene and technically he should get Carmel Peach's permission to enter, but she was still at the Nersessians' and, anyway, he'd kept a copy of the padlock key. Donegal Crescent was quiet — no cars passed. The only sounds were a TV in a lit-up living room next door and a dog barking in one of the back gardens. He carried the torch in his pocket. He liked its heaviness.

Inside, the hallway was dark, the air bitter and salty, sealed up, heated and reheated. He reached for the light and even as he did he remembered — *Shit*. The electricity key: Souness had removed it when they left and placed it on top of the meter. He switched on the torch, followed the beam quickly to the kitchen, and pushed the key back in. The lights came on, the fridge started up noisily. He stood for a moment, blinking in the light, his senses quivering. The walk down the hallway — the silent living room on his right, the door to the basement — had set the hair on his neck straight up. *Not like you — not like you —* It took a moment for his heart to stop racing.

He flipped open the fridge — it was covered in DS Quinn's fingerprint dust and a black and grey crust of microbes. The smell was of riverbeds and mushroom fields, but there was another smell in the house. The smell that Souness had been troubled by the last time they were here. This time it was stronger, still faint but distinctive. He switched off the fridge at the plug, anxious to preserve whatever electricity was left, and went back to the kitchen doorway, finding the light switch for the hallway. It was just as he'd remembered it — the framed prints on the wall, the plastic runner to protect the carpet, Rory's turbo water-gun on the stairs. And the smell. Stronger now.

He sniffed, trying to imagine the receptor that very particular smell stroked. It was almost, *almost but not quite*, the sweetly familiar smell in Penderecki's house. Almost the smell of death. *Is it something the science unit missed? Something else in the house no one's seen?*

Something else in the house. Yes. Someone else had been in the house with the Peaches. He was sure.

He put the torch in his trouser pocket and went to the bottom of the stairs. The last thing Peach said he remembered was standing here, looking up the staircase. Caffery hung his jacket on the newel post and went slowly up the stairs. The higher he got, the stronger the smell. He stood on the landing, resting his hands on the cupboard door. The message was still there, smudged and scraped where DS Fiona Quinn had cut samples from the paint. *Female Hazard*. This little cupboard had been Carmel Peach's home for more than three days. Here she had lain, crunched up and in pain, listening to her son crying below, her wrists bleeding.

If she was to be believed.

Come on, then.

He pushed open the door. There was a lagged tank at the back of the cupboard and slatted shelves above. On the top shelf, a stack of towels. Caffery sniffed. He crouched down, sniffing the carpet. Here, even outside the cupboard, it had been soaked in Carmel's urine and the sharp alleyway smell of it came up to him now, almost making him cover his nose. *But that isn't the smell you're after — it's something else . . .* He straightened and turned, looking up and down the landing.

The master bedroom was at the front of the house, the bathroom facing it. The boards creaked as he walked to the end of the landing, flicking on the lights and looking in both rooms. Silence. The street-light shone orange on the bedroom curtains. A copy of *Hello!* magazine lay on the dressing-table, Carmel's cosmetics stood in a silent little line, a cardigan and a pair of socks were on the floor. In the bathroom Rory's bath toys were piled in a plastic laundry basket under the sink. Caffery turned off the lights and went back on to the landing. *He watches them — he watches them in bed*. Past the cupboard, *Carmel's cupboard*, down to the back of the house. This was Rory's room. He pushed open the door and stood for a moment.

It was a neat square stuck on the house over the kitchen, with a big casement window. DS Quinn had pulled the curtains to stop curious eyes, but there was enough of a gap to see the trees in the park moving in the wind. The smell was stronger in here.

Caffery had the sudden sensation that something was standing in the hallway behind him. He turned quickly.

The corridor was silent, just the street-lights glowing from the bedroom. *You're imagining things now. Making things up* . . . He moved quietly into the room, bending to pick up toys, turn things over, trying to imagine someone in the park looking through the window and watching Rory play. Wolverine stared silently down at him from an X-men poster next to the bed, Gundam and WWF models lay scattered on the floor — *try to imagine Rory crouched here playing with his toys and being watched*. He turned. In the little sliver of window-pane between the curtains the bare bulb glared back. He snapped the light off and opened the curtains. The trees on the other side of the broken fence were less than fifty yards away.

He said he liked watching me in bed . . .

It was one of those odd cloudless nights in which the wind keeps the stars clean and the sky never seems to get properly black. In the park the trees moved as one, shivering where the wind licked at them. Caffery stood quite still, letting his attention move around the room behind him, up the walls, around the doorway then up, across the ceiling, over his head and out through the window, touching the sides of the house, down the garden path, over the fence and out, out into the night — into the woods. Could someone sitting in one of those trees see into this room? Someone who liked climbing?

He went to Rory's bed and lay down, taking the torch out of his pocket and resting it on his stomach, conscious of the cold, bare window on his right. He put his hands behind his head and stared at the ceiling, wondering if he was expecting something to happen — something to hurtle through the window and land on him on the bed. *Secret places. There is always somewhere to hide things*. Not the place you expect. His movement in the room had set up a small rotation of the lightbulb above the bed. He watched it dreamily, circling circling, thinking of Ewan — does everything circle back? Rory's *South Park* duvet smelt of fabric softener and faintly of leaves, and Caffery half closed his eyes, enjoying that smell, remembering the tree-house. Tracey Lamb . . . was she really lying . . . did she know?

He sat up, the torch rolling off and banging loudly on the floor. A fly had crawled out of the plastic rose at the base of the light fitting.

He jumped up on the bed, reaching inquisitive fingers to it, turning the rose on its axis to face him. There was a small square hole in the plastic — he poked his fingers in, feeling the roughness of the edge. The square had been excised as if with a Stanley knife.

Fiona? His pulse was racing now, pressing on his ears in the silence. *Fiona, this isn't you, is it? What would the science unit want with a sample of the light rose?*

"Hal, I hope you're having fun in Cornwall, it's Darren, mate. Look, I'll see you when you get back but Ayo wanted me to call and say that she never got round to coming over to your house, see, and she's sorry — but the fing is our baby got here last night." He paused for a moment and Benedicte had a picture of him, embarrassed, trying to be cool, shifting from foot to foot, being the big man. "He's a bit early, our baby, right, a month early, cos she, you know, someone went and got her all stressed up at work over somefink, some *filth*, Josh, you're right about them, Josh man, and anyway little Errol, that's gonna be his name, little Errol, he's in one of them premie things — he's OK, like, but . . ." He paused and seemed to be wondering what to say. "Oh, man, don't get worried, he's OK, it's just we couldn't water no plants, and I'm sorry. We're going to open something together, the four of us, when you get back, and celebrate." He coughed. "Anyway, that's all, homeys. See you."

Benedicte lay against the radiator with her face in her hands.

She had a headache, cramps in her limbs, and even with the dribble of water her mouth was still so filled with a glue-like substance that closing it was uncomfortable. The papers said that Carmel Peach would have been dead within twenty-four hours in that heat if she hadn't been found. Smurf's breathing was laboured and Benedicte knew that she was deteriorating fast. She was such an old dog, a poor old dog, and so confused — her eyes were dull and crusted and in the last few hours she had stopped moving, except to pant or whimper. Ben dropped her hands and took deep breaths, trying to stop herself crying. Ayo had a new baby, and she and Josh and Hal were all going to die.

Caffery found a mop in the kitchen cupboard and took it upstairs. He switched on all the lights on the first floor and stood on the landing, looking up at the hatch in the ceiling. Secret places. The attic is one of the most common places for "missing" children to hide — *Always check behind the water tank*. The first attending team had searched the attic at number thirty looking for Rory. Had they missed something?

He switched on the light and prodded the hatch. It swung open smoothly, and when he stood on tiptoe and pushed up his hand, he found a light switch and the rubberized feet of a stainless-steel fold-down ladder suspended in the opening. The light came on and the ribbed vault of the roof lit up like a church. Tucking the flashlight in the back of his waistband he pulled down the ladder and began to climb.

Caffery was six foot on the nose and the roof was too low for him: he had to bend his head slightly to stand. The attic was neat — tea chests from some long-ago move, "Rory/clothes" written on one, "Kitchen" on another, rolls of orange insulating material and in the corner, where the shadows ran down from the walls, leaned a plastic Christmas tree and a Woolworth's bag full of red tinsel. Cobwebs strung across the ceiling clung to the lightbulb like a fairground ghost-train prop. He could feel the prickle of insulating material on his skin — and that high, warm smell in his nostrils. Something was up here — something that all the people who had come through the house had missed. He made a slow 360-degree turn, taking in every incongruity, and immediately he saw what he was looking for.

It was at the other end of the attic, right above Rory's bedroom: a small, indistinct pile of something, smeared like mud into the shadows, flies buzzing above it.

He picked his way across the joists, hand covering his mouth — *afraid of what you might find?* He stopped half a yard away from the pile, waving away the flies. He was looking at a long, wet deposit of food — half-eaten food slumped over polystyrene fast-food boxes, slimy hamburgers, a small pile of McDonald's cups, a pile of scrunched tissues. Off to one side a faecal mound, a tissue on top of it. And in the middle of it all a circle had been cleared in the insulating material, from the centre of which a single spiral of yellow electric light poked up into the room. When he went and stood above it he found he was looking through a hole straight down at a *South Park* duvet.

Someone had made a camp here — someone had relaxed here, lived here, shat here, watched Rory from here, probably *masturbated* here. *You fucker.* He straightened up and looked around. Two yards away, leaning against next door's shared wall, was a piece of fibreboard. When he tried to move it he found it was light — it came away easily and he pushed it to one side. He put one hand on the bare wall and leaned over to inspect what had been behind it.

Fucking hell — you clever bastard.

Nine or ten breeze blocks had been removed. Bracing his feet on two joists Caffery rolled up his sleeve, and slowly, slowly, as if he was feeling for something sharp, he put his hand into the hole. In the silent, unblinking darkness of the neighbouring attic his disembodied hand clenched and unclenched, patted blindly up the walls. He retreated and pulled the torch from his waistband, leaning forward a little to shine it into the darkness, and found he was staring into an identical attic. This one was unused — there was no bric-à-brac piled up and the only chink in the geometry was the access hatch outlined in light from the hall below and the sound of a television playing downstairs. He shone the torch against the far wall and saw what he was expecting: another piece of MDF propped against the far wall.

Someone had burrowed along the top of the houses until they could get to Rory Peach.

Quickly he switched off the torch, climbed down the ladder and went into the street, walking backwards into the middle of the road, hands in his pockets, head back, looking at the roofs. These were terraced houses, low-pitched roofs: none of the attic spaces was big enough to convert, and if someone had a mind to, and an understanding of the flesh and bones of a building, they could probably make their way from one end of the street to the other. If they could find a way into one of the other houses from the street —

He stopped.

Two doors down from the Peaches was the boarded-up shell he and the TSG officer had searched on the first day. *Shit — yes*. He reached in his pocket for his mobile, trying to find DS Fiona Quinn's number in the memory.

CHAPTER TWENTY-EIGHT

A hyena, DS Quinn knew, leaves its footprints — she had always known its tail had brushed the walls somewhere inside number thirty: she just hadn't known exactly where to look. This was a familiar problem for forensic investigators: without good witness statements to direct them they were walking blind — they couldn't cover an entire house with fingerprint dust, they had to be told where to focus. But now, with this strange eyrie, all sorts of possibilities had opened up. She knew she could get mitochondrial DNA from the pile of faeces; she also believed there might be other body fluids up here — saliva, blood or semen — that could give her a full profile.

Now she moved carefully around the attic, dressed in the ghostly protective suit that shielded her from the UV light she was using. The equipment she'd brought was her bazooka — the "Scenescope": a combined longwave UV source and camera on a jointed wand, it could detect the smallest amount of body fluid.

Caffery remembered a time when these alternative light sources needed four men to carry them, remembered hearing how the technicians at the Brighton bombing sat in the corridor and used their feet to push the Scenescope's baby brother, the Crimescope, into the lift. Now the equipment arrived coolly in a tiny portable black box. But safety restrictions were still tight. The rest of the SSCU team had set up in the front bedroom, as far as possible from the light source, and sat with Caffery and Souness, crowded around the monitor, watching the screen, the only sound the big Scenescope fan whirring and the creak of joists as Quinn moved around overhead. The camera transmitted a distinctive blue circle to the monitor, a spotlight sliding along textured surfaces that looked like nothing more than skin under a microscope, until it slipped over a dab of something organic and a cold white flare raced down the wand to the screen and Quinn knew where to scrape for a sample.

"See that?" Caffery tapped the screen. "That's the hole in the floor — for him to watch Rory."

"What the hell is going on?" Souness said softly. She had been called away from a charity gala in Victoria and was still dressed in a black silk suit and bow-tie. She'd grumbled about having to leave the event, but if Caffery had expected proof that she knew about Paulina and Lamb, if he'd expected tension in her voice, it wasn't there. She had driven over immediately, stopping on the way at Brixton station to pick up PC Palser — the first attending officer who'd searched the attic. Now Palser was sitting awkwardly in the corner, staring at his hands, embarrassment written all over him. Souness was showing him her back, allowing him to stew a bit.

"And what's all this about our dentist friend?" she asked Caffery, unhooking her bow-tie and undoing the wing collar, letting it sit gaping around her neck. "And Champ?"

"Peach's cast doesn't match either bite. Champ doesn't recognize him. He's absolutely one hundred per cent certain it's not him."

"So what's going on with the DNA? Is there a mistake?"

"Quinny says they'll run it again, but . . ."

"But what?"

"I don't know." He chewed the cuticle on his black thumb. "I just don't know."

They wanted to take PC Palser into the attic to get his version of events, so when Fiona Quinn had finished they all went on to the landing. She met them at the bottom of the ladder looking positive.

"We've got a lot. A lot." She pulled off the lightweight TV-screen goggles and blinked: for the first time in forty minutes her view of the world wasn't via the cathode-ray tube. "Jack, I promise you, I'll have got something out of this."

"Can you get me anything in twelve hours?"

"Why? What's going on?" She unzipped the front of her suit — the "Area 51 radiation suit", she called it — and shrugged it down off her T-shirt. "Someone's not telling me something — the goalposts have moved."

"You can say that again." He drew his hand down over his chin, feeling the incipient stubble there. "If I told you what we're thinking you wouldn't believe me."

"You want the lab to rerun the DNA test?"

"Yes."

"Will do." She turned to PC Palser and gave him a sympathetic look. "All right, son?"

"Yes," he mumbled, not meeting her eye.

"Good. It's clear up there, so go ahead."

Palser was silent as the three of them climbed up to the loft. It was only as he began to show them how he'd done the original search of the attic that he got his blood back. "No one said it was food I was looking for," he protested. "I was looking for a kid. No one said nothing about food."

"But this was all here when you searched the attic — all of this?"

"Yes. But I was in a hurry, I mean, I don't remember the . . ." He pointed, embarrassed. "It didn't smell like this then."

"How about this? Did you see this when you came up?"

Caffery was crouched at the very edge of the roof, where it sloped down to the joists, resting his weight forward on his knuckles and staring down at the soffit — the section under the joists on the roof overhang. Someone had removed the weatherboarding and he could see directly down into the back garden. There were two unwashed milk bottles on the patio twenty feet below. Someone had cut themselves a hunting hole — if they had lain flat here and hung a small way through that hole their face would have been directly in front of Rory's window.

* * *

Outside, the night was unusually cool. As if all the heat had risen into the sky. Caffery and Souness stood for a while looking up at the clear stars, letting the wind ruffle them a little and take the smells away. The SSCU van's doors were open, and they could see the technicians busily chopping up samples, freezing what they could in the on-board freezers. These days, they routinely froze most samples — no one quite understood why, but DNA just popped right out of the frozen stuff in a way that it didn't when it was at room-temperature. Caffery rolled a cigarette and stared up at the sky, at the sickle-shaped moon — so luminous and solid, it appeared cut out and pasted on the sky. He imagined Tracey Lamb looking at the same moon. *Not now — not that now* — He looked sideways at Souness. "Danni?"

"Aye?"

"Is there something you want to tell me?"

She looked at him, surprised. "No. Should there be?"

"No."

"What's this? What's with all these glaekit questions? What's going on?"

"Oh, nothing." He lit the cigarette. "Really, nothing." He believed her — she didn't know. If there was a connection between Paulina and what had happened to Lamb that morning, Souness knew nothing about it.

Rebecca knew that today her life had changed utterly. Like a time-lapse film she had actually been able to feel the process, sense a new colour creeping over her. A thaw, maybe. The heroin must have worn off by now, but she felt unnaturally calm — as if she was facing in the right direction at last. In one phone call to her agent she had cancelled the Clerkenwell exhibition and arranged to accept all the offers outstanding on work she'd chosen not to sell. As the day wore on the rumour seeped out, tagging some passing interest, and slowly, slowly it built until her agent had whipped them up: "I speak to you, Rebecca, looking out of my office window at the streets of Soho, and all I can see is the thrash of fins and tails — it's a feeding frenzy down there. Blood running down their chins. I could have sold your fucking lavvy seat, darling."

She spent the day at Caffery's, lying on her back in the garden, smoking cigarillos, mobile to her ear, astonished that the fairy-tale figures being fed down the phone line could really be attached to her. *Are you sure there isn't a mistake?* She watched the smoke curl up to the blue and pondered this odd shift in her life. She wondered how he would see it — how he'd feel about her now. *I wouldn't blame you if you just told me to fuck off, Jack, I wouldn't blame you.*

When he came home late that night, his face was grey. He seemed exhausted. "There are some clever bastards in the world," he said, getting a beer from the fridge and emptying the change out of his pockets, stuffing his jacket in the dry-cleaner's bag. "Some clever, clever bastards." But when she pressed him he wouldn't say any more. He took off his trousers, put them in the bag, too, and went up to the bathroom in his socks and shirt.

While he showered she opened some wine. It was a tall blue bottle, and because she liked the way it looked in the light, she brought it upstairs. She filled both glasses, put his on top of the toilet cistern with the bottle, and sipped at hers, wondering where to start.

"I've cancelled the show," she said eventually, leaning against the sink, looking at his silhouette in the shower.

"What's that?"

"I said I've cancelled the show at Zinc."

He pulled back the shower curtain, trying to rub the soap from his eyes. "What?"

"I'm selling the pieces that I'd got offers on — the ones I thought I wanted to hold on to. Actually, I've already done it — I've sold them."

"Becky . . ." He turned off the shower, groped for a towel, wiping the soap and water off his face so that he could see her properly. "You can't. You can't do that."

"I can, you know." She leaned over, took his glass from the cistern and handed it to him. Soap dripped from his arms and legs and stomach. A few days ago she would have stared, made a comment, told him what a total turn-on his body was, but she wasn't going to be flippant tonight. "I can and I have. And guess what." She turned her glass around, looking down into it, a little embarrassed. "I'm going to go and see a therapist too." She stuck out her tongue and smiled. "I know, *yuck*, promise you won't tell a soul."

He didn't answer. He sat down on the edge of the bath, his back to her, staring down into the wine-glass. She couldn't tell what he was thinking. After a while he turned, swung his legs out of the bath, put the glass on the floor and held out his hand to her.

"Come here."

She took his hand and he pulled her on to his lap, wrapping soapy arms around her. "That's good," he said. "That's really good."

She bent her head and smiled secretly against his neck, getting soap on her face. The water was soaking into her T-shirt.

"My T-shirt's wet," she said. "Look at me."

"Shall we go to bed? See if it works this time?"

She smiled. "Except you're covered in soap."

"I don't care. Come on."

And they crawled between the sheets, wet and soapy, and he pulled her T-shirt over her head and used it to wipe the soap off his chest, his stomach, his legs, then threw it on the floor and fell forward, groping at her bra. "If this is what a little smack does for you . . ."

"Oh, stop it." She kicked him in the shin. "Don't tease me. You know it's not that."

"I know." He was smiling as he pulled at her shorts, as he pressed his hard, damp body against hers, and she had to stop herself turning to him and saying it out loud like an idiot: *I am so sure, so, so sure it's going to be OK*.

CHAPTER TWENTY-NINE

(27 July)

Tracey Lamb had to go to the Narey hearing that morning — but she didn't want to come back and find Steven had made another mess in the caravan. "Come on." She put down some bits and pieces on the bunk, some Cokes, some Caramel bars, some biscuits. "Come and sit down here and we'll play a game."

The chocolate and the idea of a game cheered him up. He sat down on the bed, on top of his tangled sleeping-bag, and started to rock back and forward, grinning, showing the gaps in his teeth where they'd rotted from too many sweets. "Gaaayhb. Gaaayb."

"That's it. Now give me your hands."

He held them out, delighted that Tracey was paying him attention.

"Good. Now keep still, while I . . ." She used the electric flex to fasten his hands together. "Good." She reached around his back to pass it behind him and slowly wound it around his body. She kept things light, laughing and poking him in the ribs to keep him smiling. "Come on — this is fun. See, what the game is, is that Tracey ain't all that good at tying Steven up — see? Steven can always get out, can't he?"

"Yeeeeth." He nodded, grinning. "Yeth." He stared in rapt attention as she tightened the electric flex so that one arm was fastened at his side. She stood and fed the remaining lead first around the handles of the cupboards, then around the window catches and the base of the table. Now he could move around in a circle of only about two or three feet. He could reach the sink but he couldn't reach the windows or the door or do any harm.

"There." She stood back, wiping her hands on her leggings. "Now, I bet Steven can get out of that — I bet Steven's too clever for Tracey, ain't he?"

"Ye-ehth!"

"Let's see, then. Let's see him get out of that."

"'Kay, 'kay." He grinned, rocking back and forward, his eyes rolling in his head. He struggled and writhed, the flex becoming tighter around his hands until the flesh bulged and the veins in his neck stood up. Tracey folded her arms and watched, her head on one side. *Yeah — get out of* that *you little shit*.

Then suddenly he was free. He jerked forward, arms flailing like a baby trying to get out of his high chair, a big rotten-toothed grin. "Dud id!"

Oh, you fucking piece of shit. She kicked the bottom of the table. "Yeah — you done it, didn't you?"

"'Gain, 'gain."

"OK — again. We'll try again."

"'Kay — 'kay." He jolted forward, excited. "Gaaaybb!"

"But this time," she pushed his hands back in his lap, "this time Tracey's going to try harder."

This time she used a second piece of flex and an oily towrope from the boot of the Datsun. She left one of Steven's hands free but this time, although he struggled for ten minutes, while she stood at the door and watched with a cool smile, he couldn't get out. Eventually, trussed up on the bunk like a Christmas turkey, he looked up at her and grinned. He was out of breath but he was thrilled that the game was going so well.

"Well done." Tracey nudged the slop bucket towards him with her toe. "Right. I ain't going to be long. I'll be back this afternoon. And then, if you've been good" — she put her face near his and grinned — "if you've been good, maybe you'll meet someone special."

"On your list number 103, number seven, sir." The list caller allowed the district judge to find the case on his list. "This is Ms Tracey Jayne Lamb. Kelly Alvarez is representing."

Bury St Edmunds' combined crown and magistrates' courts were housed in a high-vaulted red-brick building tucked away behind the grounds of the ruined abbey. The interior was full of wood veneer and wall-to-wall carpeting. Kelly Alvarez, dressed in a slightly scruffy off-white suit and a red silk blouse, sat on the defence side of the big bench, directly under the huge central atrium. To her right, in the dock, Tracey Lamb stood patiently, clutching her sputum cup and chewing a ball of strawberry bubble-gum.

The clerk read out the charges. "Tracey Jayne Lamb, you are charged with conspiracy to commit an act of indecent assault with others unknown, contrary to common law."

The district judge frowned at Lamb as if he hadn't noticed her in the dock and now was slightly offended to see her — as if she had just walked in unannounced.

"Miss Lamb." He took off his glasses, pressed his hands flat on the desk and sat forward in the high-backed leather chair. "You understand that this is a very serious offence and it can't be tried here. We're here today only to set a date for a transfer hearing and talk about bail."

Lamb gave him a sarcastic smile as if he was asking her whether she knew the alphabet. "Ye-es." She pushed the gum into the corner of her mouth, spat a gobbet of phlegm into the cup, and straightened up, allowing herself a small smile. "I know."

"Right." He closed his eyes in disgust and turned back to the CPS solicitor. "You've said you won't oppose bail?"

"That's right."

"Are you sure you don't want to oppose?"

"Yes, I'm quite sure."

"You know I have the right to overrule that decision."

"Yes — I —"

"Good." He tapped his pen loudly. "Because I think that's what I might well do."

"Sir." Alvarez half stood, accidentally knocking a pen off the table. "Sir, it's important to recognize that this offence is very old, there's no evidence that the defendant is still in contact with the victim."

Tracey chewed a little harder, narrowing her attention on the district judge. No one had said she might not get bail. She hadn't even thought about it. Now the CPS solicitor was standing, nodding at the judge. "That's common ground, sir, we agree with the defence."

"And," Alvarez pushed her hair behind her ears, "the defendant has no offences for the last eight years. Miss Lamb was given police bail and appeared on time today for the Narey hearing. There is absolutely nothing to suggest that she might fail to appear. Um . . ." She scanned the papers in the Narey bundle. "She has been living in the same place for thirty years, and the alleged offence took place over twelve years ago. And my learned friend, the prosecution, has already indicated that he won't be obstructing or asking for conditions."

"Just a moment, just a moment." The judge scratched his head. "This is a very serious offence we're talking about. This isn't a shop-lifting charge. We need to think about it very carefully."

"Sir," Alvarez interrupted, "leave to speak to my client?"

"Oh, well." He threw his pen on the bench and leaned back, one elbow on the arm of the ornate chair. "I suppose so." He flapped a hand at her. "Go on. Go on."

At the dock Alvarez stood slightly angled away from him, one hand resting on the handrail. She looked up at Lamb with bulging eyes. "I want to offer him some security," she whispered. "Do you know anyone who could put forward something —"

"*I thought you said I was going to be out of here.*"

"You are, you are, I just didn't expect this." She bit her lip. "And look at the prosecution — they didn't expect it either. Now, I need something to offer him. Do you have someone who could put some money down on your be —"

"*No, I fucking haven't.*" This was all wrong. If she wasn't bailed then Steven . . . *he'll get out of that rope — won't he? Won't he get out?* But when she thought about him tugging at the flex, chewing it madly, she knew there was a chance he wouldn't. "*You never said I wasn't going to be out of here.*"

Alvarez lowered her eyes and rubbed the bridge of her nose. "Tracey, just think, please — is there anyone who —"

"Miss Alvarez?" The judge was getting impatient.

"Yes, sir, I'm just trying to establish if I can offer any security." She turned back to Tracey, her head bent closer. "Are you sure you can't —"

"*No. I just said no.*"

"Miss Alvarez, I don't know if anyone will be able to offer your client security, but it's academic anyway." He cleared his throat, pressing his fingers to his lips. "Because I have a feeling that Miss Lamb — I have a feeling she might be tempted not to turn up for the next hearing."

"That ain't true —"

"Sir!" Alvarez went quickly back to the bench. "Sir, the defendant came to court today, sir. She was perfectly aware of the seriousness of the charges, and yet she still came to court. I'm sure Miss Lamb would comply with any conditions you'd like to impose. She would be prepared to report at such times as you think appropriate. She would keep residence at her home address."

"Look," the district judge shook his head regretfully, "it's not for me to teach you your jobs, but this is a serious offence." He shook a biro in Lamb's direction. "She's got previous convictions."

"Yes, but not related to this."

"She *knows* the length of sentence . . ." He waited for Alvarez to subside. "She knows the length of sentence were she found guilty, so . . ." The judge made a note in the court register, leaned over to murmur something to the justice's clerk, then looked up at the court again. "So — *no*. No." He ratcheted his body round until he was facing Lamb. "None of the conditions you could offer me would suffice. So, Miss Lamb, stand up, if you would."

She stood, eyes narrowed bitterly, chewing the gum, hating him.

"I've told you that I can't deal with this case here, and because of the nature of the case and the witnesses who might be called, I think it's safest to transfer the proceedings to somewhere where they can give video evidence if need be — do you understand?" He didn't wait for her to answer. "In the meantime, because I feel there's a serious risk you might simply decide not to return to court, I'm going to remand you in custody. You can come back and see us here one week from today — that's the third — and we'll have another look at the situation. Thank you." He turned back to the court clerk and raised his eyebrows. "Shall we continue?"

Morning. Her arms were weak as water and there was something new: a strange wavering of the air as if the room was splitting in two. In the night Smurf had vomited up something that looked like coffee grounds in water and when Benedicte saw the flat eyes, the crusty mucus around Smurf's mouth, she knew. She put an arm around the dear old neck and pressed her lips against the ear. "Smurf, I am so sorry."

Benedicte had found Smurf twelve years ago as a shiny puppy at Battersea Dogs' Home and brought her home on a red canvas lead. She had danced around her ankles at the bus stop, rear end fishtailing from side to side with excitement, claws ticker-tackering on the pavement. Smurf made washing day hell. Every pair of socks disappeared. She liked to doggy-paddle in the sea with Josh when they went to Cornwall and since they weren't sure when she was born they gave her Valentine's Day for her official birthday. Now there was ammonia on her breath and her breathing was laboured, her lips puffing out with each breath.

"I love you, old Smurf." She lay next to the dog, and pressed her face against the velvety head, feeling the eye blink, the soft rusty smell of the fur, the rasp of the greying muzzle hairs. She kissed the dog once, just under the ear where the skin was soft and Smurf shifted slightly, sighed. She half lifted her tail and dropped a thin paw on Benedicte's bare foot.

There is no point in trying, at the end is only evil, no matter what you do, no matter how hard you work, you can't build a wall strong enough . . .

When she looked up, half a minute later, Smurf had stopped breathing.

Caffery woke early, before he meant to, with Alek Peach's face in his head. Rebecca was next to him, asleep. He rested his head on his arm and watched her breathing in and out, her little pixie face quite smooth and untroubled, thinking about last night and wondering if he should wake her and do it all over again. But Peach's face came back suddenly, and when he couldn't fade it or get rid of it he rolled out of bed and went into the bathroom.

Something unspeakable had happened at number thirty Donegal Crescent, and he was starting to think that Alek was the primary living victim. He forced it along his mind as he showered, had coffee, ironed a shirt. Rebecca was still asleep when he left. He didn't wake her, and regretted not kissing her all the way to Shrivemoor, but by the time he got to the incident room, it was still Alek he was thinking about.

He went through the two DCs' statements from yesterday and set their parameters for day two. "Call me for anything, OK? Absolutely *anything*." When they had gone he asked Kryotos to chivvy up General Registry with Peach's paper record. She had it by 11a.m. "You ready for this?" She sat down in the SIO's room, the docket on her lap. She looked astonishingly healthy that morning, as if all the light in the room was reflecting from her skin. It made him feel even more tired. "I found out who the victim of his indecent assault was."

"Go on, then."

"Carmel Regan. His wife. She was two days short of her thirteenth birthday and he was nineteen. Her dad didn't like it, obviously, and shopped Peach. They stuck together even while he was doing time. And something else."

"Oh, God."

"Quinn got some preliminary results from the stuff in the attic."

"And?"

"They don't match Peach's profile."

"Yup. Thought that's what you were going to say." Caffery laced his hands together, rolled his head from side to side as if to get rid of a neck crick. "God," he said, after a while, scratching his neck. "Damn and fuck, Marilyn. I can't believe this is happening — the wheel's coming off."

"I know. And there's more."

"More?"

"They reran the DNA tests on whoever raped Rory, and —"

"Oh, no," he groaned. "Don't tell me."

"It came back the same as last time. Exactly the same. Alek Peach."

When Souness arrived at the incident room Caffery was waiting for her at the door. He'd been thinking about it. Thinking the impossible. "We need to go and see Alek Peach. I think I know what happened. And I think we should appoint a SOIT officer for him."

"SOIT? But that's for —"

"For victims of sexual assault. That's right."

Tracey Lamb's name was on the board in the reception wing of Holloway Prison. It said she had a legal visit that afternoon at two o'clock. At one forty-five they took her with the other girls down to the holding cell: "Cunts' Corner", it was still called, just as it had been the last time she was here.

"You're in room one." Room one: that made sense — the one with the TV for video evidence, nearest to the kangas' station so they could keep her under their noses. "Here's your drawer." Lamb scowled at the officer, held wet fingers to the end of the roll-up to stop it burning, and slung it in the drawer to smoke later. "And the rest." The officer rattled the drawer. Obediently Lamb reached into the breast pocket of her T-shirt for her roll-ups. She had a tiny amount of tobacco — as a remand prisoner she was allowed thirty pounds a week and that had to buy toiletries and all her tobacco.

Three K. Just think — three grand, straight through your fingers.

"Come on, room one, let's be having you."

She was shepherded out of the cell, down the glass-lined corridor and into the room where Kelly Alvarez waited with her papers spread out on the table.

"Hi, Tracey."

"Yeah, what do you want?"

"I want to just tie up some loose ends about your bail next week — I want to be ready for them this time. Want to have a package to offer." She gleamed across at her client, anxious for a response.

Tracey sat down opposite and scowled. "You never told me I might not get bail today."

"I know, I know. I'm sorry about that, Tracey."

"I'd of skipped if I'd known this was going to happen."

"Tracey, that particular judge has got a reputation for it. I spoke to Prosecution afterwards and he was as surprised as I was." She smiled. Yellow teeth. "But we'll make a new application next week and then there'll be no problem."

"Yeah?" She raised her chin a little and looked carefully at Alvarez. In a week Steven might not be alive — if he hadn't got out of the ropes he might still be there, bound to the cupboards and the table in the caravan. *Seven days — how long would it take? What the fuck would you do with a body?* What did he have for water and food? The Cokes and chocolate she'd brought him this morning, and a little water in the bottle under the sink. "How can you be so sure I'll get out next time?"

"Ah, because I've got some inside info." She winked broadly. "Today's judge will be on holiday next week and it'll be someone else. There'll be no problem, I promise you."

Lamb nodded thoughtfully. Accustomed to looking over her shoulder, spotting the sleight-of-hand in every encounter, her senses were perfectly tuned in to certain frequencies and she could tell that Kelly Alvarez was not suited to this profession. She could tell that Alvarez was an idealist who wanted badly to please her clients and she knew exactly how to make this fundamental flaw work for her. "Did you find out how they got me?" she said.

"They had a video of you."

"Just one?"

"Just the one." She held up her copy. "Want to see it?"

"No." She shifted in her chair. "What am I doing in it?"

"You are . . ." She coughed neatly into a big fist. "You are indecently assaulting a small boy."

"Have you seen it?"

"Yes."

"And? Where are we? What am I wearing?"

"You're on a bed."

"Leopardskin cover?"

"That's the one. They'd had it for years." Alvarez put her head on one side, her eyes sympathetic. "I think it was always going to happen, Tracey. The only good thing is that it's all a long time in the past. They haven't got anything recent — a jury will be convinced you've put it all behind you."

"No internet stuff?"

"Uh . . ." Alvarez started to look uncomfortable at the direction of the conversation. "No," she said cautiously. "The video was the only piece of evidence that's come to light so far."

"OK." *There are at least four more videos of you in the stuff Penderecki was holding — and a whole pack of Carl's internet stuff.* Caffery would have surrendered all of that if he'd been connected. Lamb rubbed her hands over her face and looked over her shoulders at the kangas' station. "Right." She turned back, leaning forward, her voice lower. "I asked you about DI Caffery."

"Yes." Alvarez seemed happy to change the subject. "I was interested in that — I asked Prosecution and he hadn't heard of him."

"You *sure*?"

"Certain. I did a bit of asking around and he's with a totally different unit, absolutely nothing to do with the paedophile unit and certainly nothing to do with the investigation. Why? What're you thinking?"

"Nothing." But she was. Her thoughts were pounding along. Something in her kept stretching, stretching as hard as it could towards that money — every sinew, every cell. "You reckon I'll get bail next week, then?"

"Oh, yes. I can *guarantee* you will."

CHAPTER THIRTY

It didn't take long for Caffery to recognize that Carmel Peach was on medication. During the night, Alek had been moved to an annexe room in a new ward, and Carmel sat at the end of his bed painstakingly picking the onions out of a bowl of minestrone soup and placing them in a napkin. She looked as if the pigment had been sucked out of her, as if what was left standing was just the dried-out hide. She had chipped her nail polish into flakes that lay across her T-shirt and jeans, and when Caffery and Souness came into the ward she looked up but didn't recognize their faces. Her mind flicked past them easily and she went back to the soup.

"Alek." Souness sat down next to him on the bed. Caffery closed the door and pulled down the blind. "Alek," Souness said gently, "do ye know why we're here, son?"

"To give me more grief?" He was wearing a black and silver Elvis T-shirt and two or three pillows supported his back. His sideburns had been trimmed, right up to the grey, and next to him, on the side of the bedside cabinet, a child's crayon drawing had been taped. Kenny from *South Park*, "Rory" written in brown felt tip at the bottom. "You can't hurt me now."

He stared at his big hands, his head drooping. "Not any more. Just do what you have to do."

"We're sorry." Caffery mirrored Souness and sat down on the bed, conscious of the intimacy of sitting so close to Peach. "We're here to say that we're sorry — *I*'m sorry, but there's still something you're not telling us, Alek. Something happened in your house . . ." He cleared his throat. "Something happened before Rory was kidnapped. We've got an idea what but we'd like to hear it from you because —"

He stopped. Carmel had suddenly sat bolt upright. Without a word she slammed down the napkin, got to her feet, stuffed her feet into a ragged pair of trainers, the backs pressed down under her heels, and walked jerkily around the room, humming loudly to herself, a snatch of music from a car advert, picking things up and putting them down, opening the bedside cupboard and pulling objects out, noisily rearranging them. Seeing her expression Alek put his face in his hands and shook his head despairingly. Caffery leaned forward and spoke in a low voice, above the noise, "I'm sorry, Alek, if this seems insensitive, but it has to be done."

"Da — da da *da*!" Carmel sang the tune out loud. Caffery looked up to find her glaring angrily at him. "Da-da — da-*da*!"

"Carmel, love," Peach said, "go and wait outside."

Furiously, silently, she grappled in her handbag for cigarettes and a lighter, not taking her eyes off Caffery, and stalked out of the room, slamming the door behind her. It took him a moment or two, staring at the closed door, to get rid of that angry, war-mask image. He shifted a little, and glanced over at Souness, who shrugged.

"Mr Peach . . ." He tried again, straightening up his voice. "Alek."

Peach's jaw moved, as if his tongue was a piece of obstinate gristle that he'd like to swallow or spit out. He pushed away the bowl of soup and didn't answer.

"We do understand how you feel. We've got a specially trained officer — he's done a course, a special course for, uh, this sort of thing."

Peach pointedly turned his head to Souness. "Is that all he's come here for? To tell me about your training schemes?"

Caffery sighed. "I understand why it's difficult, Alek."

"Oh, yeah?" He turned cold eyes back to Caffery. "You really think you understand, do you?"

"Yeah, I think I —"

"You really think you understand." He bunched up his fists. "Fucking filth come here and tell *me* they can *understand* what happened to *me*. You haven't got a *clue* what we went through . . ."

"What I mean is —"

"*No!*" He pointed a finger in Caffery's face. "No, let *me* tell *you* about understanding." His head was twitching, the sinews on his neck stood out. "Because I'll tell you this for nothing, I hope one day you *do* understand. I hope one day the same thing happens to you. I hope you feel this way so someone can come mincing in and preaching to *you* about under-fucking-standing. You've *never* had a choice like I had — *never*." He dropped back against the pillow, breathing hard. "You haven't got children — I can see it in your eyes."

Caffery stared at Rory's drawing of Kenny. He knew he was supposed to be feeling sympathy for Alek Peach, knew he was supposed to be terribly, terribly sorry for what had happened to him, but there it was again, that maddening, bright anger moving down his limbs — as if it had been injected like adrenaline from a gland into his heart. All he'd expected from his extended hand of sympathy was a straightforward, honest acceptance. He tried again. "Mr Peach, all I —"

"Don't tell me."

"I just want to —"

"I don't *want* your understanding."

Shit. Caffery jumped to his feet, furious, pacing around the bed, opening his hands to appeal to Souness. "I'm only trying to help," he mouthed at her.

She turned her face away from Peach and reached over to touch Caffery on the wrist: "Let me deal with this, OK?"

"Go on, then." Caffery dropped into a chair in the corner. He'd given up with Alek Peach. He sat, his legs pushed out in front of him, his head dropped on one hand, and watched.

"Right . . ." Souness rubbed her forehead, trying to think how to put it. "Alek, we think the intruder made ye do something to Rory . . ." She paused. Peach was breathing hard, staring angrily at his hands. "Now, we've never come up against something like this, so we need you to work with us, and what I think we need to start with is an allegation."

Silence. Caffery watched sullenly from the edge of the room. *She won't get through to him — he's a dickhead.*

"We're sorry, young man." She put her hand on his and squeezed it. "But we need to hear it in your own words."

Peach suddenly put his head back and tears lit up in the corners of his eyes, running down his face. He heaved in a breath. "It doesn't matter anyway. I've died now," he muttered. "I've died now, so it doesn't matter what I tell you. I'm dead. I know you can see me." He lifted one bruised hand and touched the fingertips to his chest. "You can see me, sitting here, inside my skin, but really I'm not *here*, see? I'm not really here." He used the heel of his hand to press the tears back into his eyes. "Oh, God, oh, God —"

When it was over Caffery and Souness paused outside the ward to check their watches. They were both pale. When Peach had finally begun to talk he had given them the whole ugly thing at once: dragged it out by its tail and slapped it down in front of them, teeth, blood and claws. He'd admitted it all — admitted that somewhere there were photographs of what had happened, that he'd lied about not hearing or seeing Rory, said that he hadn't been dehydrated because he and Rory had both been given a little water in those three days, because the intruder had a reason to keep them strong. And finally, his head drooping, tears falling on to his pyjamas, like a child, he admitted he'd been forced to do the worst, most unspeakable thing. The troll had told Alek he'd throw Rory out of a first-floor window on to the concrete patio if he didn't.

By the time the interview was over all three of them were shaking. Caffery realized now how little he'd thought through what it had been like in number thirty. To hear it come out of Peach's mouth awed and silenced him. Maybe that was why Peach had given him the bullshit about his eyes — maybe he'd been afraid that Caffery would look right into him and see all the lies he'd had to tell about Rory.

They walked down the stairs in silence. Souness bought them both coffee from a vending machine and they went out into the shocking sunshine. The car was too hot to drive, so they opened the doors and sat on the seats with their feet on the tarmac, sipping their drinks.

"So," Souness said, after a while, pulling the rearview over to check her face, removing a little fleck of dirt from the corner of her eye, "where does that put us now?"

Caffery was silent. He sat with his feet apart, elbows resting on his knees, staring into the coffee. Peach had told them how panicky the troll had got when the doorbell rang, how he'd whimpered and barged around the kitchen trying to get out. But Peach had still been blindfolded and was unable to give them a better description of him. Still, *one* thing he had said was jammed in Caffery's head.

"Jack? I asked you a question."

"Yeah — sorry." He drank his coffee down and crumpled the plastic cup. "How are we doing for tick-tocks?" He checked his watch. "Right, my lads'll be back from door-to-door by now — you feel like going through their statements for me?"

"And where are ye going to be?"

"I'm going home."

"Ye're just going tae dump me here — in the middle of shagging Camberwell?"

"No. I'll drive you back first." He took the keys out of the door and put them in the ignition. "You deserve a lift after what you just did."

Souness, who was holding her collar out and blowing air down it to try to cool down, stopped when she heard that. She turned to him, a suspicious look in her eyes. "Jack? That wasn't a wee compliment slipped through there, was it now?"

"Don't let it go to your head. Now, come on, shut the door."

It was the first time Caffery had been home this early for a long time. The sunlight illuminated unused dusty corners of the house, and the windows needed cleaning. The answerphone was blinking — he put his briefcase on the sofa, opened the french windows and listened to the message while he sat at the top of the garden steps pulling off his shoes and socks.

"It's me, Tracey. I got remanded."

"I'm not interested, Tracey." He padded into the kitchen. "You're a fucking liar and I've stopped playing."

"They never give me bail and I got custody instead and I'm in Holloway, if you want to see me." She hesitated as if she was about to say something and Caffery, in the kitchen, reaching into the back of the fridge to retrieve a solitary old can of Heineken, paused and looked round into the hall. "And, anyway, that's where I am. You could bring me some fags," she added pathetically, "if you wanted. And a phone card."

Yes, you slag. He slammed the fridge. *Yes, you're still a wind-up merchant.* He padded into the hallway to wipe the message and found Rebecca waiting for him on the stairs.

"Who's Tracey?"

He stood, surprised and open-mouthed, guilty to be standing here in his own hallway. "I didn't see your car."

"I had to park round the corner. It's jammed outside." She came down two steps so she was eye to eye with him. "Who's Tracey?"

He sighed, avoiding her eyes.

"Well?"

"It doesn't matter." He turned away, starting towards the kitchen. He knew that if he told her it would start an argument — what Rebecca wanted to hear was that he was doing something in return for her gesture, that he was giving up Ewan. She certainly didn't want to know the sort of bait he was still taking. "She's no one."

"Jack, tell me." She came down two more steps. "Jack —"

"No — you don't want to hear."

"Please."

"*What?*" He turned back to face her. "I've just said you don't want to know, so leave it at that."

She didn't flinch. "Just tell me who she is."

"Someone who's got me here." He grabbed his balls. "If you really want to know she's someone who's got me here and's enjoying jerking me around."

"Why?"

He took a breath to reply, but changed his mind. "No, leave it — it's all about Ewan."

"Oh." She was silent. She tucked her bottom lip under her teeth and dug a little hole in the wooden banister with her thumbnail. He turned to go but she stopped him. "Jack."

"What?"

"It's OK, you know."

"What?"

"About Ewan — it's OK. You can't change your life just because your dumb, neurotic girlfriend wants you to."

He was humbled. They sat at the kitchen table and talked and he was honest with her: he told her about finding the videos — "They've been in the hall cupboard all along" — about going to see Tracey, about the arrest, about the way he'd gone to the Soho bank with the cash, paid it in and promised himself to forget it all. She sat opposite him, smoking thoughtfully, occasionally stopping him to ask a question. From time to time he had to remind himself that this was really happening, that they were sitting talking about it, and Rebecca wasn't just dismissing it, or sliding in cutting comments here and there.

"Jack," she said, looking at the tip of her cigarillo, "you know, it's true, it all really winds me up." She wiped her face and pressed the bridge of her nose between thumb and forefinger. "But," she dropped her hand and looked up, "it's only because I get *scared*. Only because I get scared of how tense you get. I get scared you'll hurt someone — or yourself."

"Me too." He sighed, shaking his head. "I get scared too." He covered her hand with his. "Rebecca . . ."

"What?"

"We'll have to talk about it later."

She held up her hands. "That's OK — that's fine, really."

"I've got to get on — I'm in the middle of something."

"Yes." She put out the cigarillo and started to get up. "Don't let me stop you."

"I think you should go out."

"Why?"

"Trust me — I think you should go out."

Roland Klare took the camera from the tin, bundled everything into a bag and left the flat, fumbling with his keys and nearly dropping them. He was anxious, he was sweating, but he had made up his mind. It was time.

The lift took him all the way to the ground floor without stopping once. He walked calmly out of Arkaig Tower, pausing in the street, his mouth moving, uncertain which was the best way. One or two passers-by looked at him suspiciously, but he was used to these odd stares and he just flapped his tongue out at them — *leave me alone, I am doing the right thing, doing what ought to be done* — and turned right, away from them, clasping the bundle to his chest, heading off down Dulwich Road.

The passers-by paused to look at the eccentric figure in ill-fitting, dirty clothes, hurrying in the direction of central Brixton. But they soon continued on their way and didn't think much more about it. That was the thing about Brixton — always expect the unexpected.

It was 5p.m. when he found it. As soon as Rebecca had gone to the bottom of the garden, with a cup of tea and a magazine and a promise to knock on the french windows if she wanted to come in, he got the videotapes from the cupboard and found the notes he'd made. Somewhere in his tearful, dreadful rambling, Peach had said something that had stuck and wouldn't go away. "He kept saying that everything smelt of milk. He went around sniffing everything and complaining about it. Everything smelt of milk." Caffery knew it had been among the tapes somewhere, but he couldn't automatically link that snatched piece of vocabulary to a specific scene. He consulted the notes he'd scribbled in the incident room and eliminated most of the tapes — several had no soundtrack, or only a solitary, directorial voice whispering instructions to a small child blinking at the camera. *That's really beautiful, that is* . . . But three of the videos had muffled conversations off-camera, and these were the ones that Caffery sat and watched. It was a snippet, a tiny, inconsequential sliver of conversation he was looking for and when he found it his heart sank.

It would be in this one.

He disliked this video in particular because the child in question — a boy who seemed to be about nine — was so patently trying to be brave, so patently trying to please the camera and, worst of all, was so clearly ashamed of his body. He was overweight for his age and it wasn't the abuse he seemed most unhappy about: he seemed more afraid that he wouldn't be good enough, that he might be too fat to please.

The video was set in a bathroom — it was a surprisingly clean room. In fact, it was a typical suburban bathroom from some time in the eighties. The walls were a pale, ragwashed pink, and there was a pink and grey floral border around the door, fluffy pink and white towels on the rail. The sink was in the shape of a shell, and the taps were gold-coloured. It might have been shot in winter because at times the child appeared to be shivering with cold. The other people in the video, two adult men, wore rubber masks.

"What an oinker," someone whispered off-screen. Then something Caffery couldn't understand which ended clearly with the word "flabby".

"Squeal like a pig," someone else giggled. "Ah sayed squayeel lahk ah payig."

"What do you think, Rollo?" Another male voice.

Caffery inched forward a little on the sofa.

"He smells." It was a dull and uninterested voice. "He smells like milk." A shuffling sound and something off-screen fell over. The tape was paused, and when the picture came back the bath was full and the boy was lying on his back in the water, propping himself up so that his immature genitals were exposed above the water-line.

"OK, that looks good — now let's have you just touch yourself . . ."

Caffery stopped the tape and rewound a few frames, started the tape again.

"*What an oinker ******* flabby.*"

"*Squeal like a pig, I said, squeal like a pig.*"

"*What do you think, Rollo . . .*"

"*He smells. He smells like milk.*"

"*OK, that looks good . . .*"

He rewound again.

"*. . . pig.*"

"*What do you think, Rollo?*"

"*He smells. He smells like milk.*"

"*OK, that —*"

Rewind. Play.

"*He smells. He smells like milk.*"

"*OK —*"

Rewind. Play.

He smells, he smells like . . . smells like milk . . . smells, smells like milk, smells . . . Rollo? He smells. He smells like milk. OK, that looks good . . . What do you think, Rollo? He smells, smells like milk, what do you think, Rollo, Rollo, Rollo.

Caffery groped in his jacket pocket for his mobile. He just had time to register his visit and drive through the traffic to North London before Holloway visiting hours started.

He registered under Essex's name, Mr Paul Essex, and used Essex's driving licence as ID. He didn't want anyone seeing the name Jack Caffery on the roster of visitors, and he didn't want anyone knowing he was job. He switched off his mobile and put it with his other belongings in the glass-fronted locker in the visitors' centre and let the officer stamp him — an invisible visitor's pass tattooed on the back of his hand — like a teenager going to a nightclub.

He'd been here dozens of times before, but something odd happened on this visit. He realized it as he walked along the line of tape that led visitors through the system, passing them under the cold, programmed attention of the screws, past the drugs amnesty boxes, past the mouth search — "Lift your tongue, please, sir, and now just turn your head, this way, good, and now this way." He realized that this afternoon he was seeing it with new eyes — *because you're on the other side now, like it or not you are on the other side*. This was what it was like to be on the outside, to see clearly the towering, bureaucratic engine, to feel its threat. The female officer didn't meet his eye as she ran her hand around the waistband and shook the front of his trousers. "Thank you, sir." She held out a hand to show him the way through.

Waiting outside the visitors' room an officer walked a passive drugs dog down the queue — the animal must have smelt Caffery's discomfort because it paused next to him, turned its head slightly, eyeing him coldly — *just as if it knows which side you're really on*. Discomfited by the dog's naked stare he loosened his collar and turned away his eyes, conscious of the officer's attention on the side of his face. *For God's sake, move on, move on* . . . Eventually the dog did turn away. It continued down the line, finally coming to sit at the end of the queue, next to a woman with a baby in a car seat. "Madam." The baby might have been what had made the dog stop. Sometimes drugs came in in babies' nappies. "If you'd like to come with me."

"Mr — uh — Essex." The officer at the door ticked off the bogus name on the clipboard and unlocked the door, nodding towards the nearest table. "You're on reception one."

The first "reception" desk, on the row reserved for new inmates still in reception week, was the closest to the senior officer. Caffery sat on the red plastic visitor's chair, his back to the officer, and looked around the room. Polystyrene tiles hung from the ceiling, the carpet was shiny with tea stains — in an emotional encounter the first thing to go on the floor was the tea, he'd seen it happen time and time again. The officer unlocked the holding cell and the quiet, bass murmur of conversation crescendoed as the inmates came out, a cloud of trapped cigarette smoke coming with them. Caffery rested his hands on the little wooden table and didn't look up. He sat and stared at his hands and waited, and soon here she came, out from the back of the group, in a pale blue T-shirt, her jogging trousers rolled up to mid-calf, bare ankles, trainers and an ankle chain. Her hair was held back severely from her face, her earrings were in place. She took a polystyrene cup from the tea bar and dropped into the blue inmate's chair opposite him, her glittering little eyes taking in his clothes, his face, his eyes.

"You come in under a different name," she said. "I asked the kangas who it was, they said Essex."

"An old friend of mine." He felt in his pocket for change. "What do you want, Tracey? Tea? Coffee?"

"Nah — did you bring my fags?"

"You know I can't bring them in here — you know that."

"OK," she said lightly. Caffery could tell she was glinting with satisfaction at getting him here with just one phone call. But she wasn't going to be the first to show her hand. "What're you here for, then?"

He leaned forward, his hands clasped on the little child's table between them. "Who's Rollo?"

"*Eh?*"

"Rollo. From Carl's videos."

"Not *him* again? You don't want to get anywhere near him — he blades your sort."

"He lives by the park in Brixton, doesn't he?"

"So?" She frowned, scratching nervously at the inside of her arm. "So what?"

"What's his real name?"

"What am I? A cunt? I'm not telling you anything."

"You'll tell me, Tracey — or that trouble we talked about is going to come back to haunt you."

She stared furiously across at him. "Nah . . ." she said. "Nah — you're more scared of the dirty squad than I am. You're not going to let them have the rest of those vids because you don't have them any more — you've traded them already." She spat into her polystyrene cup, wiped her mouth and looked up. "I know your game. I know your connections."

He didn't speak. He pressed both hands palm down on the table. Behind her, in the crèche, children screamed and ran in circles. A baby lay on its back, kicking its legs and arms, having its nappy changed. Lamb might think she had him straddled, but she'd already given him more than she knew.

"Right." He stood up to leave. "Always nice to see you, Tracey."

"Wait!" She half stood, her eyes bright and desperate.

"What?"

She glanced nervously at the guard and lowered her voice to a hiss: "*You never asked me about the boy, you never asked me about Penderecki's boy.*" Lowering herself back into the chair, she pushed her hair behind her ear, and dropped her eyes to the table. "I thought we was going to talk," she murmured, out of the side of her mouth.

"No." He bent over and put his hands on the table, his face close to hers. "No, Tracey. I'm tired of being dicked by your sort."

"*I know something*."

"I don't think so. You're lying to me, but it's not the first time and, believe me, it's no novelty to me."

"1975," she said, "in the autumn."

Caffery, who was taking a breath to reply, stopped. He stared at her, his eyes moving across her face. He shouldn't let himself be pulled in again — she was just putting up another smokescreen and if Penderecki had told Carl about Ewan then there'd be no mystery about *when* it happened. But, of course, *you can't let it go, can you*. He sat down again, subdued, crumpling into the chair and putting his head in his hands. He sat like this for over a minute, resenting her, hating her, and wanting to hit her. "Go on then." He looked up, wearily drawing his hands down his face, knowing. "Roll out the spiel."

"Nah." Lamb looked sullenly at him. She scratched under her armpit and sniffed loudly, looking around the room with her nose tipped up. "Nah," she said, looking at the ceiling. "You need to try a little harder than that. 'S not that easy, is it?" She summoned up phlegm, spat into the polystyrene cup, wiped her mouth and raised her eyebrows at him. "*You*'ve got to convince *me*. You've got to prove you ain't nothing to do with the dirty squad. Because it's funny how they come sniffing around right after you did, isn't it?"

He nodded, and sat looking at her, stroking his chin, a therapist assessing a patient. Had Tracey Lamb known more about him she would have stopped there. She wouldn't have blatantly fed his mood pure oxygen. "Well?" she asked, cocking her head and smiling. "Come on. It's your turn to be nice to *me*."

And with that she'd crossed the line. It was too late. He sat forward and spoke very quietly: "Don't dick with me, Tracey." He said it into her face. "Because if I ever see you on the street I'll kill you."

"Oh," she said archly, her lips white. "Well, fuck you, then, cos maybe I don't know anything after all."

"Well, what a surprise." He got to his feet. "The only difference is *I* mean what I say."

He walked to the door, pulling up his sleeve to reveal the little security stamp. An officer appeared at his side, jangling keys on a long chain and guided him to a small black box, pushing his hand under the UV. "Under the light. That's it." The stamp on his hand lit up and she looped the keys, unlocked the door and held it open for him. He paused, half turning to look back to where Lamb stood, her hands on the table, glaring at him. She mouthed something and raised her eyebrows, but Caffery turned away, thanked the officer and carried on out of the door. He was trembling.

Fuck. Lamb fell back into the chair, kicking angrily at the table legs. She couldn't believe he'd gone. She had been so close. *So fucking close*. She looked around her, at all the mothers and the daughters and the babies, and knew she was alone. Totally alone.

She was sullenly sticking her fingernails in the side of the styrofoam cup when she saw the senior officer watching her. “Yeah?” she said, raising her eyebrows sarcastically at her. “What you staring at?”

CHAPTER THIRTY-ONE

The incident room was emptying for the day. Most of the computers had been turned off and Kryotos had washed up all the cups. She was already halfway out of the office, pulling on her jacket, when she saw him coming out of the lift. She knew Caffery. She knew not to argue with him when he had that look on his face. *My God, that look*. "Come on, then," she said, taking off her jacket without even waiting for him to speak. They went back into the incident room where she booted up the ageing PC and tapped in the new fields he gave her: prison sentences beginning in 1989, attacks on police officers using a knife or razor blade, and addresses in SW2, specifically addresses on the perimeter of Brockwell Park.

"Where'd you get all this, Jack?" Souness was in her braces and shirt-sleeves, a cup of coffee in one hand, a docket in the other. She'd wandered out of the SIO's room and come to stand behind Kryotos and Caffery. "Where's this all been massaged from?"

"I dunno." He didn't meet her eyes. "Just a hunch."

Even as he said it he felt her eyes snap down on him, in that wry, all-seeing way of hers, and he had to turn his head slightly sideways so she couldn't look in through his face.

"Jack?" He moved away, towards the SIO's room, but Souness had him by the tail and she knew it. She could take her time working her way up, hand over hand. "Don't walk away from me, Jack." She followed him calmly. "I know you too well."

"Just a bit of fucking privacy, Danni." He sat down at his desk. "*If that's not too much to ask*."

But she stood in the doorway, leaning against the frame, sipping her coffee. "Jack Caffery's got a wee secret." She looked over her shoulder, closed the door and came into the office. She put the coffee on the desk and bent down to him, her voice a low whisper: "Jack, I wish ye'd tell me more."

He pushed his face nearer hers, his voice matching hers. "*What am I supposed to tell you?*" he whispered. "*Danni?*"

"You're supposed to tell me if something's happening to ye — something that could affect your future in the force."

"OK, then," he said, sitting back and opening his hands. At last it was happening. "Come on — out with it. I've been waiting for this."

She shushed him, holding her finger to her lip. "Why's the love of my life suddenly so interested in you, Jack? Why's Paulina started subtly bringing you into the conversation all the time?" She jerked her chin at the phone. "I've just had her now, in her snaky little way bringing the conversation back to you."

"I don't know, Danni. Do you?"

"Don't be sarcastic with me." She looked at him, her chin dropped, her eyebrows raised. "If she was just shopping around, looking for a bit of quick recreational dicking, I'd understand. You look like you could do the honours, I'll give ye that. But it's not that, is it? It's something else."

He didn't answer. Souness's face was close to his. He dropped his eyes and stared at his hand where it lay on the desk, opening and closing it. He didn't want to be the first to say it. He wanted her to have the opening shot.

"Who is it?" she said eventually. "Eh? Who is it's got you looking like you want to blatter someone?"

"No one."

"You're lying. You've been gone all afternoon and now you come back with a face ready to take someone apart. And it's the same person gave you those new parameters."

He shook his head. "No."

"If something's happening I won't be coming to your aid. Ye do know that?"

"You won't have to."

"I'll forget your *name* if it means I can cover my own arse."

He nodded. "It won't come to that. I promise."

"Jack." Kryotos was at the door, a cool smile on her face. Souness straightened like a guilty child, immediately dropping this hard-faced, ping-pong match.

"Marilyn," Caffery pushed back his chair, "what?"

"This." She was holding a single page printout. "Detained under Section 41 — a genuine loony tunes. Can I go home now?" She was right to be so smug. She had poured all the new search parameters into the database and out of the soup one name had bobbed up.

When Caffery saw it he shook his head. "Shit." He handed the paper to Souness. "I know that name."

No one answered the door. They'd hammered and called, and now, in the little uncarpeted landing, they had a silent audience of neighbours standing in the doorways, arms folded, the *Brookside* titles playing in living rooms behind them. Caffery lifted the letterbox and peered in.

"What do you think?" Souness murmured next to him. Neither she nor Caffery had mentioned Paulina all the way here. It was just as if they'd agreed to drop it until this was dealt with. "Well?"

"He's not here."

"You sure?"

"Yes." He straightened and pulled off his jacket. "He's off somewhere." He handed Souness the jacket and began loosening his tie. "With someone else, probably."

"Oh, Christ Almighty." She saw what he was going to do and turned hurriedly to the audience. "If ye'd all just like to go inside. That's it." She made shooing gestures at them, as if to sweep them all back into their flats. "Come on now, nothing to see here." Slowly, reluctantly, they closed their doors and she turned back. "Jack," she hissed, "we don't even know if this is him."

"We will soon." He emptied his pockets, handing her his keys and some loose change.

"Oh, Jesus — I hope you remember how to fill out a PropDam."

"Remember?" He took a step back. "I could do it in my sleep." He rammed his foot into the door. "*Police!*" His voice echoed around the small dank landing. Letterboxes opened slyly behind them. A second kick. The door shuddered, seemed for a moment to bow at the centre, but the two locks held.

"That bottom one's a deadbolt, Jack."

"I know. POLICE!" He slammed out his foot, landing the kick perfectly along the line of the locks, jarring the tendons in his knee. The top Yale sprang out of its footing but the bottom one held. He hopped backwards, getting his balance. "*Fucking thing.*"

"Och, look," Souness said impatiently, patting her pockets for her mobile. "You'll never hoof it down. We need the ghostbusters, Jack. I'll give them a call."

"OK, OK — just give me a —" He stepped back, pushing his hair off his forehead, and landed the third kick where he wanted it, about four inches to the right of the locks. The thin outer skin of the door crumpled. The next kick went straight through. "There." He hopped back, dragging away long splinters of wood, and began ripping at the opening, breathing hard, dropping pieces of honeycombed interior on to the floor. He pushed his hand into the hole and patted along the inside, his face hard against the door.

"Good." He looked at Souness. There was a thumb-turn at the back of the deadbolt. "Got it." The lock rotated easily. He and Souness were in.

Neither spoke. They stood, peering cautiously into the darkened hallway.

Souness took a deep breath. She pocketed her mobile, handed Caffery his jacket and keys, and stepped across the threshold. From somewhere inside, somewhere in the darkness, came a stale smell. She hesitated, felt in her pocket for the sturdy torch she'd brought. "You sure he's not here?"

"I'm sure." But his voice was low. Cautiously he flicked on the light and they both stood, looking into the hallway. It was an unremarkable, council-block hallway, ending a few feet ahead in a doorway. No carpet on the floor, the boards were bare. The walls were woodchip and on either side of the hallway were two painted doors. "Hello?"

Silence.

"This is the police, Mr Klare."

Silence.

From the landing behind them came the creak of another letterbox opening. "Nosy wee fuckers." Souness closed the battered door with her foot and turned back to Caffery, who was standing at the first door, his hands up, palms facing the door, an odd softness in his expression as if there was warmth coming from it.

"Jack?"

He didn't answer. The hair on his arms prickled, standing straight up against his shirt. In biro, in tiny, almost invisible letters, someone had written very plainly the word *Hazard*.

He turned to Souness and smiled.

Outside it was getting dark. From the window in the living room they could see the weather rolling in for miles around — clouds as big as cathedrals stalked above the park, pink evening light prismed up from the horizon. Souness put some calls in to mobilize the locals, to get a bulletin out to the area cars, to mount surveillance on the flat and to get the SSCU over to Arkaig Tower to see if they could pick up some DNA to match to their target. "Right," she said. "Let's give the place a wee spin, then. Before the cavalry arrive."

They brought the lifts to the top floor, jammed them and propped open the door to the staircase — if Roland Klare decided to come home between now and the time new officers arrived, they wanted to hear his footsteps on the stairs. They zoned the flat roughly between them: Souness wrapped polythene freezer bags around her hands and took the living room and bathroom while Caffery did the kitchen and the bedroom. They used lights only in the rooms that didn't have windows; in the others they relied on what daylight remained. Klare's flat, they soon found, was a warehouse: every imaginable object was hoarded here, from a collection of vacuum-cleaners to a tawny owl in a glass dome. Some areas were filthy — the smell of the bathroom made Souness put her hand over her mouth — and the fridge was full of rotting food: they could well imagine Klare was responsible for the mess in the

Peaches' attic. But in erratic ways the flat had been kept scrupulously clean. The kitchen had been scrubbed: in some places the worktop had been so manically scoured that small scoops of the Formica had worn through and showed chalky white. Cloths sat in a large boiling-pan on the hob. The floors, none of which had carpets, were obsessively clean.

With the first stone Souness turned she found something of interest. "Hey, Jack," she called, "have a deek at this."

He went into the living room and found her standing at a metal-framed desk, silhouetted against the sunset, staring into an opened drawer. "What's that?"

"Fuck knows." She picked it up and they both peered at it. It was a battered notebook, a rubber band around it. "What d'you make o' that, then?"

He took her elbow and lifted it higher, tilting it towards the window so he could see better. The words "The Treatment" had been carefully stencilled in a box on the front cover, and the curling pages were covered with detailed drills and formulae, all written in a tiny, hectic scrawl. Newspaper clippings had been pasted inside, articles on the Rory Peach case. Caffery's skin tingled. "Grab it, then."

"Right." Souness slipped the notebook into a freezer bag, put it inside her jacket and turned back to the living room. "Come on, snap-snap."

They worked for another ten minutes, neither sure exactly what they were looking for. In a magazine rack Souness found a card picturing a toddler in a nappy with the caption: "I HATE TO BOTHER YOU WITH A

PERSONAL PROBLEM . . ." She opened it and read the punchline: "BUT I'M HORNY." In the bedroom, deflated and tucked into a drawer, Caffery found a blow-up doll of a male child, a tag in Japanese attached on the seam at the ankle. They were definitely in the right place, and it was all so *weird*, he thought, like an out-of-hours museum, all Klare's collection neatly ordered on fold-out tables — metal, the sort you might see at a jumble sale. Caffery noticed that none of the collection touched the floor, everything rested on these tables — it made him think about how Rory Peach had been stored, off the ground, the way a big cat would drag a carcass into a tree.

He was still wondering about this when, ten minutes later, he pushed open a cupboard door in the bedroom and found what he knew they were looking for. "Hey, Danni," he called, "got a moment?"

"What?" She came in from the living room, puffing, holding her arms above her head and squeezing past the tables to get to him. "What you got?"

"I don't know." He reached inside and switched on the light.

"Red bulb," Souness muttered, peering suspiciously into the cupboard. "Freaky."

"It's a darkroom."

"Eh?"

"It's a darkroom — look." He pointed to a small plastic table covered in equipment: bottles of chemicals, a pair of rubber gloves, trays, a lamphouse mounted on a stand that he guessed was for printing film. Set aside from the clutter, at the far end of the table, was a biscuit tin, sealed with brown tape. "Darkroom equipment." He reached in his pocket for his Army knife, slit the tape on the tin, popped the lid off and looked at what was inside. "Oh, shit."

"What?"

"Here we go." He handed the torch to Souness and started pulling out prints. "Photos."

"What?"

"Look."

Souness came into the cupboard and shone the torch onto the photos. Human faces stared up at her. "Oh, God," she said, tipping back a bit on her heels. The images were blurred but she thought she knew what she was looking at. She recognized the cross-hatched lino on the floor. "Rory Peach?"

"I think so."

"Jesus." She picked up the top photograph and stared at it. "Poor wee mite." She had Alek and Rory, and the truth of what had happened to them in number thirty Donegal Crescent, in her hand, and it made the blood go from her face. "Not enough that he's dead," she said quietly. "He had to go through that first."

"I know." Caffery was rummaging in the tin. Underneath the pictures of Rory Peach he found an old Polaroid of a child wrapped with torn sheets, a gag on his face, his hands placed across his chest like a pharaoh. He knew what this was. He recognized the wallpaper. And the Teenage Mutant Ninja Turtles poster. "He was right," he said, handing the photo to Souness. "He was fucking right — it wasn't a hoax."

"*Who* was right?"

"DI Durham." There were more pictures of the same child underneath. "See? It's the Half Moon Lane family."

"Jesus, Jesus, Jesus, what the fuck ever happened to them then?"

"I don't know. I just don't know." Further down, under the Polaroids, he found a photograph of a boy — face down in a scatter of dead leaves, his trousers and underwear pulled down to his knees. This, he felt sure, was Champaluang Keoduangdy twelve years ago — one of Roland Klare's earliest victims. "Jesus," he muttered, "it's all here." He lifted the tin and found underneath it four more Polaroids. These pictured a boy tied to a radiator, a white radiator against a tangerine-coloured wall. The boy, it was clearly a boy, lay on his side. He was white, he looked about Rory Peach's age and he wore sandals, a blue T-shirt and shorts — just like the child in the Half Moon Lane photograph. The child's face was half hidden; there was a glimmer of brown tape on the side of his cheek where he'd been gagged and his shorts had been half unzipped to show his underwear. It wasn't Rory Peach and it wasn't the Half Moon Lane child. This time when she saw it Souness began stamping her feet. "Oh, my God," she muttered. "Oh, my God, I smell trouble. My God, I think you were right —"

"*The next family?*" He looked up at her. "Do you think that's the next family?"

"Aye, aye — I wouldn't be surprised. Come on — let's get them back to Shrivemoor." She tucked the torch into her waistband and started gathering up the photos, stuffing them into the tin. "Come on."

She squeezed her way back past the tables to the bedroom window and glanced out. In the street below cars were arriving — subtly as ants from a nest, clustering around the foot of the building. "Good, they're here."

"Right." He closed the door and came out from behind the tables. "I want to look in the cupboard in the hall."

"I thought you'd done it."

"Nope. Come on."

In the hallway he stood for a moment, his hands resting on the door. Logan had been up here on the first day of the investigation, Caffery remembered seeing Roland Klare's name in his statements, but this writing "*Hazard*" was so small Logan could easily have missed it. He tried now to picture the size of the room beyond. Another bedroom? No door handle — just a brass knob, so maybe a cupboard? *Just like Carmel Peach, sealed away in a cupboard, a warning scrawled across it*.

"Come on, Jack." Souness stood next to him, clutching the tin to her stomach. "We haven't got all —"

"OK." He pushed the door. It opened smoothly and he found he was looking at another small cupboard. The bulb was out and it took a moment for his eyes to get used to the light, but when he did he put his hands on the edges of the doorframe to keep his balance.

"What is it?"

"Uh." He wiped his mouth. "I don't know. Give us the torch."

Souness passed the torch to him. He clicked it on and let the beam play around the small area. At the back of the cupboard was a waist-high glass tank. Like a fish tank. "There's something at the back of the cupboard."

"Then go and have a look."

"Yeah." *Yeah, sure, no problem.* The tank was about two-thirds full of liquid, semi-opaque, and near the surface something clogged floated. *Sure, something's fucking floating in it but that's no problem* —

"Come on, Jack, let's get on wi' it."

"It stinks — sure you don't want to do it?"

"Ye wee coward."

"You do it, then."

"No fucking way — that's a man's job."

"Right." He took a deep breath and stepped inside. "First off, there's something on the floor here." He let the torch play across the wall to the right. "Clothes," he said. "A pile of clothes on the floor." He could come back to those later. "And, uh, then, this tank . . ." He stepped nearer, let the light play over it, and immediately saw that the object floating in the yellowish fluid was a tangle of clothes. Clothes floating in — he bent nearer — clothes floating in — "Jesus." He took an involuntary step back.

"What?" Souness said. "What is it?"

"Piss. It's only about a hundred gallons of piss."

"Jesus —"

"Crazy fucking bastard." Caffery shone the torch into the tank. Men's clothes, a nylon zip-up top, a hooded tracksuit, three pairs of trainers. Roland Klare had been storing clothes in two feet of urine. "Crazy, crazy fucking bastard —"

Benedicte was fevered, lightheaded. Her skin was scratchy, there were sores inside her mouth from her manic suctioning of the copper pipe, and her fingerpads were raw from digging into the floor. It had been a day's work to push Smurf's corpse as far away as she could. She had covered her with Hal's shirt, but the bluebottles had managed to find their way under it and were feeding on the lushest, choicest food they had ever known. They proliferated, doubling their numbers it seemed, in her fever, every time she opened her eyes.

Sometimes she knew she was awake, and sometimes she wasn't sure. Her eyes raced around inside their sockets, lights floated in and out, and sometimes she could see her life before this — flickering along so happily, so happy and smooth, only soft edges and milky comfort and, *look*, there she was with Josh and Hal and Smurf, the whole family, sitting on the lawn. It was summer time — they were wearing shorts, Josh's Pocari Sweat canister was on the steps, a radio played, fresh cut grass stuck to the back of Josh's legs when he got up to jump into the paddling-pool. Then she could hear Josh downstairs crying. *Josh?* Was that really Josh? And the other noise? What was that? An animal grunting. Or was it a man? Sobbing?

Ben — come on now, come on — wake up.

Josh? Sweating, her heart thudding, she opened her eyes in the dark room. Moonlight on the ceiling. Over in the corner the grey shape of her poor dead puppy. She was awake. Really awake. Had that been Josh, crying? She rolled on to her side so that her ear was pressed against the floorboards and listened to the house under her. Silent.

She'd imagined it.

She crunched up her eyes and tried to go back to the picture of Josh and Hal — sitting on the grass. But her brain seemed swollen, as if it was pressing against her eyes, and she just couldn't do it. She couldn't see their faces. In just five days her son and her husband had been reduced to a few blurry images — Josh a tiny, defenceless shadow with grasping hands, and Hal a dark landscape in bed next to her at night.

"Oh, Josh," she whispered. "Hal, Josh, I love you."

The house was silent as she closed her eyes again. Over the roof she could hear a plane. She had a sudden image of the light in the cabin, the lovely rosy light of sunset racing around the cabin — Hal and her on the way to Cuba in the days when no one went to Cuba, a travel agent would laugh if you asked to go to Cuba, and you had to fly through any number of Caribbean islands just to get there. And he had wanted to go because he wanted to see the furniture factories in Holguín. She held her hands across her face and imagined a sea she had always wanted to visit — a magical sea, the Sea of Cortez maybe — a mysterious sea where whales come to mate and strange singing could be heard coming across the water at dusk . . .

As she dreamed she twitched, lying on the floor, chained to the radiator, the flies landing on her eyes.

Coming down the front steps of Arkaig Tower Souness started to walk more slowly. In the lift she had been flipping through "The Treatment", the odd little *vade mecum* from the desk drawer, shaking her head in amazement, and now she was so absorbed in it she almost came to a halt. Caffery stopped and turned to look at her: "Danni?"

"Fucking beautiful." She shook her head and gave a low whistle. "Fucking beautiful."

"What is?"

She looked up. "It's all here — everything."

He came to stand behind her, leaning over her shoulder to read: " 'Exposure to female hormones' — what the fuck is that?" He tried to pull it away from her but she shrugged him off.

"Get off." She held it nearer, reading carefully. " 'Milky smells — offensive. Prolactins are heavy —' "

"What're prolactins?"

"I don't fucking know, do I?" She closed the book, put it in her pocket. "We'll get it back to Shrivemoor and have a proper look. It might tell us where those poor wee fuckers are." She looked around the deserted streets. "Now. Where did we put the car?"

They arranged an emergency meeting to hammer out plans for hunting down Roland Klare, and while they waited for everyone to arrive they made coffee, sat in the SIO's room and Caffery called Rebecca to make his excuses — "No, honestly, Jack, it's OK. I'm watching *Eurotrash* repeats anyway." He wanted to kiss her for it. Souness called Paulina with the same story and as she talked Caffery sat, staring at his reflection in the window, listening to the conversation, waiting to hear his name mentioned. But it wasn't, and when Souness put down the phone she immediately turned her attention to the book. He was relieved — the silent pact held; Roland Klare was all they were going to talk about tonight.

They sat, shoulder to shoulder, like children at school, and read "The Treatment" from cover to cover, hardly exchanging a word. They knew they were looking at the minute cataloguing of Klare's mind, his reasoning scraped out on paper. For the amount "The Treatment" told them about his motives and compulsions, Souness could have opened the drawer and discovered, nestled among bits of paper and elastic bands, Klare's naked, beating heart. It told them about his rituals and fears, about his love for shadowy air pockets high above the ground, about the manner in which he'd subdued Carmel Peach. It told them about his impotence, it told them why he'd wanted to watch Alek Peach rape his own son, it told them about his compulsion to use his urine to "purify and neutralize". It even told them why he'd worn gloves, and it wasn't because he was clued up about forensics as they'd assumed. Then, on one of the final pages, Caffery saw something that woke him up like an adrenaline jag:

Identification of new sourse/family achieved . . .
..check and nuetralize all places habituated by female (done!)

He grabbed the book.

New family: Child observed good, Father good, Problems: 1. Wife. 2. Dog is female.

"It's nae the Peaches he's talking about, is it? They didn't have a dog."

"No. It's the next ones." Caffery sat quite still, feeling his memory dilate towards something. A dog — where did that fit in? And these photos of a boy against a radiator — the walls, a pale tangerine colour, the radiator, modern, straight-lined, white — *and there was a shape in this memory too. A hill out of a window? Trees?* He didn't know how many doors he'd knocked on in the first days, and either the two specially assigned DCs or Logan had revisited them all since — they had all checked out — but his memory kept on pushing. Then, just when he thought it might nudge up a name, the lift bell pinged in the corridor and he lost his train of thought and was back to looking at a simple photograph of a nameless child in a nameless room and a notebook filled with scribble. "Fuck."

Fiona Quinn and two exhibits officers appeared in the doorway, looking around the deserted incident room as if they'd expected a welcoming committee. "Are we the first ones?"

"Yes." They both stood. "Come in."

Caffery and Souness made everyone coffee, then they sat Fiona down. "Was Carmel Peach tested?" they wanted to know. "Did you test her?"

She frowned. They made her nervous, these two senior detectives with adrenaline on their breath. "Tested for what?"

"Drugs? A sedative? GHB?"

"No one told me to. By the time I got the statements I —"

"Have you still got a blood sample?"

"Yes — there's still a sample. I'll get it tested."

"And did we get any urine from the Peaches' house? Had he pissed on stuff in the house?"

"There was piss everywhere — don't you remember?"

"Did you get any?"

"We were at the mercy of your statements. No one told us he'd pissed on things."

"But you said it was everywhere."

"We thought it was them — the Peaches."

Caffery and Souness both sat back with their fingers to their foreheads.

"Well, I didn't know, did I?"

"No. It's OK — it's not your fault."

The emergency strategy meeting took until 2a.m. — the DAC attended and the borough commander cut short a golf club dinner to come to Shrivemoor. All the way through the meeting Caffery couldn't stop staring at the Polaroids, at the child crunched up against the white radiator. Tangerine walls. Where did he know those walls from? And when he switched his attention to the blurred face of the man in the Half Moon Lane photos *again* he felt that tickle in his memory. There was something about the shape of his head, the position he'd been bound in, his arms folded across his chest. If he was less tired, if he'd been sleeping better recently, he might be able to remember. But he couldn't. After the meeting he drove back to Brixton, to Arkaig Tower, and tapped on the window of the blue Mondeo parked just in view of the entrance. The surveillance team leader let him in and they all sat in silence, Caffery in the back, smoking, swallowing mints and pain-killers and staring out at the empty streets, listening to his memory ticking away. *The dog — the dog goes somewhere too — where the fuck does the dog go?* It was 5a.m. when he finally fell asleep, his glasses on, his head tipped back on the seat, a roll-up between his fingers.

CHAPTER THIRTY-TWO

(28 July)

Tracey Lamb hadn't slept much last night. She had lain awake on her bunk in the reception-wing dorm annoying the three other inmates by sucking on her raw cuticles and lighting the same roll-up every ten minutes, taking carefully rationed puffs, then pinching it out. She was regathering her confidence. She was going to be bailed in just under six days — and then she wanted to make her getaway. That would mean another bid to DI Caffery — there had to be a way of cracking that little nut.

She had convinced herself that Steven would still be alive — that the Cokes, the chocolate and the bottle of water under the sink would be enough if he had been unable to get out of the ropes, and by the morning she'd got the confidence to make the next move. The screws had decided that she wasn't high risk — that if she was allowed a phone card she wouldn't snap it in two and use it to carve up the inside of her arms — so as soon as bang-up was over she went to the phones and used two units on her card to call Caffery. She'd left his mobile number at home and all she had was his home number from directories. It was early but his answerphone picked up. She paused for a moment, then began to mumble into the receiver. "It's me — Tracey . . ."

It was raining. Caffery woke to the steady beat of it on the car roof and the low, bored whistling of the surveillance officer in the driver's seat. He sat up, yawning, moving his head from side to side. The radio was on low and the dashboard clock said a quarter to ten. *Shit*. He pressed knuckles into his eyes. He had slept longer than he'd meant to.

Outside it was dull. Rain drifted down the steamed-up windows and the dashboard air vents had blown a clear silver hole in the windscreen. The second officer was asleep, her head crunched down sideways on her shoulder, her earring stuck into the flesh of her cheek. Maybe because she was the only woman in a car with two men, in her sleep she had instinctively crossed her hands protectively over her chest.

Caffery leaned forward to look out of the windscreen. "Nothing moving out there?"

The officer met his eyes in the rear-view. "Nothing."

"Right." He began searching his pockets for tobacco, blinking, trying to crank his mind forward. He rolled a cigarette, lit it, and was about to settle back when the posture of the sleeping woman suddenly tilted off a thought.

He stopped, the cigarette halfway up to his mouth, and stared at her — at those hands crossed pharaoh-like across her blouse, as if she should be holding an amulet. He was so silent and naked in his fascination that, after a while, the other officer began to get irritated.

Brixton was soaking. Rain washed a thin soup of juices and fish blood out of the market and into the gutters. There were few hints of the huge operation that was taking place in the hunt for Roland Klare — a couple of extra uniforms on the street, a couple of squad cars on the one-way system. Caffery stood outside the Rec swimming-pool, looking at the steamed-up windows. All the chlorine and shouts from the pool seemed to have ended up flattened against those windows. With Kryotos's help, and with the help of a neighbour in Effra Road, Caffery had tracked down Chris Gummer to this pool. When Gummer had stopped him on the station forecourt four days ago and talked about Rory Peach being tied up, he had made a strange dipping gesture and crossed his arms over his chest. Caffery remembered it vividly now: it was the same way that the Half Moon Lane father and son had been fastened, with their arms across their bodies. The photos were blurred and old, but Chris Gummer was a believable match for the father.

He stood for a moment, behind the glass, looking at the swimmers. Two large women dressed in pink-flowered swimming caps sat in the shallows, swirling water around their hips, and nearby a group of bald men, hunched and thin in arm, talked in a small circle. In the deep end children shrieked and jumped off the diving boards. Chris Gummer seemed oblivious to them all.

He wore a bathing cap and was pulling his long, oily white body through the pool with a fatigued breaststroke, his head held up high above the water, eyes half closed, mouth working like a fish —

It's him, Caffery thought, *it's him* —

He knocked on the window. Gummer looked up, saw Caffery and trod water for a while, as if deciding what to do. Then his face changed. He took a gulp of air and continued swimming to the far end of the pool. Caffery knocked again, and this time Gummer didn't even look round.

"Fair enough." He pushed the red emergency handle and stepped out on to the pool edge. Somewhere an alarm screamed, and the lifeguards at their station looked around in confusion. Gummer reached the side of the pool and suddenly realized what was happening. The lifeguards were blowing whistles. He clung to the edge, wiping his eyes and staring at Caffery walking towards him.

"What?" He moved along the side towards the shallow end, looking up at him. "Stop following me."

"Get out of the pool. I need to talk to you."

"About what?"

"Get out and I'll tell you."

A cropped-haired woman in shorts and flip-flops jumped in front of Caffery and stood, heels together, back erect, like a traffic *gendarme*, her hand extended at shoulder height, palm out, as if Caffery might stop through the pure ferocity of her expression.

"Yeah, c'mon, c'mon." He pulled his warrant card from his pocket and flicked it at her. "Out of my way."

"I have to think about the health of the other swimmers . . ." But she was already backing off, her confidence punctured by the card, wondering if their speculations about Gummer had been right after all. "Your shoes, sir . . ." she finished lamely.

"Come on, Chris." Caffery kept pace with him. Bloodshot eyes in a white face, the slick rubber cap corrugating the skin on his forehead. "We need to talk. There's something you forgot to tell me."

"Go away." Gummer stretched his feet down in the water until he found the bottom. "When I wanted to talk to you, *you* wouldn't talk to me." He pushed himself off the side and began to wade away, out into the centre of the pool, his thin white arms held straight out at the sides. Caffery walked calmly down to the shallow end and before the lifeguard could stop him he had stepped, fully dressed and still in his shoes, into the shallow end of the pool. Swimmers scattered, shocked by this lean man wading out among them, and in the centre of the pool Gummer saw that the game was up. He turned, holding up spade-like hands, his mouth quivering. "All right, all right! That's enough."

They talked in a corner of the café. Both of them smelt of chlorine — Caffery's trousers were wet to the knees. A group of teenage boys in FILA sports jackets were using a gluestick to fake bus passes at another table. They kept jumping up to buy chocolate and Red Bulls from the vending machine, and Caffery sat with his back to them, looking across the table at Gummer, who had bought a cup of coffee and two chocolate bars, which he unwrapped, broke into four pieces and positioned on a paper plate in front of him. The chocolate remained untouched for the rest of the conversation.

"Chris, look." His tobacco had survived the swimming-pool. He sprinkled a little into a cigarette paper. "I'm sorry about that. But I needed to talk to you."

"*I* really needed to talk to *you*." Gummer had dressed in a worn checked shirt, frayed in places, his fine baby hair dripping on to the collar. His face was as shiny as a peeled egg. "That's why I came all the way to Thornton Heath. But that didn't make any difference, did it?"

"I'm sorry. I learned my lesson."

He shrugged and let his gaze wander away somewhere over Caffery's head. Blood rimmed his eyes. Caffery lit the cigarette and pulled the little foil ashtray towards him. "Chris, tell me something. How did you know about Champaluang?"

"I told you. It was in the paper."

"And that's the first time you heard someone mention the troll?"

He nodded. "You should have listened to me."

"You're right." He turned the cigarette round and round in his fingers, looking at it thoughtfully. "Chris, tell me if I'm wrong, but when you heard about Champaluang, you must have wondered, I mean, help me out here, but when you heard about the troll you must have wondered if it wasn't the same person who was in your house . . ."

Gummer took a sharp breath. His mouth moved a little, but no sound came out. He dropped his eyes and hunched his shoulders forward, his hands wedged between his knees. Caffery saw that he was shaking.

"Chris?"

He didn't look up. Caffery tapped ash into the little foil ashtray, looking at the top of his head — at the skin through the hair — wondering where to go next. "I think that the troll was in your house once, Chris. Maybe a long time ago. Am I right?"

He didn't respond. Caffery thought about the Half Moon Lane photos in his pocket. *Show him the photographs? What if you're wrong?* "Let's put it this way. People have some screwed-up fantasies — don't they?" he began. "Don't you think it's amazing the things that some people get off to?"

Gummer shrugged. He kept his eyes fixed on the chocolate.

Oh, Christ, he's going to be difficult —

"For example, some people . . ." He shifted in his chair and crossed his legs. "Some people's fantasy might be — uh — watching a man rape a child, say. Do you think that's possible?" Gummer gave a little cough and put his hands up to his face, pressing the tips of his thumb and forefinger into the corners of his eyes. Caffery could see the scalp flush red with blood. "A boy, for example. Some people might have a fantasy about that — do you think?"

Gummer dropped both hands flat on the table and took deep breaths through his nose. His eyes were closed and Caffery could see the corneas moving beneath the eyelids like a shadow show.

Don't give up —

"A father raping a son, for example."

"I'm not a paedophile," he said suddenly, opening his eyes. "I loved my son more than anything."

"Why didn't you go to the police?"

"I tried to — I tried to talk to you. You wouldn't listen."

"I mean before. When it happened."

He took in a sharp breath and shook his head convulsively. "No, no, no, no, no." He swung his head from side to side, overemphasizing it like a child. "No — my wife said no. We weren't to go to the police."

"She didn't want the truth to get out?"

"Are you surprised?"

"They could have done something."

"Could they?" He fiddled with the fraying cuff of his shirt and stared at the chocolate. "Could they have stopped her going? Could they have stopped her taking my son away?"

"I don't know," Caffery said. "I don't know."

"She took him away — she couldn't bear me to get near him afterwards. I don't know where they are now." He reached inside his zip-up holdall and pulled out a photograph. It was battered and had been mended with Sellotape. He pulled his shirt down over his hand, carefully rubbed clean a small area of the table and put down the photograph, lovingly, smoothing down the edges.

"Your son?"

"My son. Nine. I've got more pictures at home but this one's my favourite. Look at it." He tried to hold the edges down with his long white fingers. "It's in a mess. I try, but I can't help it getting in a mess after all this time. She's wrong about me, my wife. I'm not a paedophile, you know, I'm not a paedophile. Just because a person does something like that doesn't mean he wanted to — or wants to again. I'm not a paedophile."

"But the kids . . ." Caffery nodded over his shoulder at the swimming-pool. "Why do you work here?"

"I don't touch them! Not ever. But I love them, you see — I do — they're the only contact I have — she took my —" He shook his head. "I'm not a paedophile."

"I know that. I know you didn't have a choice." He watched Gummer's nearly motionless head. He wasn't enjoying this — he didn't like making people cough out their pain like this. "He said he'd kill your boy if you didn't — am I right?"

He nodded. A milky tear dropped out of his eye on to the table. Caffery edged a little nearer. "That's what he did, isn't it. Chris? He said he'd kill your boy?"

"He was going to crush his head with a paving-stone. A paving-stone out of the back garden if I didn't. Oh, God —" He suddenly reached inside the holdall and pulled out a bottle of pills, tapped out two on to the palm of his hand and swallowed them.

"What's that?"

"Calms me down." He stuffed the bottle back in the bag, then sat forward and turned his hands over, showing Caffery the insides of his wrists. He looked up. His eyes were red and swimming in tears — as if they were bleeding. "It's wrong, I know, it's wrong to give up. But sometimes life just seems to be going on for such a long time."

The boys at the vending machine had noticed that Gummer was crying. One by one they turned to stare. Caffery leaned forward and lowered his voice. "Chris, I think we should take this somewhere else, don't you? Will you come to the station with me?"

He nodded and gazed out of the window at the rainy streets, biting his lip. "Is it what happened to that family? The Peaches?"

Caffery didn't answer. He got to his feet, put his hands on the table, and spoke in a low voice. "I wish you'd talked to someone back then."

"The world was a different place back then."

Champaluang's attack had happened a few days after Gummer's wife had left. Gummer had read about the attack in the South London press and was seized with the notion that the man Champ called "the troll" was the same teenager responsible for destroying his life. He watched the papers like an owl after that, but until the intruder at Donegal Crescent he hadn't seen one incident with the hallmarks of the troll on it. When he and Caffery got to Shrivemoor they found out why.

Klare had been in high-security psychiatric facilities for eleven years. Kryotos had the file on her desk and was photocopying pages from it. "Stabbed a WPC in Balham in 1989. He'd tried to abduct a little boy from outside a supermarket." This was his "index offence", the offence that first put him into the mental-health system. It had happened when he was just eighteen. The WPC had cornered him in a stairwell on a council estate and he'd jumped at her with a penknife. The child was unharmed but the WPC had suffered severe cuts to her hands.

"The abduction charge fell through." Kryotos spoke quietly. Gummer was sitting on a chair next to the SIO's room, just out of earshot. He looked as if he might cry. "The boy's parents didn't press charges, didn't want to put him through the trial, so they charged him with the assault on the WPC." For this he had been convicted and held for over ten years under Section 41 of the Mental Health Act, until fifteen months ago when he was considered stabilized on clozapine, and the Home Secretary lifted the restriction order, sending him for a year to a halfway hostel before, in April, releasing him back into the community. "Even if I'd had time to feed all the house-to-house interviews into HOLMES and seen his CRO —" She shook her head. "It was for assault. It never went down as an abduction. He'd've still slipped through." She paused, and looked at him, standing there in front of her all dishevelled. "You stink, Jack. You smell like a swimming-pool."

"Thanks, Marilyn."

"That's OK. Want some shortbread?"

"No thanks, Marilyn."

"One day I'll stop asking."

"No, you won't."

Souness and the rest of the team were in Brixton so Caffery took Gummer into the SIO's room, sat him down and got the story from the beginning.

It had started in 1989. The Gummers had planned their holiday quite openly and none of their friends ever found out that they hadn't made it to Blackpool, that they had never even left Brixton. *But something went wrong on that holiday*, everyone agreed, *they were never the same afterwards*. No one knew about the tall youth who had appeared out of thin air in the hallway of the little terraced house. No one knew how he'd tied Gummer's wife in an upstairs bedroom, "X" spray-painted on the door. No one knew about the act Gummer was forced to perform on his own son, nor that afterwards, curled up in the corner and crying, he'd had to watch Klare make his own attempt on the nine-year-old. Klare had been impotent. Frustrated, full of rage, he had bitten a hole in the boy's back.

"Did he use a belt?" Caffery felt sorry for Gummer, who sat with his arms wrapped around his knees as if it was cold, his shoulders hunched up, staring blankly out at rainy Croydon. But he knew he had to ask. "Did he use a belt? Around your son's neck?"

"No. Not a belt. But he beat him. And he bit him."

So that's a skill you learned later, in prison, you bastard. "Anything he said? Anything in particular you remember?"

"No. I've gone through it a hundred times. Oh, I mean of course there were *excuses*, you can imagine the sort of thing, said he didn't mean it — that he had to do it — etcetera, etcetera."

"He *had* to do it?"

"Oh yes." Gummer twisted his mouth up as if the memory was a sour spot on his tongue. "Oh yes. A few times he said it — said he couldn't help it — had to treat himself — it was all madness to me, all just an excuse —"

"The Treatment."

Gummer paused. "What?"

"The Treatment," he said softly, thinking about the little notebook in Souness's drawer. He looked up at Gummer. "I'm sorry — it's nothing — he's schizophrenic, we think. He's —"

"He's mad — that's what he is."

"Yes. Maybe." Caffery tapped his fingers on the desk. "Anyway — go on, Chris, go on."

After the attack Gummer had tried to persuade his wife to go to the police but she had resisted and, in a few bitter and well-chosen words, spelled it out to him: if he went to the police then the rest of the world would know he was a *child molester*. A child molester! *Never ever ever let anyone know. It will stay with us until the day we die*. But keeping the secret eventually got too much and she had packed up her records, her Jane Fonda workout videos and her son, and left, leaving Gummer in London with nothing: no pillows, no sheets, no towels — just a sticky bottle of tomato ketchup in the fridge and the round conviction that he was a pervert because of what he had managed to achieve. "With my son, my own son, I wouldn't have thought it possible, if it hadn't happened."

"Did you have an attic?"

"Yes. There was an attic in that house."

Caffery pictured Klare, in the attic like a patient spider, just watching and waiting, waiting for a moment when he could scamper out and do what he wanted without interruption. "I think that's where he came from."

"I know."

"You know?"

"Found out afterwards. He left by the front door — just opened it and walked out — but how did he get in? I found the mess he left afterwards when I got a ladder up there." He shrugged. "Looking back I realized my wife had sensed something was wrong."

"Before?"

He nodded. "She kept saying she could smell something — she said there was a smell in that house. I couldn't smell it but it was driving her crazy trying to get rid of it before we went on holiday — she said something had died under the floorboards. If she'd got her way she would've had me rip the place apart. Now I wish I had —"

He stopped. Caffery had just sat back so fast it was as if someone had wrenched him by the collar. "Your wife smelt the stuff in the attic *before*?"

"She kept moaning about it — I couldn't smell it myself, but they say women have a better sense of smell than men."

Caffery stood and went into the incident room, rapping his knuckles on Kryotos's desk. "Marilyn. How far's Danni?"

"She just called — she'll be back in fifteen or so."

“Right. Can I leave Gummer with you until she’s back? You could make him some tea or something.”

“I’ll give him some shortbread. Where are you going?”

“Brixton. Tell Danni I’ll call her later.”

CHAPTER THIRTY-THREE

What pitched her out of that long, trancy sleep? The voice? Benedicte thought so. A man's voice, murmuring. She opened her eyes. A bluebottle was picking its way carefully through the crust on Smurf's nose. She stared blankly at it, lying on her side, trying to decide if she was dreaming or really hearing a man's voice in the kitchen below.

Hal? Was it Hal? *What's happening?* She raised her head. Maybe the troll had gone. Maybe Hal was talking to Josh. *Yes, that's what it sounds like — he's gone and I missed it because I was asleep.* She rolled on to her front and fanned her hands out on the splintered boards. The skin on her arms had taken on the papery, transparent look that dried honesty got — she almost expected to see the little veins in her hands turn blood-black and noded like seeds. Her throat was so dry it seemed no longer a functioning part of her body, but a long, living welt running under the muscles.

Another sentence spoken from below.

Hal?

Moving painfully she shuffled sideways and dropped her face into the gap between the boards. Everything was taking longer than it should, every move made her vision swim, the edges of light and matter blur. She wriggled her hand out until it cupped the light fitting. The light was on, she could feel the heat of it against her palm as she applied a silent, steady pressure downwards on it. With a quiet *sloosh* it fell down into the room below, circling wildly on the wire. She lay for a moment, panting, exhausted by the effort. *I'm ill*, she thought. *He's killing us*. Gathering all her energy she inched her face into the gap, and immediately she could feel different air on her face, dry, full of the kippery smell of an animal's bedding.

My God. Is he still here?

And then she saw. She wanted to jerk back out of her hole but she found she couldn't move. She was transfixed.

Hal was gone. Only the man-shaped stain where he had been. And in his place the upholstered armchair that belonged next to the window in the living room. Sitting in the chair, facing away from her, into the family room, just ten feet below her, the troll. He had stripped down to a T-shirt and was crouched on the chair like a bird, his hands between his legs.

Silently, carefully, she sucked in a breath. *You should have known — should have known*. All the lights in the two rooms were on, the curtains were drawn. A camera lay on the floor next to him. He hadn't heard her push the light through because he was intent on watching something out of sight in the living room. His face was creased and reddened, there was a diamond point of saliva on the lower lip, and now that she looked closer she saw his belt and flies were open and he was using one hand to massage himself. *Oh, God*. A bubble of nausea rose in her throat. *Oh, God — the bastard*. He stopped masturbating for a moment to spit on his palm and Benedicte got a glimpse of the little white pudding of his penis — not even hard.

"Do it," he murmured. "Do it."

What's he watching? Christ, what's he watching? Can Josh see?

"Just do it," he was saying. "Do it now." His bottom lip was loose and moist, his loamy hand a blur, the saliva lengthened downwards from his mouth. *Who's he talking to?* Ben closed her eyes, the darkness in her head switching and flickering. *Am I imagining it? Is this still a dream? My God, Josh. Where's Josh?*

From the living room came a wail. Her eyes snapped open. That was Hal. Screaming something in a thick voice she couldn't understand: "Ican'tdoitIcan'tIcan'tIcan't. *PleaseGODkillmeinstead* . . ." He wrenched in a breath and this time she heard the words clearly. "KILL ME. *Please. Kill me instead*."

"Get off. Get off." The troll got down from the chair and kicked something that lay on the floor just out of Ben's view. Something heavy. He began to pull the belt out of his jeans. "Get off." He wrapped the belt around one fist, pulling the other end taut. The jeans slid down to his ankles, his legs bowed out like a mountain goat's. He dropped to his knees.

My God, what's he doing? He looks as if he's going to . . .

She could see only his lower body, the jeans crumpled around his feet, dirty grey Y-fronts. But there was something in the tension of his buttocks, something that made her think of an animal feeding. The way a cat's hindquarters would twist when it was . . .

When it was chewing *something* —

A thin cry. The troll's buttocks twisted again. Now Benedicte understood. Josh. "NO!" She jammed herself blindly forward into the hole. "*No!* Leave him alone!"

A sudden silence. The feet below became still.

"*I mean it. Leave him alone or I'll kill you. I'll kill you.*"

Silence. All she could hear was the swollen knocking of her heart. Then suddenly, out of nowhere, his face shot up next to hers — she could smell his breath, see blood on his teeth. *Ohmigod.* She jolted back. Jammed her ear against the edge of the boards, the pain boomeranging her back into the hole. *No!* She scrabbled for purchase, the plasterboard cracking, her free leg cycling crazily, trying to get a foothold on the carpet, expecting the foul breath on her at any second. She could hear him panting, almost as if he was afraid — *What's* he *afraid of?* — got a hurried, hectic glimpse of his eyes, panicked, nervous, his hands up to his mouth as if *she* terrified *him*, then *sniff, sniff, sniff*, and he started whimpering, lips quivering, and this time, with the last of her strength, her hands scrabbling weakly at the carpet, she wrenched herself out of the hole, back into the room, and even as she did she heard the doorbell ringing in the hallway.

Caffery stood on the doorstep, the rain pattering down around him. He was breathing hard. He had walked around the perimeter of the Clock Tower Grove building site, passing heavy machinery and a saturated bundle of electrical conduit — *Champ, I'll never be able to look at conduit again without thinking of Champ* — until he could see Clock Tower Walk beyond the security fencing. All the houses were unoccupied, all except number five. Number five's curtains were drawn, and when he saw that he started to move a little faster, breaking into a trot along the little brick street, slamming his thumb on the doorbell.

"Mrs Church?" He rang again, the heel of his hand flat against the bell. The house was silent. Standing on tiptoe he looked through the garage door. A lemon yellow Daewoo was parked in the gloom. He knew he might be wrong. He remembered the woman who had answered the door to him here, more than a week ago. He remembered her talking about the smell in her house, just as Gummer's wife had done, just as Souness had done at the Peaches'. He remembered the dog. He lifted the letterbox.

"Mrs Church?"

And then, on the air in the hallway, he smelt urine. *My God, an animal's in there*. Food containers littered the hallway. A TV played somewhere in the back of the house. And at the top of the stairs something had been spray-painted in red.

He dropped the letterbox and turned, reaching in his pocket for his phone, his heart racing.

"Jack, listen." Souness was adamant. "Don't go in, Jack, don't go in. Wait for us. Are ye listening to me?"

"I won't. I swear."

He meant it. He put the phone in his pocket, and stood on the doorstep, his jacket held over his head to protect him from the drizzle, shifting tensely from foot to foot, looking up at the house then back along the road for the area cars. Minutes ticked by, and suddenly, from behind, came a noise. He shot to the letterbox in time to see something bolt out of the kitchen, through the hallway and hurtle up the stairs. Blurred and huge, he was carrying something in his arms and immediately Caffery knew that there was blood. He ripped off his jacket, wrapped it around his arm and rammed his elbow through the glass panel, loosened the bolt under the Yale, flicked the catch down, and now he was in, racing into the kitchen, flinging the door back on its hinges. The kitchen was hot — full of that familiar smell — *Jesus, what's happened in here?* — the lights were on, the curtains closed, and here, lying on the floor, shaking and covered in his own dirt, lay something Caffery assumed was Mr Church. *Oh, Christ* — Church saw him and closed his eyes, turning his head away. *Ignore him, find the child*. The boards overhead groaned and sighed and Caffery snapped his head up. Now he knew what Klare was carrying.

"*Police!*" He threw himself into the hallway, grabbed the banisters, swung himself around, slamming his feet into the stairs, clearing two at a time. At the top of the first flight he stopped, hands out, pulse thundering.

"Here." A woman's voice. "Here." He spun around. The landing was dark and silent, it smelt of urine — ahead of him another staircase led up into the gloom, behind him was a door, to his left a door, and to his right a door, the word *Hazard* scrawled across this one in red.

"Mrs Church?"

"Here." Her voice was weak. "Here . . ."

"Keep still — I'll be right there."

"My little boy —"

"It's OK — just hold on."

She started to sob but Caffery had to turn away. *Assess your areas of responsibility. Not her — she's OK — it's the child you want*. The landing above creaked. He whipped back to face the staircase. *Where's the fucking light switch?* He patted the walls, found nothing. Another board creaked and now he heard, as clear as sound over water, a child crying above. Not calling or screaming but weeping, as if he didn't expect to be heard. *What was his name? What was his fucking name? Come on now — think*. He put his hand on the stair rail and there, at eye level on the wall, hung a framed photograph, a little boy feeding a goat. Grinning. And suddenly he had it. *Josh*.

"Josh?" he shouted up the stairs. "Josh. I can hear you. This is the police — it's OK now, Josh. Just you keep still, OK?"

The crying stopped. Silence. He took a deep breath and quietly mounted the first two steps. "Josh?" Nothing above him, only a breathing so faint he thought he was imagining it. "Josh?"

Something toppled from the darkness above.

Jesus —

He flattened himself against the wall, wasn't quick enough and was hit square in the stomach, the impact shooting him back down the stairs. He grabbed vainly at the walls, slammed against the bathroom door, his phone spinning out of his pocket and away down the next flight of stairs. Silence. He blinked. "*Josh?*" The boy had landed at the foot of the stairs about a yard away. Naked, winded and shocked. He had brown packing tape on his mouth. "Josh?" Caffery hissed. "You OK?" The child looked up at him, frozen with shock. Tears had made white tracks on his face and his wrists were taped. "Here." Caffery got to his feet and pushed open the bathroom door. "In here. Go on. Quick." He didn't have to be told twice — he scampered inside in a crouch, a naked, bloodied little savage, tilting and tipping as if he was drunk. There was enough light to see a raw hole in his back. A bite. Caffery's heart sank. "Keep the light off," he hissed. "I'll be back." He pulled the door closed and turned back to the stairs.

"KLARE, YOU FUCKER."

He waited. Nothing.

He turned for the stairs, taking one at a time, stopping to listen to Klare moving around overhead. *What the — ?* The buckle and creak of aluminium. *The loft ladder — the fucking loft ladder*. He threw himself forward up the last stairs, moving too fast to stop and take in the surroundings: a tiny landing, a door open into a bedroom beyond, the ladder rising up into the attic, Klare halfway up, trying to crawl slyly away. "STOP, YOU FUCKER —" He charged at the ladder and Klare sprang up the next few rungs, moving fast, Caffery behind, grabbing at his heels, their combined weight making the ladder creak. Klare was through the hatch and in the attic, and Caffery lost him for a moment, saw the underside of his trainers disappear away from the hatch, smelt him, heard the joists wheeze under his weight. *Fuck*. He launched himself up the last few rungs, into the darkened loft, the rain pattering on the tiles above, Klare disappearing in the gloom at the far end — *yes, of course, of course, that's where you'd go — next door* — a quick breath of rotting food in his lungs as he followed, slammed into the rough breeze-block wall, found the gap and ducked — through it in one, ripping his trousers, banging his head against the breeze blocks, dropping instinctively into a crouch in the adjoining attic, his hands out.

No light. It was completely black in here. He was still for a moment, getting his breath back, listening for Klare's breathing. At the far end of the attic a sudden shaft of sunlight shot into the darkness, illuminating Klare from below. He had ripped up the attic door.

"*Stop!*"

But he was standing astride the hatch, dropping the ladder on to the landing, his hands leapfrogging over the spooling aluminium. Caffery picked his way agilely across the joists, his heart slamming away — *you're closing the reactionary gap here, remember your training — reactionary gap — it's there to save your life, if you close it you have to know exactly why and what you expect. Is this a good place to —*

Klare was quick: without a sound he had turned and dropped out of sight, so fast he almost didn't touch the ladder. "*Stop!*" Caffery was seconds behind, sliding down the ladder, battering his knees on the rungs, landing in a nearly finished hallway, cord carpet, magnolia-painted plasterboard and a glimpse of a bathroom, the sink and toilet still swaddled in plastic. On his right Klare's head disappeared down the stairs, crashing into brittle walls, plaster shaking out on to the air, leaving behind his yeasty smell. Caffery bolted after him, reaching the first landing and spinning back against the wall to face the next flight, clearing three steps at a time, landing on the ground floor with his foot half turned under him, getting his balance back, the cardboard taped on the floor by the builders slithering away under his feet, as Klare darted ahead into the kitchen, Caffery after him again, screaming and yelling, "*You fucker*," into the kitchen, identical to the Churches' next door, and at last Caffery slid to a halt in the doorway, breathing hard.

Roland Klare was at the back door, gripping the handle, one foot rammed against the base, his centre of gravity slung back as he tugged. The door was locked.

"STAY THERE!" Caffery yelled. *Assess your areas of responsibility, Jack — come on, a bit of fucking discipline — what's your focus in this environment? The subject, the door* — "JUST STAY THERE!"

Klare turned, panting, his grey T-shirt riding up over his stomach, his soft woman's hair stuck to his face. "No —" He held his hands up. "No! *Don't touch me!*"

"*What d'you mean don't fucking touch you? I'm going to arrest you, you little shit.*"

"*No!*" His jeans were unzipped, hanging loose as if he'd pulled them on in a hurry. "No no no — please

please please don't." He took a step back, covering his ears. "I didn't mean it." He sank down suddenly under the sink, his hands over his face. "I didn't mean it."

"You didn't *mean* it? I don't fucking believe this. *You didn't mean it?* What *did* you mean, then? What *did* you mean, then, eh?" He stepped forward and gave Klare an experimental kick in the side. Klare sighed a little, but didn't try to resist, so he did it again. "I said *what did you mean*?"

"Leave me alone." His face crumpled in self-pity. He dug his nails into his hair. "Don't —"

"What did you mean when you left an eight-year-old to *die*? Eh? *What did you mean?*" He kicked him harder, once in the side and once, when Klare turned slightly away, in the kidneys. "I'm talking to you, you piece of shit. *What did you mean?*"

"*Please* don't, *please* don't." He wiped tears from his face and rubbed his eyes. "I didn't mean to. I had to — it's the only way — I never meant to —"

"You already fucking *said* that!" He gave him two kicks in quick succession, one in the chest and one in the face. This time when his foot came away blood rushed out of Klare's nose. "You already fucking said you didn't mean it. You *stinking* piece of shit." He swung himself away, walking up and down the length of the kitchen, pressing his nails into his palms. Klare was blathering — blood was running down his chin, splashing on the floor. "What did you mean when you left that poor fucker lying next door in his own shit? Eh?"

"Please *no*, it's not my fault, I had to for the treat —"

"Shut up." Caffery ran back across the kitchen, almost skidding on the blood, and with all his strength booted Klare in the ribs. "*I said shut up!*"

"*Jack!*"

He turned, panting, sweat on his face. Souness was standing in the hallway with two TSG officers in their Kevlar tunics and riot masks. Her face was white. She stared at Klare, basted in blood, and back at Caffery, standing frozen in the centre of the room, twitchy as a circus tiger.

"Jack — what the *fuck* do ye think you're doing?"

The rainclouds, by mid-afternoon, were so heavy and low they seemed to be touching the chimneys, electric lights had come on in windows, as if evening had come early to London. Rebecca was lying in Jack's bed, half asleep. She hadn't slept well last night — after Caffery's call at 11 p.m. she had walked around with the TV on in the background telling herself not to get worried about him, telling herself he knew how to stay in control, that he wasn't a child, that he could, he really could, keep calm and look after himself. She only had two vodkas and no one had called to say, "Miss Morant, you'd better sit down." So she supposed everything was OK. She had spent the morning home making, a proper little housewife, driving the Beetle down to Sainsbury's and coming back in the rain with bags full of fruit and wine. When she came in the answerphone had been blinking. There was one message. She wasn't in the habit of listening to Caffery's messages — she wasn't that obsessive — but while she was in the kitchen unpacking the shopping the phone rang again and this time she heard the whole thing: "It's me, again. Just wanted to make sure you got the last message about Monday. Monday at one o'clock."

Rebecca had paused, a bag of tangerines in her hand, and stared down the hallway. That was Tracey's voice. *Not now, Tracey, not when it's all starting to work for us*. Slowly she put down the fruit, went into the hallway and stared at the machine. Biting her lip, she pressed the button. The first message played back. It started with a silence. Then, as if she'd got her courage, Tracey Lamb said: "It's me, Tracey, right? Uh — with what we was talking about, yeah? I'm getting bailed on Monday, so if you want to know some more about, y'know —" She paused, and Rebecca could hear her drag on a cigarette. "I'll be back at my place at one o'clock — you know where it is."

A tiny nibble of anxiety somewhere in Rebecca's stomach — horrible because today she was so determined to keep on track. She listened to both messages again then wrote in felt-tip on the back of her hand *Tracey/Monday/1.00p.m.*. Then she rewound the tape. Tracey's message would stay there until another call wiped it, but the light wasn't blinking and Caffery would have no reason to play the tape unless she told him to. *You* could *just leave it that way* — *you* could *bury it for ever — he never need know — it might all just disappear . . . now Penderecki's gone he might just forget it all and be safe and* . . . "Oh, shut up, for God's sake."

She looked at the kitchen. *Maybe a glass of something to keep you calm?* But no. No — she wasn't going to backtrack. Instead she had finished unpacking, had cleaned the kitchen, put on a load of washing, eaten a sandwich for lunch and then gone upstairs. In the bedroom she took off her jeans and T-shirt, lay down on Jack's bed and drifted off to sleep.

She was still there — drifting in and out of her dreams — when his car pulled up later that afternoon. He was much earlier than she'd expected. She jumped up, surprised, and stood in the window, the curtain hooked up on her arm, blinking and rubbing her eyes as he got out of the Jaguar. He stopped for a while at the gate and stared at the front door with an odd, preoccupied look on his face, as if he was trying to work something out — as if he was trying to remember a telephone number or recall something someone had said. Then the rain lifted on the wind, driving sideways, making the trees in the front garden hiss and bend and Jack shook off the stasis, came inside and she could hear him in the house, throwing the keys on the hall table and coming up the stairs. Quickly she pulled on one of his shirts over her underwear and went on to the landing. The bathroom door was open and he was bending over the toilet, his hands propped on the cistern, as if he was going to vomit.

"Jack?" He didn't turn. "Jack? Are you OK?"

He shook his head. She put her hand on his back and saw that the rainwater running off his trousers on to the floor was veined with red. There was thinned blood on the tiles.

"*Jack?*"

He spat into the toilet. "Mmm?"

"There's blood on you, Jack."

He looked down at the floor. "Yes — that's blood."

"Are you — are you bleeding?"

"No."

"*No?*" She felt suddenly lightheaded. "Then — oh —" She covered her mouth with her hand. Downstairs someone was ringing the doorbell. "Jack? God, no, Jack — what happened? What've you done?"

"It's OK. I stopped —"

"What do you mean you st —"

"I stopped. Before I could —"

"Before you could *what*?"

"Before I could — oh, fuck —" He dropped his face. The doorbell rang again, longer this time. "Get the door, will you?"

"I *warned* you."

"Becky —"

"*What?*"

"The door."

"The door?"

"The front door."

"Oh — God — yes. OK." She ran down the stairs, heart racing — *I need that drink, I need that drink — and, Jack, I'm definitely not telling you about Tracey now — I'm going to lie —* She opened the door and found DCI Danniella Souness standing on the doorstep, red in the face, huffing and puffing and stamping her feet.

"Danni —"

"Becky —" Souness stepped inside without waiting to be asked, dripping rain on to the floor. "Where is he?"

"What? Oh —" She put her hand to her head. "He's up there — in the bathroom — Danni, what's going on?"

Upstairs Caffery spat into the toilet again and wiped his mouth. He had wanted to kill Klare. When his foot met flesh and gristle it was Penderecki's kidneys he was connecting with. When Klare screamed and tried to protect himself, it was Penderecki's screams, the screams he had never had the pleasure of hearing. He was angry enough to kill and it wasn't going away — it was still there, stretched taut across his stomach like a new muscle.

"Are ye puking?" Souness came and stood next to him, her arms folded.

He shook his head.

"What then?"

"Just feel like it."

"Aye — I'm not surprised. I'd be puking me face up too if I'd just left my oppo in the lurch like this."

"I need a drink." Rebecca was in the doorway, her voice shaky. "Maybe I should get us all a drink?"

"No, Becky, not just now." Souness put her hands on her thighs and bent over to look at the side of Caffery's face. "I've something to deal with here. This one. He walked out on me."

"I had to." He straightened up a bit, wiping his mouth and taking deep breaths. "You know I had to."

"Not when I'm in the *middle* of it, Jack — Klare's down at Brixton factory and I need you down there. I can't do this on my tod."

"No. Take me off the case."

"*What?*"

"Take me off the case."

"Ooof!" She looked around the bathroom with her hands open, as if she was asking the walls, the mirror, the basin, to join in her disbelief. "What shite is *this* you're spouting now?"

"You saw what I just did." He pushed past her and went to the sink, turning on the tap and scooping water into his mouth. "You can't let me get away with what I just did."

"*What* did he just do, Danni?"

"You *saw* what I did, Danni."

"Aye. I saw a piece of low-life shite — a child-killer actually — I saw him resisting arrest. And ye know something funny, I double-checked with the TSG officers, asked them if that's what they saw, and you know what? I was right — I wasn't imagining it. It's exactly what they saw too."

Caffery shook his head. "No, Danni."

"Sometimes it happens when someone resists arrest — they're bound to get a few fucks thrown into them. It happens — especially to the low-lifes like that."

He looked at her steadily in the mirror above the sink. "You really think you can defend me?"

"I think so."

"You said you wouldn't."

"Aye — Paulina'll tell you all about me and my promises. It's a wee luxury I allow myself for all my hard graft."

"Right." He ran his tongue around the inside of his mouth. He needed to show her — he wanted to explain how much this case had pushed him, in visible and invisible ways. He wanted her to understand just how far his obsession could take him. "Wait there."

He clattered down the stairs, swinging into the hallway, and pulling away all the things in the cupboard under the stairs until he found the taped-up box at the back. It was all going to come out now. He was going to crash into it, face first, get it all over. He raced back up the stairs.

In the bathroom Rebecca was silent. Souness had put the lid down on the toilet and was sitting astride it, her feet pushed back as if she was in the saddle, drumming on the seat between her legs with her knuckles, drumming out the beat of a rock song in her head. He set the box on the floor, felt in his pocket for his Swiss Army knife, flicked it open and slit the tape.

"What's this?" Souness stopped drumming. "What have we got here?"

He didn't answer. In the corner he saw Rebecca cross her arms and frown. He opened the top flaps of the box and up-ended it. Penderecki's child-porn collection tumbled out on to the floor, rolling out and tiding up against the edge of the bath. One magazine fell at Rebecca's feet, open to the black-and-white image of a prepubescent girl. She was holding a vibrator to her cheek as if it was a teddy or a flower. Rebecca looked at the photograph silently for a moment, and then, not looking up or speaking, she used her toe to close the magazine and sat down on the edge of the bath, her face in her hands.

"This." Caffery straightened up and looked at Souness. "This —"

No one spoke. Rebecca massaged her scalp compulsively, staring at her bare knees. Souness crossed one boxy leg over the other, drew her jacket closed and crossed her arms.

"See? See all this?" He kicked the pile of magazines and videos. "That's why Paulina's been so interested in me. I kept it all to myself. It's Penderecki's. I should have surrendered it to the unit but I kept it to myself because I thought it might tell me *something about Ewan* —"

"Jack," Souness interrupted.

"What?"

"I know."

"*What?*"

"I said I *know*. I know all about Tracey Lamb. I've known since yesterday."

"Then why didn't you —" He broke off. "Paulina *did* tell you. You *do* know the paedo unit's on to me."

"Ahh — no. That's where you're wrong. *Paulina*'s on to you. But not the unit." She sighed and crossed her arms. "She gave the unit Lamb's name but she never said where she got it from — told her DCI she got it as a tip-off on the hotline. She's a good girl, Paulina. She knows how I feel about ye. And she knows what ye went through with that piece of shite Penderecki." Souness stood and leaned over to the small window above the toilet. She opened it and let a flash of dripping green light into the bathroom. "One of those, was it?" She nodded to the railway. "One of those over there?"

He sighed. "Yes."

"And that," Souness rested her pillowy breasts on the sill and leaned out a little further, seeing it all for the first time, "that's the railway line. The last place wee Ewan was seen?"

"Yes." He leaned past her and closed the window. "Danni."

"What?"

He looked at her closely. "Let me off the case."

"Oh, for Christ's sake . . ." She dropped her chin and rubbed her scalp with the palm of both hands. She did it rapidly, harshly. When she lowered her hands and looked up there were bright red patches on her scalp and face. "Right — OK, OK. Let's leave it for tonight. Give us all some time to calm down. I can handle Klare." She put a hand on his arm. "Have some leave, OK? When you've cooled off come in and we'll go through your arrest statement and get that squared. I don't want the funny firm looking at you — they look at you and pretty soon they're looking at the whole unit. And this" — she kicked the pile of magazines on the floor — "this, I don't want to hear any more about this. I know you'll do the right thing." She sighed and hitched up her trouser waistband. "Now, that drink, Becky, hen . . ."

Rebecca took her hands from her face and looked up. "Changed your mind?"

"What do you think?"

Souness didn't speak much while she drank the Scotch and Coke from Caffery's best crystal tumbler, standing in the living room at the french windows. She looked like a squire surveying his land, one hand in her trouser pocket, tipping her weight up on to her toes from time to time, looking out past the dripping garden to Penderecki's house. "Thank you, Becky." She handed back the glass when she'd finished. "Thank you."

Afterwards, when she was alone, Rebecca poured a glass of wine, and took it to stand in the same place, standing and staring at the garden, at the beech tree where the tree-house had been. The rain pattered down outside; the fresh smells of earth and the green juice of the garden came in through the windows. Her stomach was tight. *He's got to do something — he can't go on like this*.

"Becky?" He was standing in the doorway, looking more exhausted than she'd ever seen him. So exhausted that the skin around his eyes almost seemed inflamed — as if he was holding back an enormous pressure. "Are you all right?"

She didn't answer. *Just keep quiet — you don't have to say anything*.

"Becky?"

She bit her lip and turned away. She was aching now. She went into the hallway and pressed the answerphone button. Caffery came to stand behind her and Tracey Lamb's voice filled the little house:

"It's me, Tracey, right? Uh — with what we was talking about, yeah? I'm getting bailed on Monday, so if you want to know some more about, y'know — I'll be back at my place at one o'clock — you know where it is."

Rebecca turned back and saw Jack's face was white. White. A little flicker in his eyes. Before she could stop him Jack had stepped past her and in one movement swept the answerphone on to the floor. It lay cracked and tangled in wires, blinking and frantically winding itself back and forward. He kicked it once against the skirting-board, turned and went into the kitchen, threw open the fridge, filled a tumbler with wine and sat down at the table.

She hurried after him, sitting down opposite and trying to cover his hand with hers but he shrugged her away. He looked — *God, he looks terrible*. "You were right," he said. "You were right about me. About Bliss."

She sat back a little, shocked. "OK," she said cautiously, trying to stay calm. "You mean what I *think* happened, happened?"

He drank his wine down in one swallow, refilled his glass and looked out of the window at the dripping garden. He seemed to forget she was there for a moment. His hands, she noticed, were trembling.

"Jack? Did you hear what I —"

"Yes."

"Yes what? Yes, you heard me? Or yes, what I thought happened, happened?"

"Yes, I killed him. And you're right — I'll probably do it again. And yes, it's because of Ewan." He stared at his thumb. The black thumbnail. His stigmata. His blood stuck in the place it got stuck in twenty-five years ago and refused to flow. "You're right."

She put her hand to her head. She was starting a headache. "Jack — look." She took a deep breath and leaned forward to him, taking his hand from where it sat curled lightly around the tumbler. "Look, you've done the right thing, OK? Danni's going to take you off the case."

"And what about her?" He nodded into the hallway, to the answerphone. "What am I going to do about her?"

"I don't know. That's for you to decide."

He pulled his hand away and sat in silence for a long time.

"Jack?"

He didn't answer. He was imagining Tracey Lamb walking out of the court on Monday, coming towards him over the daisy-spotted abbey lawn with her rabbit's smile, holding out her hand for the money, and as he thought it he knew that he'd want to hurt her, do to her what he'd just done to Klare. He couldn't tolerate any more of what Penderecki had already put him through. "That stuff upstairs," he said suddenly, staring down at his thumb. "It'd be enough to stop her getting bail on Monday if I gave it all up."

"To Paulina?"

"No. She can't cover for me any more."

"Then?"

"The CPS. I'll send it anonymously. It might keep her in prison at least until —"

"Until you cool down?"

He nodded.

"Odysseus," Rebecca said gently.

"What?"

"Odysseus — it's your grand Odyssean gesture. It's you tying yourself to the mast. Resisting the sirens."

"I don't care what it is — I just care that it works."

CHAPTER THIRTY-FOUR

(3 August)

The following week the police brought the Churches back to the house. The workman caught sight of the marked area car pulling up in the driveway. Everyone knew they'd almost starved to death, everyone was talking about it, speculating about how it might have been in there. "Right under our noses — how could we not have guessed?" The workman felt a little guilty. He'd seen Roland Klare coming and going, just once or twice, and hadn't given it a second thought. Not that he was going to mention that to anyone. Now he laid his tools down and crept a little further along the RSJ to watch the Churches. He was surprised — they had lost weight. The fat family had lost weight.

A PC got out and spread his arms wide as if to protect the family from prying eyes, looking over his shoulder as they climbed out. There was no one watching, no press, no neighbours — in fact, no one paid much attention at all, except for the workman, but the officer seemed to feel it was part of his job. He stood protectively while the wife got out — she was wearing a bandage on her ankle, but apart from that she looked, the workman thought, amazing. And slim in her little blue sundress. *Christ, she looks really hot*.

She opened the car door and stretched her arms inside for the boy. He was too old to be carried really, and she had some difficulty lifting him, but he clung to her like a toy monkey, not speaking, staring at her neck. Hal Church had already got out and stood on the driveway, a little apart from them, watching with an odd look on his face, as if he didn't want to meet their eyes. He closed the car door and followed his wife and the PC up the driveway, a few paces behind, his head bent. When they reached the door he allowed the officer to accompany his wife and son into the house ahead of him.

Amazing how losing a little weight can make you look so healthy, the workman thought. That is one healthy, healthy family. He turned away and picked up his tool belt. Lucky bastards.

Souness had relented and given Caffery an extra two weeks' leave to think things through — he and Rebecca decided to spend some time in Norfolk. They had good reason. Before they left he drove over to Shrivemoor to go through the arrest statement. He went early, while Rebecca was still showering and packing, and he and Souness sat in the SIO's room and talked over coffee. It was a hot August morning, so hot that out of the window the air seemed to have been burned white by the sun, and the distant Croydon skyline had hardened to a steady silver glitter. Roland Klare, Souness said, was on the mental-health wing at Brixton Prison.

They'd forced him into clothes that didn't stink of piss. Yes, he was ill, she said, but he was still an evil radge, and Caffery should stop beating himself up over what he'd done. He's a sick piece of shite so take that guilty look off your face.

But hashing through the statement, co-ordinating their lie, felt wrong. He felt sure that whatever they did the fallout would come eventually, a God finger would appear above him in the thunderclouds. He wondered how many more Klares there would be, how many more Blisses. He wondered where it would end.

"Right." He picked up his keys and stood. "I'll be off, then."

"You away for your holidays, are ye? You and Becky?"

"That's it."

"Going anywhere special?"

"No," he lied. "Nowhere special."

In the incident room Kryotos was leaning against her desk, her arms folded, watching him come out of the SIO's room. She wore a well-starched blue dress with a sweetheart neckline, had kicked off her shoes, and now she extended a foot to halt him in his tracks. He stopped and looked at the bare foot, slightly embarrassed. She was smiling at him and he thought he knew what was coming. "Marilyn —"

"You're brilliant, Jack." Although there was no one in earshot, she leaned in to him and whispered, "You are absolutely brilliant. You got him, that bastard, you *got* him."

Caffery stood awkwardly, one hand in his pocket, one on the back of his neck, not looking at her. He wasn't going to hold up his hand and say, "No, you don't understand. You don't understand the first thing about me."

"Thank you, Marilyn, I appreciate it."

"You're welcome." She pushed herself off the desk and rummaged in a carrier-bag. "Orange cake."

"No, I —"

"Come on, Jack." She straightened and held out a Tupperware container. "You and Rebecca can eat it — go on, make me happy." She pushed it at him. "Come on, you know you want it."

He shook his head and sighed, smiling sideways at her. "Oh, Marilyn, when will you ever give up?" He took the container from her. "Go on, then. We can eat it in the car. Thank you."

It was a fine high blue day, a day for tennis — or picnicking on long lawns next to lakes, and Caffery drove up the M11, glad to be leaving London behind. Rebecca had packed walking shoes, all her paints, an easel and Kryotos's orange cake in the boot. She wore a green seersucker dress and new Ray-Bans and she sat in the passenger seat not speaking, gazing out of the window at lines of trees on distant ridges, at sunlight flashing on tractors. All week long she had kept up her determined cheerfulness. Sometimes it made her feel a little tight inside, keeping it going like this, but she wasn't going to drop it.

Caffery took a turning off the main road and soon they were on poor, weed-cracked lanes, with concrete posts and wire fencing on either side. It was as if they were crossing a deserted army base. “Look.” He slowed the car. “Her house is down there.”

They were passing a small turning. Rebecca opened the window and leaned out, peering down the little track. A rusting sign hung on the gate and beyond it the track disappeared into the trees. Then it was gone, the Jaguar had passed the turning, and Rebecca found herself looking at a disused chalk quarry, long rusty stains down the edges, an abandoned caravan in the trees at the top, four pheasants taking off in formation over it. She wound up the window and Jack put his foot on the accelerator and they continued, on to Bury, Rebecca saying a silent prayer that whatever happened today, Jack would be OK, Jack would be calm and smooth at the end of it.

The centre of Bury St Edmunds seemed to be full of flowers: impatiens and forget-me-nots tumbled out of window-boxes, roses, peonies, columbine crammed against low garden walls. When they arrived they could hear bells striking in the abbey’s Norman tower. They parked next to the court, got coffee from the WRVS shop and stood outside in the sun, waiting for Lamb’s case to start.

“It’s going to be fine,” Rebecca said. They’d chosen to stand slightly behind the white Securicor van parked in the front. Caffery didn’t want to be seen by the young barristers from the crown court who crunched around in the gravel talking on their phones and practising golf swings. He might know one of them. “I promise you, Jack, it's going to work. No one will know you — they'll have got the tapes, and *everything* will work — she won't get bailed."

"I don't know." Either the caffeine had kicked in, or he was more nervous than he realized. His hands were shaking. "I don't know."

"Well, I do, and I'm telling you. It's going to be fine."

When Lamb's case came up they put out their cigarettes in the bottom of their coffee cups, went inside and climbed the narrow staircase to the public gallery. The sun streamed down from the huge white atrium — there was nowhere to hide from the light and the court was suffocatingly hot and hushed, the clerks and probation officers' faces shiny above their collars. The public gallery was a hard little bench up behind the dock, separated from the court only by glass. Caffery and Rebecca slid into their seats, Caffery unbuttoning his cuffs, rolling up his sleeves, Rebecca tugging at the neck of her dress to let air in.

"Number 111 on your list. Tracey Lamb, Alvarez representing."

Alvarez, Caffery guessed instantly, was the pepperpot woman sitting on the right of the table — short, squat, dressed in a grubby sky-blue suit like a down-at-heel air hostess. But the CPS solicitor? He scanned the faces — he had no idea what the prosecution solicitor looked like. It took him a moment to realize it was the grey man facing Alvarez with the froggy neck, dressed as if he'd wanted to match Alvarez, in a sky-blue shirt and a yellow tie.

Caffery sat back a little so that his face was hidden by the railing. He didn't want to make himself too visible to the CPS. *Nervous, Jack? Slightly nervous?*

Lamb was brought into the court and climbed the two steps into the dock. Even through the thick glass Caffery could hear her emphysematous breathing. "Is that her?" Rebecca hissed, inching forward, trying to see her face. She wore a Nike zip top over a tight white T-shirt and had her back to them, looking straight out at the court. Someone coughed.

"This is a charge relating to a video that came into the police's possession several years ago." The CPS lawyer was on his feet, beginning his outline. "The woman in the video was subsequently identified by the investigating officer as the defendant."

Caffery shifted and Rebecca rested a cool hand over his, but he couldn't relax. Tracey Lamb's back was less than two feet away from him. She put her little polystyrene sputum cup down on the ledge in front of her and took off her jacket — the T-shirt was pulled drum tight across swells of adipose. Even now, if he closed his eyes and conjured the oiled click of a tool in his palm, he could imagine the rest. He could imagine sliding it into that back — he knew what it would look like: he'd seen enough bloodied fat sloughed away on the autopsy block. He imagined her enlarged elephant's heart squeezing the blood out through the ribs.

At that moment, as if his thoughts had reached through the air, Lamb pretended to cough. She covered her mouth and dipped her face slightly, to the side, turning sufficiently to see behind her into the public gallery. At first she seemed surprised to see him. She let her eyes wander over Rebecca and then back to Caffery. They stared at each other for a long time. Then Tracey Lamb dropped her hand from her mouth and smiled. Her long rabbit's teeth pressed into her bottom lip. She winked.

"Miss Lamb, if you could look at me, please." Bethuen, the district judge, a long woman with a regal neck, seemed to be the only person in the place not sweating. On her red leather chair, under the coat-of-arms, she sat rigid and calm in her checked Jaeger jacket, looking down over her spectacles at Lamb. "This is a very serious offence — you know that, don't you?"

"Yeah." Lamb turned back to face the court, a smile twitching on her mouth. "Yeah — I know that."

"Good. Then let's see if we can pay attention." Bethuen had found the notes of the Narey hearing and was holding the register open at that page. "I see a certain Mr Cook refused bail." She took off her spectacles and looked up. "In spite of the fact that prosecution weren't going to argue." She allowed herself a small raised eyebrow. "Nice to know that the spirit of Draco is still alive and well in the twenty-first century, isn't it? Now," she looked down at the CPS solicitor, "this is basically a new bail application. Am I right?"

"That's right."

Alvarez, who was at the solicitors' bench drawing a biro around the metal spirals of her notepad, back and forward, back and forward, nodded to herself and gave a small, confident smile. "Bethuen makes out she's a real ogre," she'd told Tracey, just before the hearing. She'd pulled back the cell wicket and thrust one of her yellow smiles into the space. "Good morning, Tracey." She had the enthusiasm of a morning DJ and she trilled a little on the "R" in Tracey. "Bethuen makes out she's an ogre but there's a secret liberal heart beating under all that houndstooth. You'll be out of here in an hour."

And Jack Caffery was directly behind her in the public gallery, dressed casually in a pale blue shirt. He'd got the answerphone message. He was early, and it was going to take some boxing and coxing to hold him off until she could sort things out at the caravan, but the important thing was that he was here. If he had the money with him they could shake hands on it today.

"The — uh — prosecution . . ." The little prosecution lawyer stood. He laid his right hand across the absurd yellow tie, as if he was swearing an oath, and half bowed to the judge. "The prosecution is in possession of . . ." He looked down and turned over a paper. "That is to say, some new *evidence* has come to light." In the public gallery Caffery squeezed Rebecca's hand. "And the Crown has no choice but to object to bail on the grounds that this new evidence *strongly* suggests that Miss Lamb is likely to commit further offences."

Alvarez jumped to her feet. "Madam."

"Yes?"

"I would have thought that if Prosecution had this information he would have had the courtesy to tell me."

"Shall we hear what the new evidence is?" Bethuen pushed her glasses up her nose and turned with a cool smile to the prosecution. "Something which strongly suggests she might reoffend? I'd very much like to hear that."

Alvarez subsided at the bench.

The CPS solicitor cleared his throat. "The investigating officer has viewed four videos, similar videos to the one brought originally, but more recent."

Lamb jiggled her shoulders nervously, looking from Alvarez to the prosecution and back again. A few feet behind her, Caffery dug his nails into his palm, making white half-moons in the skin. He didn't like Bethuen's voice — she didn't sound as if she was going to give the CPS the time of day. *But it has to work*. He let out his breath and looked up through the atrium at the blue sky, his teeth metallic in his head, hoping, hoping, *praying* it would work.

As Bethuen listened to the prosecution outlining the content of the videos, Lamb's hunched shoulders seemed to solidify and grow. She was as still as an iceberg, staring straight ahead into the court, gripping the edge of the dock, her hands white and quivering. Bethuen made a note in the court register, put the pen down and looked up: "Now, the court case has already been set for the thirtieth of September, I trust that still suits everyone." She took her glasses off, leaned forward on her elbows. "And that leaves only the bail to consider."

Rebecca reached over and rubbed Caffery's arm reassuringly. He didn't look at her. *Make it work, make it work* —

The odd, cawing sounds from the caravan echoed around the quarry, through the forest and out into the open fields. Five cows grazing nearby stopped chewing for a moment and looked up. It was a scream that could have been made by a bird, or an animal. A little brindled dog, which often crossed this field, stopped in its tracks and looked towards the quarry, its ears quivering and pricked.

Ewan Caffery didn't know how long he had been tied here — didn't know it was seven days since Tracey had left. He didn't know it was three days since he'd finished the water from the bottle under the sink. Now he stopped screaming, too exhausted to continue, and dropped sideways on the bunk — as far as the bindings would allow. He gave the ropes a few more jerks but he was too weak now to break them, so he lay patiently, on his side, his eyes rolled upwards to Britney Spears, who smiled down at him from her pickup truck in a Midwestern cornfield.

In the meadow the cows went back to their grass, ears twitching lazily at insects and the dog lost interest, sitting on its haunches to scratch under its chin.

"Now then." Bethuen lowered her glasses and looked kindly at Tracey. "Now, Miss Lamb, what to do with you?" She folded her hands and smiled. "It's complex, isn't it? But I don't have to scurry off and consult authorities to know what they'd tell me. They would tell me to take this new evidence very seriously indeed." She paused. "And so I'm sorry but under paragraphs A and B of the Bail Act you will remain in custody until we see you in court again."

"No!" Lamb shot forward.

Yes. Caffery squeezed Rebecca's hand.

"That'll be all." Bethuen nodded at the security guards, put on her glasses and began to scribble in the register. Lamb whipped round and glared at Caffery. He met her eyes coolly and she hurled herself at the glass, her hands hammering into it. "You fucking pig!" she bawled, pounding her fists on the glass. "You cheap cunt. You cheap cunt!"

"*Miss Lamb!*" Bethuen got to her feet, and the Securicor guards leaped forward.

"Please, Miss Lamb —"

"I'll fucking have yer —"

"Tracey!" Alvarez dodged between benches to get to the dock. "Calm down."

"*No!*" A guard manoeuvred one hand behind her back but Lamb was still jumping — still thumping at the glass with the other hand. "*I'll fucking have yer for it.*" She whipped round and caught up her Styrofoam cup, flinging it at Caffery. "*You fucking wanker. You piece of shit.*" The cup hit the glass and the contents slid slowly down the surface. Caffery got to his feet, took Rebecca's hand, and led her quietly to the steps, his face turned slightly so that Lamb couldn't see the victory in it.

"*Now you're never going to know*," she yelled behind them. "*You'll never fucking know!*"

They reached the bottom of the stairs, closed the door, hurried down the entrance hall, and they were out in the sun with the barristers' golf swings, the beech-tree alley, the Securicor van and all the flowers and graves of Bury St Edmunds.

CHAPTER THIRTY-FIVE

Caffery and Rebecca stayed on in Norfolk, on the borders north of Bury St Edmunds, not far from Lamb's garage. They found a B&B with a thatched roof and two sleek red setters playing in the garden. There was honeysuckle outside the window, roses on the bed linen and, arranged on a tray, a kettle, sachets of Nescafé and custard creams in cellophane. Rebecca made them coffee in the mornings and got back under the sheets with him, pressing her morning skin against him and nuzzling her new pixie hair on his chest and stomach.

Sometimes he could see their future quite clearly. Sometimes it looked like a long, open road, but other times, in Rebecca's sudden silences, in her bursts of laughter, her flashes of false bravery, he knew it wasn't going to be easy. He knew they couldn't re-invent their story overnight. Still, he smiled at her and loved her and held her hand when she was asleep at night and in the mornings sat on the bath edge talking to her as she bathed, watching her lather shampoo into her hair and massage her scalp with her strong fingers.

She bought a ridiculous man's Panama hat from an Oxfam shop, rolled up joints and stuck them in the hatband, interspersed with cow parsley. She looked bonkers, he told her. "Like an eccentric ivory dealer, or something." In Kings Lynn she bought strange lilies and white poppies and took them back to the B&B, put them in a jam-jar and made a big painting of them out on the lawn as the sun went down. On the second day they walked for miles, through the ancient land where once sandblows could cover whole villages, through the old, abandoned rabbit farms, past mysterious, ever-moving sink holes. They talked about the dreams they could buy if he sold the house: "Now that you've really moved on, Jack" — the blue futures they could sign up for with her money and his freedom. He could buy a flat in Thornton Heath without a mortgage, she could buy a cottage in the country somewhere, in Surrey maybe, or something bigger out here in Norfolk. They could have a holiday — "Somewhere like South America," she said. "Or Mexico, I could get really precious about the muralists." On and on they went, Rebecca in her crazy hat and Caffery quiet at her side, thinking, *I can't, Rebecca, I can't.*

As the sun began to set they stopped for a moment, on the slope above a shallow valley. The oblique, orange rays found a reflective surface in the trees on the other side of the valley, something artificial, a piece of glass, or a window maybe, and suddenly, as if a spotlight had swung round, a reflected image of the sun shot across the land towards Caffery and Rebecca, dipping their faces in gold. A caravan, he saw now, it was a caravan reflecting the light, and with a numb jolt he realized it was standing above the quarry near Lamb's garage. He hadn't realized how close they'd been all day. It made him want to take Rebecca straight back to the B&B, away from here.

"You're wavering," Rebecca said suddenly. "You're not going to sell the house — I can tell." She didn't look at him as she spoke. She stood at his shoulder, staring at the sunset. "You've changed your mind about Ewan."

"No, I haven't." He reached for her hand. It was time to go. "I haven't changed my mind."

"You have. You want to go and see Tracey in Holloway again."

"I don't. Really I don't."

But he was lying. Of course he was lying. He couldn't explain it to her. He couldn't explain that everything he saw on the flinty, sandy heathland where they walked, everything he saw and everything he did, still made him think about Ewan. If anything it was worse out here, all this way from London. They drove back to the B&B in silence and Rebecca didn't mention it again all week.

Then suddenly, for no apparent reason, one morning he woke up with the impression that Ewan had walked into the room.

He sat up. The clock said 6.20, the sun was outlining the flowers on the curtains, and next to him Rebecca was asleep. He looked around the little B&B room, confused, his heart thumping, fully expecting to see Ewan sitting in the window seat, dressed in his mustard T-shirt, shorts and Clarks sandals, swinging his legs.

"Ewan?" Everything seemed different. Everything in the room seemed to have a weightlessness, everything seemed to have become detached from its meaning. His limbs were light, as if he had been carrying a heavy object and had just released it. He felt as if he might float up towards the ceiling.

"Ewan?"

"Jack? What is it?" Rebecca, half asleep, dropped her hand on his back and idly scratched his shoulder-blades. "What's up?"

"Nothing." He dropped his head back on the pillow and put his hand over his chest, over his thumping heart. "I had a dream, I think. That's all."

THE TREATMENT

Date. 5th June (2 months out of hostel - one year and 2 months out of Broadmoor)
Mood. - Good (I have made up my mind to ~~act~~) (action)
Symptoms. Got erection at 6.00 am. ~~Not~~ viable
Causes and/or Stresses.

Notes. Have been given acess to Broadmoor 'Responsible Medical officers' report to Special Hospital Services Authority after MY petition in 1996 to Secretary of state for lifting of my Section 41 restriction order
Now I can see all MISTAKES and LIES told about me.

NOT DELUSION FACT

means that I can't "come"

6th December 1996
Subject reports erectile dysfunction and anorgasmia.
Experiences delusional conviction that symptoms are a
direct result of traumatic insult to subject's Vas Deferens
duct as a result of exposure to female hormones (especially
prolactin and the luteotropic hormones (lth)). Subject
routinely hallucinates female voices outside his cell and
believes that female patients are secretly being mingled
with the male patient population. RMO is undecided on real
cause of symptoms (neurophysical evaluation inconclusive).
Although patient presented with symptoms (therefore
unlikely to be extrapyramidal or associated with
medication) as a caution have recommended immediate
transfer to cloxapine (300mg twice daily, in consultation
with British National Formulary) 600mg carbamazepine in
conjunction with an anticholinergic (suggest Disipal).
Recommend ongoing leucocytes and agraulocytosis monitoring
by Clozaril Patient Monitoring Service. Patient has made it
clear that he does not consent to this treatment, that he
does not believe that neuroleptics will have effect on what
~~he believes to be~~ IS dysfunction of his endocrine system and
not a psychosis. However RMO is authorised, under Sections
57 and 58, to overrule dissent. No recurrence of macropsia,
micropsia, dissociation, hypergraphia. However, still
reports olfactory hallucinations which seem to be
associated with above delusions (specifically reports
persistent smell of milk.)

♀

RMO's treatment was always fruitleless
Don't have to SUBMIT to NAZI pharmacuticle REGIME now!!

IS

how can ~~administection~~ administration of antipsichotic medicine have affect on what is a dysfunctionalisation of my ENDOCRINE system and NOT a psychosis?? SCIZOFRENIA IS NOT an issue!!!

Decisions made, lessons learnt, things to be done today.
decided to STOP taking Clozaril!!!
decided to START on my own TREATMENT of symptoms

Things to be brought from shop or got by means. Blank today

Date: 19th June (2½ months out of hostel)
Mood: Anxious due to no relief of symptoms
Symptoms: Continue. No erection. Chafing due to exessive masturbat
Causes and/or Stresses: Don't know. I have taken every precaution against exposure to females ♀

Prolactins ~~[struck out]~~ as recurrent pathogen, !

Prolactin (or luteotropin) acts with other hormones to initiate the secretion of milk by mammary gland.

female breath

prolactins increased by 'motherhood'

female sweat

HORMONES

- progesterones
- progestins
- estrogens(eggm
- estradiol
- estrone
- estriol

milky smells

from here

ALL MA
MILK
SMEL
(offensi

prolactins
The short half life of ~~[struck out]~~ (A-I x 2 where H = half life in years OR MHL = ln G,) means tha

especially from here

- when hormones leave female they will DIE within 36 hours

D
M
co
pr

prolactins are heavy fall to earth and become COWARDLY

prolactins are he
fall to earth if ca
cling t
some

Decisions made, lessons learnt, things to be done today.

Its Time to look for new stimulation!!!
New stimulation source!!!

Things to be brought from shop or got by means.

Date. 1st July (3 months out of hostel)
Mood. No Change
Symptoms. No change
Causes and/or Stresses.
Have tried use of photographic material from 1989 as stimulus. No result. Need live source/stimulus. Problem with single source – not
Notes. clear if subject is PURGED. Also – if unrelated 3rd party present (e.g. Mr. Cort Lamb) risk of introduction of MORE pollutants off his lack of personal hygene – i.e. does not wash hands after contact with female ♀. I wore rubber gloves when handling subject who's HISTORY was unclear (i.e. MOST VIDEOS AND THIS ATTEMPT FROM 1989)

HAM ADVERT

89 Part of the South London Weekly News Group Est 1982 No.

Parents warned – do not allow children into park unattended

11 Year Old in 'horrific' attack in Brockwell Park

'This was a very violent crime,' he added. 'And in my opinion there is every chance that the child's attacker may have committed this offence before.'

Bogu
Ruli

→ !!!

→ LIAR!! WAS NOT "PLAYING"

robable reason for failure to get
ction. Child was still contaminated off of contact with female ♀

Decisions made, lessons learnt, things to be done today.
Better for subjects to be ♂ + ♂ and not single source.
Should be purged for sometime in absence of female ♀
Must (1) Identify subjects/source (2) Prepare camera

~~**Things to be brought from shop or got by means.**~~
1. Household match box in AREA i.e. QUADRANGLE 4
2. WIRELESSES TO BE STACKED FACE OUT IN AREA 2A
3. CATALOGUE ALL RADIO TIMES
4. CLEAR OUT ROOM 2.

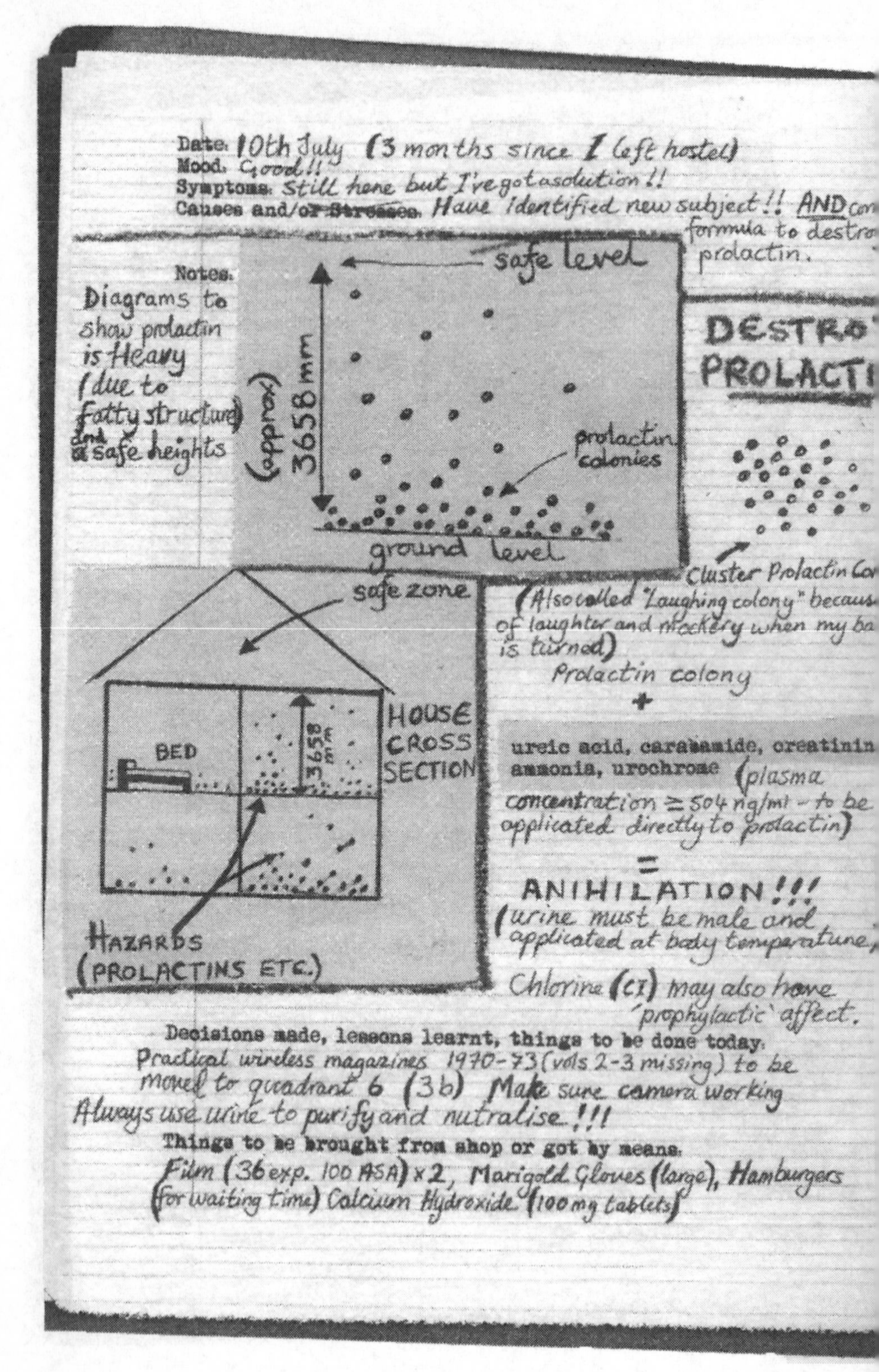

Date: 10th July (3 months since I left hostel)
Mood: Good!!
Symptoms: Still here but I've got a solution!!
Causes and/or Stresses: Have identified new subject!! AND
formula to
prolactin.
Notes:
Diagrams to show prolactin is Heavy (due to fatty structure) and safe heights
safe level
(approx) 3658 mm
prolactin colonies
ground level
Cluster Prolactin
(Also called "Laughing colony" because of laughter and mockery when my
is turned)
Prolactin colony
+
ureic acid, carabamide,
ammonia, urochrome (plasma concentration ≥ 504 ng/ml – to be applicated directly to prolactin)
=
ANIHILATION!!!
(urine must be male and applicated at body temperature
Chlorine (Cl) may also have 'prophylactic' affect.
safe zone
BED
3658 mm
HOUSE CROSS SECTION
HAZARDS (PROLACTINS ETC.)
Decisions made, lessons learnt, things to be done today:
Practical wireless magazines 1970-73 (vols 2-3 missing) to be moved to quadrant 6 (3b) Make sure camera working
Always use urine to purify and nutralise!!!
Things to be brought from shop or got by means:
Film (36 exp. 100 ASA) x2, Marigold Gloves (large), Hamburgers (for waiting time) Calcium Hydroxide (100 mg tablets)

Date. 17th July
Mood. EXTREME irritation, EXTREME nervousness, EXTREME agravation
Symptoms. EXTREME failure of erection
Causes and/or Stresses. INTERUPTION!! (By ringing on door)

Notes. Forced to store subject.

Diagram to show emergency storage of subject/source

♂ shows position of subject

SAFE

ground level

prolactins and other female hazards

Anxiety over impotence
+
Presense of PROLACTINS and female (treated) in house
+
Reluctance of subjects
+
Interuption
+
Dropped recording equipment at scene of storage (camera)
+
Camera is broken
=
NO VISUAL STIMULATION

Decisions made, lessons learnt, things to be done today.
Must have either acess to subject or retreive film.

Things to be brought from shop or got by means.

Date: 19th July
Mood: AGITATED
Symptoms: Blood Pressure AND NO ERECTION!
Causes and/or Stresses: MAJOR STRESS (apart from females and cannot access subject) include: HAVING TO TALK TO POLICE (who are PERSECUTORS and JUDGES and not very CLEVER!!!)
Notes:

Not able to acess subject/source due to what is UNACCEPTIBLE level of interference off of police

TIME RUNNING OUT FOR RORY

[illegible]

Police admit 'with every hour that passes we become more concerned for his safety'

EXCLUSIVE

[illegible]

Prayers

[illegible]

End

[illegible]

Cannot get to source/subject

KEEP CALM by following routine

Decisions made, lessons learnt, things to be done today:

Reserve camera for repairs

Things to be brought from shop or got by means:

Phytosterols, Bleach (2x2 litres), tuna (canned - 140mg) 4x2 litre containers, WD40 (small), Household matches (wipe clean) New rubber gloves.

Date. 21st July

Mood. ANXIOUS. VERY UPSET. Acute sense of <u>FAILURE</u>

Symptoms. No RELIEF. FEAR OF prolactin at <u>UNMANAGEABLE</u> level

Causes and/or Stresses. LOSS OF SOURCE (<u>see below</u>) Absence of direct visual stimulation. Drying of VAS DEFERENS tract (<u>ACUTE</u>)

Notes.

REST IN PEACE, RORY

Scotland Yard: 'Now it's a murder inquiry'

EXCLUSIVE

[illegible]

Nightmare

[illegible]

Source removed by authorities. Having difficulty ajusting to loss of what was MINE. My <u>CURE</u>. <u>FOUGHT</u> for, and <u>EARNED</u>.

Decisions made, lessons learnt, things to be done today.

Keep trying to free film. Try to locate <u>NEW</u> SOURCE/SUBJECT

Things to be brought from shop or got by means.

Jacket, staples, more calcium, rubber bands

Date 22nd July
Mood Improving
Symptoms Still no relief. But hopeful. See below!
Causes and/or Stresses New source identified for ♂ and ♂ visual stimulation. Recording equipment salvaged!!!
Notes Areas and prolactin colonies already nutralised: Some milk products in house, female bathroom ♀, females side of bed ♀
Identification of new source/family achieved!!!

NEW SOURCE/SUBJECT PLANS AND LOCATION

Alley
empty
empty
Empty
empty
Number Five
Empty
Park
Gardens
Clock Tower Grove
BUILDING SITE
To Effra Road

FRONT VIEW
Number Five
Garage

BACK VIEW
Number Five
source bedroom

New family:
Child (observed) Good ✓
Father Good ✓
Problems: 1. Wife 2. Dog is female ♀
check and nuetralise all places habituated by female ♀ (dn

Enter new source location tomorro

Decisions made, lessons learnt, things to be done today.
Immdetiate nutralisation of all previously untreated dairy and n products. Isolation of female ♀ hazard and nutralisation using u (1ml per 5sq.cm) All clothing to be adequately checked and protective gloves (r worn as precaution.

Things to be brought from shop or got by means.
GHB (for introduction in to females coffee) Got from outside MASS (Brixton). Araldite (Resin and hardener 15ml) Kodak D76 powder, red light bulb.

Date. 25th July
Mood. Restless due to waiting for purge time to finish
Symptoms. No relief (Yet!)
Causes and/or Stresses. Milky smells (offensive) due to female still in house

Notes. Sedation of female? – acheived
Imobilisation of two male sources ♂♂ – acheived
Imobilisation of dog (female) – acheived
Also photographic record of previous sources now acheived – available

Suspected prolactin colonies	Nutralised?	Still Active?
Door to female hazard room	YES	NO – DEAD!!
Curtains in living room	YES	YES (laughter heard today when my back was turned – coming from curtains)
Carpet in stairway number one	YES	DON'T KNOW
Carpet in stairway number two	YES	DON'T KNOW

TAUNTING COLONIES (LAUGHING COLONIES) BECOME COWARDLY WHEN KNOCKED FROM PERCHES

Decisions made, lessons learnt, things to be done today.
Do not introduce camera until all colonies dead (due to risk of contamination). Keep calm (look out of window at park from target's house to control RESTLESS feeling)

Things to be brought from shop or got by means.

Date: 27th July
Mood: ~~Optim~~ ~~Optim~~ Hopeful
Symptoms: No relief BUT TOMMORROWS THE DAY FOR
Causes and/or Stresses: THE TREATMENT TO START!!!

Notes:

Suspected prolactin colonies	Nutralised?	Still Active?
Door to female hazard room	YES	NO (DEAD)
Curtains in living room	YES	NO (DEAD)
Carpet in stairway number one	YES	NO (DEAD)
Carpet in stairway number two	YES	NO (DEAD)

ALLMOST READY TO GO!!!

Decisions made, lessons learnt, things to be done today:
Start <u>treatment</u> tommorrow!! (Do not anticipate interup
Bring camera to house

Things to be brought from shop or got by means:

Acknowledgements

Thank you to the following who made time in their lives to help me: **AMIT, Beckenham:** DCI Duncan Wilson and DC Daisy Glenister (also André Baker and John Good at OCU Eltham). **The Air Support Unit, Lippits Hill:** Inspector Philip Whitelaw, PC Terry White, Paul Watts, PC Howard Taylor and Richard Spinks. **The Metropolitan Police Paedophile Unit:** DCI Bob McLachlan and Marion James. **HMP Holloway:** David Lancaster (Governor) and Senior Officer Peter Collett. **South London Scientific Support Command Unit:** Dave Tadd. **Also:** D Supt Steve Gwilliam, Adrian Millsom, Neil Sturtivant, Neil Fairweather, Ashley Smith, Dr Heywood of the Neurology Department, Yeovil District Hospital, everyone at the Intensive Care Unit, Kings Hospital, London (especially Maura Falvey), the West Somerset Coroner's Office and all the staff and students at Bath Spa University, Faculty of Humanities. A special thank you to DI Cliff Davies at the OCG, who gave of his time with faultless generosity.

Thank you also to Jane Gregory and Lisanne Radice, Patrick Janson-Smith, Simon Taylor, Jo Goldsworthy,

Selina Walker, Prue Jeffreys, Jim Brooks, the Laydons, the Heads, Rilke D., Norman D. and the wise women: Margaret Murphy, Caroline Shanks, Linda and Laura Downing.

Most of all, a heartfelt thank you to the ones who keep me sane: Mairi Hitomi, my wonderful family and Keith Quinn.

Also available in ISIS Large Print:

The Chemistry of Death

Simon Beckett

Fresh and original . . . perfectly captures the claustrophobic horror of a rural community in crisis . . . absolutely compelling — and so deliciously scary

Mo Hayder

A human body starts to decompose four minutes after death. The body, once the encapsulation of life, now undergoes its final metamorphosis. It begins to digest itself. Cells dissolve from the inside out. Tissue turns to liquid, then to gas. No longer animate, the body becomes an immoveable feast for other organisms.

Young Neil and Sam learn this disturbing information first hand when they come across a maggot trail on the edge of Farnley Wood. Although country boys, aware of the cycle of life and death, the discovery of the naked, unrecognisable body of Sally Palmer sickens them to their core.

ISBN 0-7531-7602-5 (hb)
ISBN 0-7531-7603-3 (pb)

Priest

Ken Bruen

Amongst writers, Ken Bruen has become the crime novelist to read **George P. Pelecanos**

Bruen's writing is lean, mean, and deliciously sharp **Time Out**

Ireland, awash in cash and greed, no longer turns to the Church for solace or comfort. But the decapitation of Father Joyce in a Galway church horrifies even the most jaded citizen.

Jack Taylor, devastated by the recent trauma of personal loss, has always believed himself to be beyond salvation. But a new job offers a fresh start, and an unexpected partnership makes him hope that his one desperate vision — of family — might yet be fulfilled.

Bleak, unsettling and totally original, Ken Bruen's writing captures the brooding landscape of Irish society at a time of social and economic upheaval.

ISBN 0-7531-7610-6 (hb)
ISBN 0-7531-7611-4 (pb)

The Dispossessed

Margaret Murphy

There's a murderer out there getting personal . . .

Bled to death and left in a rubbish bin, the teenaged prostitute is just the first victim.

DI Jeff Rickman's investigation into the Afghan refugee's sordid death leads first to the heart of a community who can't — or won't — talk to him. Then the investigation comes home to Rickman's own private life. As the body count starts rising he is framed for a crime he didn't commit. A murderer is trying to make things personal. Very personal.

Is he on the trail of a serial killer? Or something even more sinister?

ISBN 0-7531-7329-8 (hb)
ISBN 0-7531-7330-1 (pb)

Falling Off Air

Catherine Sampson

A first-rate read **Publishers Weekly**

From the warmth of her living room, her infant twins safely tucked up in bed and a storm raging outside, Robin Ballantyne is horrified to witness the suicide of Paula Carmichael, prominent social activist and highly respected community figure. Paula's death soon reveals that she had been haunted by dark secrets and unanswered questions, and that this mysterious figure had known all about Robin, her family and the estranged father of her twins, TV producer Adam Wills.

When Robin ends her extended maternity leave and returns to work at the Corporation, tragedy moves even closer to home, and she finds herself at the centre of a murder investigation, hounded at every turn by police and press. With her solitary, cosy life transformed into a nightmare, Robin must clutch at her reputation and her sanity, whilst unearthing the truth before she loses everything, forever.

ISBN 0-7531-7339-5 (hb)
ISBN 0-7531-7340-9 (pb)